John Cuming Walters

# Tennyson, Poet, Philosopher, Idealist

Studies of the life, work, and teaching of the Poet Laureate

John Cuming Walters

**Tennyson, Poet, Philosopher, Idealist**
*Studies of the life, work, and teaching of the Poet Laureate*

ISBN/EAN: 9783337068646

Printed in Europe, USA, Canada, Australia, Japan

Cover: Foto ©Raphael Reischuk / pixelio.de

More available books at **www.hansebooks.com**

# TENNYSON

## POET, PHILOSOPHER, IDEALIST

# TENNYSON

## POET, PHILOSOPHER, IDEALIST

*STUDIES OF THE LIFE, WORK, AND TEACHING*
*OF THE POET LAUREATE*

BY

## J. CUMING WALTERS

AUTHOR OF "IN TENNYSON LAND"

WITH PORTRAIT ON STEEL BY ARMYTAGE
*After a Photograph by Mrs Cameron*

LONDON
KEGAN PAUL, TRENCH, TRÜBNER & CO., Ltd.
1893

# PREFACE.

LEST misunderstanding should arise, it is perhaps as well that I should explain at the outset that I have not attempted to supply a biography of the late Lord Tennyson. I have given prominence to his literary career, and preference to those facts which illustrated the literary side of his character. Believing, as I do, in the far-reaching and permanent effects of early environment, I have recounted with some detail the events of Tennyson's youth; but in succeeding chapters I have only casually caught up the main threads of his personal history.

Each chapter is a separate and complete study of some phase of Tennyson's work, and I have particularly endeavoured to deal adequately with his religion, philosophy, and politics. Some doubtful points I hope to have set at rest by undertaking original investigations and by careful reference to standard authorities. The criticisms of Tennyson's contemporaries, especially those of his youth, are quoted at some length because of their interest and value.

I have not, however, deemed it necessary in a work of this kind to repeat for the thousandth time the " small talk " of which great men are so often the victims; and I must ask pardon in advance of those readers who do not find in these pages a full and true account of Tennyson's sayings and doings in private life. Nearly every poem he published is referred to, and every important public act of his life is chronicled, while I have not hesitated in some half dozen cases to repeat a story which illustrates his methods and his character. By giving as many specimens of Tennyson's poetry as would be allowable I have hoped to re-kindle old enthusiasms and arouse new admirers. But those who desire to read about the tobacco he smoked, the hats he wore, and the beer or wine he drank at dinner, must turn to those volumes where such unconsidered trifles are held to be worthy of chronicling. I have excluded parodies also—even the clever ones of Mr Swinburne, Sir Theodore Martin, and the late C. S. Calverley; for I agree with Sir Arthur Helps, that he who makes a parody lacks reverence. And it is in love and reverence that these pages have been prepared, and whatever their demerits the pleasure of writing them remains.

*August* 1893.

# CONTENTS.

# TENNYSON

## POET, PHILOSOPHER, IDEALIST.

### CHAPTER I.

#### EARLY DAYS: "POEMS BY TWO BROTHERS."

> " What vague world-whisper, mystic pain or joy,
>    Thro' these three words would haunt him when a boy
>        Far-far-away ?
>
> " A whisper from his dawn of life? a breath
>    From some fair dawn beyond the doors of death
>        Far-far-away ?
>
> " Far, far, how far? from o'er the gates of Birth,
>    The faint horizons, all the bounds of earth,
>        Far-far-away?"
>                    —*Far-Far-Away.*

THE poet of yore was a "maker," a "doer"; not a seer of visions or a dreamer of dreams; not the idle singer of an empty day. He was a leader of men, standing out pre-eminent as prophet and sage—a beacon in times of darkness, casting a living light along the path of duty. Such a man is, in many cases, the sole or central figure in a dark or shadowy picture looming through the past. His influence does not die: it is transmitted from bard to bard, each of whom catches the last notes of melody only to begin anew and in deeper tones the long-continued theme. We can hear these hero-minstrels always above the rush and roar of battle, the tossing and tumult of years, the changes and chances of time. When man groaned under tyranny, the

A

strains of these sweet singers soothed the madness of despondency, and inspired the combat for redress. When the rights of a people were menaced, from their midst would rise the bard to give a tongue to their wrongs and a voice to their desires. He roused up heroes whom the times demanded and the wretched sought, and often in the hour of peril would himself seize axe or sword, and, putting himself at the head of hosts he had thrilled, would rush forth "to strive a happy strife." As soldier and as guide the man's double nature was asserted. Whilst, as he denounced oppression, his "words did gather thunder as they ran," he could attune his lyre to softer strains and higher themes, teaching of hope and patience in the hour of trial, and honour in the time of adversity. The poet was the exponent of national feeling. Legislation is the product of a high civilisation ; and in a rude and growing state, when government is unsettled and authority vested in a few, the wants and aspirations of the multitude can only be revealed in some huge outburst of long-pent feeling. What wonder that the poet became " the people's voice "? Song is often but history, accurately recording or reflecting predominating sentiments and popular movements. The poet's mission is undeniable, and great is he who realises and fulfils it. He may cull, preserve, and hallow the beauty and sublimity of the past ; treasure olden forms and ancient saws ; safeguard the laws which led to good and progress ; prepare the way for future excellence. Conservative and pioneer, watcher and adviser, ever to the fore, yet revering the past, he is the supreme counsellor, sympathiser, guide—

> Dower'd with the hate of hate, the scorn of scorn,
> The love of love.

It is the poet who, with the "viewless arrows of his thought," has

> Bravely furnish'd all abroad to fling
> The winged shafts of truth,
> To throng with stately blooms the breathing spring
> Of Hope and Youth.

Never had poet loftier conception of his duty, never did poet live up to a higher ideal, than Alfred, Lord Tennyson, the last and greatest of England's Laureates. With an intuitive perception of his destiny he chose and lived his poet-life, never swerving from his course, never diverting his glance from the goal, far-off, towards which he journeyed. He was poet all in all, from his earliest youth unto that dark hour when, with an open volume of Shakespeare before him, he passed into the silent land. As his work had been conceived, so had it been wrought. His belief in the poet's consecration was indisputable ; the end and purpose he was designed to serve were fully recognised. He compared the poet's mind first to a crystal river, " bright as light, and clear as wind," and then to " holy ground," where

> Leaps a fountain
> Like sheet lightning,
> Ever brightening
> With a low, melodious thunder ;
>
> .    .    .    .    .
>
> It springs on a level of bowery lawn,
> And the mountain draws it from Heaven above,
> And it sings a song of undying love.

Alfred Tennyson was born on the sixth day of August 1809, a year which is also memorable for giving birth to Mendelssohn and Chopin, masters in the world of music ; Darwin, who has left an enduring mark upon the annals of science ; Gladstone, scholar and statesman ; Abraham Lincoln, the American president ; Elizabeth Barrett Browning, unrivalled as poetess ; Edgar Poe, the great strange genius ; Dr Oliver Wendell Holmes, who stands at the head of living American poets, and takes rank with the greatest. Among others born in 1809 were Mary Cowden Clarke, John Stuart Blackie, Charles Lever, and Lord Houghton. Such constellations of genius are not without parallel ; in fact, nature seems to love to surprise the world with sudden prodigality and abundance of good gifts. The *annus mirabilis* 1809 is almost comparable with that time of splendour when Shakespeare was the brightest star in a wondrous galaxy; and the Victorian era will most fitly bear comparison with the lustre of the period associated with the royal sway of Elizabeth. But none could have foreseen that the infant child of a Lincolnshire rector living in a remote hamlet, was destined to contribute so bountifully to the glory of his age. Somersby, the birth-place, was at that time a sequestered nook, nestling among the wolds, and containing a population of about one hundred. There in the white rectory-house opposite an old square-towered church lived Dr George Clayton Tennyson, a scion of the house of D'Eyncourt, and his wife, a daughter of the Rev. Stephen Fytche, of Louth. Their first-born son died, but two others, Frederick and Charles, had already been born, and the fourth was baptised and named Alfred three days after his birth.

Emerson, in his essay on Plato, tells us that great geniuses have the shortest biographies; and in his essay on Shakespeare he adds that " it is the essence of poetry to spring, like the rainbow daughter of Wonder, from the invisible, to abolish the past, and refuse all history." Whether the days of Alfred Tennyson were deficient in event, or whether his isolation from the world was such that no real insight into what constituted his life as a man and a poet could be obtained, is not now capable of determination. Suffice it that chroniclers have at most times had to depend upon current gossip and occasional personal revelations. Few indeed are the facts made known by the poet himself, and the most diligent gleaner will find the harvest disappointing. Sir Henry Taylor records in his autobiography that in the course of conversation the Poet Laureate told him that he " believed every crime and every vice in the world were connected with the passion for autographs and anecdotes and records; that the desiring anecdotes and acquaintance with the lives of great men was treating them like pigs to be ripped open for the public; that he knew he himself should be ripped open like a pig; that he thanked God Almighty with his whole heart and soul that he knew nothing, and that the world knew nothing, of Shakespeare but his writings: and that he thanked God Almighty that he knew nothing of Jane Austen; and that there were no letters preserved either of Shakespeare's or of Jane Austen's that they had not ripped open like pigs." The same extraordinary feeling made itself manifest in more than one of the Laureate's poems, especially in his lines of congratulation to a friend who had " miss'd the irreverent doom Of those that wear the Poet's crown."

> For now the Poet cannot die,
>     Nor leave his music as of old,
>     But round him ere he scarce be cold
> Begins the scandal and the cry :
>
> " Proclaim the faults he would not show :
>     Break lock and seal : betray the trust :
>     Keep nothing sacred : 'tis but just
> The many-headed beast should know."
>
> Ah shameless ! for he did but sing
>     A song that pleased us from its worth ;
>     No public life was his on earth,
> No blazon'd statesman he, nor king.

The bitterness and the morbidness of the stinging lines are but too apparent ; but though the poet's injunction may be regarded as too severe, in these pages at least we will not " tear his heart before the crowd."

Alfred Tennyson was happy and fortunate in his parents and surroundings. Of his father and mother nothing but good is known. The "owd Doctor," as he was not irreverently called in the locality, was a learned unworldly man of whom we probably get a portrait in *The Village Wife.* He was "hallus aloän wi' 'is boöks," and if he had a fault, it was that he "niver looökt ower a bill, nor 'e niver not seed to owt." We are told that he was "something of a poet, painter, architect, musician, linguist, and mathematician." His wife was a gracious and excellent woman, with a heart of genuine kindness and tenderest sympathy—"No angel, but a dearer being, all dipt In angel instincts, breathing Paradise." "A sweet and gentle and most imaginative woman," is Mrs Ritchie's tribute. To these two were born in all eight sons and four daughters, most of whom proved in after years to possess the poetic temperament more or less developed. Little is known of the poet's youth, but the perfect harmony of the home life is attested in many ways. The strongest ties of friendship seem to have bound the brothers and sisters to one another, and the references to early days in the poems of Alfred and of Charles Tennyson are of such warmth and tenderness that the meaning cannot be mistaken. The boys had their dreams and desires, the poetic instinct striving to make itself felt, and leading them to the love of all beauty. They sang and played together, they told marvellous tales, they loved to dwell upon themes which set their fancy flying, and in imagination their home became an enchanted castle and themselves Arthurian knights. It is recorded that Alfred's first verses were written upon a slate and shown to Charles who approved them. The "great artist Memory" pictured in colours most rich and beautiful those Lincolnshire scenes where the "prime labour of its early days" was wrought. First there was the home with its hoard of treasured recollections—the "well-belovèd place Where first we gazed upon the sky," where stood the gray old grange, and where might be seen the lonely fold, the sheep-walk up the windy wold, the woods that belt the gray hill-side, and

> The seven elms, the poplars four
> That stand beside my father's door.

How great an influence Lincolnshire scenery had upon the poet has already been traced. One, knowing nothing of Alfred Tennyson's origin, but knowing the characteristics of his county, could easily have singled him out as a Lincolnshire man. "All great poetry," said Russell Lowell, "must smack of the soil, for it must be rooted in it, must suck life and substance from it, but it must do so with the aspiring instinct of the pine that climbs forever toward diviner air." If further evidence of the use of environment were needed, what could be more significant and appropriate than the unrestrained admission of Charles Tennyson in the beautiful sonnet which I extract from the rarest of his volumes ?—

> Hence with your jeerings, petulant and low,
> My love of home no circumstance can shake,
> Too ductile for the change of place to break,
> And far too passionate for most to know.—
> I and yon pollard-oak have grown together,
> How on yon slope the shifting sunsets lie
> None know so well as I, and tending hither
> Flows the strong current of my sympathy ;
> From this same flower-bed, dear to memory,
> I learnt how marigolds do bloom and fade,
> And from the grove that skirts this garden glade
> I had my earliest thoughts of love and spring :
> Ye wot not how the heart of man is made,
> I learn but now what change the world can bring !

Tennyson, like his two elder brothers, received the first part of his education at "Cadney's"—a schoolhouse in Holywell Glen of some repute at that time. It was opened about 1815 by Charles Clark, who, on leaving Somersby, was succeeded by William Cadney. Locally this worthy is now remembered on account of his placing a Latin inscription—a mixture of Horace and Virgil—over the entrance to the Glen,[1] and any particular merit he may

[1] William Howitt was the first to describe Tennyson's native place, and his words are worth quoting :—"The native village of Tennyson is not situated in the fens, but in a pretty pastoral district of softly sloping hills and large ash-trees. It is not based on bogs, but on a clean sandstone. There is a little glen in the neighbourhood, called by the old monkish name of Holywell. Over the gateway leading to it some by-gone squire [an error : it should be Cadney] has put up an inscription, a medley of Virgil and Horace ; and within, a stream of clear water gushes out on a sand rock, and over it stands the old schoolhouse almost lost among the trees, and of late years used as a wood-

have possessed, or whatever his special qualification for his work, cannot be related. Until the Tennyson brothers were sent to Louth Grammar School their education may have been partly under the supervision of their father, though it is not unlikely that no regular or systematic course of training was entered upon. I have already disposed of the fiction that Alfred and Charles Tennyson received the major portion of their education at Louth.[1] As a matter of fact Alfred was only just eleven years old, and Charles was only thirteen when they returned to Somersby, and Cadney was entrusted with the care of them. Their sojourn at Louth had been absolutely uneventful, and they brought back with them only bitter recollections of the headmaster's severity. Cadney's duty was to teach the boys arithmetic, but a quarrel with the Doctor abruptly terminated the engagement. William Clark, a sharp Bag Enderby boy, only two years Alfred's senior, was then called upon to act as tutor, and having a special aptitude for mathematics, he succeeded in the task. As for Cadney, misfortune appears to have dogged his steps. He was turned out of his cottage in the Glen because the boys in his charge disturbed the game, such as there was ; and eventually the schoolmaster ended his days in Spilsby Union-house at Hundleby, at the age of eighty-four. William Clark, the " boy-schoolmaster," is still living at Tetford, near Somersby ; and it is interesting to relate that his brother Charles was for some time employed at the Hall at Gantby, which was often regarded as the original of Dickens's " Bleak House."

house, its former distinction only signified by the Scripture text on the walls, ' Remember thy Creator in the days of thy youth.' There are also two brooks in this valley, which flow into one at the bottom of the glebe field, and by these the young poet used to wander and meditate." I have given a full description of these scenes as they present themselves in later times, and subsequently other "localizers" have done the same. Some interesting facts about Cadney's school were published in the *Pall Mall Gazette* of June 19, 1890. Previously the history of that interesting place was very obscure.

[1] See " In Tennyson Land," pp. 35-37.

It can easily be understood that during the interval between their leaving Louth Grammar School and entering College, very little restraint was exercised over Dr Tennyson's sons. They were sturdy, spirited lads, and appear to have been left to their own devices. We can imagine them wandering about the Lincolnshire Uplands, taking long journeys across the wolds, exploring knoll and copse, and occasionally walking as far as the sea. Now and then they visited Boston, where a relative lived, and in the summer they spent a few days at Mablethorpe in the "lowly" white cottage, whence they could see

> Stretch'd wide and wild the waste enormous marsh,
> Where from the frequent bridge,
> Like emblems of infinity,
> The trenched waters run from sky to sky.

All these scenes were knowledge and inspiration to the young poets, nor was it long before their thoughts found expression. It was Charles Tennyson who declared how good were all things in the poet's eyes, and who, while still a youth, felt that he and his kin were marked off from the common race. In his exquisite Book of Sonnets we read :—

> No trace is left upon the vulgar mind
> By shapes which form upon the poet's thought
> In instant symmetry : all eyes are blind
> Save his, for ends of lowlier vision wrought ;
> Think'st thou, if Nature wore to every gaze
> Her noble beauty and commanding power
> Could harsh and ugly doubt withstand the blaze
> Or front her Sinai Presence for an hour ?
> The seal of Truth is Beauty—When the age
> Sees not the token, can the mission move ?
> The brow is veil'd that should attach the tie
> And lend the magic to the voice of Love :
> What wonder then that doubt is ever nigh
> Urging such spirits on to mock and to deny ?

The love of Lincolnshire was deeply rooted in the hearts of these poets, and in truth there is no wonder that it should be.  For Somersby is an enchanted spot, bright, luxurious, and beautiful.  Wooded hills rise before it and lie behind it; a merry brook gleams in the glen, and " swerves to left and right through meadowy curves," as it draws

> Into [its] narrow earthen urn,
>   In every elbow and turn,
> The filter'd tribute of the rough woodland.

All the air is melodious with the songs of birds—the rapturous lark, the trilling linnet, the joyous thrush, and the wrangling daw; and the long lonely lanes, like avenues, are cool and shady, and odorous with many flowers.  How all these scenes and sounds influenced the mind of Alfred Tennyson, and suggested to him story and song has already been told.  "What oftenest he viewed He viewed with the first glory," as every poet has done; and like a necromancer he has ever caused to pass before our eyes the lovely tints and golden hues of a glorious vanished past.

It was during this somewhat unsettled and aimless period that Alfred and Charles Tennyson composed those poems which were afterwards to be published as the work of " Two Brothers."[1]  There may be some truth in the curious story related to me that publication was decided upon in order that a little money might be obtained to enable the boys to carry out a long-cherished project of visiting the Lincolnshire churches.  Suffice it that a selection of the compositions was made and taken to Jackson of Louth, who sometimes risked the printing of books.  The Tennysons would be acquainted with Mr Jackson, or would know him well by repute, on account of their occasional visits to Louth, and they could scarcely fail to remark his superior establishment in the centre of the town.  Mrs Tennyson and her sons had resided for some time in Harvey's Alley, now known as Westgate Place, the little domicile being situated close to the church in which the Rev. Stephen

---

[1] Frederick Tennyson was responsible for one poem, *The Oak of the North.*

Fytche preached. Alfred and Charles Tennyson found Mr Jackson kind-hearted and sympathetic. Not only did he arrange to bring out the poems in book form, but he offered them £10 for the copyright. To this the boys agreed, but, with the confidence of youth, afterwards informed the publisher that £10 was "none too high a price," whereupon that excellent person considerately doubled it. Twenty pounds was the sum actually received by the two lads for their poems. Already, therefore, they had proved the falseness of that disastrous prophecy of their uncle, who, on giving Alfred a half-sovereign for some verses, declared that that was the last money he would ever receive for a like reason. The original manuscript of this interesting work was sold for £480 last December (1892).

The *Poems by Two Brothers* made their appearance in a small drab volume, priced at seven and sixpence, in 1827. The "copy" had been put into the printer's hands early in the year, so that Alfred was only seventeen when the last of his contributions to the pages was made. It was originally intended that the two brothers' initials, "C. T." and "A. T.," should appear upon the title-page; but while the work was passing through the press the authors changed their minds, and told Mr Jackson that this was no part of the agreement, and would "not assist the sale of the book any more than if there was no signature at all." Thus it happened that when the book appeared there was no indication of who the two intrepid poets were.

"Hæc nos novimus esse nihil" was the motto modestly chosen by the brothers for their first work; and their "Advertisement" was written in the same vein. "The following poems," the public were informed, "were written from the ages of fifteen to eighteen, not conjointly, but individually, which may account for their difference of style and matter. To light upon any novel combination of images, or to open any vein of sparkling thought untouched before, were no easy task; indeed, the remark itself is as old as the truth is clear; and, no doubt, if submitted to the microscopic eye of periodical criticism, a long list of inaccuracies and imitations would result from the investigation.  But so it is.  We have passed the Rubicon, and we leave the rest to fate, though its edict may create a fruitless regret that we ever emerged from 'the shade,' and courted notoriety."  Then follow some forty introductory lines of no great merit as a whole, though with here and there a striking line or a flashing image.  We are told that

> When the mind reflects its image true—
> Sees its own aim—expression must ensue ;
> If all but language is supplied before,
> She quickly follows, and the task is o'er.

Then, with a recollection of November the Fifth festivities, the youthful poet illustrates his meaning as follows :

> Thus when the hand of pyrotechnic skill
> Has stored the spokes of the fantastic wheel,
> Apply the flame—it spreads as is design'd,
> And glides and lightens o'er the track defined.

A rhapsody on poetic pleasures is better.

> I know no joy so well deserves the name,
> None that more justly may that title claim,
> Than that of which the poet is possess'd
> When warm imagination fires his breast,
> And countless images like claimants throng,
> Prompting the ardent ecstasy of song.

Even at this early period we find that the boys, instead of dashing off their verses in a frenzy, were accustomed to pace the study "in a dreaming mood," and form "with much toil the lab'ring lines," a confession which does them great credit.

> Such are the sweets of song—and in this age,
> Perchance too many in its lists engage ;
> And they who now would fain awake the lyre,
> May swell this supernumerary choir :
> But ye, who deign to read, forget t' apply
> The searching microscope of scrutiny :

> Few from too near inspection fail to lose,
> Distance on all a mellowing haze bestows ;
> And who is not indebted to that aid
> Which throws his failures into welcome shade ?

I judge this Introduction to be the work of Charles Tennyson, being more in conformity with his style. It is true that the line, "Distance on all a mellowing haze bestows," finds its echo in *In Memoriam*, but Campbell had already given currency to the idea in the well-known "Distance lends enchantment to the view." Of the hundred and two poems which follow it is difficult to say much either in praise or blame. They are not commonplace, stilted, or ill-conceived ; but, at the same time, they reach no great height and excite little real emotion. Above all, they never seem to come direct from the heart. Whatever power they possess, and whatever grace they display, are purely of the intellectual kind, and the cold, carefully-measured lines are strangely unlike most boyish outbursts into verse. How curious it is to hear these lads between fifteen and eighteen gravely discoursing on philosophy, and from the depths of their experience teaching mankind the severe duties of life. It is scarcely natural to be tutored by youth and told that "life is but a scene of fallacy and woe," that "mortal man" should not "complain of death," and that "never from a wither'd heart The consciousness of ill shall part." The subjects of the poems are always sombre. Death, sorrow, pain, exile, rage, remorse, and despair are the most constant of themes. We are told by these artless juveniles that

> 'T is a fearful thing to glance
> Back on the gloom of misspent years ;

and at another time one of them, as if that gloom could never be dissipated, devotes a whole poem to explaining how he "wanders in darkness and sorrow." He asks—

> In this waste of existence, for solace
> On whom shall my lone spirit call?
> Shall I fly to the friends of my bosom?
> My God ! I have buried them all !

The poet then courts a terrible doom.

> Like the voice of the owl in the hall,
>   Where the song and the banquet have ceased,
> Where the green weeds have mantled the hearth,
>   Whence arose the proud flame of the feast;
> So I cry to the storm, whose dark wing
>   Scatters on me the wild driving sleet—
> " Let the war of the wind be around me,
>   The fall of the leaves at my feet !"

Thomson, Scott, and Byron, had up to this time been the " masters " whom the two poets reverently regarded, and it is not surprising to find that the influence of all the three can be detected in their juvenile works. Alfred Tennyson was but fifteen years of age when he heard of Byron's death at Missolonghi. The effect of the news upon the susceptible mind of the lad was such that he " thought the whole world was at an end." " I thought everything was over and finished for everyone—that nothing else mattered," he related long afterwards. " I remember I walked out alone, and carved, ' Byron is dead ' into the sandstone." In view of this we may conclude that it was Alfred who wrote the lines *On the Death of Lord Byron* in the metre afterwards employed in *The Two Voices.*

> The hero and the bard is gone !
> His bright career on earth is done,
> Where with a comet's blaze he shone.
>
> He died where vengeance arms the brave,
> Where buried freedom quits her grave,
> In regions of the eastern wave.
>
> Yet not before his ardent lay
> Had bid them chase all fear away,
> And taught their trumps a bolder bray.
>
> Thro' him their ancient valor glows,
> And, stung by thraldom's scathing woes,
> They rise again, as once they rose.
>
> As once in conscious glory bold,
> To war their sounding cars they roll'd,
> Uncrush'd, untrampled, uncontroll'd !

Each drop that gushes from their side,
Will serve to swell the crimson tide,
That soon shall whelm the Moslem's pride !

At last upon their lords they turn,
At last the shame of bondage learn,
At last they feel their fetters burn !

Oh ! how the heart expands to see
An injured people all agree
To burst those fetters and be free !

Each far-famed mount that cleaves the skies,
Each plain where buried glory lies,
All, all exclaim—" Awake ! arise !"

Who would not feel their wrongs ? and who
Departed freedom would not rue,
With all her trophies in his view ?

To see imperial Athens reign,
And, lowering o'er the vassal main,
Rise in embattled strength again—

To see rough Sparta train once more
Her infant's ears for battle's roar,
Stern, dreadful, chainless as before—

Was Byron's hope—was Byron's aim :
With ready heart and hand he came :
But perish'd in that path of fame !

There is a poem on *Greece*, full of martial vigour, which
no doubt was inspired by Byron's mission, while the better-
known lines *On a dead Enemy* are in the true Byronic
vein.

I came in haste with cursing breath,
　And heart of hardest steel ;
But when I saw thee cold in death,
　I felt as man should feel.

For when I look upon that face,
　That cold, unheeding, frigid brow,
Where neither rage nor fear has place,
　By Heaven ! I cannot hate thee now !

Charles Tennyson's was the gentler muse ; and we must ascribe to him most of the poems of a tender melancholy and a chastened religious feeling.  The pretty stanzas on *Boyhood* remind us of the thought pervading some of the sonnets subsequently published.

> Boyhood's blest hours ! when yet unfledged and callow,
>     We prove those joys we never can retain,
> In riper years with fond regret we hallow,
>     Like some sweet scene we never see again.
>
> For youth—whate'er may be its petty woes :
>     Its trivial sorrows—disappointments—fears,
> As on in haste life's wintry current flows—
>     Still claims, and still receives, its debt of tears.
>
> Yes ! when, in grim alliance, grief and time
>     Silver our heads and rob our hearts of ease,
> We gaze along the deeps of care and crime
>     To the far, fading shore of youth and peace ;
>
> Each object that we meet the more endears
>     That rosy morn before a troubled day ;
> That blooming dawn—that sunrise of our years—
>     That sweet voluptuous vision past away !
>
> For by the welcome, tho' embittering power
>     Of wakeful memory, we too well behold
> That lightsome—careless—unreturning hour,
>     Beyond the reach of wishes or of gold.
>
> And ye, whom blighted hopes or passion's heat
>     Have taught the pangs that care-worn hearts endure,
> Ye will not deem the vernal rose so sweet !
>     Ye will not call the driven snow so pure !

Happy boy, that for him, as he wrote these lines, there still remained the light of sunrise and the rosy hue of morn—that the sadness was only anticipated and the pleasure at that moment enjoyed !

I have quoted these poems chiefly because of the index they constitute of the state of the minds of the two youthful authors.  The *Poems by Two Brothers* plainly reveal that Alfred and Charles Tennyson were conscious of their gifts, and that if they had little knowledge of the world and its ways, they at all events possessed in compensation an abundance of imagination. Their poems lack humanity and, even in many cases, spontaneity. They were exercises, tasks, and truly "lab'ring lines," and though the execution of them was worthy, they remained inanimate and dull. It is perhaps needless to record that the volume dropped almost unheeded from the press. The *Gentlemen's Magazine* for July 1827 contained a brief and kind critique, in which the verse was commended as "promising." The *Literary Chronicle* said the volume exhibited "a pleasing union of kindred tastes." Beyond that there was nothing. Not until it was a relic was that little volume to become treasured and famous, and many years were to pass before the two brothers were to " emerge from the shade," as in boyhood they had dreamed they might do. The literary partnership cemented the friendship between them. A community of thought and likeness of temperament had already drawn them closely to each other, and how loving and genuine their attachment was can be learned from the beautiful tribute which was paid to Charles Tennyson in *In Memoriam—*

> Thou and I are one in kind,
>     As moulded like in nature's mint ;
>     And hill and wood and field did print
> The same sweet forms in either mind.
>
> For us the same cold streamlet curl'd
>     Thro' all his eddying coves ; the same
>     All winds that roam the twilight came
> In whispers of the beauteous world.
>
> At one dear knee we proffer'd vows,
>     One lesson from one book we learn'd,
>     Ere childhood's flaxen ringlet turn'd
> To black and brown on kindred brows.

Charles Tennyson, under the name of Tennyson-Turner, was yet to win renown as a sonneteer ; but of many happy days those were among the happiest when, with his poet-brother, he roamed about the Lincolnshire wolds, or stood by his side listening to the roar of the northern sea.

# CHAPTER II.

AT CAMBRIDGE: "TIMBUCTOO."

> " Old wishes, ghosts of broken plans,
>     And phantom hopes assemble;
> And that child's heart within the man's
>     Begins to move and tremble.
>
> " Thro' many an hour of summer suns,
>     By many pleasant ways,
> Against its fountain upward runs
>     The current of my days:
> I kiss the lips I once have kissed;
>     The gas-light wavers dimmer;
> And softly thro' a vinous mist,
>     My college friendships glimmer."
>
> *—Will Waterproof's Lyrical Monologue.*

THE time came when the two brothers were to leave Lincolnshire for the first time. Frederick, the eldest of Dr Tennyson's sons, had been for two years at Cambridge University, where he had maintained the reputation won at Eton for dexterity in Latin and Greek verse-writing. In 1828 Charles and Alfred Tennyson entered Trinity College, an epoch-marking event in the lives of both. From sleepy, out-of-the-world Somersby to the centre of intellectual activity was a change which could not fail to leave its impress upon the minds of the Lincolnshire rector's sons. They arrived at Cambridge when, by fortuitous circumstances, there were gathered within the University a number of young men upon whom the seal of a high destiny had been fixed. The magnetism which draws man to man, and which causes them to seek their affinities, attracted into one small circle the Tennysons, Richard Chenevix Trench, Monckton Milnes (afterwards Lord Houghton, who towards the close of his life meditated writing the Laureate's biography), William Makepeace Thackeray, George Venables (sometimes supposed to be the "George Warrington" of *Pendennis*), James Spedding, J. M. Kemble, W. H. Brookfield ("Old Brooks"), and Kinglake the historian. But above and beyond these was Arthur Henry Hallam, son of Hallam the historian, of Clevedon Court, Somerset, who in October 1828 entered Trinity College, being then in his eighteenth year. Undergraduate life was not a dull and wearisome round of study, and these kindred spirits found plenty of opportunity for communication. Tennyson was not a resident in the College—he lived first in Rose Crescent and afterwards at Corpus Buildings—but Hallam had a room within "the reverend walls," and there the brilliant young men were wont to meet for interchange of thought.

In 1829 a number of them were set in friendly competition for the Chancellor's gold medal for a poem, the subject, oddly chosen, being Timbuctoo. Hallam and Monckton Milnes were believed to stand the best chances of success, and each was fairly confident of the prize. Milnes wrote with pride to his father to say that his verses were admired by his own friends, while Hallam boasted that he had written "in a sovereign vein of poetic scorn for anybody's opinion who did not value Plato and Milton." His poem, which was afterwards published among his collected works, is in the difficult *terza rima* of Dante. Alfred Tennyson hung aloof from this contest, but urged by his father to compete, he revised and adapted a poem on Armageddon, finished some years before, and submitted it for judgment. This poem was in blank verse, and Tennyson thus overcame the obstacle of rhyme, which had been viewed with consternation when the subject was first announced. A protest had, indeed, been made that there was no rhyme to Timbuctoo, but Thackeray with ready wit immediately scribbled down the lines—

> In the vale of Cassowary,
> By the plain of Timbuctoo,

> There I ate a missionary,
> Body, bones, and hymn-book, too.[1]

In the *Cambridge Chronicle and Journal* of June 12, 1829, the award was made known in the following words :—
"On Saturday last the Chancellor's gold medal for the best English poem by a resident undergraduate was adjudged to Alfred Tennyson, of Trinity College." There is a strange story related that Tennyson sent in two *Timbuctoos* for the medal : one to please the examiners, and one to satisfy himself, and it was the *latter* which won the prize.[2]  Sir George Trevelyan, in recording Macaulay's failure to win the medal ten years before with his poem *Waterloo,* somewhat bitterly remarks that "the opening lines of Macaulay's exercise were pretty and simple enough to ruin his chance in an academical competition."  What the cynic would have said to that peal of music with which *Timbuctoo* opens, we can only conjecture.  The poet imagines himself surveying a vast and beautiful domain.

> I stood upon the Mountain which o'erlooks
> The narrow seas, whose rapid interval
> Parts Afric from green Europe, when the Sun
> Had fall'n below th' Atlantic, and above
> The silent heavens were blench'd with faery light,
> Uncertain whether faery light or cloud,
> Flowing Southward, and the chasms of deep, deep blue
> Slumber'd unfathomable, and the stars
> Were flooded over with clear glory and pale.
> I gazed upon the sheeny coast beyond,
> There where the Giant of old Time infix'd
> The limits of his prowess, pillars high
> Long time erased from earth : even as the Sea
> When weary of wild inroad buildeth up
> Huge mounds whereby to stay his yeasty waves.[3]

As he gazes upon the wondrous scene, "legends quaint

[1] I give the likeliest of several versions, one of which has been attributed to Sidney Smith.

[2] Another story, perhaps the invention of an enemy, is that one of the examiners marked on the MS. "v. q." (meaning "very queer"), and it was mistaken for "v. g." ("very good").

[3] *Cf.* "yeasty surges" in *The Sailor Boy.*

and old" come to his mind, and he muses upon the time
when Atalantis was "a center'd glory-circled memory," and
when imperial Eldorado was a dream to which "men clung
with yearning hope which would not die."

> As when in some great city where the walls
> Shake, and the streets with ghastly faces thronged
> Do utter forth a subterranean voice,
> Among the inner columns far retired
> At midnight, in the lone Acropolis,
> Before the awful genius of the place
> Kneels the pale Priestess in deep faith, the while
> Above her head the weak lamp dips and winks
> Unto the fearful summoning without :
> Nathless she even clasps the marble knees,
> Bathes the cold hand with tears, and gazeth on
> Those eyes which wear no light but that wherewith
> Her phantasy informs them.

The poet, too, finds the desire glowing within him to know
where the vanished splendours are. "The moonlight
halls," the "cedarn glooms," the "blossoming abysses"—
where are they?

> Then I raised
> My voice and cried, "Wide Afric, doth thy Sun
> Lighten, thy hills enfold a city as fair
> As those which starred the night o' the elder world?
> Or is the rumour of thy Timbuctoo
> A dream as frail as those of ancient time?"

There was "a curve of whitening, flashing, ebbing light,"
and a rustling of white wings, and a young Seraph stood
beside the questioner.

> I looked, but not
> Upon his face, for it was wonderful
> With its exceeding brightness, and the light
> Of the great Angel Mind which looked from out
> The starry glowing of his restless eyes.
> I felt my soul grow mighty, and my spirit
> With supernatural excitation bound
> Within me, and my mental eye grew large
> With such a vast circumference of thought,

> That in my vanity I seemed to stand
> Upon the outward verge and bound alone
> Of full beatitude.   Each failing sense,
> As with a momentary flash of light,
> Grew thrillingly distinct and keen.   I saw
> The smallest grain that dappled the dark earth,
> The indistinctest atom in deep air.
> The Moon's white cities, and the opal width
> Of her small glowing lakes, her silver heights
> Unvisited with dew of vagrant cloud,
> And the unsounded, undescended depth
> Of her black hollows.   The clear galaxy
> Shorn of its hoary lustre, wonderful,
> Distinct and vivid with sharp points of light,
> Blaze within blaze, an unimagined depth
> And harmony of planet-girded suns
> And moon-encircled planets, wheel in wheel,
> Arched the wan sapphire.   Nay—the hum of men
> Or other things talking in unknown tongues,
> And notes of busy life in distant worlds
> Beat like a far wave on my anxious ear.

A marvellous description of mental doubt and perplexity follows, and then the poet tells how his vision was cleared and his thought uplifted until he felt "unutterable buoyancy and strength" to penetrate "the trackless fields of undefined existence far and free."   The mists passed away, and in the clear light of a new morn he saw the enchanted city of Timbuctoo.

> Then first within the South methought I saw
> A wilderness of spires, and crystal pile
> Of rampart upon rampart, dome on dome,
> Illimitable range of battlement
> On battlement, and the Imperial height
> Of canopy o'ercanopied.
>                                      Behind
> In diamond light up spring the dazzling peaks
> Of Pyramids, as far surpassing earth's
> As heaven than earth is fairer.   Each aloft
> Upon his narrowed eminence bore globes
> Of wheeling suns, or stars, or semblances
> Of either, showering circular abyss

> Of radiance.  But the glory of the place
> Stood out a pillared front of burnished gold,
> Interminably high, if gold it were
> Or metal more ethereal, and beneath
> Two doors of blinding brilliance, where no gaze
> Might rest, stood open, and the eye could scan,
> Through length of porch and valve and boundless hall,
> Part of a throne of fiery flame, wherefrom
> The snowy skirting of a garment hung,
> And glimpse of multitude of multitudes
> That ministered around it—if I saw
> These things distinctly, for my human brain
> Staggered beneath the vision, and thick night
> Came down upon my eyelids, and I fell.

What the Seraph said to him when he had raised him up is told in a luxury of language which afterwards was found perfected in the *Idylls of the King*. The Spirit had been sent to sway the heart of man and teach him "to attain, by shadowing forth the Unattainable." It was he who with every changing season played about the human heart, visited man's eyes with visions, "and his ears With harmonies of wind and wave and wood."

> And few there be
> So gross of heart who have not felt and known
> A higher than they see : they with dim eyes
> Behold me darkling.  Lo I have given thee
> To understand my presence, and to feel
> My fullness : I have filled thy lips with power.
> I have raised thee nigher to the spheres of heaven,
> Man's first, last home : and thou with ravished sense
> Listenest the lordly music flowing from
> The illimitable years.

The Seraph, too, was the permeating life coursing through the labyrinthine veins of fable, and with beautiful impressiveness he told the mortal by his side the doom of all things glorious and fair.

> Child of man,
> Seest thou yon river, whose translucent wave
> Forth issuing from the darkness, windeth through

> The argent streets o' the city, imaging
> The soft inversion of her tremulous domes,
> Her gardens frequent with the stately palm,
> Her pagods hung with music of sweet bells,
> Her obelisks of rangéd chrysolite,
> Minarets and towers?   Lo! how he passeth by,
> And gulphs himself in sands, as not enduring
> To carry through the world those waves, which bore
> The reflex of my city in their depths.
> Oh city: oh latest throne! where I was raised
> To be a mystery of loveliness
> Unto all eyes, the time is well-nigh come
> When I must render up this glorious home
> To keen Discovery: soon yon brilliant towers
> Shall darken with the waving of her wand;
> Darken and shrink and shiver into huts,
> Black specks amid a waste of dreary sand,
> Low-built, mud-walled, barbarian settlements.
> How changed from this fair city!

The poem, good as it is, must chiefly be regarded as an omen.   It was the true gold of morning—the opening of a long and cloudless day.   We could have wished that the poet had seen fit to include *Timbuctoo* in his collected works, but perhaps the incongruity of the subject made him decide upon its exclusion rather than the defects of treatment.   Hallam and Milnes were among the first to congratulate their friend upon his triumph, and John Sterling or Frederic Maurice—it is not certain which— hailed the dawning genius in the pages of the *Athenæum*. After quoting a long passage the critic asked, " How many men have lived for a century who could equal this?"   The poem was printed for the first and last time with the author's consent in the College Magazine; but in the *Ode to Memory* (" written very early in life," but first published in 1830) two of the lines have been preserved—

> Listening the lordly music flowing from
> The illimitable years.

The Prize Poem was not to escape the cruel fate of burlesque, and Thackeray's was the hand to inflict the blow. In *The Snob* an anonymous letter appeared with an enclosure of verses, and the whole is so amusing and good-natured that I cannot refrain from reproducing a portion of the skit.

### TO THE EDITOR OF "THE SNOB."

Sir,—Though your name be " Snob," I trust you will not refuse this tiny *Poem of a Gownsman*, which was unluckily not finished on the day appointed for the delivery of the several copies of verses on *Timbuctoo*. I thought, sir, it would be a pity that such a poem should be lost to the world ; and, conceiving *The Snob* to be the most widely-circulated periodical in Europe, I have taken the liberty of submitting it for insertion or approbation.—I am, Sir, yours, &c.

## TIMBUCTOO.

### THE SITUATION.

In Africa (a quarter of the world),
Men's skins are black, their hair is crisp and curl'd,
And somewhere there, unknown to public view,
A mighty city lies, called Timbuctoo.

### THE NATURAL HISTORY.

There stalks the tiger—there the lion roars
Who sometimes eats the luckless blackamoors ;
All that he leaves of them the monster throws
To jackals, vultures, dogs, cats, kites, and crows ;
His hunger thus the forest monster gluts,
And then lies down 'neath trees called cocoa nuts.

### THE LION HUNT.

Quick issue out, with musket, torch, and brand !
The sturdy blackamoors, a dusky band !
The beast is found—pop go the musketoons—
The lion falls covered with horrid wounds.

### THEIR LIVES AT HOME.

At home their lives in pleasure always flow,
But many have a different lot to know.

### ABROAD.

They're often caught, and sold as slaves, alas !

### REFLECTIONS ON THE FOREGOING.

Thus men from highest joys to sorrow pass.
Yet though thy monarchs and thy nobles boil

> Rice and molasses in Jamaica's isle ;
> Desolate Afric ! thou art lovely yet ! !
> One heart yet beats that ne'er thee shall forget.
> What though thy maidens are a blackish brown,
> Does virtue dwell in whiter breasts alone?
> Oh no, oh no, oh no, oh no, oh no !
> It shall not, must not, cannot, e'er be so.
> The day shall come when Albion's self shall feel
> Stern Afric's wrath, and writhe 'neath Afric's steel.
> I see her tribes the hill of glory mount,
> And sell their sugars on their own account ;
> While round her throne the prostrate nations come,
> Sue for her rice, and barter for her rum.

In one portion of his *Timbuctoo* Tennyson had supplied an explanatory footnote—a habit to which he was greatly addicted in his youth. Thackeray, not to be behind, supplied voluminous explanations, such as : " Line 1—The site of Timbuctoo is doubtful ; the author has neatly expressed this in the poem, at the same time giving us some slight hints relative to its situation." " Lines 15 and 18—A concise but affecting description is here given of the domestic habits of the people. . . . The author trusts the reader will perceive the aptness with which he has changed his style. When he narrated facts he was calm ; when he enters on prophecy he is fervid."

Tennyson had the greatest objection to ridicule of this sort, and it is not improbable that he resented Thackeray's playfulness, though, happily, there was no break in their friendly relations. As a proof of the poet's sensitiveness it may be related that at a college symposium he read to his assembled friends the lines on the Kraken, with the fine conclusion that the monster will not emerge from the sea-depths "until the latter fire shall heat the deep "—

> Then once by man and angels to be seen,
> In roaring he shall rise and on the surface die.

As the poet finished reading, one of the friends, more ribald than the rest, exclaimed, "That will be a pretty kettle of fish !" Tennyson glared at the speaker in silence, and left the room. But at the next meeting he produced the poem beginning—

> Vex not thou the poet's mind
> With thy shallow wit.

Those who remembered the preceding incident gave the lines a personal application.

In the copy of *Poems*, by Alfred Tennyson, 1833, which is in the Dyce Collection at South Kensington Museum, an autograph manuscript is inserted containing the following sonnet :—

> Therefore your Halls, your ancient Colleges,
>   Your portals statued with old kings and queens,
> Your gardens, myriad-volumed libraries,
>   Wax-lighted chapels, and rich-carven screens,
>   Your doctors, and your proctors, and your deans,
> Shall not avail you, when the Day-beam sports
> New risen o'er awakened Albion—No !
>   Nor yet your solemn organ-pipes that blow
>   Melodious thunders thro' your vacant courts
> At morn and eve—because your manner sorts
>   Not with this age wherefrom ye stand apart—
> Because the lips of little children preach
> Against you, you that do profess to teach,
>   And teach us nothing, feeding not the heart.

There is a note appended to this which serves as comment and explanation :—" I have a great affection for my old university, and can only regret that this spirit of under-graduate irritability against the Cambridge of that day ever found its way into print." This note forbids further reference to the subject.

There were to be many reminiscences of these college days—life-long influences of friendship and of sorrow. The poet had become as close a student of men and manners as he had formerly been of nature. In volumes which the future was to bring forth, his love and his scorn were to be shown for those he knew, though it is gratifying to observe that his love was for the many and his scorn for the few. There are the touching lines of consolation to James

Spedding, and the stirring sonnet to J. M. Kemble, "a latter Luther;" the lines to "Old Brooks, who loved so well to mouth my rhymes," and the masterly delineation of that Character who

> Canvass'd human mysteries,
> And trod on silk, as if the winds
> Blew his own praises in his eyes,
> And stood aloof from other minds,
> In impotence of fancied power.

Who was he ?   What was the name of him who

> With lips depress'd as he were meek,
> Himself unto himself he sold ;
> Upon himself himself did feed :
> Quiet, dispassionate, and cold,
> And other than his form of creed,
> With chisell'd features clear and sleek?

The identity of this person has remained a mystery, the nearest approach to a discovery being made when a manuscript note appended by the late Master of Trinity College to a copy of the poem was found to contain the information that "the original was a certain eloquent speaker at the Cambridge Union, of whose subsequent career little or nothing is known." This is vague and disappointing, and, like the fool's story, signifies nothing. A short time ago a beautiful copy of the original edition of Tennyson's Poems (1830) passed through my hands, and turning to this poem I saw with astonishment the record in faded ink, and *in the Tennysonian caligraphy*, that the " Character " was none other than "Thomas Sunderland, M.A. of Trinity College."

Those college-days were full of rare delight and profit. Who would not have loved to hear Tennyson reading a new poem, Kemble the "soldier-priest" advancing his "cross-worded proof," Brookfield, the "man of humorous melancholy mark," the "kindlier, trustier Jaques," uttering his words of cheer, and Arthur Hallam drawing all to his converse with

> Seraphic intellect and force
>   To seize and throw the doubts of man ;
>   Impassioned logic, which outran
> The hearer in its fiery course ?

How inspiring it must have been to hear that "band of youthful friends" holding debate on mind and art, labour and state :—

> When one would aim an arrow fair,
>   But send it slackly from the string ;
>   And one would pierce an outer ring,
> And one an inner, here and there ;
>
> And last the master-bowman, he
>   Would cleave the mark.

"So sad, so fresh, the days that are no more!" Brookfield, who remained a cherished friend of the poet's, was a clergyman of the Church of England, a distinguished preacher, Chaplain-in-Ordinary to the Queen, and one of Her Majesty's Inspectors of Schools. He was especially favoured in his literary friendships. It was at his death, in memory of these days, that the Laureate wrote the sonnet beginning

> Brooks, for they call'd you so that knew you best,
> Old Brooks, who loved so well to mouth my rhymes,
> How oft we two have heard St Mary's chimes !
> How oft the Cantab supper, host and guest,
> Would echo helpless laughter to your jest !

In later years his friends included many names famous in the ranks of literature—Carlyle, Kinglake, Lord Houghton. Miss Thackeray (Mrs Richie) wrote to Lord Lyttleton that Mr Brookfield was the "Frank Whitestock" of her father's sketch, *The Curate's Walk.*

No marvel is it that the doings of those Cambridge days passed into a cherished memory, that the "dawn-golden times" lost none of their radiance or beauty as they were pushed further back into the past. Alfred

Tennyson, who, like Thackeray, left without taking his degree, on one ever-memorable occasion returned to Cambridge.

> I past beside the reverend walls
>   In which of old I wore the gown ;
>   I roved at random thro' the town,
> And saw the tumult of the halls ;
>
> And heard once more in college fanes
>   The storm their high-built organs make,
>   And thunder-music, rolling, shake
> The prophets blazon'd on the panes ;
>
> And caught once more the distant shout,
>   The measured pulse of racing oars
>   Among the willows ; paced the shores
> And many a bridge, and all about
>
> The same gray flats again, and felt
>   The same, but not the same ; and last
>   Up that long walk of limes I past
> To see the rooms in which he dwelt.
>
> Another name was on the door :
>
>     .     .     .     .     .     .
>     .     .     .     .     .     .

# CHAPTER III.

## A LYRICAL PRELUDE.



*—Parnassus.*

ONE of those apocryphal stories, usually related of men of mark, is to the effect that Alfred Tennyson as a little boy was asked what he would like to be when he grew up. "A poet !" said the child.   However much we may be inclined to doubt the fact, there is no escape from the conclusion that Tennyson as a young man had no serious aims of earning a livelihood.   Even in his day, when poetry was more in demand, and when it was something of a marketable commodity, no one with a practical mind could have thought it possible to obtain a satisfactory revenue from this source.   Dr Tennyson was not a rich man, and with his large family could not have saved money, so that it seemed a pressing necessity for the elder sons to choose a business or profession.   Charles entered the Church, but Alfred, after leaving College, had apparently no definite plans.   He had written in 1827-8 *The Lover's Tale*, which had been privately printed in 1833 and suppressed, the author "contenting himself with giving a few copies away." Thomas Powell, the author of a book on English writers, thinks the poem "decidedly unworthy" of Tennyson's reputation at that time—a lamentably rash judgment.   Of this poem Arthur Hallam possessed a copy, and as the whole piece was republished in 1879, its merits may be judged by readers for themselves. It is sufficient to relate in Tennyson's own words under what circumstances the long-concealed poem was brought into the light. "The original Preface to *The Lover's Tale,*" he wrote, "states that it was composed in my nineteenth year. Two only of the three parts then written were 'printed, when, feeling the imperfection of the poem, I withdrew it from the press. One of my friends, however, who, boy-like, admired the boy's work, distributed among our common associates of that hour some copies of those two parts, without my knowledge, without the omissions and amendments which I had in contemplation, and marred by the many misprints of the compositor. Seeing that those two parts have of late been mercilessly pirated, and that what I had deemed scarce worthy to live was not allowed to die, may I not be pardoned if I suffer the whole poem at last to come into the light, accompanied with a reprint of the sequel—a work of my mature life—*The Golden Supper ?*" It is worth noting here that *The Lover's Tale* supplied one line to *Timbuctoo*—" A center'd, golden-circled memory "—early evidence of the poet's economy. The author of *Tennysoniana* has pointed out that this early work of the Laureate's bears some resemblance to Browning's *Pauline,* which was also published in 1833. The *Berenice* of Edgar Allen Poe also treats of the same subject in a more sensational manner. *The Lover's Tale* was to have been included in the volume of 1833, and part of it was in type when Tennyson again decided that it was unworthy in its present condition to see the light.

At College, as we have seen, Tennyson was in the habit of reading his poems to a select circle of companions. It was on one such occasion that Alford, afterward Dean of Canterbury, heard "some very exquisite poetry of his entitled *The Hesperides.*" The enthusiasm of his friends may have finally decided the poet on his course, and the judgment of Hallam, who was one of his warmest admirers, no doubt largely influenced him. With this friend he had journeyed under romantic circumstances to the Pyrenees, the object of the two zealous youths being to carry succour to the patriots engaged in a struggle for liberty in Spain. Mrs Ritchie, who has special information of this incident in the poet's life, tells a strange story of how, when Tennyson and Hallam were taking money and letters written in invisible ink to certain conspirators who were then revolting against the intolerable tyranny of Ferdinand, they met, among others, a Senor Ojeda, who confided to Alfred his intentions, which were to *couper la gorge à tous les curés.* Senor Ojeda could not talk English or fully explain all his aspirations. "Mais vous connaissez mon cœur," said he, effusively. "And a pretty black one it is," thought the poet. The friends were soon convinced that the patriots were too bloodthirsty to be pleasant companions, so they took their departure. But two and thirty years later, when Tennyson saw again the valleys and the flashing streams, the memory of that time rose up, and

> All along the valley, by rock and cave and tree,
> The voice of the dead was a living voice to me.

The journey ended prematurely, but left Tennyson unexhausted. He was at this time, according to Edward Fitzgerald, "a man at all points of grand proportion and feature, significant of that inward chivalry becoming his ancient and honourable race," and he determined to expend his superfluous energy in a walking tour through Wales. We learn that he went one day into a little wayside inn, where an old man sat by the fire, who looked up, and asked many questions. "Are you from the army? Not from the army! Then where do you come from?" said the old man. "I am just come from the Pyrenees," said Alfred. "Ah, I knew there was a something," said the wise old man.

About this time Tennyson and Hallam had decided to issue a volume of their poems jointly, but Hallam's father did not favour the project.  Consequently, in the year 1830, a small but well-printed volume made its appearance with the title, "Poems, chiefly Lyrical.  By Alfred Tennyson." The 154 pages contained fifty-three poems, only thirty of which were preserved, though, in the latest authorised edition of the Laureate's works, *Supposed Confessions of a Second-rate Sensitive Mind not in unity with itself*, and *Leonine Elegiacs* have been restored.  Among the best-known poems which this volume contained were the series of portraits—*Lilian, Isabel, Madeline*, and *Adeline ; The Merman* and *The Mermaid*, the *Recollections of the Arabian Nights*, the *Ode to Memory, Oriana, The Sea-Fairies*, and *The Dying Swan*.  The volume was received with a chorus of praise.  Coleridge, in his "Table Talk" of April 18, 1830, wrote, "Tennyson's sonnets, such as I have seen, have many of the characteristic excellencies of those of Wordsworth and Southey."  Arthur Hallam, as might be expected, found much to applaud, and singling out the *Supposed Confessions* (to the lumbering title he objected), he declared that it was "full of deep insight into human nature, and into those particular trials which are sure to beset men who think and feel for themselves at this epoch of social development."  Leigh Hunt thought the poem might have been written by Crashaw "in a moment of scepticism, had he possessed vigour enough"; and a much later critic, after subjecting the poem to minute analysis, has declared, "It is a fine poem, at whatever period it was written."  Few of the other pieces in the volume were such a mixture of religion and metaphysics, and the judgment of John Stuart Mill upon the book stands forth as the most discerning and impartial of the time.  In the *Westminster Review* he wrote—

"That these poems will have a very rapid and extensive popularity we do not anticipate.  Their originality will prevent their being generally appreciated for a time.  But that time will come, we hope, to a not far distant end.  They demonstrate the possession of powers, to the future direction of which we look with some anxiety.  A genuine poet has deep responsibilities to his country and the world, to the present and future generations, to earth and heaven. He, of all men, should have distinct and worthy objects before him, and consecrate himself to their promotion. It is thus that he best consults the glory of his art, and his own lasting fame. Mr Tennyson has a dangerous quality in that facility of impersonation on which we have remarked, and by which he enters so thoroughly into the most strange and wayward idiosyncracies of other men. It must not degrade him into a poetical harlequin. He has higher work to do than that of disporting himself amongst 'mystics' and 'flowing philosophers.' He knows that ' the poet's mind is holy ground,' he knows that the poet's portion is to be

> Dower'd with the hate of hate, the scorn of scorn,
>     The love of love.

He has shown, in the lines from which we quote, his own just conception of the grandeur of a poet's destiny ; and we look to him for its fulfilment. It is not for such men to sink into mere verse-makers for the amusement of themselves or others. They can influence the associations of unnumbered minds ; they can command the sympathies of unnumbered hearts ; they can disseminate principles ; they can excite in a good cause the sustained enthusiasm that is sure to conquer ; they can blast the laurels of the tyrants, and hallow the memories of the martyrs of patriotism ; they can act with a force the extent of which it is difficult to estimate, upon national feelings and character, and consequently upon national happiness. If our estimate of Mr Tennyson be correct, he too is a poet ; and many years hence may be read his juvenile description of that character, with the proud consciousness that it has become the description and history of his own work."

This candid but complimentary criticism was followed by one of twelve pages in the *Englishman's Magazine*, penned by Hallam, and bearing the daring title " On some of the Characteristics of Modern Poetry, and on the Lyrical Poems of Alfred Tennyson." Part of this glorious tribute deserves to find its place here :—"Alfred Tennyson," wrote Hallam,

"has yet written little and published less ; but in these 'preludes of a loftier strain' we recognise the inspiring God. Mr Tennyson belongs decidedly to the class we have already described as Poets of Sensation. He sees all the forms of nature with the 'eruditus oculus,' and his ear has a fairy fineness.

There is a strange earnestness in his worship of beauty which throws a charm over his impassioned song, more easily felt than described, and not to be escaped by those who have once felt it. We think he has more definiteness and soundness of general conception than the late Mr Keats, and is much more free from blemishes of diction and hasty capriccios of fancy. He has also this advantage over that poet and his friend Shelley, that he comes before the public unconnected with any political party or peculiar system of opinions. Nevertheless, true to the theory we have stated, we believe his participation in their characteristic excellences is sufficient to secure him a share of their unpopularity. The volume of 'Poems, chiefly Lyrical,' does not contain above one hundred and fifty-four pages ; but it shows us much more of the character of its parent mind, than many books we have known of much larger compass, and more boastful pretensions. The features of original genius are clearly and strongly marked. The author imitates nobody ; we recognise the spirit of his age, but not the individual form of this or that writer. His thoughts bear no more resemblance to Byron or Scott, Shelley or Coleridge, than to Homer or Calderon, Furdúsi or Calidasa. We have remarked five distinctive excellences of his own manner. First, his luxuriance of imagination, and, at the same time, his control over it. Secondly, his power of embodying himself in ideal characters, or rather moods of character, with such extreme accuracy of adjustment, that the circumstances of the narrative seem to have a natural correspondence with the predominant feeling, and as it were, to be evolved from it by assimilative force. Thirdly, his vivid, picturesque delineation of objects, and the peculiar skill with which he holds all of them *fused*, to borrow a metaphor from science, in a medium of strong emotion. Fourthly, the variety of his lyrical measures and exquisite modulation of harmonious words and cadences to the swell and fall of the feelings expressed. Fifthly, the elevated habits of thought, implied in these compositions, and importing a mellow soberness of tone, more impressive, to our minds, than if the author had drawn up a set of opinions in verse, and sought to instruct the understanding rather than to communicate the love of beauty to the heart."

Soon after the appearance of this article the *Englishman's Magazine* ceased to appear, and it was this fact which enabled Professor Wilson—"Christopher North"—to insert an additional sting in his famous review in *Blackwood*. "The *Englishman's Magazine*," he said, "ought not to have died, for it threatened to be a very pleasant periodical. An essay 'On the Genius of Alfred Tennyson' sent it to the grave. The superhuman—nay, supernatural—pomposity of that one paper incapacitated the whole work for living one day longer in this unceremonious world. The solemnity with which the critic approached the object of his adoration, and the sanctity with which he laid his offerings on the shrine, were too much for our irreligious age. The 'Essay on the Genius of Alfred Tennyson' awoke a general guffaw, and it expired in convulsions. Yet the essay was exceedingly well written, as well as if it had been on 'The Genius of Sir Isaac Newton.' Therein lay the mistake. Sir Isaac discovered the law of gravitation; Alfred had but written some pretty verses, and mankind were not prepared to set him among the stars. But that he has genius is proved by his being at this moment alive; for had he not, he must have breathed his last under that critique. The spirit of life must indeed be strong within him; for he has outlived a narcotic dose administered to him by a crazy charlatan in the *Westminster*, and after that he may sleep in safety with a pan of charcoal."

This ominous note of warning prepared Tennyson for the reception which his next volume might expect in certain quarters. Nearly three years elapsed, however, before the second volume made its appearance. His was not the mind to reel under buffets however rude. He knew with Wordsworth that "every author, as far as he is great and at the same time original, has the task of creating the taste by which he is enjoyed: so has it been, so will it continue to be. . . . The predecessors of an original genius of a high order will have smoothed the way for all that he has in common with them, and much he will have in common; but for what is peculiarly his own he will be called upon to clear and often to shape his own road; he will be in the condition of Hannibal among the Alps."[1] Little could the veteran Laureate have known, when he penned those words, how exactly they applied to the man who was to succeed him.

Dr Tennyson was to know almost nothing of the ripening

---

[1] Essay on Poetry.

greatness of his son.  He died on March 18th, 1831, at the age of fifty-two, and was buried in the little Churchyard opposite the old home.  Not long afterwards the brother of James Spedding died, and Tennyson, "flowing in words" towards his bereaved College friend, was able tenderly to touch upon his own loss.

> 'Tis strange that those we lean on most,
>   Those in whose laps our limbs are nursed,
> Fall into shadow, soonest lost :
>   Those we love first are taken first.
>
> God gives us love.  Something to love
>   He lends us ; but, when love is grown
> To ripeness, that on which it throve
>   Falls off, and love is left alone.
>
> This is the curse of time.  Alas !
>   In grief I am not all unlearn'd ;
> Once thro' mine own doors Death did pass ;
>   One went, who never hath return'd.
>
> He will not smile—not speak to me
>   Once more.  Two years his chair is seen
> Empty before us.  That was he
>   Without whose life I had not been.

This poem was the last of thirty pieces which formed the volume dated 1833, published by Edward Moxon.  The more noted of the compositions are *The Lady of Shalott* (since entirely revised), *Mariana in the South, Eleanore, The Miller's Daughter, Œnone, The Palace of Art, The May Queen, The Lotos-Eaters,* and *A Dream of Fair Women.* Among suppressed poems were *The Hesperides, Rosalind, O Darling Room,* and *To Christopher North.*  The publication of this volume secured for the poet the recognition of Samuel Taylor Coleridge, and one of the heaviest castigations on record from the *Quarterly Review.*  Coleridge showed himself fully aware of the faults as well as the merits of the young poet, and in reading the criticisms of that time one must remember that many of the original versions of the now justly esteemed poems were very different to those now read. Weak lines appeared which have since been strengthened ; awkward words and phrases were actual blemishes, and in some cases whole verses, now omitted, detracted from the effect. For example, four introductory stanzas to *A Dream of Fair Women*, contained an image which is only once removed from the ridiculous—

> As when a man, that sails in a balloon,
>   Downlooking sees the solid shining ground
> Stream from beneath him in the broad blue noon,—
>   Tilth, hamlet, mead, and mound :
>
> And takes his flags and waves them to the mob,
>   That shout below, all faces turned to where
> Glows rubylike the far-up crimson globe,
>   Filled in a finer air :
>
> So, lifted high, the Poet at his will
>   Lets the great world flit from him, seeing all,
> Higher thro' secret splendours mounting still,
>   Self-poised, nor fears to fall,
>
> Hearing apart the echoes of his fame.
>   While I spoke thus, the seedsman, memory,
> Sowed my deep-furrowed thought with many a name,
>   Whose glory will not die.

Only the last three lines are worthy of preservation. Again, the original introductory stanza to *The Miller's Daughter* was—

> I met in all the close green ways,
>   While walking with my line and rod,
> The wealthy miller's mealy face,
>   Like the moon in an ivy tod.
> He looked so jolly and so good—
>   While fishing in the milldam water,
> I laughed to see him as he stood,
>   And dreamt not of the miller's daughter.

Taking these as specimens of the poet's shortcomings, we can understand Coleridge's reserve of praise when he wished to be friendly, and the *Quarterly* reviewer's excess of blame when he wished to be hostile. Writing in April 1833, the author of *Christabel* said—

"I have not read through all Mr Tennyson's poems, which have been sent to me ; but I think there are some things of a good deal of beauty in what I have seen.  The misfortune is, that he has begun to write verses without very well understanding what metre is.  Even if you write in a known and approved metre, the odds are, if you are not a metrist yourself, that you will not write harmonious verses ; but to deal in new metres without considering what metre means and requires, is preposterous.

"What I would, with many wishes for success, prescribe to Tennyson,—indeed without it he can never be a poet in act,—is to write for the next two or three years in none but one or two well-known and strictly-defined metres, such as the heroic couplet, the octave stanza, or the octosyllabic measure in *Allegro* and *Penseroso*.  He would, probably, thus get imbued with a sensation, if not a sense, of metre without knowing it, just as Eton boys get to write such good Latin verses by conning Ovid and Tibullus.  As it is, I can scarcely scan his verses."

But there was one man who had early recognised all the inherent power of the young poet.  "Some of our readers, we would fain hope," wrote Charles Kingsley in *Fraser's Magazine* in 1850, "remember, as an era in their lives, the first day on which they read those earlier poems ; how, fifteen years ago, *Mariana in the Moated Grange, The Dying Swan, The Lady of Shalott*, came to them as revelations.  They seemed to themselves to have found at last a poet who promised not only to combine the cunning melody of Moore, the rich fullness of Keats, and the simplicity of Wordsworth, but one who was introducing a method of observing nature different from that of all the three, and yet succeeding in everything which they had attempted, often in vain."  Those who write of Tennyson's early poems now can only repeat these opinions and confirm these impressions.

"Alfred Tennyson," wrote Bayard Taylor in May 1877, when he was able to look back upon these early efforts, and trace the poet's progress from a promising beginning to assured success, "must be classed among the most fortunate poets of all time.  He discovered the true capacities of his genius while still in the first freshness and ardour of youth, overcame doubt and hostile criticism before his prime, and has already lived to see his predominant influence upon the poetic literature of his day. Whatever judgment may be passed upon his work, his position and influence are beyond dispute. Posterity may take away a portion of what he has received, but cannot give him more. We have as yet but little knowledge of his life from the age of twenty-two to thirty-two; but that very fact indicates that this period was marked by no serious vicissitudes of fortune. As far as the world knows, his days have preserved a singularly even tenor. What emotional experiences, what periods of spiritual anxiety and suffering, he has passed through we do not know, and do not need to know; but for thirty years we have seen him moderately prosperous in external circumstances, and leading a quiet life of surrender to his art. Compared with the resounding platitudes of Heber and Milman, his poems express an independence of conception remarkable in one so young. In fact, the lines—

> Divinest Atlantis, whom the waves
> Have buried deep, and thou of later name,
> Imperial Eldorado, roofed with gold;
> Shadows to which, despite all shocks of change,
> All onset of capricious accident,
> Men clung with yearning hope which would not die,—

might have been written at any later period of his life. They illustrate the first distinct characteristic of his genius—an exquisitely luxurious sense of the charms of sound and rhythm, based upon an earnest, if not equal, capacity for sober thought and reflection. These two elements co-existed in Tennyson's mind, but were not developed in the same proportion, and are not always perfectly fused in his poetry. Take away either, and the half of his achievement, falling, leaves the other half utterly insecure. The aim of his life has been to correct and purify a power which he possessed almost in excess at the start, and to add to its kindred and necessary power by all the aids of study and science. The volume of 1832-3 is a remarkable advance in every respect. We see that indifference or ridicule has been powerless to stay the warm, opulent, symmetrical growth of his best powers. In the *Lady of Shalott*, *Œnone*, the *Lotos-Eaters*, the *Palace of Art*, and the *Dream of Fair Women*, we reach almost the level of his later achievement. In some of these the conception suffices to fill out the metrical form; the exquisite elaboration of detail is almost prescribed by the subject; and the luxuries of sound and movement, while not diminished, are made obedient to an intelligent melodic law. Rarely has a young man of twenty-two written such poetry or justified such large predictions of his future. We may conjecture that more was written in these years than he has preserved, for when we reach the volume of 1842, we find every former characteristic of his verse heightened and purified, not changed.  Only a sportive element, which does not quite reach the humorous, is introduced ; it is another chord of the same strain.  The fastidious care with which every image was wrought, every bar of the movement adjusted to the next and attuned to the music of all, every epithet chosen for point, freshness, and picturesque effect, every idea restrained within the limits of close and clear expression,—these virtues, so intimately fused, became a sudden delight for all lovers of poetry, and for a time affected their appreciation of its more unpretending and artless forms."

The indiscretion of youthful friends was directly responsible for the ferocious onslaught on Tennyson in the *Quarterly Review.*  He had been over-praised at one time, and now he was to be over-censured.  Looking calmly and dispassionately at the volumes of 1830 and 1833, noting both the strength and the weakness of the poems, observing the faults—faults which the poet's subsequent emendations show he became conscious of—I cannot honestly declare that the *Quarterly* strictures were unjustified.  They were severe to cruelty, and not altogether discriminating, and, as it happened, the sinister prophecies of the critic were unfulfilled.  But the praise lavished by too-ardent admirers upon Alfred Tennyson was more likely to injure him than the remorseless exposure of his demerits.  It was the custom in the old " slogging " days to use the sledge-hammer for crushing butterflies, and the " hang, draw, and Quarterly " had become specially notorious owing to its attack on Keats.  But Tennyson, after reading the pitiless satire of the reviewer (supposed to be none other than the editor, Lockhart), might have thought much the same as Disraeli in *Tancred :* " Failure is nothing ; it may be deserved or it may be remedied ; in the first instance it brings self-knowledge ; in the second it develops a new combination, usually triumphant."

A copy of the famous critique lies before me as I write. It abounds in scornful epithets and satiric phrases.  The reviewer adopted the good old-fashioned plan of publishing every weak line and drawing attention to its defects, easily distinguishable or otherwise.  He ridiculed the sentiments,

burlesqued the mannerisms, and did his utmost to make
bad worse. "Our task," he began, "will be little more
than the selection, for our readers' delight, of a few specimens of Mr Tennyson's singular genius, and the venturing
to point out, now and then, the peculiar brilliancy of some
of the gems that irradiate his poetical crown." The "few
selections" consisted of copious extracts from nearly every
poem in the volume. Immaturity and inexperience were
no doubt responsible for the blemishes, the want of accuracy,
the occasional false notes and the imperfect images of the
early poems. Thus, when he wrote in a *Dream of Fair
Women* of Iphigenia—

> One drew a sharp knife through my slender throat
> Slowly, *and nothing more,*

the poet exposed himself to the critic's gibe : "What
touching simplicity—what pathetic resignation—he cut my
throat—'*nothing more !*' One might indeed ask what *more*
she would have ?"

Tennyson never forgave the critics, and to the end of his
life he could not tolerate strictures. It is related that a
promising poet presented his book to Tennyson, accompanying it with a letter expressing admiration of his
genius. For reply, the Laureate returned him a cutting
from a newspaper of no recent date, embodying the epitome
of a lecture on one of the *Idylls* given by the younger poet,
containing some adverse criticisms. "I am like a traveller
in a lonely desert," said Tennyson ; "when suddenly there
appears on the horizon a figure which shoots an arrow that
reaches me, enters the flesh, and remains there. Although
the wound is small, 'tis a smart I cannot forget." To "indolent reviewers," "irresponsible, indolent reviewers" of
"blatant magazines," he dedicated his *Experiment* in
hendecasyllabics ; in *Sea Dreams* he declared—

> He had never kindly heart,
> Nor ever cared to better his own kind,
> Who first wrote satire, with no pity in it ;

and in *The Sisters* the poet tells how

> The critic's blurring comment makes
> The veriest beauties of the work appear
> The darkest faults.[1]

But he profited by criticism, and to what extent was seen when, in 1842, after an almost unbroken silence of nine years, he issued in two volumes his " Poems." In the meantime he had almost disappeared from public life. The shadow of his life-sorrow had enveloped him, and only once or twice had he emerged from his retirement to give the world a sonnet or such stanzas as *Oh, that 'twere possible* and *St Agnes.* " He moves on his way," said William Howitt, " heard, but by the public, unseen. Many an admiring man may have said, with Solomon, ' I have sought him, but I could not find him; I called him, but he answered not.' If you want a popular poët, you know pretty well where to look for him; but in few of those places will you find Alfred Tennyson. You may hear his voice, but where is the man? He is wandering in some dreamland, beneath the shade of old and charmed forests, by far-off shores, where

> All night
> The plunging seas draw backward from the land
> Their moon-led waters white;

by the old mill-dam, thinking of the merry miller and his pretty daughter; or he is wandering over the open wolds, where

> Norland whirlwinds blow.

From all these places—from the silent corridor of an ancient convent; from some shrine where a devoted knight recites his vows; from the drear monotony of the moated grange, or the ferny forest, beneath the ' talking oak '— comes the voice of Tennyson, rich, dreamy, passionate, yet not impatient; musical with the airs of chivalrous ages, yet mingling in his songs the theme and the spirit of

---

[1] See also *Poets and Critics* in the last volume, *The Death of Œnone.*

those which are yet to come." We have it on the authority of Frederick Tennyson, the eldest brother, that so careless was the poet at this time, that he lost the whole of the manuscript of his volume, and had to re-write all the poems from memory. These poems, now gathered under the head of *Juvenilia*, found immediate favour with the public and the critics alike. At a bound he had surpassed most of the singers of the day. Such poems as *A Dream of Fair Women*, *Œnone*, *The Lotos-Eaters*, and *The Palace of Art*, with their delicious cadences, their dreamy sensuousness, and their suffusion of exquisite colour, were at once a revelation and an enchantment. The song-like stanzas had haunting melodies; the very words seemed to sparkle to the eye; a sense of luxury and rest was borne on the languorous lines. There had been nothing like this since the music-laden verses of the *Faery Queen* gushed from the soul of Edmund Spenser, and the consummate art of the new poet could not fail to obtain instant acknowledgment. Among new poems were the *Morte d'Arthur*, *The Gardener's Daughter*, *St Simeon Stylites*, *The Talking Oak*, *Ulysses*, *Locksley Hall*, *The Two Voices*, and *The Golden Year* —all "preludes of a loftier strain." Wordsworth at once declared, " He is decidedly the first of our living poets," and, we may almost take it, saluted his successor. In those days what a spell the burst of harmony exercised, what new emotions it stirred !

> Music that gentlier on the spirit lies
> Than tir'd eyelids upon tir'd eyes ;
> Music that brings sweet sleep down from the blissful skies.

All Tennyson's poetry is such music, bearing with it an undercurrent of mystical and deep feeling. Who can read the *Lotos-Eaters* without seeming to hear the drowsy, murmurous phantom-song that " softer falls Than petals from blown roses on the grass "? or without seeming to feel the breath of elfin-winds, when " All round the coast the languid air

did swoon, Breathing like one that hath a weary dream "?
Even nature is hushed and motionless—

> Full-faced above the valley stood the moon,
> And like a downward smoke, the slender stream
> Along the cliff to fall and pause and fall did seem.

Then follows this exquisite verse, with its metrical cadence
and soft syllabic flow of words, descriptive of the strange
enchanted land in which the mild-eyed melancholy lotos-
eaters dwelt—

> A land of streams ! some, like a downward smoke,
> Slow-dropping veils of thinnest lawn did go ;
> And some thro' wavering lights and shadows broke,
> Rolling a slumbrous sheet of foam below.
> They saw the gleaming river seaward flow
> From the inner land : far off, three mountain-tops,
> Three silent pinnacles of aged snow,
> Stood sunset-flush'd : and, dew'd with showery drops,
> Up-clomb the shadowy pine above the woven copse.

This is the real lotos-music—thin, subtile, dreamy, yet how
wonderfully rich and sweet! Tennyson fits the melody to
the theme, and his art in onomatopœia is unexcelled. He
is a master of expression and harmony. His first productions were melodies in words. *Claribel* is only a combination of sweet sounds ; *Sea-Fairies* is a susurrant wave-like
song, beautiful and alluring, but with no more significance
than the rhythm of the sea ; the *Merman* and the *Mermaid*,
companion poems, are suggestive as the murmuring in sea-
shells, and mimic in metre the pulsation of restless waters :
but in none of them is stored the little crystal of thought
to make them more than idle melodies. These were the
notes ringing in the heart of a young man in whose bosom
music in all its power and grandeur was throbbing and
surging like a full tide. The sonnets of Charles Tennyson
also reveal his passionate love of melody and song—

> We must have music while we languish here,
> Loud music, to annul our spirits' strife,
> To make the soul with pleasant fancies rife,
> And soothe the stranger from another sphere.

The minor poems of Alfred Tennyson belong to four classes—song, narrative, fancy, sentiment—the products of various moods, the "random sport of sun and shade." Just as his music haunts the listener, so do the vividness and beauty of his pictures enchant the sight. One can never read Tennyson's poems without a refrain lingering in the mind or a vision forming before the eyes. In those eight lines *We are Free*, light as the breeze, the very words seem to tinkle and chime, to rise in refrain, to subside in a murmur. Sometimes the cadence falls into a minor key, as in that half-wailing poem—

> Flow down, cold rivulet, to the sea,
>   Thy tribute wave deliver :
> No more by thee my steps shall be,
>   For ever and for ever.
>
> A thousand suns will stream on thee,
>   A thousand moons will quiver :
> But not by thee my steps shall be,
>   For ever and for ever.

There is that world-famous lyric, too, familiar to every heart, which for pregnancy of thought, wealth of suggestion, and undefinable tenderness, is unmatched. It consists of sixteen lines, each a bar of music—a prelude, a theme, a passionate burst of agony, a closing cry of anguish and despair. The poem can scarcely be read in silence and alone without tears.

> Break, break, break,
>   On thy cold gray stones, O sea !
> And I would that I could utter
>   The thoughts that arise in me.
>
> O well for the fisherman's boy,
>   That he shouts with his sister at play !
> O well for the sailor lad,
>   That he sings in his boat on the bay !
>
> And the stately ships go on
>   To their haven under the hill ;
> But O for the touch of a vanish'd hand,
>   And the sound of a voice that is still !

> Break, break, break,
>   At the foot of thy crags, O sea !
> But the tender grace of a day that is dead,
>   Will never come back to me.

In these lines one sees the poet bowed down with an unnamed woe, watching the continual roll and rush of waters, hearing anon the laughter of heedless youth, catching the echoes of a song that speeds over the waves. He views the disappearing ships as one by one they cross the line and pass to their haven. Then swells up in the heart of the mourner a vain hope, a passionate yearning, an all-consuming desire, to feel once more the touch of a vanished hand, to hear again the sound of a voice that is still. And the monotonous waves rise and break and fall impotently on the stony beach, they exhaust their strength against the crags : and the despair of truth seizes on the poet's heart, shutting out every comfort and hope—

> The tender grace of a day that is dead,
>   Will *never* come back to me.

In many other examples it could be shown how the poet in these early volumes touched various chords—how by the happy blending of notes he produced the most beautiful of effects—how, in *Claribel*, words broke into melody, the theme deepening, and then, as if the pedals of an instrument had been pressed, softening again and ceasing on the repetition of the first line.

In narrative he had equal skill. Two verses sufficed to condense all the story of King Cophetua and the Beggar Maid. It would be impossible to compress the details into smaller compass, and this poem—which appeared in a later volume—may be taken as representative of the narrative style to which *Oriana*, *The Sisters*, *Lady Clare*, the *English Idylls*, and even *Enoch Arden* belong. The poet himself spoke of his own "deep-chested music" while modestly decrying the worth of his "faint Homeric echoes" ; but the force, vigour, concentrated strength, and measured power of the style he made his own attest to the genuine merit which that style possesses. It was not long before his flashed-out thoughts, his single-line aphorisms, and his couplets stored with grains of philosophic truth, began to be "current coin"—the surest sign of acceptability and worth. The story of *The Miller's Daughter* won the ear of the Queen, but perhaps *Locksley Hall* exercised the greatest influence and charm over the majority of the poet's admirers. The splendid passion of the hero, the subtle touches, the alternate scorn and sorrow, produce an emotion which is hard to define and can never again be wholly suppressed. Charles Kingsley wrote—" In saying that *Locksley Hall* has deservedly had so great an influence over the minds of the young, we shall, we are afraid, have offended some who are accustomed to consider that poem as Werterian and unhealthy. But, in reality, the spirit of the poem is simply anti-Werterian. It is man rising out of sickness into health—not conquered by Werterism, but conquering his selfish sorrow, and the moral and intellectual paralysis which it produces, by faith and hope—faith in the progress of science and civilisation, hope in the final triumph of good." Perhaps I may be pardoned a personal note in regard to this poem. I was but a boy, just beginning to feel the stirring of hope and prompting of ambition some twelve years ago, when a volume of Tennyson's poems was first put into my hands. By a happy chance I turned to *Locksley Hall*, and never shall I forget the thrill, the ecstasy, with which I read and re-read the passionate lines until they seemed to burn themselves into my memory. New feelings of ardour were aroused in me, my mind seemed to open to splendid revelations, and I realised the intense truth of Keats's declaration on first "looking into" Chapman's Homer—

> Then felt I like some watcher of the skies
> When a new planet swims into his ken.

How are we to account for the magic influence of

*Locksley Hall?* Surely the explanation lies in the fact that in ringing lines it proclaims the aspirations and voices the desires of all youthful natures yearning for action. It is " the passionate chant in which are so vividly uttered all the undisciplined thoughts, the wayward fancies, the lofty but vague aspirations, that effervesce in the spirit of the cultivated youth of the nineteenth century," says Professor Ingram, and as such it is not only an inspiration and incentive, but it is a revealing to the young of the thoughts that surge in their expanding minds. The hero of *Locksley Hall* was fiery, impulsive, and unrestrained, but his nature was none the less noble and his ideal none the less worthy and true.

Another poem which has exercised a great charm upon all readers is *The May Queen*, and I cannot refrain from quoting James Spedding's clever and appreciative comments upon that poem, occupying as it does, a unique place in the category of Tennyson's works.

" The homely pleasures, the sports, the cares, the vanities of her little life," he said, "the familiar places she must leave, the familiar process of the seasons, hitherto bringing to the delighted spirit only a succession of delights, now sad and sacred because watched for the last time—all her shining world, as it was when she moved the centre of it, as it will be when she is no longer there—pass over her mind like shadows, and are touched with exquisite sweetness and simplicity.

" But the poet saw in the situation materials for a deeper and loftier strain. Hitherto so full of life, what would she know of death ? A blank negation it seemed ; the non-existence to her of all that existed ; no positive image. But as she grows familiar with the thought of total separation from all she knows, new interests disclose themselves, and death appears but as the passage to a new life. That life she has long known of indeed, and looked forward to ; but idly, as a thing far off, which did not yet practically concern her ; a proposition assented to, but not comprehended ; a book possessed and known to contain precious things, but not yet read—or at most read with a truant attention,

> Like words
> That leave upon the still susceptive sense
> A message undeliver'd, till the mind
> Awakes to apprehensiveness, and takes it.

"But now the formless void takes shape and substance as she gazes into it, and draws her whole spirit that way, until already in imagination death is swallowed up in victory."

For a fancy-picture of utter isolation and dejection we have but to turn to *Mariana in the Moated Grange* whose weary watching and waiting had no end. The poem was written before Tennyson was twenty, and Bayard Taylor has the following interesting note upon it: "*Mariana* is an extraordinary piece of minute and equally-finished detail. Tennyson, once, in talking with a fellow-author about his own reluctance to publish his poems, said, 'There is my *Mariana*, for example. A line in it is wrong, and I cannot possibly change it, because it has been so long published; yet it always annoys me. I wrote:

> The rusted nails fell from the knots
> That held the peach to the garden wall.

Now, this is not a characteristic of the scenery I had in mind. The line should be: 'That held the *pear* to the *gable*-wall.'" Edward Fitzgerald wrote to his friend Allen, "I have bought A. Tennyson's poems. How good *Mariana* is"; and Carlyle, most impressed with this poem, wrote to Emerson—"Alfred, you see in his verses, is a native of moated granges." The *Recollections of the Arabian Nights* afford us insight into the poet's more fantastic imaginings; and *A Dream of Fair Women* discloses the luminant beauty of the phantom shapes of our visions. The grace and chasteness of Tennyson's ideals are revealed in magic touches. One by one he leads before us out of shadow into light Helen of Troy, Iphigenia, Cleopatra, Jephthah's Daughter, Fair Rosamund, Margaret Roper, Joan of Arc, and Queen Eleanor. The pellucidness of diction is in this poem brought to perfection. What could be more stately, solemn, and befitting than the superb conception of King Priam's Daughter ?—

> I saw a lady within call,
> Stiller than chisell'd marble, standing there ;

> A daughter of the gods, divinely tall,
>     And most divinely fair.
>
> Her loveliness with shame and with surprise
>     Froze my swift speech : she, turning on my face
> The star-like sorrows of immortal eyes,
>     Spoke slowly in her place.

Artist, sculptor, and musician could do no more.

It is when reading such lines that we can appreciate the outburst in *Alton Locke*—that fine tribute which the greatest novelist paid to the foremost poet.

"In a happy day, I fell on Alfred Tennyson's poetry, and found there, astonished and delighted, the embodiment of thoughts about the earth around me which I had concealed, because I fancied them peculiar to myself. Why is it that the latest poet has generally the greatest influence over the minds of the young? Surely not for the mere charm of novelty? The reason is that he, living amid the same hopes, the same temptations, the same sphere of observations as they, gives utterance and outward form to the very questions which, vague and wordless, have been exercising their hearts. And what endeared Tennyson especially to me, the working man, was, as I afterwards discovered, the altogether democratic tendency of his poems. True, all great poets are by their office democrats ; seers of man only as a man ; singers of the joys, the sorrows, the aspirations common to all humanity ; but in Alfred Tennyson there is an element especially democratic, truly levelling ; not his political opinions, about which I know nothing, and care less, but his handling of the trivial everyday sights and sounds of nature. Brought up, as I understand, in a part of England which possesses not much of the picturesque, and nothing of that which the vulgar call sublime, he has learnt to see that in all nature, in the hedgerow and the sandbank, as well as in the Alp peak and the ocean waste, is a world of true sublimity—a minute infinite— an ever fertile garden of poetic images, the roots of which are in the unfathomable and the eternal, as truly as any phenomenon which astonishes and awes the eye. The descriptions of the desolate pools and creeks where the dying swan floated, the hint of the silvery marsh mosses by Mariana's moat, came to me like revelations. I always knew there was something beautiful, wonderful, sublime, in those flowery dykes of Battersea Fields ; in the long gravelly sweeps of that lone tidal shore ; and here was a man who had put them into words for me ! This is what I call democratic art—the revelation of the poetry which lies in common things."

*The Gardener's Daughter* was another of the perfect idylls which at once seized the popular fancy, for where shall we find richer painting or better interpretation of the feelings of the heart?

> Were there nothing else
> For which to praise the heavens but only love,
> That only love were cause enough for praise.

Trite enough is the idea, but its beauty of exposition is fresh. Take this for felicitous imagery—

> The heavens between their fairy fleeces pale
> Sow'd all their mystic gulfs with fleeting stars,

or this, the most charming of conceits—

> Night slid down one long stream of sighing wind,
> And on her bosom bore the baby, Sleep.

The volumes contained infinite variety, for greater contrasts there could scarcely be than those between *Will Waterproof's Lyrical Monologue* and *The Vision of Sin, St Agnes* and *Amphion, Ulysses* and *The Talking Oak.*

It fell to the lot of James Spedding, a year later, to review the works of the new poet, the article being written, as he explained in a prefatory note in his volume of *Reviews and Discussions,* "in pursuance of an engagement, made when Mr Tennyson's two first volumes were out of print, that if he would publish a new edition I would try to get leave to review it in the *Edinburgh.* Upon my assurance that, though an intimate friend and an advanced believer, I would not commit the *Review* to any praises or prophecies that would endanger its reputation, the editor consented." Spedding began by observing that

> "One of the severest tests by which a poet can try the true worth of his book, is to let it continue for two or three years out of print. The first flush of popularity cannot be trusted. If, on the other hand, a new edition be perseveringly demanded, and when it comes, be eagerly bought, we may safely conclude that the work has something in it of abiding interest and permanent value; for then we know that

many people have been so pleased or so edified by the reading that they cannot be content without the possession."

Proceeding to consider Tennyson's poems, he said :—

"The book must not be treated as one collection of poems, but as three separate ones, belonging to three different periods in the development of his mind, and to be judged accordingly.

"Mr Tennyson's first book was published in 1830, when he was at college. His second followed in 1832. Their reception, though far from triumphant, was not inauspicious ; for while they gained him many warm admirers, they were treated, even by those critics whose admiration, like their charity, begins and ends at home, as sufficiently notable to be worth some not unelaborate ridicule. The admiration and the ridicule served alike to bring them into notice, and they have both been for some years out of print. As many of these productions as Mr Tennyson has cared to preserve are contained in the first volume of the present edition. The second consists entirely of poems not hitherto published ; which, though composed probably at various intervals during the ten intervening years, have all, we presume, had the benefit of his latest correcting hand. In subject, style, and the kinds of excellence which they severally attain or aim at, they are at once so various and so peculiar, that we cannot affect to convey any adequate idea of the general character of the collection ; unless we should go through the table of contents, giving as we go a description and a sample of each poem. . . . The indications of improving taste and increasing power exhibited not only in the results of his later labours, but in the omission of some and the alteration of others among his earlier, lead us to infer that Mr Tennyson's faculties have not yet reached their highest development ; and, even as they are now, he has not yet ventured upon a subject large enough to bring them all into play together.

"His earliest published volume—though it contains one or two poems, as *Mariana*, for instance, which must always rank among his very best—is to be referred to rather as a point from which to measure his subsequent progress, than for specimens of what he is. The very vigour and abundance of a poet's powers will commonly be in his way at first, and produce faults. But such faults are by no means unpromising. Indeed it is better that the genius should be allowed to run rather wild and wanton during its nonage ; for a poet will hardly have the free command of his faculties when full grown, unless he allow them free play during growth. . . . We cannot, however, conclude without reminding Mr Tennyson, that, highly as we value the Poems which he has produced, we cannot accept them as a satisfactory account of the gifts which they show that he possesses ; any more than we could take a painter's collection of studies for a picture, in place of the picture itself. Powers are displayed in these volumes, adequate to the production of a very great work ; at least we should find it difficult to say which of the requisite powers is wanting. But they are displayed in fragments and snatches, having no connexion, and therefore deriving no light or fresh interest the one from the other. If Mr Tennyson can find a subject large enough to take the entire impress of his mind, and energy persevering enough to work it faithfully out as a whole, we are convinced that he may produce a work, which, though occupying no larger space than the contents of these volumes, shall as much exceed them in value, as a series of quantities multiplied into each other exceeds in value the same series simply added together."

"The poet's narrow circle of admirers," wrote Bayard Taylor, "widened at once, taking in so many of the younger generation that the old doubters were one by one compelled to yield. I still remember the eagerness with which, as a boy of seventeen, I sought for the volume ; and I remember also the strange sense of mental dazzle and bewilderment I experienced on the first perusal of it. I can only compare it to the first sight of a sunlit landscape through a prism : every object has a rainbowed outline. One is fascinated to look again and again, though the eyes ache."

Well might Emerson say—" O cherish Tennyson with love and praise, and draw from him whole books full of new verses yet ! " Well might aged Wordsworth with half prophetic instinct declare that this young poet would "give the world still better things." Well might Edgar Allen Poe ("the first American author to welcome Tennyson ") express a doubt that he was not already the "greatest of poets." And well might Dickens, with his large-hearted sympathy and his generous feeling, relate with joy how he had spent a whole morning on the sea-shore reading the little volumes, and had seen once more "the mermen and mermaids at the bottom of the ocean, together with millions of queer creatures, half-fish and half-fungus, looking down into all manner of caves and seaweed conservatories." The new star had arisen, and all eyes were turned to watch its radiance.

# CHAPTER IV.

## A "LOFTIER STRAIN": "THE PRINCESS."

"And I too dream'd, until at last<br>
Across my fancy, brooding warm,<br>
The reflex of a legend past,<br>
And loosely settled into form.<br>
And would you have the thought I had,<br>
And see the vision that I saw?"

*—The Day Dream.*

ALFRED TENNYSON'S history for at least forty years of his life is fragmentary. Like a comet, he appeared unexpectedly upon the horizon, and he mysteriously disappeared again. Where he was in these dark intervals is now only partially known. His early life at Somersby and his career at Cambridge have been already briefly sketched, but after his father's death, and until the time of his marriage, he was a wanderer. Dr Tennyson's widow remained at the old home, for the new rector of Somersby was non-resident. To the little Lincolnshire village Tennyson returned when his University life was over, and he was often visited by Arthur Hallam, who was now more closely linked with the Tennyson family by reason of his engagement to Miss Emily Tennyson, the second daughter. It was to Richard Trench that Hallam wrote in 1831, announcing—" I am now at Somersby, not only as the friend of Alfred Tennyson, but as the lover of his sister. An attachment on my part of nearly two years' standing, and a mutual engagement of one year, are, I fervently hope, only the commencement of an union which circumstances may not impair and the grave itself not conclude." After Arthur Hallam's death in January 1833, the family appears to have been separated. Charles became curate at Tealby, and he and

Alfred spent part of their time with their great-uncle at
Caistor, the Rev. Samuel Turner, vicar of Grasby, three
miles distant.  To that living Charles succeeded in 1835;
and, finding that Mr Turner had bequeathed to him the
major portion of his property, he assumed his name.  Alfred
betook himself to London, where it is on record that he
lived "in poverty, with his friends and golden dreams," and
it was during this period that he experienced, like Will
Waterproof, "that eternal want of pence which vexes public
men."  There is probably good reason for believing that
until the publication of the poems of 1842 he was "passing
rich" on seventy pounds a year.  But the London sojourn
was rich in the formation of friendships; for the Cock
Tavern ("to which I most resort") became a veritable
Mermaid Tavern, and as Shakespeare and Ben Jonson and
their friends met of old and "tippled canary wine," so did
Tennyson and Carlyle drink their pint of port, and " look at
all things as they are, But thro' a kind of glory."  "Worth
cries out to worth," said Emerson, and it was not long
before a circle was formed by such men as John Stuart
Mill, Thackeray, Sterling, Forster, Landor, and others who
made separate names for themselves.  Once or twice he
met Wordsworth, who had been introduced to him by
Moxon the publisher.  Emerson records in his *English
Traits* that he, too, had met Tennyson in London about
this time, and when he interviewed Wordsworth at Amble-
side soon afterwards, their conversation turned upon the
new poet.  Tennyson, the philosopher chronicles, was, in
Wordsworth's opinion, "a true poetic genius, though with
some affectation.  He had thought an elder brother
[Charles?] at first the better poet, but must now reckon
Alfred the true one."  Dickens, who "never faltered in his
allegiance to Tennyson," was also among the poet's personal
acquaintances.  The poet has been somewhat irreverently
described as a "Fleet Streeter," and a "Bohemian of Bo-
hemians," noted for "the poetic emphasis of his dress and
the Parnassian width of his hat-brim."  He was even known

at that little (and now not very choice) tavern, where the memory of Dr Johnson is treasured, the " Cheshire Cheese," at which place the poet could be seen with a huge meerschaum filled with the strongest and most pungent of tobaccos. In Lord Houghton's Biography there is an interesting letter in which Spedding begged Monckton Milnes (as he was then) to subscribe to Carlyle's lectures on German literature, and the following passages occur :— " Yesterday I dined with Alfred Tennyson at the Cock Tavern, Temple Bar.[1]   We had two chops, one pickle, two cheeses, one pint of stout, one pint of port, and three cigars. When we had finished, I had to take his regrets to the Kembles ; he could not go because he had the influenza."

From 1844 to 1850 the poet's visits to London must have been sporadic and casual, for his home was in Gloucestershire.   Tennyson's residence at Cheltenham is an episode in his life which has escaped many of those who have sketched his history.   He lived with his mother at 10 St James's Square—a " tall, old-fashioned villa, built in the most approved doll's house style of architecture."   It is stated that after the railway station was built, Tennyson " bribed one of the officials for the temporary possession of a highly-educated parrot, which was a pet of the railway men, and was wont to impart unauthorised information to the passengers.   A love of animals was a conspicuous trait of the Tennyson family ; and Mrs Tennyson, who is remembered in Cheltenham as a handsome, bright, sympathetic, and rather unconventional old lady, seldom went out of doors unless accompanied by two at least of the three or four dogs which—not to mention a monkey—belonged to the establishment."   Several unmarried brothers and sisters were also staying in the house at Cheltenham, and they drew around them many friends, chief of whom were Sydney Dobell, Mr Alan Ker (who married Mary Tennyson), and Robertson.   *In Memoriam* shows traces of

---

[1] This is further confirmation of the fact that the Cock was not in the Strand, as has been so frequently asserted.

the influence of the country upon the poet's mind. The Cotswolds are said to be described in the stanzas commencing—

Calm and deep peace on this high wold,

though I prefer to think the picture is Lincolnshire; but "the geological changes which have occurred in the Severn Valley are described with literal exactness." The poet himself might have demurred to this "localisation," but it is not possible to dispute the fact that Tennyson throughout his works described what he saw, and has left us the best of all pictures of the land in which he dwelt.[1]

The lyrical poems had been received with so much favour that edition after edition had been called for, and it was only five years later that the contents of the two volumes were incorporated and the first one-volume edition issued. Tennyson had been busy all this time not only with further revisions of the poems, and occasional additions to their number, but with a work on a far larger scale. There had been an emphatic call for a great, sustained poem, and expectation was general that in good time Tennyson would produce a piece which would at once entitle him to take his place among the poets of commanding height. Such a premonition was thoroughly justified: tentative chords had been struck preluding an outburst of sublimer music. Yet, after the promise of *Locksley Hall, The Two Voices*, and the *English Idylls*, there was some disappointment when, in 1847, *The Princess*, eagerly awaited, was given to the world. This gorgeous mosaic was deemed a splendid waste. The power was there, but it had been misdirected. Only the art of a master-poet could make the subject inviting; only the perfection of workmanship could save so fantastic a story from ridicule; only the riches lavished on the lines and the lessons drawn from a grotesque and unnatural situation could atone for the lack of human interest alike in the characters and the theme.

[1] See Appendix A.

Fitzgerald preferred Tennyson's earlier lyrics to *The Princess.* "I wish," he said in one of his quaint letters, "I had secured more leaves from that old 'Butcher's Book,' torn up in old Spedding's room in 1842, when the Press went to work with, I think, the Last of old Alfred's Best." In his eyes *The Princess* was only "dignified trifling." "I found A. Tennyson," he said, "in chambers at Lincoln's Inn, and recreated myself with a sight of his fine old mug, and got out of him all his dear old stories, and many new ones. He is re-publishing his poems, *The Princess*, with new songs interposed. I cannot say I thought them like the old vintage of his earlier days." Again, he asked a friend—" Have you seen *The Princess?*" and went on—" I am considered a great heretic for abusing it ; it seems to me a wretched waste of power at a time when a man ought to be doing his best, and I almost feel hopeless about Alfred now—I mean about his doing what he was born to do." Even when *Gareth and Lynette* had appeared, Fitzgerald complained. " A. T.," quoth he, "was born to do more than idylls." On the other hand, Sir William Rowan Hamilton, the famous mathematician, and himself a poet, was once heard to remark, " It deeply presses on my reflection how much wiser a book is Tennyson's *Princess* than my 'Quaternions'"—the name given to the method of mathematical investigation which he had discovered. The comparison was a curious one, but full of significance.

It has since been generally admitted that *The Princess* alone, or its like, could never have supported Tennyson's claim to rank with the masters ; it serves now as a single pillar strengthening the tower of fame which has been upreared. "There comes a time," writes Edmund Clarence Stedman, "in the life of every aspiring artist, when, if he be a painter, he tires of painting cabinet pictures—however much they may satisfy his admirers ; if a poet, he says to himself : 'Enough of lyrics and idylls ; let me essay a masterpiece, a sustained production, that shall bear to my

former work the relation which an opera or oratorio bears
to a composer's sonatas and canzonets.'  It may be that
some feeling of this kind impelled Tennyson to write *The
Princess.* . . . But not often has a lovelier story been recited.  After the idyllic introduction, the body of the
poem is composed in a semi-heroic verse.  Other works of
our poet are greater, but none is so fascinating as this
romantic tale: English throughout, yet combining the
England of Cœur-de-Lion with that of Victoria in one be-
witching picture.  Some of the author's most delicately
musical lines—'jewels five words long'—are herein contained, and the ending of each canto is an effective piece of
art."  The poet himself in calling the piece "A Medley,"
and in writing the Prologue appears to have been convinced
that an explanation would be required; but whether the
explanation is sufficient is an open question.  The poem
is made—

> To suit with time and place,
> A Gothic ruin and a Grecian house,
> A talk of college and of ladies' rights,
> A feudal knight in silken masquerade.

In spite of gleaming lines and lofty thought, in spite of
the exquisite intercalary songs (an after-thought), and that
miracle of beauty, the "small sweet Idyl" which the
Princess read—the poem never has been, and never will
be, truly popular.  It is an exercise rather than a pleasure
to read it, and though it dazzles with brilliancies and is
affluent in thought, it satisfies but little and leaves the
heart untouched.  "Faultily faultless, splendidly null" is
the comment one feels disposed to pass when this noble
but inanimate work of art is surveyed.  Yet a majestic
truth lies enshrined in this casket.

> Woman is not undevelopt man
> But diverse: could we make her as the man,
> Sweet Love were slain: his dearest bond is this,
> Not like to like, but like in difference.
> Yet in the long years liker must they grow;

> The man be more of woman, she of man ;
> He gain in sweetness and in moral height,
> Nor lose the wrestling thews that throw the world :
> She mental breadth, nor fail in childward care,
> Nor lose the childlike in the larger mind.
> Till at the last she set herself to man,
> Like perfect music unto noble words.
> And so these twain, upon the skirts of Time,
> Sit side by side, full-summ'd in all their powers,
> Dispensing harvest, sowing the To-be,
> Self-reverent each and reverencing each,
> Distinct in individualities,
> But like each other ev'n as those who love.

Mrs Ritchie tells us that *The Princess* was written "among the fogs and smuts of Lincoln's Inn," an instance of how little the environment of the moment influences thought and operates upon the mind. The second edition, called for in 1848, gave the poet an opportunity of dedicating *The Princess* to Henry Lushington, admittedly the most suggestive of his critics, and not the least ardent of his admirers from the first. It is said, moreover, that the mansion, Vivian-place, where

> On the pavement lay
> Carved stones of the Abbey-ruin in the park,
> Huge Ammonites, and the first bones of Time,

was the home of the Lushington family, near Maidstone. One of the favourite haunts of Tennyson, after the departure of the family for Kent, was the district between Rochester and Maidstone and over Blue Bell Hill, whence could be seen

> The happy valleys, half in light and half
> Far-shadowing from the west a land of peace

with the

> Gray halls, alone, among their massive groves ;
> Trim hamlets ; here and there a rustic tower
> Half lost in belts of hop and breadths of wheat ;
> The shimmering glimpses of a stream ; the seas ;
> A red sail, or a white ; and far beyond,
> Imagined more than seen, the skirts of France.

It was this part of the country which Dickens, writing
to Forster, declared to be "one of the most beautiful walks
in England"; and the famous "Kit's Coty House" (the
"Tomb in the Wood") dating from Saxon times, which
Dickens knew so well,[1] is believed to have suggested to
Tennyson his similitude of the "eight daughters of the
plough," each "like a Druid rock." The prototype of Sir
Walter Vivian was Edmund Henry Lushington, and his
son, "an Edmund too" (to retain the idea and change the
name), became the husband of Cecilia Tennyson, whose
marriage is the theme of the concluding stanzas of *In
Memoriam.* The poet's tribute to his brother-in-law, "the
most learned man in England after Thirlwall," will be
immediately recalled :

> And thou art worthy, full of power ;
> As gentle, liberal-minded, great,
> Consistent ; wearing all that weight
> Of learning lightly like a flower.

Princess Ida has devoted herself to the task of

> Raising the woman's fallen divinity
> Upon an equal pedestal with man.

"The statement of this enterprise," says Professor Ingram
in his "Dublin Afternoon Lecture," "brings us face to face
with one of the great practical problems of our age; and
we find in Tennyson's selection of this theme a new
example of the attraction which draws the eminent natures
of each period towards the questions which are then most
important to Humanity."

*The Princess* is particularly important to the student,
affording him as it does an insight into Tennyson's
peculiar, but not erratic, ideas of woman. "She is the
second, not the first." No one reverenced more than he
the daughters and mothers of the race. But at the same

---

[1] Mr W. R. Hughes in his *Week's Tramp in Dickens-Land* thinks that
Kit's Coty House gave rise to the famous archæological episode of the stone
with the inscription, "Bill Stumps, his mark," in *Pickwick.*

time no one was more strongly convinced than he that women must not be allowed to usurp the privileges of men.

> When the man wants weight, the woman takes it up,
> And topples down the scales ; but this is fixt
> As are the roots of earth and base of all :
> Man for the field and woman for the hearth ;
> Man for the sword and for the needle she ;
> Man with the head and woman with the heart ;
> Man to command and woman to obey ;
> All else confusion.

In his early poems he had given us a series of skilfully drawn pictures of women of many types of beauty, pictures upon which we could gaze with delight, but the prototypes of which we do not yearn to know. But in *The Princess* he sets before us woman as she is, declares what she should aspire to, indicates her duty, informs us of her limits.

> The bearing and the training of a child
> Is woman's wisdom.

Tennyson once admitted half regretfully that " the public did not see that the child was the heroine" of the poem, not Princess Ida. The fate of Psyche's babe is the pivot upon which the whole story revolves. It is Psyche's babe who teaches Ida that she has a woman's heart, and such influence as a child may exercise, when all other influences fail, is revealed in the song beginning " Home they brought her warrior dead." Women are not to be hard and inexorable, are not to despise the love of worthy men, are not, indeed, to trust to themselves in their journeying along life's rough by-ways. They must yield themselves to the stronger, trust themselves to the wiser, find support and protection in the enfolding arms of the mightier. Woman's part is " sweet humility." Her " cause is man's : they rise or sink together." Said the Prince—

> She that out of Lethe scales with man
> The shining steps of Nature, shares with man
> His nights, his days, moves with him to one goal,

> Stays all the fair young planet in her hands,—
> If she be small, slight-natured, miserable,
> How shall men grow ?      .      .      .
>
> .      .      .      .      .      .
>
> .      .      .      .      .      .
>
> .      .      .      Each fulfils
> Defect in each, and always thought in thought,
> Purpose in purpose, will in will, they grow,
> The single pure and perfect animal,
> The two-cell'd heart beating, with one full stroke,
> Life.

*The Princess* was a protest against the rhapsodical falsity of such views as Shelley held. It showed woman her proper sphere, it forbade presumption and lawlessness, it silenced foolish discontent which had its origin in mistaken purposes, and it corrected the tendency of "advanced" womanhood to direct her aims to unprofitable and unappropriate ends. Tennyson's argument is that if woman be the lesser man she must be content with a lesser sphere and an inferior place—yet not with a sphere or place without dignity. She is not to be the drudge and slave, she is not to be "something better than a dog, a little dearer than the horse," but a being with a soul, a being "dipt in angel instincts," a being to whom man may be "yoked in all exercise of noble end."

Tennyson has been greatly misunderstood upon this subject, especially by those who cannot discriminate between the false and true ideals of womanhood. As well treat women as playthings as treat them as divinities. We have to choose between the extravagant and impossible and the natural and practical. An ideal is none the worse for being attainable. The dissolute lyrists of the seventeenth century sang of women as goddesses and treated them like slaves. Tennyson takes a perfectly human view of the sex; and perhaps in comparison with the views of many of his predecessors his opinions seem commonplace, lacking in warmth and enthusiasm. He has even been deemed to hold women in contempt: Mr Salt, with his mind fixed on Shelleyian ideals, thinks that *The Princess*, as a contribution to the discussion of female education, is "sadly trivial and commonplace, being the merest caricature of the ideas it is supposed to combat, and a repetition of the immemorial fallacies by which men seek to divert attention from the real issue, culminating, of course, in the hypocritically evasive injunction, 'Lay thy sweet hands in mine and trust to me.'"  The poet's aim, as I conceive it, was to avoid in this, as in other questions, the falsehood of extremes.  He perceived the true office of woman, and plainly indicated where her duty lay and where her powers could be best directed.  A more glorious-seeming but utterly impossible ideal would have won for him unstinted praise, but what was Tennyson if not a plain dealer?  He abhorred woman's wrongs without subscribing fully to the modern programme of woman's rights.  He had the candour to combat some of her claims and the courage to deny some of her pretensions.  Less as a matter of principle than as a matter of propriety and expediency he showed where the impulsive Ida would fail.  All men know, and all women realise, that there are inevitable limitations to the progress of the weaker sex in certain directions, and if the boundary line is overstepped, it is at the risk of losing certain womanly attributes and leaving certain womanly functions unfulfilled.  It is not those who talk most fulsomely of women's destiny who treat women most kindly.  Laon is seldom just to Cythna; but Ida was not the sport of a wanton or the slave of a libertine.  Tennyson's love was pure and unimpassioned; his type and ideal of the good and perfect woman was an Edith Aylmer, a gentle Enid, a Lilia Vivian, and a Dora.  These were gracious, tender, loving, the best to love and the best to wed—models of English wives and mothers who remain unexcelled.  Those who have gazed long upon the gaudy foliage of the tropics may at length fail to appreciate the delicate perfection of a pale pink rose; and those who have been accustomed to the resplendent beauty and the ardours of Zuleika, Parisina, Cythna, Zelica, Haidée, and the other damsels ravishing as the houri and as remote as they from human nature, will be dissatisfied with a simple Letty meeting her lover by the lake, or with Maud who sends her swain a rose. Tennyson's women are a protest against the Oriental creatures who are deemed fit for a Sultan's harem, and who the early poets of the century would have us believe exceed in charms and character our own English maids. But reaction has set in, and most of us are now prepared to echo the song of the Foresters—

> There is no land like England
>   Where'er the light of day be ;
> There are no wives like English wives
>   So fair and chaste as they be.
> There is no land like England
>   Where'er the light of day be ;
> There are no maids like English maids
>   So beautiful as they be.

Let us remember also with gratitude and admiration that Tennyson was a woman's champion. He sought not only to save them from themselves by correcting distorted aims and subduing ambition that was akin to rebellion against law and their ordained lot ; but he strove most earnestly to protect them from the awful wrongs of a corrupt age. How often was his voice raised against loveless marriages and against marriage forbidden when true love was inspired ! No more terrible sermon against the paltry pride that would sacrifice happiness to selfish, seeking ambition is to be found than in *Aylmer's Field*, where the fury of the poet is so great that he spares not the parents who have broken the heart of their child, but makes them pay a penalty heavier than death. So in *Romney's Remorse:* the man who obeyed his cynical master's behest and "lost salvation for a sketch" finds the retribution almost too great to suffer. What is more pitiable than the broken-hearted man's last cry to the deserted wife ?—

> I am a trouble to you,
> Could kneel for your forgiveness.   Are they tears ?
> For me—they do me too much grace—for me?
> O Mary, Mary !      .      .      .      .      .
> .      .      .      .      I have stumbled back again
> Into the common day, the sounder self.
> God stay me there, if only for your sake,
> The truest, kindliest, noblest-hearted wife
> That ever wore a Christian marriage-ring.
>
> My curse upon the Master's apothegm,
> That wife and children drag an Artist down !

So firm a believer was Tennyson in holy marriage that he could tell of the happiness of the leper's wife ; he cherished women so much, felt so deeply for them in their feebleness, that he could rouse pity for the Magdalene ;[1] he hated so fiercely the cruelty of man that he did not scruple to defend the faithless wife of a vexing and loveless husband ;[2] and with all the burning scorn of a noble nature he denounced the iniquity of forcing a pure maiden to wed a rich and unscrupulous creditor of her needy father.[3]   Such a poet could have no debased and unworthy ideas of women ; and even if his heroines may half-contemptuously be classed as "quiet and domestic," they are sweet and pure, faithful and true, and perfect in beauty because perfect in honour and virtue.   As time goes on and the new light increases, it will be found that Tennyson's doctrines will bear the strongest of all tests.   As in other matters, he spoke the plain and honest truth of women, their mission, and their future, heedless alike of praise and blame, but serenely confident of ultimate justification.

One of Tennyson's friends (Mr Fields) complained that the poet had mediæval ideas of women.   Like the "fat curate," Edward Bull, the poet may have half-believed that

> God made the woman for the man
> And for the good and increase of the world,

[1] See *Forlorn* in the *Demeter* volume.

[2] See *The Wreck* in the *Tiresias* volume.

[3] See *The Flight.*

although, when these words were uttered, the expostulation followed :

"Parson," said I, "you pitch the pipe too low."

So runs the controversy between the Prince and his father, the rough King Gama, in *The Princess.*

> "Not war, if possible,
> O King," I said, "lest from the abuse of war,
> The desecrated shrine, the trampled year,
> The smouldering homestead, and the household flower
> Torn from the lintel—all the common wrong—
> A smoke go up thro' which I loom to her
> Three times a monster : now she lightens scorn
> At him that mars her plan, but then would hate
> (And every voice she talk'd with ratify it,
> And every face she looked on justify it)
> The general foe.   More soluble is this knot,
> By gentleness than war.   I want her love."
>
> .   .   .   .   .   .   .   .   .
> .   .   .   .   And roughly spake
> My father, "Tut, you know them not, the girls.
> Boy, when I hear you prate, I almost think
> That idiot legend credible.   Look you, Sir !
> Man is the hunter ; woman is his game :
> The sleek and shining creatures of the chase,
> We hunt them for the beauty of their skins ;
> They love us for it, and we ride them down.
> Wheedling and siding with them !   Out ! for shame !
> Boy, there 's no rose that 's half so dear to them
> As he that does the thing they dare not do,
> Breathing and sounding beauteous battle, comes
> With the air of the trumpet round him, and leaps in
> Among the women, snares them by the score
> Flatter'd and fluster'd, wins, though dash'd with death
> He reddens what he kisses : thus I won
> Your mother, a good woman, a good wife,
> Worth winning."

Here is mediævalism indeed, but it is not Tennyson's. The whole poem revolts against the King's low estimate of woman and the brutality of man.   The son does not woo or win Princess Ida in his father's barbarous style.   Professor Ingram declares that Tennyson throughout this poem "feels nobly, as well as thinks justly, about woman.  Even whilst we are made to understand the hopelessness of Ida's project, justice is done to her high aspirations, and to the cause which she has undertaken to vindicate.  He has managed to suggest to our memories in one way or other almost all the historic glories of the sex—almost all those more or less exceptional natures amongst women which stand out conspicuous on the canvas of the past: Miriam and Deborah, and the questionable barbaric glory of Jael; Judith and Vashti, Sappho and Corinna, Cornelia and the Spartan Mother, Joan of Arc and Elizabeth. . . . Beautifully has the poet shown the development of the true womanly elements in her nature.  The tender domestic instincts are first awakened by the care of Psyche's child.  Then, when glorying in the triumph of her champions, she comes forth to offer hospitality to those who have suffered in her cause, she sees the old King's haggard face stooped over the prostrate body of his son—the son who had saved his life—and she is overwhelmed with a sudden storm of pity."   Pity is akin to love.   Out of the gracious acts, the

> Lonely listenings to his mutter'd dreams,
> And often feeling of the helpless hands,
> And wordless broodings on the wasted cheek,

springs up the flower of earnest friendship, quickly yet coyly maturing into love.  Tennyson shows what is the *best* office for women, not necessarily what is the *proper* one.

As to *The Princess* as a whole, opinion may always be divided upon its merits.  A verdict was delivered at the time of its original publication, which has always seemed to me to be singularly fair and instinctively correct; and it is worthy of recording, inasmuch as it represents very faithfully the general view taken of a work which is remarkable alike for its excellences and its faults.

"There is so much to admire in this volume," said the *Athenæum*, "that we cannot wish it unwritten; but so much also to censure that, while we could recognise the whole if tendered as a pledge of genius, we cannot accept it as a due consummation of that faculty. To those whom occasional revelations of rare and genuine beauty compensate for much that is marred by affectation, wasted by neglect, or destroyed by incongruity, *The Princess* will be welcome ; but it will be read with some disappointment by all who expected from its author harmony of design and sustained merit in its exposition.

"We find in these pages little which denotes advance. In many shorter poems from the same source the aim is as exalted, the insight as deep, as in this elaborate one. No wholesome severity has discarded former puerilities. Nor does the poet in all cases retain his admitted and peculiar excellences. That charming modulation which gave added effect to his felicitous conceptions, and not seldom substituted them, is often remorselessly violated in the book before us. False or deficient quantities occur with a frequency which suggests that they have been deliberately adopted. If, as we suspect, they have been introduced for relief, we would caution Mr Tennyson that correct monotony is less displeasing than awkward and unmusical licence. The only new attribute of the writer's mind revealed in *The Princess* is a certain fertility of incident,—which, however, does not extend to happiness of combination.

"The absence of this latter quality is, indeed, the chief defect in the poem. Notwithstanding passages of occasional baldness, harsh or careless versification, and sentences so inverted or elliptical as frequently to be ambiguous, there is in this production a wealth and pictorial beauty and a delicate apprehension of motive and feeling to which our current poetry can furnish few parallels. The grand error of the story is the incoherency of its characteristics. Its different parts refuse to amalgamate. They are derived from standards foreign to each other. The familiar and conventional impair the earnestness of the ideal ; and what might else have been appreciated as genial satire loses its force from its juxtaposition to tragic emotion. Nor are these opposite elements used as contrasts to each other. It is sought to identify them ; but in the attempt to fuse both, each parts with its distinctiveness."—The same critic refused to admit that the consciousness of an eccentric plan—as manifested by the poet's Prologue—could excuse it. "We fancy," he said, "that the Prologue is in reality an apologetic supplement. If so, there is hope that an error spontaneously discerned and confessed will in future be avoided." He admitted the plaintive beauty of *Tears, idle Tears*, and believed that the "small, sweet Idyl" breathes the very luxury of tenderness, and floats to us in sighs of music. The critic thus concluded :—"Lecture rooms and chivalric lists, modern pedantry and ancient romance, are antagonisms which no art can reconcile. With the power which Mr

Tennyson has here evinced for the familiar and the ideal, regarded separately, it is much to be deplored that by their unskilful combination he has produced simply—the grotesque."

This judgment stands.   Yet, such is the beauty and power of the poem, we can endorse the high praise awarded it by Charles Kingsley, whose brief analysis of the poet's scheme and whose expounding of his meanings have done so much to make *The Princess* acceptable and admired among a larger class of readers.

"The idyllic manner," he said, "alternates with the satiric, the pathetic, even the sublime, by such imperceptible gradations and continual delicate variations of key, that the harmonious medley of his style becomes the fit outward expression of the bizarre and yet harmonious fairyland in which his fancy ranges.   In this work, too, Mr Tennyson shows himself more than ever the poet of the day.   In it more than ever the old is interpenetrated with the new—the domestic and scientific with the ideal and sentimental.   He dares, in every page, to make use of modern words and notions, from which the mingled clumsiness and archaism of his compeers shrinks as unpoetical. Though, as we have just said, his stage is an ideal fairyland, yet he has reached the ideal by the only true method—by bringing the Middle Age forward to the present one, and not by ignoring the present to fall back on a cold and galvanised Mediævalism; and thus he makes his *Medley* a mirror of the nineteenth century, possessed of its own new art and science, its own new temptations and aspirations, and yet grounded on, and continually striving to produce, the forms and experiences of all past time.   The idea, too, of *The Princess* is an essentially modern one.   In every age women have been tempted, by the possession of superior beauty, intellect, or strength of will, to deny their own womanhood, and attempt to stand alone as men, whether on the ground of political intrigue, ascetic saintship, or philosophic pride. Cleopatra and St Hedwiga, Madame de Staël and the Princess, are merely different manifestations of the same self-willed and proud longing of woman to unsex herself, and realise, single and self-sustained, some distorted and partial notion of her own as to what the 'angelic life' should be.   Cleopatra acted out the pagan ideal of an angel; St Hedwiga, the mediæval one; Madame de Staël hers, with the peculiar notions of her time, as to what 'spiritual' might mean; and in *The Princess* Mr Tennyson has embodied the ideal of that nobler, wider, purer, yet equally fallacious, because equally unnatural, analogue, which we may meet too often up and down England now.

He shows us the woman, when she takes her stand on the false
masculine ground of intellect, working out her own moral punishment,
by destroying in herself the tender heart of flesh : not even her vast
purposes of philanthropy can preserve her, for they are built up, not
on the womanhood which God has given her, but on her own self-will ;
they change, they fall, they become inconsistent, even as she does
herself, till, at last, she loses all feminine sensibility ; scornfully and
stupidly she rejects and misunderstands the heart of man ; and then
falling from pride to sternness, from sternness to sheer inhumanity,
she punishes sisterly love as a crime, robs the mother of her child, and
becomes all but a vengeful fury, with all the peculiar faults of woman
and none of the peculiar excellences of man.

"The poem, being, as its title imports, a medley of jest and earnest,
allows a metrical licence, of which we are often tempted to wish that
its author had not availed himself; yet the most unmetrical and apparently careless passages flow with a grace, a lightness, a colloquial
ease and frolic, which perhaps only heighten the effect of the serious
parts, and serve as a foil to set off the unrivalled finish and melody of
these latter.  In these come out all Mr Tennyson's instinctive choice
of tone, his mastery of language, which always fits the right word to
the right thing, and that word always the simplest one, and the perfect
ear for melody which makes it superfluous to set to music poetry
which, read by the veriest schoolboy, makes music of itself."

When revised and re-written, and with the delicious lyrics
interspersed, *The Princess* exhibited so much of the poet's
power that, despite the pervading sense of disappointment,
a future of great achievement was confidently predicted for
its author.  What form his next work would take was
wholly problematical, but the power of the man was not to
be questioned.  His admirers waited and were confident.

# CHAPTER V.

POET LAUREATE: PATRIOTISM AND POLITICS.

> " For some cry 'Quick' and some cry 'Slow,'
>     But, while the hills remain,
>   Up hill 'Too-slow' will need the whip,
>     Down hill 'Too-quick' the chain."
>
> —*Politics.*

WORDSWORTH died in 1850, and the question of his successor as Poet Laureate aroused considerable interest. The office was either created under a misconception of a poet's powers, or it was abused. Its actual origin is uncertain. Kings in old days had their minstrels just as they had their fools, and probably the one was esteemed no higher than the other. Skelton was the first actually to bear the title "Laureate," but he used the word simply in the sense of meaning that he had been crowned with bays at the University. Edmund Spenser heads the list of Laureates who had an office and duties assigned to them, and who received payment for writing to order. Samuel Daniel succeeded him, and thereafter came Ben Jonson, whose salary was a hundred marks and a tierce of wine.

> Who would be a Laureate bold,
>   With his cask of sherry
>   To keep him merry?

asked Sir Theodore Martin in the "Bon Gaultier" parody of Tennyson's poem on *The Merman.* As a matter of fact, the cask of sherry is now a myth, for in the time of the "poet Pye" the allowance of wine was commuted for £27 a year. Part of the duty of the Laureates was to write an ode on the monarch's natal day, "his quit-rent ode, his peppercorn of praise," as Cowper scoffingly termed it;

but in the time of George III. this absurd practice fell into abeyance. Looking down the list of Laureates one comes across names quite forgotten, and the inevitable conclusion is reached that the office, ridiculous in its inception, has been disgraced by many who held it. Who cares for Whitehead, Pye, Laurence Eusden, Nahum Tate, or Thomas Shadwell?—who respects Colley Cibber or Thomas Warton?—who reads any of their works save in a spirit of curiosity? Yet these are the men who were crowned Laureate. Men like Spenser, Jonson, Dryden, Southey, and Wordsworth, were too great for the office, and the others were too mean. A poet who is willing to sing to order is in truth no poet at all, and if he is unwilling he ought not to have the task forced upon him. Prince Albert's letter to Rogers offering him the Laureateship very cleverly explained why, and under what circumstances, the office was to be retained.

"MY DEAR MR ROGERS,—The death of the lamented Mr Wordsworth has vacated the office of Poet Laureate. Although the spirit of the times has put an end to the practice (at all times objectionable) of exacting laudatory odes from the holder of that office, the Queen attaches importance to its maintenance from its historical antiquity and the means it affords to the Sovereign of a more personal connection with the poets of the country through one of their chiefs. I am authorised, accordingly, to offer to you this honorary post, and can tell you that it will give Her Majesty great pleasure if it were accepted by one whom she has known so long, and who would so much adorn it ; but that she would not have thought of offering it to you at your advanced age if any duties or trouble were attached to it.—Believe me always, my dear Mr Rogers, yours truly, ALBERT."

"BUCKINGHAM PALACE,
"8th May 1850."

To this letter Rogers replied—" How can you forgive me, Sir, for having so long delayed to answer a letter which I have had the honour to receive from your Royal Highness? But I was so affected by it as to be utterly unable to do justice to my feelings." In the end he declined the honour. Sir G. C. Lewis proposed that Sir Henry Taylor should be appointed Laureate, on the ground that Tennyson was "but little known." Rogers himself deprecated the appointment of Tennyson and advocated the claims of Charles Mackay. Leigh Hunt, "Barry Cornwall," and Browning all had the suffrages of a section; but the first-named wrote in his *Journal*—" With regard to the Laureateship, the editor of this journal has particular reasons for wishing to give his opinion on the subject in his own person; and his opinion is, that if the office in future is really to be bestowed on the highest degree of poetical merit, and on that only (as being a solitary office it unquestionably ought to be, though such has not hitherto been the case), then Mr Alfred Tennyson is entitled to it above any other man in the kingdom, since of all living poets he is the most gifted with the sovereign poetical faculty—Imagination. May he live to wear his laurel to a green old age, singing congratulations to good Queen Victoria and human advancement long after the writer of these words shall have ceased to hear him with mortal ears."

This noble tribute of a brother-bard may have assisted to bring about the final result; but Tennyson had an admirer also in the Queen, whose heart he had won with *The Miller's Daughter*, and Prince Albert himself took a conspicuous part in urging Tennyson's claim by merit to the office. Sydney Dobell told the story that a servant, opening the door to a visitor when the poet was out, asked what message she should give. "Merely say Prince Albert called," was the reply. So far as the Laureateship was concerned, however, it seemed likely that Tennyson would have been completely overlooked by the Premier, Sir Robert Peel, who, on learning from Monckton Milnes that "Tennyson was certainly the man," replied, "I am ashamed to say that, busied as I have been in public life, I have never read a line of Tennyson's. Send me two or three of his poems." Milnes selected *Locksley Hall* and *Ulysses*. Peel was delighted with both, but especially with *Ulysses*, and promptly made the appointment. On March 6th, 1851, "Mr Tennyson was presented" at Buckingham Palace.

He wore the same court-costume that Wordsworth and Southey had worn before him at their installations, and Sir Henry Taylor in his Autobiography has an amusing story to tell in connection with this. In 1869, when the veteran poet was knighted, he was in great difficulty about a fitting costume in which to do homage, and he wrote, " I have a new cause to lament the loss of my old friend Samuel Rogers. Two successive Poets Laureate went to Court on their appointment in borrowed plumes, and the plumes were borrowed from him. I well remember (how can I forget it ?) a dinner in St James's Place, when the question rose whether Samuel's suit was spacious enough for Alfred. The elder poet turned to his man waiting behind his chair. ' I dare say, Edmund, you remember how Mr Wordsworth wore them when he went to Court ; I think it was you who dressed him on the occasion ?' ' No, sir, no,' said Edmund, ' it was Mr and Mrs Moxon, and they had great difficulty in getting him into them.' No such suit remains for me, nor, if it did, would the same assistance be available."

Monckton Milnes had been Tennyson's best friend, and the Poet Laureate was soon to be again indebted to him for timely service. In Mr Wemyss Reid's account of that remarkable man of letters, an amusing piece of history may be found as to how Tennyson obtained his pension :—

"' Richard Milnes,' said Carlyle one day, withdrawing his pipe from his mouth, as they were seated together in the little house in Cheyne-row, 'when are you going to get that pension for Alfred Tennyson ?' 'My dear Carlyle,' responded Milnes, 'the thing is not so easy as you seem to suppose. What will my constituents say if I do get the pension for Tennyson ? They know nothing about him or his poetry, and they will probably think he is some poor relation of my own, and that the whole affair is a job.' Solemn and emphatic was Carlyle's response. 'Richard Milnes, on the Day of Judgment, when the Lord asks you why you didn't get that pension for Alfred Tennyson, it will not do to lay the blame on your constituents ; it is *you* that will be damned.'

" Nobody knew better than Carlyle that there was not the slightest danger of Milnes incurring the Divine wrath on this score. As a matter of fact, Peel was already in communication with him on the subject of Tennyson's pension, and very singular were the circumstances surrounding the question. Two applications had been made to Peel for a pension of £200. One was on behalf of Tennyson, a young man in whose glorious future comparatively few in that time believed, whilst the other came from the friends of Sheridan Knowles, the dramatic author, on whose behalf age and infirmity, as well as past services to English literature, were the reasons pleaded. Peel consulted Milnes as to the course which he ought to take, accompanying the appeal by the statement that for himself he knew absolutely nothing either of Mr Tennyson or of Mr Knowles. ' What?' said Milnes, ' have you never seen the name of Sheridan Knowles on a playbill?'

" ' No,' replied Peel.

" ' And have you never read a poem of Tennyson's?'   ' No,' was again the answer.  Milnes offered the opinion that if the pension were merely to be bestowed as a charitable gift, Sheridan Knowles, infirm and poor, and past his prime, was the proper recipient of it ; but that if, on the other hand, it were to be bestowed in the interests of English literature and of the nation at large, then, beyond all question, it should be given to Alfred Tennyson, in order that his splendid faculties might not be diverted from their proper use by the sordid anxieties of a struggle for existence.  Peel took the public view of the question, and bestowed the pension upon Tennyson, though it is satisfactory to know that before very long he was enabled to confer a pension of the same amount upon Sheridan Knowles."

Of the spiteful letter of Rogers on Tennyson's "unfitness" for a pension nothing need here be said.  On a first view it seems inconsistent on the part of a man who had expressed himself strongly on the subject of pensions, and who had exhorted his fellowmen not to

> Toil for title, place, or touch
> Of pension,

that he should himself accept both title and pension. But at least the pension was earned, and we know now that Tennyson only consented to be ennobled at the earnest and repeated request of his friend the Premier, Mr Gladstone.[1]

The new Laureate, immediately on his appointment,

[1] See *Talks with Tennyson* in the *Contemporary Review*, March 1893.

composed a dedicatory poem to the Queen which has since been prefaced to all complete editions of his works. The lines are apt and graceful; admiration is expressed without a taint of sycophancy, and praise is awarded without fulsomeness. The reference to Wordsworth is particularly good—

> Your Royal grace
> To one of less desert allows
> This laurel greener from the brows
> Of him that utter'd nothing base.

The last three verses, which are now almost familiar as household words, are models of fine taste and elegant expression.

Mr Stedman, in his judicious and discriminating essay, remarks that the Poet Laureate was never at ease in handling subjects of the day—" To his brooding and essentially poetic nature such matters seem of no more moment, beside the mysteries of eternal beauty and truth, than was the noise of catapults and armed men to Archimedes studying out problems during the city's siege." An additional reason for non-success is to be found in the fact that Tennyson was not in the busy world, did not mingle with the crowd, and seldom felt the throbbing of the heart of great humanity. Yet, though I have spoken of his non-success, I could not speak of his failure, and in more than one instance he achieved a positive triumph. His *Ode*, sung at the opening of the International Exhibition,[1] with the aspiration that each man should

> Find his own in all men's good,
> And all men work in noble brotherhood ;

—his *Welcome to Alexandra*, his *Welcome to the Duchess of Edinburgh;* his suppressed poems, *The War, Britons, guard your Own*, and *Hands all Round;*—all these, to the last lines on the Death of the Duke of Clarence, form no unworthy addition to our patriotic literature and to his

---

[1] A sonnet on the same subject was written by Charles Tennyson-Turner.

own works.  But above them all stands the *Ode* on the Death of the Duke of Wellington,—one of the six grandest odes in the English language.  Noble in conception, lofty in language, rich in sentiment, and musical with resonant lines for which Handel alone could have found the organ-chords, this *Ode* was, in its original form, veritably the inspiration of the moment.  Knowing how slow a worker Tennyson was, this fact alone is proof of the intensity of his feeling.  The death of the "last great Englishman" stirred his heart to the depths.  He paid not only his tribute to the great warrior and statesman, but he made the *Ode* an appeal to the loyalty of all Englishmen.  Since the poem appeared in the *Times*, with all the weakness caused by haste and the blemishes made more conspicuous by irritating printers' errors, it has been elaborated and constantly revised.  Remarkable to relate, however, the poem was far from giving satisfaction for some time.  Sir Henry Taylor, the man who might have been Laureate, was one of the first to send his congratulations to his successful rival when the *Ode* appeared.  In reply Tennyson wrote—"Thanks, thanks!  In the all but universal depreciation of my ode by the press, the prompt and hearty approval of it by a man as true as the Duke himself is doubly grateful."

Phrases in the *Ode* have passed almost into by-words, particularly the ringing refrain—

> Not once or twice in our rough island-story,
> The path of duty was the way to glory.

The picture of the Iron Duke seems to breathe and live.  The recounting of his deeds has all the energy and pride with which we can imagine the old bards spake to stimulate their heroes to mighty deeds.  The lines are deep and pealing, and now and then, as swept by some strong gust, they gather into a warlike thunder, or burst into impetuous torrent.  We seem to hear at times the toll of bells, at times the clamour and clangour of war, at times the acclamation of the people, at times the low roll of music and the wail of the Dead March. The *Ode* is a triumph of sounds, and with these sounds come the words we would utter in "eternal honour" to the name of the victor at Waterloo. *The Charge of the Light Brigade* alone among the patriotic lyrics can be spoken of in the same breath. "No writing of mine," said Tennyson in sending a thousand copies of the poem to the soldiers before Sebastopol, "can add to the glory they have acquired in the Crimea." Certain it is that the stirring lines have made that question still more difficult to answer—"When can their glory fade?" As further proof of the poet's practical sympathy with the Crimean heroes, his "Balaclava Letter" of 1875 may be put in evidence. "I cannot attend your banquet," he wrote, "but I enclose £5 to defray some of its expenses, or to be distributed, as you may think fit, among the most indigent of the survivors of that glorious charge; a blunder it may have been, but one for which England should be grateful, having learnt thereby that her soldiers are the bravest and most obedient under the sun." This autograph letter was discovered a year or two ago inserted in a copy of the first edition of *Maud* which was offered for sale. It is interesting to know that the manuscript of the whole poem is in the possession of a Torquay lady, who has stated that the latter part of the fourth verse originally stood as under—

> Right thro' the fire they broke ;
> So was the Russian line
> Struck by the sabre stroke,
> Shattered and sundered.

But the marginal correction gives the present improved rendering. Two lines following alone formed the fifth verse—

> Then they rode back, but not,
> Not the Six Hundred.

The most extraordinary story told in connection with this memorable poem was published after Tennyson's death.

A New England preacher, it was said, in the middle of a sermon suddenly began to recite *The Charge of the Light Brigade*. The congregation listened breathlessly to the end, but before the service had concluded elders and people were loud in their anger at the way in which the chapel had been profaned. Their murmurs found the minister wholly unprepared. He had gone into the pulpit intending to speak about the need for charity, and was wholly unconscious of what he had done. Convinced at length by testimony which he could not withstand, he was filled with remorse, went sadly to his room that night, and watched through all the hours till the morning, seeking consolation, and not finding any. At daybreak they brought him word that a man, looking like a tramp, wanted to see him urgently. The minister, half from habit, decided to see him. The stranger came into the room and said, simply, "I come to thank the man who has saved my soul." The minister stood in silence, wondering whether this was some new mockery of his senses. The stranger went on: "I was all through the Crimea, and I was in the thick of the fight at Gettysburg, but never till I heard you recite that poem in the chapel yesterday did I know what I had to thank God for. Sir, from that hour I determined to change my life, and I want to thank the man to whom I owe my salvation."

A chaplain to Her Majesty's forces has recorded that after the battle of Balaclava, when the wounded were in hospital, he read to them *The Charge of the Light Brigade*, and their pleasure was so manifest that he could not refrain from writing to the poet to tell him of the circumstance. For reply the Laureate sent him two hundred copies beautifully printed, with an autograph letter, which unfortunately was lost in a shipwreck before the conclusion of the war.

In all, Tennyson wrote some thirty patriotic poems. Of these, there are a number which have a political bearing and significance, or, at all events, political meanings may be

strained from them. But Tennyson, while at times exerting
a political influence, held aloof from politics. He detested
partisanship, and in his earliest volumes denounced factions.
So late as 1880, when he had consented to be nominated
for the Rectorship of Glasgow University, he wrote the
following letter directly he heard that he was being "run"
as a Conservative :—

"I only consented to stand for your Lord Rectorship when informed
by the letter of introduction, which your agreeable deputation brought,
that my nomination was 'supported by a large majority, if not the
totality, of the students of Glasgow.' It now seems necessary that I
should, by standing at your invitation, appear what I have steadfastly
refused to be—a party candidate for the Conservative Club. The mere
fact of a contest between the supporters of a nominee of a Liberal and
that of a Conservative Club leads, I suppose, inevitably to this conclusion in the minds of the public, and therefore I must beg to decline
the honour of your candidature. You are probably aware that some
years ago the Glasgow Liberals asked me to be their candidate, and that
I, in like manner, declined; yet I would gladly accept a nomination,
after what has occurred on this occasion, if at any time a body of
students, bearing no political party name, should wish to nominate
me, or if both Liberals and Conservatives should ever happen to agree
in foregoing the excitement of a political contest, and in desiring a Lord
Rector who would not appear for installation, and who would, in fact,
be a mere *roi fainéant*, with nothing but the literary merits you are
good enough to appreciate."

He only once voted in the House of Lords, his support
then being given to the County Franchise Bill ; and had
his health been better, he intended to vote for the Deceased
Wife's Sister Bill, of which he heartily approved.

Tennyson must be regarded more as patriot than poli-
tician. Philosophers cannot cramp their minds and stunt
their faculties in order to be partisans. Faction and sect
are too small for men who can think. "Forward, forward,
let us range," was his cry in *Locksley Hall*, and "In its
season bring the law," was his only qualification of incen-
tives to progress. He deemed those the best statesmen who

> Knew the seasons when to take
> Occasion by the hand and make
> The bounds of freedom wider yet—

lines which Mr Gladstone once quoted with great effect in the House of Commons.  His dramas gave him the opportunity of frequently expressing his opinion of statecraft and policy, and he has compressed many a political truth into the speeches of the great men who figure in *Harold*, *Becket*, and *Queen Mary*.  Perhaps the clue to his somewhat confusing political position may be found in *The Princess*, where he says,

> Ourselves are full
> Of social wrong ; and maybe wildest dreams'
> Are but the needful prelude of the truth.

We cannot assign Lord Tennyson any definite place in political parties, but we can truly regard him as a political thinker.  This may be maintained in spite of Sir Henry Taylor's dictum that Tennyson was scarcely competent to form opinions on political questions : "I should think he is too childlike and simple to see them on all sides," said his brother-bard.  But one great principle underlies all the Laureate's utterances on this subject.  His intense patriotism, his love of England as "the land that freemen till," as "a land of settled government," as

> The land where girt with friends or foes
> A man may speak the thing he will ;—

this is the predominating sentiment to which all other considerations are subservient.  He knew in a vague and general way that

> Two parties still divide the world—
> Those that want and those that have ;

he believed that

> For some true result of good
> • All parties work together ;

but from his high standpoint he failed to perceive the extent or the importance of diversity and conflict on the political surface.  Being in the world, he realised that antagonistic forces are ever at work, and that

> Age to age succeeds
> Blowing a noise of tongues and deeds,
> A dust of systems and of creeds ;

he had learnt that "raving politics" are "never at rest," and that "tonguesters" and "rivals of realm-ruining party"

> Pluck the mighty from their seat, but set no meek ones in their place,

—but, though he sometimes doubted whether the world improves, he always found a refuge in idealism :

> My faith is large in Time
> And that which shapes it to some perfect end.

All this might seem to militate against the acceptance of Lord Tennyson as an appreciable factor in practical politics. He saw visions and dreamed dreams. His hope was that the Golden Year would speedily dawn when "all men's good" shall be "each man's rule," when "the kindly earth shall slumber lapt in universal law,"

> When wealth no more shall rest in mounded heaps,
> But smit with freer light shall slowly melt
> In many streams to fatten lower lands,
> And light shall spread and man be like a man.

Here, truly, the fair and shining ideal of the poet seems un-attainable, and the vast aspiration may be "wild as aught of fairy lore." But the craving and the hope are legitimate, though they remain unsatisfied ; and, after all, it is to be remembered that the Laureate did not gaze incessantly upon the desired but too-distant goal. He was no less the poet of the Present than of the Future; still more was he the eulogist of the Past. Whenever a great wave of political feeling swept over the land he was drawn into the current. Too little importance is often attached to the part that poets have played in politics. They have voiced the wishes of a race, aroused heroes, inspired action, commemorated deeds. Tennyson could scarcely have escaped the in-fection of the politics of his time. They enter into most subjects, temper the thoughts of the age, and excite the closest of interests. We have no evidence that the Laureate ever tried to keep aloof from the controversies which absorb public attention and affect the national welfare. On the contrary, he voluntarily entered the arena and made the might of his pen felt. He satisfied himself of the power of "one poor poet's scroll." His words have been the lashes of scorn and the ardent eloquence of praise. His verses have strengthened resolutions, aided causes, encouraged projects. "Form! form! Riflemen form!" was the in-spiriting cry he raised when "the storm in the South darkened the Day," and he feared it might "roll our way."

> Let your Reforms for a moment go,
>    Look to your butts and take good aims.
> Better a rotten borough or so,
>    Than a rotten fleet or a city in flames.
>          Form! form! Riflemen form!
>          Ready, be ready to meet the storm!
>          Riflemen, riflemen, riflemen form!

The same spirit glows in the *English War-Song*—a trumpet-call to the brave to crush "an ancient enemy"; it animates every quivering stanza of *Britons, guard your Own*, and beats in the stirring refrain of *Hands all Round.*

> First drink a health, this solemn night,
>    A health to England, every guest;
> That man 's the best cosmopolite
>    Who loves his native country best.
> May Freedom's oak for ever live
>    With stronger life from day to day:
> That man 's the best Conservative
>    Who lops the mouldered branch away.
>          Hands all round!
>    God the tyrant's hope confound!
> To this great cause of freedom drink, my friends,
>    And the great name of England, round and round.

The Laureate did not weary of reminding us that "there is no land like England," "no hearts like English hearts," "no men like Englishmen." This conviction, indeed, lay at the root of his political opinions and guided his political aspirations. No man had a greater confidence than he in his country. He loved it for its independence, admired what it had grown to, revered its past, believed in its future. If he had a fear, it was that

> The braggart shout
> For some blind glimpse of freedom [may] work itself
> Thro' madness, hated by the wise, to law
> System and empire;

or that, with a full recognition of their power, the people may "wink in slothful overtrust." Wordsworth had spoken of the same danger which arises from too keen a realisation of greatness; confidence begets unreadiness and neglect. We may be too conscious of our capacity, and deem it needless to prepare for further effort. Useless is strength if we are asleep when the enemy comes.

Nor did Tennyson forget in that most impressive epilogue to the Arthurian *Idylls*, the lines to the Queen, to warn his age of danger from another source. It was a thought intolerable to him that Britain should ever be a "sinking land "—

> Some third-rate isle half-lost among her seas,

a puny people, and an unheeded voice. Therefore he said—

> The loyal to their crown
> Are loyal to their own far sons, who love
> Our ocean-empire with her boundless homes
> For ever-broadening England, and her throne
> In our vast Orient, and one isle, one isle,
> That knows not her own greatness : if she knows
> And dreads it we are fallen.

Unity, growth, power too vast for full comprehension : these are the essentials for imperial greatness. For the Colonies he had always a cheering message, and during his life he ever strove to tighten the bonds of federation. "One of the deepest desires of his life," wrote the poet's son to the Council of the Royal Colonial Institute, "was to help the realisation of the ideal of an Empire by the most intimate union of every part of our British Empire.   He believed that every different member so united would, with a heightening of individuality to each member, give such strength and greatness and stability to the whole as would make our Empire a faithful and fearless leader in all that is good throughout the world."   When Canadian loyalty was in question some years ago, it was Tennyson who came to the rescue of the "true North" and gave utterance to the thought predominant in the minds of those who did not find "love a burden" or the bonds irksome.   "Is this the tone of Empire?" asked the Laureate; "here the faith That made us rulers?"   A famous Canadian has left on record how deeply the hearts of the people of the Dominion were touched by the noble vindication of the poet; and the "true North" has remained true.   The story of how Tennyson came to write those lines has seldom been told, and is so little known that no excuse is needed for here setting it forth.   Tennyson himself is the authority for the details.

When articles appeared in the *Times* affirming that Canada's loyalty was an illusion, and that the Dominion itself was too costly an appanage of the Empire, Lady Franklin, who was then a guest in the Laureate's house, and felt an intense interest in North American affairs, indignantly remarked upon the injustice of the declarations made.   She urged the poet to "express the true feelings of Englishmen in the poem he was about to publish," and he, being in fullest sympathy with Lady Franklin's views, acted upon the suggestion.   Thus we find the unanswerable question asked—

> This, indeed, her voice
> And meaning, whom the roar of Hougoumont
> Left mightiest of all peoples under heaven?
> What shock has fool'd her since, that she should speak
> So feebly?

"Slothful overtrust" is no phantom-fear of the alarmist, no foolish cry of dread, no unworthy aspersion upon some party leaders.  After Wellington's victories the tendency of statecraft was to be less active, less resourceful, less alert.  Those passages in *Maud* which have aroused so much controversy, were the indignant outbursts of a man who could see the corruption and stagnation incident to a prolonged period of peace.  "However we brave it out, we men are a little breed," and only the call to arms can awaken the dormant powers and arouse the finer emotions in the large body of aimless, shiftless men who sink into infamy while peace sits "under her olive, slurring the days gone by."

> Why do they prate of the blessings of Peace? we have made
>     them a curse;
> Pickpockets, each hand lusting for all that is not its own :
> And lust of gain, in the spirit of Cain, is it better or worse
> Than the heart of the citizen hissing in war on his own hearth-
>     stone?

It is not for love of war, but for pity of man, that the Laureate decried unhealthy peace—the breeder of villainy, cheating, lies, and civil war

> The viler, as underhand, not openly bearing the sword.

Men may "preach our poor little army down," but can they tell

> Whether war be a cause or a consequence?

Better to risk life and limb in the fierce combat against an invader, than to allow ambition, avarice, pride, jealousy, and all hateful passions to "make earth Hell."  Better that war should arise in defence of the right than that "Britain's one sole God be the millionaire" and "Commerce be all in all."  Better to crush out the "love of a peace that was full of wrongs and shames," and better "to fight for the good than to rail at the ill."  Such was the Laureate's line of argument.  In the ardour of youth he had sung the glory and perfection of peace, and eagerly looked forward to a time when the war-drum should throb no longer, when the battle-flags should be furled, and when a federation of races and a Parliament of man should grow to possibility. But the war against supineness and self is more righteous than the peace which corrodes social life and makes men forget to cleave to the causes which are pure and true.

Similar feelings have made the Laureate the fierce censor of tyranny in all its forms and the champion of those who rebelled against oppression. The Russian invasion of Poland was "a matter to be wept with tears of blood," the successful resistance of Montenegro to the Turks was celebrated in vaunting lines, the downfall of Buonaparte was hailed with delight—

> He thought to quell the stubborn hearts of oak,
> Madman !—to chain with chains, and bind with bands
> The island Queen who sways the floods and lands
> From Ind to Ind. .   .   .   .   .   .
>
> .   .   .   .   .   .   .   .   .   .
> We taught him lowlier moods.

In the Laureate's eyes the despot was the most hateful of beings. He deprecated the least infringement of popular privileges, and bade the monarch

> Keep the throne unshaken still
> Broad-based upon the people's will.

At the same time he recognised the futility of extreme action. Moderation begets moderation, and the same duty lies before the rulers and the ruled.

> He that roars for liberty
> Faster binds a tyrant's power,
> And the tyrant's cruel glee
> Forces on the freer hour.

Conciliation and sympathy are necessary on all sides; violence is fatal to every purpose, and spitefulness recoils upon those who use it for infliction. Lord Tennyson recognised that each side has its rights and its privileges. Beware, he says, how you assail them. Neither those who govern nor those who are governed are to be hastily deprived of their gains or their inheritance. Here, in spite of his idealism, in spite of his cry of "Forward, forward," the poet's inherent conservatism manifested itself. Professor Dowden has well explained that he "belonged to the party of movement, but not to the party of revolution. He gladly accepted change, but he would build the new upon the bases of the old; like Bacon he would make the supreme innovator, Time, our model, which innovates greatly, yet slowly and by degrees." Again and again he deprecated "raw haste," which is not true progress, but "half-sister to delay." To the statesman, to the citizen, to the king, and to the democrat, he gave the same sage counsel to avoid the falsehood of extremes.

> Not clinging to some ancient saw ;
>   Not master'd by some modern term ;
>   Not swift nor slow to change, but firm ;
> And in its season bring the law.

There could be no safer rule for legislation. Hurried and ill-considered reforms may be both unacceptable and useless ; therefore—

> Statesman, be not precipitate in thine act
> Of steering,

but learn a lesson of Ulysses, who sought

> By slow prudence to make mild
> A rugged people, and thro' soft degrees
> Subdue them to the useful and the good.

The poet is no enemy to progress and change. But reform and destruction are not synonyms ; he would advance and protect, lop away the mouldered branch, but preserve the tree. "Perilous is sweeping change, all chance unsound," said Wordsworth, and Tennyson's temperate proposition was—

> So let the change which comes be free
> To ingroove itself with that which flies.

There are extreme politicians who know no improvement but by violent upheavals and general demolition ; the Laureate saw it in a wise and sure method of amendment, in circumspect development and the maturing of plans, in necessary operations carried out with discretion. Effete institutions and needless reforms may go, but wholesale abolition and the ruthless extermination of customs and means of government are not the policy to safeguard popular rights or secure the national integrity.

> Of many changes, aptly join'd,
>   Is bodied forth the second whole,

and when self is discarded, place and " touch of pension " unheeded, watchwords not dealt in overmuch, Law will assuredly be found

> Set in all lights by many minds
>   To close the interests of all.

With such ideas of policy Tennyson could scarcely fail to form an ideal of the statesman best calculated to live and to work up to his standard of excellence. Hating chicanery, duplicity, subterfuge, tergiversation, and recklessness ; despising weakness and ineptitude ; denouncing vain-glory and self-aggrandisement—he prayed for

> A man with heart, head, hand,
> Like some of the simple great ones gone
> For ever and ever by,
> One still strong man in a blatant land,
> Whatever they call him, what care I,
> Aristocrat, democrat, autocrat,—one
> Who can rule and dare not lie.

If one "simple great one " were more in his mind's eye than another when he drew the vivid picture we may be almost certain that it was the Duke of Wellington. The *Ode* on that soldier-statesman's death is instinct with the same passionate feeling of regret that the unconquered hero, the shameless citizen, the truth-loving statesman

> Whose eighty winters freeze with one rebuke
> All great self-seekers trampling on the right,

has gone " for ever and ever by " :—

> The last great Englishman is low.

The Iron Duke undoubtedly approached the poet's ideal of the statesman. He was the model great one who

> Cared not to be great
> But as he saved or served the State,

the man who found glory in duty, "whose life was work," who as state-oracle and statesman-warrior was "whole in himself, a common good," and " our greatest, yet with least pretence." It was to such a man the Laureate ever looked to guard and to guide this Empire. He asked for a scorner of the party cry, and appealed against the violence and bitterness of faction. He did not desire wordy demagogues who by clap-trap and sophistry can set class against class, delude the ignorant, pamper a hasty time, and " feed with crude imaginings the herd"; nor did he favour the rhetoric and grandiloquence which pass for knowledge and take the place of deeds.

> Step by step we rose to greatness—thro' the tonguesters we may
> fall.

The test of good legislation is its requisiteness. The practical statesman must watch what main-currents draw the years, and while ever heedful of the present be not unmindful of the Spirit of the years to come " yearning to mix itself with life." In this the Past, with its multitudinous lights, may be his guide. The consultation of the popular will is imperative, and that statesman who consults it oftenest and endeavours to give the best effect to the judgments of the many has the highest claim to be considered wise and worthy of a nation's confidence.

> Not he that breaks the dam, but he
> That thro' the channels of the State
> Convoys the people's will, is great ;
> His name is pure, his fame is free.

The poet's long life was one, however, of disillusion. In youth a sublime yearning possessed him to rush forward. The distance beaconed, the future allured. His spirit was stirred with the visionary ideals of the party of advance, and he joined in the grand but half-meaningless cry of "Forward." But this youthful ferment was to subside, and in the Laureate's later works we notice a deeper, truer, steadier tone. Half the marvels of his morning had been "staled by frequence, shrunk by usage," and he had learnt that though the heart may be shaped to "front the hour," it is vain to dream that the hour will last. Sixty years after! What a retrospect, what a vista of diminishing brightness as the cold, grim, realities of the Present rise and shut out the glory and visions of the Past! Sixty years after! How great, how terrible the change! Hope turned to despair, the hot blood languid, the fire of enthusiasm burnt out, and nothing left but the smouldering embers, the cold gray ashes of age. This is the sorry conclusion we derive from the Laureate's latest political poem—for the sequel to *Locksley Hall* is as largely political as any of his works. Mother Age, which he trusted, and which appeared to be pregnant with happiness, honour, glory, and greatness, is barren or wasteful. The poet's gleaming vision fades into the gloom of reality. The music that fell upon his ears becomes the wail of misery or the shriek of crime. The blissful future of yesterday is now the agonising to-day. Lord Tennyson lived long only to see his hopes wither, only to find his high ideals more remote. Yet, such was the confidence within him, such was his belief in the ultimate good of mankind, that he refused to yield to the temptation of pure pessimism, and dared to the end to indulge in hopes. From such a man, with such an experience, his last words have a wealth of splendid suggestion, a ring of manly resolve; they avow a sublime faith in humanity as it is used, influenced, and guided by the Divine Will; they bring a light of comfort to those who, like the poet, may in dark despair have confused cosmos and chaos and feared that "among the glooming alleys Progress halts on palsied feet." But it is darkest before dawn, and, as Keats has finely said, there is a budding morrow in midnight. Thus the poet questioned, not idly and not without hope—

After madness, after massacre, Jacobinism and Jacquerie,
Some diviner force to guide us through the days shall I not see?

When the schemes and all the systems, Kingdoms and Republics fall,
Something kindlier, higher, holier; all for each and each for all.

All the full-brain, half-brain races, led by Justice, Love, and Truth ;
All the millions one at length, with all the visions of my youth.

Earth at last a warless world ; a single race, a single tongue
I have seen her far away—for is not Earth as yet so young

Every tiger-madness muzzled, every serpent-passion kill'd
Every grim ravine a garden, every blazing desert till'd.

Robed in universal harvest up to either pole she smiles.
Universal ocean softly washing all her warless isles.

This is the old dream re-dreamed : how long will it remain a dream only, or how soon will the vision of peace and beauty be overclouded? Not, however, that it was particularly gratifying, in these days of advance, for our premier poet to be perpetually reminding us that we are the ancients of the earth and in the morning of the times. If our actions, our policy, our tendency only prove this, we have indeed little to be proud of. But were this not an essential part of the Laureate's creed, his contradictory utterances, his conflicting hopes and fears, would be well-nigh inexplicable and irreconcilable. His faith was largely rooted in the Past— the Past which is a silent and undisturbed treasury, not tomb, of early grandeur, of growing power pregnant with wealth that is slowly revealed in the process of years—the Past which contains the first seeds of a national prosperity whose full fruition is of the future ; the Past in which are

rooted the people's loyalty, patriotism, religion, and hope.
He had thought for the Future too—the Future that opens
out to us as a promised land ; and, with his hero in *The
Promise of May*, he thought that

> When the tide
> Of full democracy has overwhelmed
> This Old world, from the flood will rise the New,
> Like the Love-goddess, with no bridal veil,
> Ring, trinket of the Church, but naked Nature
> In all her loveliness.

This is the new dawn for which every poet waits, and which
constitutes at once the essence and the development of his
political creed.

# CHAPTER VI.

## "IN MEMORIAM": A STUDY OF TENNYSON'S RELIGION.

> " What use to brood?   This life of mingled pains
> And joys to me,
> Despite of every Faith and Creed, remains
> The Mystery."
>
> *—To Mary Boyle.*
>
> " I too would teach the man
> Beyond the darker hour to see the bright,
> That his fresh life may close as it began,
> The still-fulfilling promise of a light
> Narrowing the bounds of night."
>
> *—The Progress of Spring.*
>
> " Sleep sweetly, tender heart in peace:
> Sleep, holy spirit, blessed soul,
> While the stars burn, the moons increase,
> And the great ages onward roll.
>
> Sleep till the end, true soul and sweet,
> Nothing comes to thee, new or strange,
> Sleep full of rest from head to feet,
> Lie still, dry dust, secure of change."
>
> *—To J. S.*

SEVENTEEN years were occupied in the composition of *In Memoriam*. The poem made its appearance anonymously in the month of June 1850. It could be attributed to only one living poet, and, despite a rigid silence maintained by the author, critics and readers were unanimous in assigning it to Alfred Tennyson. Apart from its greatness as a literary work, *In Memoriam* is the most interesting of all the Laureate's productions, because it is essentially a personal revelation. Through this poem we become acquainted with the man himself. He was the less reserved because originally it was not his intention to publish to the world those words, which like weeds, were to

G

" wrap him o'er Like coarsest clothes against the cold
There was a use in measured language for him.  His great
grief needed vent ; the bitter waters of sorrow flowed forth
in verse.  Yet words " half reveal And half conceal the soul
within," and the student of *In Memoriam,* though dis-
covering much, must not delude himself that all the mystery of that clouded life can be learnt.  The poem gives
us an understanding of Tennyson as a mourner only, and
we can trace the course of his thoughts during a long
period of darkness and doubt.  Those thoughts lead us onward to light, hope, and cheerfulness, and they show how
a great soul was saved from the wreck of despair.  As the
poet Coleridge beautifully expresses it—

Sometimes
'Tis well to be bereft of promised good,
That we may lift the soul, and contemplate
With lively joy the joys we cannot share.

The Poet Laureate was a type of the age.  He touched
every note in the gamut of belief.  His creed underwent
much modification and change.  He alternated between
denials and affirmations, acceptances and rejections, faith
and despair.  But with all his successive hopes and fears,
his dismay and his doubts, his wavering convictions, assents
and dissents, he was always craving after the highest good
and searching for the surest truth.  Man cannot seize the
robes of purity and excellence at once.  He will follow
phantoms and be deluded by imposture ; and he has to
profit by experience and pass through ordeals before the
best opens unto him.  Never to be satisfied until he has
gained the topmost pinnacles and can gaze with purified
vision upon the light, is his duty and his privilege.  Tennyson's training, and the influences to which he was early
subjected, inclined him from the first towards religion.
His father and grandfather were clergymen, his mother was
a woman of simple, fervent piety, his favourite brother was
a man of most orthodox views.  Tennyson's own acquaint-

ance with the Bible was remarkable. His poems contain upwards of four hundred and fifty Scriptural references and parallelisms. He was imbued and permeated with Bible lore and Bible language. Some of his poems are veritable sermons—*Aylmer's Field, Sea Dreams, The Two Voices, Flower in the Crannied Nook.* Yet such was his latitude and such the varying state of his mind that he was claimed as a Christian and decried as a materialist and agnostic. This is due to the fact that Tennyson revealed, not concealed, his progressions from stage to stage; he has left the traces of his wandering along a winding way. Detesting ready-made dogmas and despising second-hand opinions, he threaded his course through a labyrinth of doubt and bewilderment, and only towards the end found the clue to happiness and the solution of mystery. Hard and cold doctrine does not suffice; the heart must have its hopes. *The Two Voices* is an argument so skilfully conducted that to which side the balance inclines is not easy to determine. The poet saw two roads to travel, and knew not which to choose. There was a battle royal in his mind between reason and temptation. Only appeal to the man's better self bidding him " be of better cheer " brought him to a decision. He could " see the end and know the good," a " hidden hope " stirred within him, and he felt

> Although no tongue can prove,
> That every cloud that spreads above
> And veileth love, itself is love.

Robert Browning lifted the argument into a higher sphere and gave a richer view of and a fuller insight into the operations and manifestations of the Divine Will—

> There shall never be one lost good ! What was shall live as before ;
> The evil is null—is naught—is silence implying sound ;
> What was good shall be good, with, for evil, so much good more ;
> On the earth the broken arcs, in the heaven a perfect round.

Doubts may be resolved for a while, but they will recur.

To thinking minds this is inevitable. Tennyson convinced himself that it was a marvel "how the mind was brought to anchor by one gloomy thought," but in his old age he still asked—

What is it all but a trouble of ants in the gleam of a million million of
  suns?
Lies upon this side, lies upon that side, truthless violence mourn'd by
  the Wise,
Thousands of voices drowning his own in a popular torrent of lies
  upon lies;
Stately purposes, valour in battle, glorious annals of army and fleet,
Death for the right cause, death for the wrong cause, trumpets of
  victory, groans of defeat;
Innocence seethed in her mother's milk, and Charity setting the martyr
  aflame;
Thraldom who walks with the banner of Freedom, and recks not to
  ruin a realm in her name.
Spring and Summer and Autumn and Winter, and all these old
  revolutions of earth;
All new-old revolutions of Empire—change of the tide—what is all of
  it worth?
What the philosophies, all the sciences, poesy, varying voices of
  prayer?
All that is noblest, all that is basest, all that is filthy with all that is fair?
What is it all, if we all of us end but in being our own corpse-coffins
  at last,
Swallow'd in Vastness, lost in Silence, drown'd in the deeps of a
  meaningless Past?
What but a murmur of gnats in the gloom, or a moment's anger of
  bees in their hive?

Questioning is natural and legitimate; one of man's privileges is to doubt, and, in doubting, to investigate. There is no virtue in blind acquiescence, no profit in a faith not understood. Oliver Wendell Holmes has summed up all in the words, " I claim the right of knowing whom I serve, Else is my service idle; He that asks My homage asks it from a reasoning soul. To crawl is not to worship." Children may accept dogmas; men must know why. To one who told him "doubt was devil-born," the poet replied—

> I know not ; one indeed I knew
> In many a subtle question versed,
> Who touch'd a jarring lyre at first,
> But ever strove to make it true.

It is a principle in music that the sweetest harmony is derived from discords. And, on the same principle, we have learnt the wise and comforting truth from Tennyson that there is more faith in honest doubt than in half the creeds. Doubt brings us step by step to the cross-roads, where we may once and for all choose between darkness and light. Who never fights can never win ; "who never doubted never half believed." Whatever form of faith is rejected or accepted, we have an assurance that " his can't be wrong whose life is in the right." While " perplext in faith," we may still be " pure in deed "; but greater still is the satisfaction and complete is the triumph when purity of life is fitted to perfection of faith—faith which satisfies and fortifies, faith which stimulates like a cordial, faith which is made fruitful by sunshine and dew. Doubt is at length resolved into steadfast belief like the nebulous mist which concentrates into the round and shining star.

A score of short, disconnected, and separate poems serve as prelude to Tennyson's majestic religious work, *In Memoriam.* These, like the prelude to a sonata, hint of the greater theme to follow, and lead into the proper key. The hatefulness of human pride and the impossibility of human independence are enforced in *The Palace of Art ;* the holiness of mercy is preached in *Sea Dreams*, while in *St Simeon Stylites* we learn that true religion is not fierce, and does not bid us live unlovely lives. *Aylmer's Field* exposes the evils of worldliness, and holds up to scorn those who devote themselves to

> Sowing hedgerow texts and passing by,
> And dealing goodly counsel from a height
> That makes the lowest hate it.

In *St Agnes' Eve* and *Sir Galahad* we find invocations to purity, but in poems which preceded and followed *In*

*Memoriam* the poet taught that man's religious impulses—like his passions, his intellect, his affection—require to be chastened and held in subjection. The highest life is the conscientious discharge of manifest duty, not the search after the marvellous and the transcendental. Be pure and be dutiful, we hear Tennyson constantly saying, and prizes unexpected and unconceived will be attained. In the great religious poem which was issued anonymously to the world in 1850 it was a comparatively easy task to trace the same mind at work, only its operations were broader and deeper and its final achievements more triumphant.

There are three, or, at the most, four great elegies in the English language, each written by a master poet and each having for its subject a rarely-gifted man snatched away in youth. Milton's *Lycidas* commemorates the drowning of a young genius, Edward King, at Cambridge; Shelley's *Adonais* commemorates the early decline of the richly-endowed poet, John Keats; Tennyson's *In Memoriam* commemorates the sudden death from fever of Arthur Hallam, the most promising scholar of his time.[1] *Lycidas* could only have been written by the mightiest master of metre and one of the few giants in the use and control of language. It is the "building" of "lofty rhyme," flooded with the streaming sunshine of poetry, luminous with incomparable imagery; every long-drawn and musical line of stately beauty and majestic diction. *Adonais* is also in its way unapproached. It is a threnody chanted with passionate mourning, a gush of exquisite sadness from a bleeding heart. Shelley lamented the death of a brother-bard as a mother might lament the death of a favourite child. The lines throb with agony, but comfort comes in idealism. Both these dirges are specimens of the finest art, gloriously conceived, suffused with feeling, skilfully embellished and shaped to perfection. They reach

[1] Gray's Elegy is of a more general character, and is not strictly "in memoriam" at all; while Coleridge's and Wordsworth's Odes on Chatterton are inferior.

the height of picturesque poetry, and are dignified and impressive as monarch-mountains with the stainless snow upon them, sparkling in the crystalline splendour of sunlight. If they have a defect it is that their very excellence and symmetry remind us more of the sculptor-poet than of the mourner. In this respect Tennyson excels his masters. *In Memoriam* belongs to a nobler range. It is thoroughly human. It leads us to the towering Alps of thought. The ascent is perilous; there are dark ways, yawning chasms, sunless precipices, overhanging avalanches, and driving snow and storm—symbols of the terrors and the obstacles in the way of reaching the sovereign eminence of Faith.

*Lycidas* and *Adonais* are, as it were, elaborate monuments carved in marble, cunningly wrought, beautified and adorned by the chisel of the master-hand. But these monuments are cold, severe, inanimate. *In Memoriam* may better be likened to a tree of deepest root, watered by the springs of human sorrow, spreading out a hundred branches, green with multitudinous leaves, casting a far, thick shadow, exhaling sweet perfume—a living work of nature awful in its mysteries, pregnant in its meanings. This is the tree which waves its branches over a grave, drawing life and vigour from the darkened recess where the eye of man cannot penetrate. It is better to have raised the tree than to have designed the monument; better to have added to the glory and consecration of life than to have bemoaned the terrors of death. And thus *In Memoriam* achieves the highest purpose and secures the foremost place. It is an eloquent sermon of life preached from the text of inscrutable death. It rises from the depths of despair to the serenity of hope and faith. It shows the "budding morrow in midnight"; it points to the vivid rainbow arched across the storm-darkened firmament.

"In this volume," said Charles Kingsley, "the record of seventeen years, we have the result of those spiritual experiences in a form calculated, as we believe, to be a priceless benefit to many an earnest seeker in this generation, and perhaps to stir up some who are priding themselves on a cold dilettantism and barren epicurism, into something like a living faith and hope. Blessed and delightful it is to find, that even in these new ages the creeds which so many fancy to be at their last gasp, are still the final and highest succour, not merely of the peasant and the outcast, but of the subtle artist and the daring speculator. Blessed it is to find the most cunning poet of our day able to combine the complicated rhythm and melody of modern times with the old truths which gave heart to martyrs at the stake ; and to see in the science and the history of the nineteenth century new and living fulfilments of the words which we learnt at our mother's knee. Blessed, thrice blessed to find that hero-worship is not yet passed away ; that the heart of man still beats young and fresh ; that the old tales of David and Jonathan, Damon and Pythias, Socrates and Alcibiades, Shakespeare and his nameless friend, of 'love passing the love of women,' ennobled by its own humility, deeper than death, and mightier than the grave, can still blossom out, if it be but in one heart here and there, to show men still how, sooner or later, 'he that loveth knoweth God, for God is love.'"

"Have you read *In Memoriam ?*" wrote Sir Henry Taylor to Mrs Fenwick in 1850. "It is a wonderful little volume. Few—very few—words of such power have come out of the depths of this country's poetic heart. They might do much, one would think, to lay the dust in its highways and silence its market towns, but it will not be felt for a while, I suppose ; and just now people are talking of the division of last Friday." Fourteen years later Sir Henry again wrote :—"I met in the train yesterday morning a meagre, sickly, peevish-looking, elderly man, not affecting to be a gentleman, and bearing rather a strong likeness to Nettleton, the ironmonger, and on showing him the photographs of Lionel Tennyson, which I carried in my hand, he spoke of *In Memoriam,* and said he had made a sort of churchyard of it, and had appropriated some passage of it to each of his departed friends ; and that he read it every Sunday and never came to the bottom of the depths of it. More to be prized this, I thought, than the criticisms of critics, however plauditory." And Professor John K. Ingram in his " Dublin Afternoon Lecture " (1866) observed that *In Memoriam* brings before us "a priceless but much neglected means of spiritual improvement, the efficacy of which not even the most sceptical can deny. I mean habitual subjective communion with the worthy and beloved dead, whom we have known with sufficient intimacy to have appreciated their excellence, and profited by their converse. We could not fail to reap from such sacred exercises the fruit of increased purity and nobleness. But, in our hurry, or pre-occupation, or dull absorption in material cares, we too often put away from us those blessed memories, or recall them but fitfully and transiently, instead of making them by deliberate cultivation an ever-present influence. And so the best effects of love upon our nature are lost—love which does but half its work if it be not stronger than death."

Had Tennyson never been a mourner he might never have been a great religious teacher. He might, indeed, never have got beyond those conflicting doubts raised in his mind by metaphysicians like his friend, Blakesley, of Trinity College—the "clear-headed friend" addressed in one of the earlier poems, whose "joyful scorn, Edged with sharp laughter, cuts atwain The knots that tangle human creeds." But the central event of his life was the loss of his gifted friend. He was a young man when the "news was brought with bier and pall" that Arthur Hallam had suddenly died :

In Vienna's fatal walls
God's finger touch'd him and he slept.

That raging sorrow was never entirely subdued; the Marah was never dry. *In Memoriam* was begun to relieve the burden of a grief-laden heart, with, at first, no intention of winning the public ear.

> For the unquiet heart and brain,
>  A use in measured language lies ;
>  The sad mechanic exercise,
>  Like dull narcotics, numbing pain.

The poet "sang because he must," and his "short swallow-flights of song," dipping their wings in tears and skimming away, were the outcome of sad hours extending over a period of many years.  It is no doubt true that Tennyson never designed publishing the tribute to his friend, that the poems had been put aside as their purpose was served, and were only rescued by other hands.  We are glad to know this.  To make a business of a life-agony is intolerable.

Arthur Hallam was the son of the famous historian, and very early gave promise of wondrous faculty.  Study was a pastime ; he mastered whatever was put before him with ease.  He was only seventeen when he met Tennyson at Cambridge ; he afterwards visited him at Somersby, travelled with him on the Continent, and was the accepted lover of his sister Emily.  The acquirement of languages was almost a passion with him, and while in Italy he made himself master of the works of Dante and Petrarch.  A profound original thinker, a deep student, a brilliant orator, a keen logician, a writer of most poetical prose, he seemed destined to be one of England's greatest.  On leaving college he proceeded to London, where, in his own words, he "slaved at the outworks of his profession" ; but he was only too glad to wander down to Somersby and shake

> To all the liberal air
> The dust and din and steam of town.

> He brought an eye for all he saw ;
>  He mixt in all our simple sports ;
>  They pleased him, fresh from brawling courts
> And dusty purlieus of the law.

His life in London studying for the Bar and dwelling

in the "long, unlovely street"—67 Wimpole Street—was not happy. He disliked the "brawling courts" after the discussions of the Cambridge Conversazione Society, and he preferred the scholarly words of youthful tongues to legal documents. But the "dawn-golden times" of Cambridge had passed away. Weary and overworked he went abroad in the autumn of 1833. At Vienna he was seized with fever, and while every day his friends were expecting to hear news of his journey he was lying dead. His body was borne to Clevedon, where the waters of the Bristol Channel break on the cold gray stones, and laid in English earth—

> And from his ashes may be made
> The violet of his native land.

> 'Tis little ; but it looks in truth
>     As if the quiet bones were blest
>     Among familiar names to rest
> And in the places of his youth.

Thus did the Danube to the Severn give "the darken'd heart that beat no more"; and thus the rarely-endowed youth whose life had perished in the green was laid by the "pleasant shore And in the hearing of the wave." All who knew Arthur Hallam bore tribute to the beauty and promise of his life. Monckton Milnes, in dedicating a volume to the bereaved father, said :—" It has pleased that high Will, to which we must submit everything, even our lives, to take him away, in whom the world has lost so much, and they who knew him so much more. We are deprived, not only of a beloved friend, of a delightful companion, but of a most wise and influential counsellor in all the serious concerns of existence, of an incomparable critic in all his literary efforts, and of the example of one who was as much before us in everything else as he is now in the way of life." The concluding words remind us of Tennyson's own confession, "he still outstripp'd me in the race," and of that touchingly beautiful remark, "he was on his way to God and could rest in nothing short of Him." Alford spoke of the

> Gentle soul
> That ever moved among us in a veil
> Of heavenly lustre ; in whose presence thoughts
> Of common import shone with light divine,
> Whence we drew sweetness as from out a well
> Of honey pure and deep ;

and Charles Tennyson-Turner in one of his first sonnets had singled out this young leader, and said—

> When youth is passing from my hoary head,
>   And life's decline steals brightness from thine eye—
> But that it cannot soon, nor quench the red
>   Upon thy cheek that hath so rich a dye—
> Then of what crowns of fame may thou and I
>   Avow ourselves the gainers ? with what balm
>   Of Christian hope, devotionally calm,
> Shall I be then anointed ? will this sigh,
> Born of distempered feeling, still come forth
>   As thus, unjoyous ? or be left to die
> Before the rapid and unpausing birth
>   Of joyous thoughts succeeding momently ?
> What would not such recoil of bliss be worth,
>   Replacing in our age this early loss of joy ?

Mrs Ritchie has also recorded that once, in conversation, Tennyson declared that Arthur Hallam was as near perfection as man might be, thus proving that it was no poetic excess which led him to speak of

> The sweetest soul
> That ever look'd with human eyes.

The predominant character of Tennyson's *In Memoriam* is its spirituality and its religious tone, its questioning and unrest. "He seems to wrestle with himself like Dante," one critic has said, "sometimes half-revealing, sometimes expressing his emotions, as the ideas which 'lie in the lake of his heart' well up and become, as it were, materially coloured by the memories he seeks severally to recall." The poem is full of moods. It starts with a low, complaining wail ; it has its outbursts of tearful passion and its seasons of calm. Little by little the con-

viction strengthens that the Judge of all the earth must
be right, His will is accepted, mysteries begin to disappear,
and the solaced singer at last finds his heart full of thank-
fulness. With faith confirmed, a purer light issuing upon
his chastened spirit, at last even "the grave is bright,"
and death is beautified. Thus, to employ a new figure,
*In Memoriam* is a symphony on death and immortality,
with tender interludes, rolling harmonies, organ peals, and
glad repetitions of a sweet refrain—

'Tis better to have loved and lost
Than never to have loved at all.

It has its rough, agitated passages and its soft flute-like
melodies ; it threads a maze of wonderful intricacy and
variety ; and finally it merges into a grand and triumphant
anthem of praise whose reverberating chords mix with the
happy pealing of wedding-bells.

Briefly put, *In Memoriam* in its personal, philosophical,
and didactic phrases is a lesson on the excellence and
divinity of human loss and disappointment. Sorrow
at the outset generates doubt, and the law of divine
compensation is not realised. The mourner questions,
for a time vainly. He searches and is unrewarded. He
is humbled, and made fit for the reception of great truth.
As a child he is taken by the hand, and experience becomes his guide. Sympathy is but a salve for wounds ;
religion is a remedy. Life at first loses its meaning and
death its significance ; but when the power of recognition
returns, meanings have been deepened and truth become
assured. The moral world is reconstructed and its basis
is firmer and truer. Sorrow, in weakening man, makes
him feel his helplessness and casts his dependence upon
a higher power. Step by step he is led upward to a
Ruler. The very inexplicability of bitter grief demands
that man should look beyond himself for reasons ; su-
premacy is not for humanity. Peace is sweeter because
the sting of pain has been felt ; light is valued because

darkness has reigned.  Behind the vale of affliction shines the welcome face of Love.  As Russell Lowell says— "'Tis sorrow builds the shining ladder up, Whose golden rounds are our calamities."  And it is at this point that Tennyson begins to speak.

> Men may rise on stepping-stones
> Of their dead selves to higher things.

No sorrow is exceptional.  Loss is common.  "Never morning wore To evening, but some heart did break." The poet's friend was great; he would have been famous; the world would have gained by his life.  This makes his doom the more insoluble,  Was the Almighty decree just? Well may the poet's faith be shaken, if not shattered.  He knew that had Arthur Hallam's life reached the allotted span he would have been "crown'd with good," and his prosperous labour would have filled "the lips of men with honest praise"

> Till slowly worn her earthly robe,
> Her lavish mission richly wrought,
> Leaving great legacies of thought,
> Thy spirit should fail from off the globe.

All this was not to be.  The promise of splendid youth was only to delude; the flower of genius was to be crushed ere it had expanded.  Was not this wanton waste?  While Hallam lived

> Hope could never hope too much,

but his

> Leaf has perish'd in the green,
> And, while we breathe beneath the sun,
> The world which credits what is done
> Is cold to all that might have been.

The contemplation of these things quickens the spirit of rebellion.  Death seems to have inflicted wanton injury, and in his first excess of woe one forgets that the "spectre fear'd of man" may be a messenger from heaven.  When passion has spent itself the reaction begins, and contrition prepares the way for resignation to the higher will. "No lapse of moons can canker love," says the poet, and when he sorrows most he still feels that

> 'Tis better to have loved and lost
> Than never to have loved at all.

These are the "low beginnings of content," and a lesson is drawn from what has occurred.

> My own dim life should teach me this,
> That life shall live for evermore,
> Else earth is darkness at the core,
> And dust and ashes all that is.
>
> What then were God to such as I?

Love for those who are lost is one of the strongest arguments for immortality. The comfort arrives that the loss itself is only temporary, that a reunion will be accomplished, and that after a brief interval friend will again greet friend—

> And love will last as pure and whole
> As when he loved me here in Time,
> And at the spiritual prime
> Rewaken with the dawning soul.

Truth, in the form of solace, has touched the bereaved man's heart, and he awakens to the blissful knowledge that

> Love's too precious to be lost,
> A little grain shall not be spilt.

It is because human love is so perfect, so enduring, so time-defying, that we must look beyond death for its crown and completion. In the brief span of life its struggles may be greater than its gain. The inexorable laws of nature, and the inexplicable decrees of fate oppose themselves to our most ardent desires. The past closes, but the future always is ours ; love is an imperishable root, and death only transplants it. The change is loss against which humanity may rebel, but it is gain in which spirituality will triumph. There are seasons when

> The sensuous frame
> Is rack'd with pangs that conquer trust ;
> And Time, a maniac scattering dust,
> And Life, a fury slinging flame.

The struggle is intense : our eyes fail in proper perception, and sorrow fills them with tears, blurring the prospect or wholly hiding the meaning. A blank is left, a void created ; there is a pause in life's music, a shutting-out of sunshine. Resignation may be delayed, and it may rise from the ashes of despair or proceed from a realisation of the divine purpose.

The death of Arthur Hallam turned, by force, the thoughts of the poet, his mourner, to the nature of death and the mysteries of life. The removal of that which was loved changed the point of view. Sorrow drew the heart upward, and love which had been materialised became idealised ; the man was spirit. Death is consecration, and the Throned Power, who in sovereignty of will, has broken the round of earthly friendship is a power of Mercy. "Our wills are ours to make them thine" the poet first learns to sing, just as Dante had grasped the truth divine—"In his will is our tranquillity." Men seldom master the meaning of the word death. "I change, but I cannot die," said Shelley ; "There is no death, what seems so is transition," was the avowal of Longfellow. Of departed Keats it was written—"He hath awakened from the dream of life. He is a portion of the loveliness Which once he made more lovely." And Tennyson, after the first cry of despair, could murmur—

> I wage not any feud with death
> For changes wrought on form and face,

and thus is led imperceptibly to the confession that he has suffered no injury by the removal of his companion. All loss has its compensation, and

> The song of woe
> Is after all an earthly song.

Moreover, death "keeps the key of all the creeds," and unlocks the mysteries of existence. With this awakening to knowledge the poet finds the long gloom passing away ; a dawn of trust and hope is breaking—there is a tremulous golden light on the eastern horizon, the shadows are dispersed, even the looming clouds take a crimson glow, and presently the blazing forehead of the rising sun will appear. The day is at hand—a day of radiance and calm. The voice of the poet grows stronger, for he is no longer filled with vague apprehensions and hopeless dread.

> Oh yet we trust that somehow good
>   Will be the final goal of ill,
>   To pangs of nature, sins of will,
> Defects of doubt, and taints of blood ;
>
> That nothing walks with aimless feet ;
>   That not one life shall be destroyed,
>   Or cast as rubbish to the void,
> When God hath made the pile complete.
>
> Behold, we know not anything ;
>   I can but trust that good shall fall
>   At last—far off—at last to all,
> And every winter change to spring.

But relapse from optimism is inevitable, and while indulging the "larger hope," the poet still felt inclined from time to time to believe the darkness impenetrable. Perhaps, like Voltaire, he may have exclaimed, "First principles will never be known. The mice that inhabit some little crannies of a vast building do not know whether that building is eternal, or whom its architect, or why he built it. We are such mice, and the divine architect who built this universe has not yet, so far as I know, told His secret to anyone." The famous poet-painter, William Bell Scott, did not believe that "God had revealed to us anything of the unseen world." "Of course," he said, "people in all ages have imagined what lies beyond death, but none know." Tennyson, wondering whether God and Nature were not at strife, and seeing Nature so "careless of the single life," must needs confess—

> I falter where I firmly trod,
>   And falling with my weight of cares
>   Upon the great world's altar-stairs
> That slope through darkness up to God,
>
> I stretch lame hands of faith, and grope,
>   And gather dust and chaff, and call
>   To what I feel is Lord of all,
> And faintly trust the larger hope.

But "death keeps the keys of all the creeds," and what creed is there to reconcile man to his fate and prove the all-wisdom of the decrees of providence?  Pantheism, scepticism, supralapsarianism, and Buddhism alike leave him unsatisfied.  Tennyson found them "faith as vague as all unsweet," and the mourner was mocked by the unreal comfort they offered.  Downcast and sorrowing, longing for rest and hungering for solace, he found nothing but the empty and unsubstantial show of good things—a laid-out feast of which he could not partake.  In his extreme agony he required actualities, a true and not a visionary compensation.  What religion grants not only the promise but supplies the balm?  Surely it is that religion, says the poet, which permits the hope of an universal restoration to life, which teaches that death has no sting and the grave no victory, and encourages the belief that

> The dead
> Are breathers of an ampler day
> For ever nobler ends.

While we may begrudge the reaper some of the fair flowers which he removes with his sickle keen, we can learn the truth above the power of science to reveal that "nothing is that errs from law."

> We pass; the path that each man trod
>   Is dim, or will be dim, with weeds:
>   What fame is left for human deeds
> In endless age?  It rests with God.

Whatever is, is right, and the "abysmal secrets of personality" rest with the Omnipotent. Once the poet had asked why a promising genius should be cut off in his prime, why he should not have been permitted to fulfil his august mission, why time was not allotted him to use great talent for the glory and the good of the world. In a quieter mood he remembered that fruit may be ripened by frost as well as by heat, and applying this truth, he reverently said—

> Death returns an answer sweet :
> My sudden frost was sudden gain,
> And gave all ripeness to the grain,
> It might have drawn from after-heat.

Therefore death had been more friend than foe : in a single hour he brought to perfection the genius which could only have slowly matured during a life-time on earth. To those remaining there is always hope.

> Eternal process moving on,
> From state to state the spirit walks ;
> And these are but the shatter'd stalks,
> Or ruin'd chrysalis of one.

> Nor blame I Death, because he bare
> The use of virtue out of earth :
> I know transplanted human worth
> Will bloom to profit, otherwhere.

The consolation of these words is for all time and for the whole race. Not only have we the assurance of reunion in the future, but we have the present knowledge—knowledge which is only ours, because we have been afflicted—that "transplanted human worth Will bloom to profit, otherwhere." So sublime a truth was worth purchasing even at the cost of Arthur Hallam's life. The wreck of the poet's happiness has been the salvation of the multitude. Tennyson's life was darkened to the end, but the perpetual cloud hovering over him did not totally exclude the sunshine.

Though a lost friend may not be replaced, the heart is not left wholly void. Other loves arise, other interests are aroused, new links are forged, new relationships are formed, and the heart,

> Tho' widow'd, may not rest
> Quite in the love of what is gone,
> But seeks to beat in time with one
> That warms another living breast.

In the same year that *In Memoriam* was published—*annus mirabilis*—Tennyson had married Emily Sellwood, the daughter of a Horncastle solicitor, and the sister of Charles Tennyson-Turner's wife. They had long been engaged, and it was the faithful, unfailing love of a good woman which saved him from misanthropy. With one so "near, dear, and true" given to him he could not abandon himself to despondency or utterly deny divine wisdom. But doubt is unavoidable. No one has more strongly insisted upon that than Tennyson. He makes doubt the concomitant of a wakeful truth-searching mind, and declines to believe that there is virtue in a faith unshaken. But by manfully combating temptation and fear, a mighty victory for truth is possible. The friend lamented had

> Fought his doubts and gather'd strength,
> He would not make his judgment blind,
> He faced the spectres of the mind
> And laid them : thus he came at length
>
> To find a stronger faith his own.

Knowledge is not the final goal ; when separated from Love and Faith, knowledge is headstrong, dangerous, and mistaken, " for she is earthly of the mind, but Wisdom heavenly of the soul." Knowledge without reverence can only lead astray, and in the day of difficulty the wanderer "cannot fight the fear of death." And the poet, from this point, is led to a beautiful explanation of how faith in his Creator was found. The revelation did not come through science.

> I found him not in world or sun,
>     Or eagle's wing, or insect's eye :
>     Nor thro' the questions men may try,
> The petty cobwebs we have spun.

Knowledge did not suffice, and the poet returns a negative to the query, " By searching can man find out God ? "  But when tempted to forsake religion, when voices whispered " believe no more "—

> A warmth within the breast would melt
>     The freezing reason's colder part,
>     And like a man in wrath the heart
> Stood up and answer'd " I have felt."

Knowledge, science, culture, were phantoms beside the reality of experience.  In the heart that had felt was stored the majestic truth which neither learning nor logic can give or take away.  Words and symbols are nothing when the heart has its inspiration, life its instinct, and the spirit its vision.  The fool may say that death ends all, and that after life comes darkness.  The heart which has grown strong by suffering cannot be dismayed, knowing that sorrow only makes "hope look through dimmer eyes," that after doubt we "find a stronger faith our own," and that

> All is well, tho' faith and form
> Be sunder'd in the night of fear.

The human view is foreshortened ; we cannot see " behind the veil."  But " all is well."  The broken and bleeding heart, feeling the touch of a healing hand, and filled with ineffable peace, beats to that refrain, and life henceforth is a psalm of gratitude and thanksgiving.  " All is well." Even suffering to come has no terror.  The divine will is vindicated, the divine lesson approved. Sorrow is the angel pointing the way to the desired goal.  Love is supreme ; it reigns in the heart, it dominates life, it forges golden bonds between man and man, it links earth with heaven.  Now can we understand that lofty prelude which some years later the poet added to his work—a hymn and a prayer preparing the mind for the reception of the truths that follow. It is "immortal love" which we "by faith alone embrace"—

> Believing where we cannot prove.

It is the God of Love who made both Life and Death, and is master of the dominion of each.

> Thou wilt not leave us in the dust:
>     Thou madest man, he knows not why;
>     He thinks he was not made to die;
> And thou hast made him, thou art just.
>
> Thou seemest human and divine,
>     The highest, holiest manhood, thou:
>     Our wills are ours, we know not how;
> Our wills are ours, to make them thine.

*In Memoriam* is not a long monotone of grief. It is a pæan of praise, growing more and more confident, and concluding with an outburst of rapturous thanksgiving. What undertone of sadness it possesses belongs to all human joy—"There's a pang in all rejoicing, And joy in the heart of pain," said Bayard Taylor long ago. But the best to be said of *In Memoriam* is in Charles Kingsley's words: "The poem enables us to claim one who had been hitherto regarded as belonging to a merely speculative and peirastic school, as the willing and deliberate champion of vital Christianity, and of an orthodoxy the more sincere because it has worked upward through the abyss of doubt; the more mighty for good because it justifies and consecrates the æsthetics and the philosophy of the present age." The eminent Christian concluded by declaring that *In Memoriam* was "the noblest Christian poem which England has produced for two centuries." Stedman's tribute is equally emphatic. "This work stands by itself," he wrote;

"none can essay another upon its model without yielding every claim to personality at the risk of an inferiority that would be appalling. The strength of Tennyson's intellect has full sweep in this elegiac poem—the great threnody of our language, by virtue of unique conception and power. . . . The grave, majestic, hymnal measure swells like the peal of an organ, yet acts as a break on undue spasmodic outbursts of discordant grief. . . . *In Memoriam* is a serene and truthful panorama of refined experiences ; filled with pictures of gentle scholastic life, and of English scenery through all the changes of a rolling year ; expressing, more-over, the thoughts engendered by these changes. When too sombre, it is lightened by sweet reminiscences ; when too light, recalled to grief by stanzas that have the deep solemnity of a passing bell. . . . The wisdom, yearnings, and aspirations of a noble mind are here ; curious reason-ing, for once, is not out of place ; the poet's imagination, shut in upon itself, strives to irradiate with inward light the mystic problems of life. At the close, Nature's eternal miracle is made symbolic of the soul's palingenesis, and the tender and beautiful marriage-lay tranquillises the reader with the thought of the dear common joys which are the heritage of every living kind." Mr Robert Buchanan aptly described *In Memoriam* as a "rainbow on a grave." Not the least interesting parts of the poem are those in which Tennyson has supplied us with fragments of his autobiography and glimpses of the old home and the places he loved.[1] Whatever awakened the memory of his lost friend was doubly dear to him ; yet, when he left Somersby in 1837, and took a last glance at the "pleasant fields and farms," seeing them from afar

> Mix in one another's arms
> To one pure image of regret,

—he was little disposed ever to renew accquaintance with them. The scenes were blotted out of his vision,

---

[1] See *In Tennyson Land*, cap. v.; also Appendix A.

but were enshrined in his memory. Let Charles Tenny-son-Turner express in words why the old home was not revisited.

> In the dark twilight of an autumn morn
> I stood within a little country town,
> Wherefrom a long acquainted path went down
> To the dear village haunts where I was born;
> The low of oxen on the rainy wind,
> Death and the past came up the well-known road,
> And bathed my heart in tears, but stirred my mind
> To tread once more the track so long untrod.
> But I was warned, "Regrets which are not thrust
> Upon thee, seek not: for this sobbing breeze
> Will but unman thee; thou art bold to trust
> Thy woe-worn thoughts among these roaring trees,
> And gleams of by-gone playgrounds.   Is 't no crime,
> To rush by night into the arms of time?"

But to the pilgrim there can be no more hallowed spot than the "dear village haunts" which breathe of that eventful past.   Here one of the great dramas of life was acted out.   Here came Arthur Hallam and read the Tuscan poets on the lawn; here wandered the friends; here the lovers plighted their troth; here were the day-dreams dreamed and the vast hopes hoped; and here was the devastation wrought and the life-long sorrow begun when with bier and pall came the revelation of irreparable loss.

No literary work has done more than *In Memoriam* to resolve doubt and "justify the ways of God to man." No one can rise from the study of it without feeling strengthened, cheered, and refreshed.   It is the history of a soul's struggle and of the victory of life and its Giver. It is the passage from darkness to light, from mystery to revelation, from fear to faith, from rebellion to resignation, and from reproof to praise.   Shelley sang in rapture—

> The splendours of the firmament of time
>   May be eclipsed, but are extinguished not;
> Like stars to their appointed height they climb,

# CHAPTER VIII.

## ENOCH ARDEN.

" To look on noble forms
Makes noble thro' the sensuous organism
That which is higher."

*—The Princess.*

TENNYSON'S tranquil life during these years supplies the biographer with very few details. He was zealously living up to his ideal and striving to miss

The irreverent doom
Of those that wear the Poet's crown.

The revision of old poems and the composition of new appears to have been his chief occupation, though "troops of unrecording friends" helped to make time pleasant at Farringford. His son Hallam was born in 1852, and two years later a second son, Lionel, was added to the family; and it was at this time that the celebrated invitation to the Rev. F. D. Maurice was sent. The lines conveying that invitation have attracted a large share of attention, because they supply us with one of the rare revelations of the poet in his private life—a privacy which we have no desire to invade save with his sanction. But the picture of the home in the Isle of Wight is too valuable to be excluded. "Come," wrote the poet,

Come, when no graver cares employ,
Godfather, come and see your boy,

.    .    .    .    .    .

.    .    .    .    .    .

Where, far from noise and smoke of town,
I watch the twilight falling brown
  All round a careless-order'd garden
Close to the ridge of a noble down.

> You 'll have no scandal while you dine,
> But honest talk and wholesome wine,
>   And only hear the magpie gossip
> Garrulous under a roof of pine :
>
> For pines of grove on either hand,
> To break the blast of winter, stand :
>   And further on the hoary Channel
> Tumbles a billow on chalk and sand.
>
>   .      .      .      .      .      .
>
> Come, Maurice, come : the lawn as yet
> Is hoar with rime, or spongy-wet ;
>   But when the wreath of March has blossom'd,
> Crocus, anemone, violet,
>
> Or later, pay one visit here,
> For those are few we hold as dear.

The character of this chosen friend, the Rev. Frederick Denison Maurice, is sketched in the same poem. He was one of "that honest few Who give the Fiend himself his due," and anathemas had been thundered at him for his candour and his freedom of thought. He had been one of the earliest to recognise Tennyson, and being himself a Trinity man, he was proud of his fellow-collegian. He had been godfather with Henry Hallam, the historian, to the poet's eldest surviving son, and Maurice soon afterwards dedicated to the Laureate his volume of "Theological Essays." "I have maintained in these Essays," he wrote, "that a Theology which does not correspond to the deepest thoughts and feeling of human beings cannot be a true Theology. Your writings have taught me to enter into many of those thoughts and feelings. . . . As the hopes which I have expressed in this volume are more likely to be fulfilled to our children than to ourselves, I might perhaps ask you to accept it as a present to one of your name, in whom you have given me a very sacred interest. Many years, I trust, will elapse before he knows that there are any controversies in the world into which he has entered. Would to God that in a few more he may find that they had ceased ! At all events, if he should ever look into these Essays they may tell him what meaning some of the former generation attached to words, which will be familiar and dear to his generation, and to those who follow his— how there were some who longed that the bells of our churches might indeed

> Ring out the darkness of the land,
> Ring in the Christ that is to be."

Maurice was the friend and fellow-worker of Mr Ruskin, and in the latter's account of his relations with the Working-Men's College (*Præterita*, vol. iii.) he makes the following remarks upon the gifted, free-thinking theologian :—" I loved Frederick Maurice, as everyone did who came near him ; and have no doubt he did all that was in him to do of good in his day. But Maurice was by nature puzzle-headed, and, though in a beautiful manner, wrong-headed ; while his clear conscience and keen affections made him egotistic, and in his Bible-reading as insolent as any infidel of them all. I only went once to a Bible lesson of his ; and the meeting was significant and conclusive. The subject of lesson, Jael's slaying of Sisera, concerning which Maurice, taking an enlightened modern view of what was fit and not, discoursed in passionate indignation ; and warned his class, in the most positive and solemn manner, that such dreadful deeds could only have been done in cold blood in the Dark Biblical ages ; and that no religious and patriotic Englishwoman ought ever to think of imitating Jael by nailing a Russian's or Prussian's skull to the ground —especially after giving him bitters in a lordly dish. At the close of the instruction, through which I sat silent, I ventured to inquire why then had Deborah, the prophetess, declared of Jael, ' Blessed above women shall the wife of Heber the Kenite be ?' On which Maurice, with startled and flashing eyes, burst into partly scornful, partly alarmed denunciation of Deborah the prophetess as a mere blazing Amazon, and of her song as a merely rhythmic storm of battle-rage, no more to be listened to with edification of faith than the Norman's sword-song at the Battle of Hastings. Whereupon there remained nothing for me—to whom the Song of Deborah was as sacred as the *Magnificat*—but total collapse in sorrow and astonishment, the eyes of all the class being also bent upon me in amazed reprobation of my benighted views and unchristian sentiments. And I got away how I could, and never went back." This glimpse of F. D. Maurice, one of the closest of Tennyson's friends, enables us to understand how the two at their meeting would discuss strange and solemn matters, "dear to the man that is dear to God," and turn at length to the social schemes in which Maurice was most deeply interested—

> How best to help the slender store,
> How mend the dwellings, of the poor ;
> How gain in life, as life advances,
> Valour and charity more and more.

Sir Henry Taylor, who was Tennyson's neighbour at this time, and often saw him, recorded that the house at Farringford was "the most beautifully situated he ever beheld." Its park, grove, and pastures in particular won his admiration, and at a later date (1860) he wrote—" In the midst of all this beauty and comfort stands Alfred Tennyson, grand, but very gloomy, whom it is sadness to see ; and one has to think of his works to believe that he can escape from himself, and escape into regions of glory and light." When the poet paid his neighbour a visit the best that Taylor could record of him was that he " grumbled agreeably for an hour or two." Fitzgerald was surprised whenever Tennyson was agreeable in the morning : " his agreeable moods are generally in the evening," he said. Lest this, and other like sayings, should be misunderstood, I may fitly say a word here on Tennyson's relations with his contemporaries. The publication of the poem called *The Dead Prophet* in 1885, drew forth the following note : " The verses are supposed to refer to somebody who lived, and to something that took place, in the reign of George the Fourth. The

Dead Prophet is represented as making the world heed his Word, as being loved by his friends and by his children, and as being a loss to his country. But one comes by who calls herself Reverence, and in the name of Truth, must find out all the weaknesses of the hero, that he may be sent stark naked through the world. The poem recalls Tennyson's previous protest against permitting the 'many-headed beast' to know the foibles of great men. But the critics want to know who the Prophet was. They are searching in their dictionaries of biography for the man of George the Fourth's reign who was a sage, and had wife and family. Tut, tut. The date and the parental point are mere blinds. Tennyson's protest refers to Thomas Carlyle, and is directed against Mr Froude's *Life* of him. That is the riddle hard to read, which our men of great insight have found so puzzling."

The friendship between Tennyson and Carlyle and his wife had been of the most intimate and enduring character. An entirely false impression is abroad that the poet was a man of few friendships, that he was a gruff recluse, of cold and forbidding manners, that it was a matter of the utmost difficulty for strangers to approach him or for acquaintances to obtain courteous treatment. It is true that the poet had a scorn (with which we must all sympathise) for the idle and vulgar curiosity of the masses ; but the whole history of his life testifies to the fact that he was a most sincere though properly discriminating companion and friend. His nature was capable of the most intense affection, and, as is always the case, of the most bitter prejudices. Once he hated he always hated, once he despised he always despised, but once he loved he loved most deeply, most tenderly, most beautifully. Assuredly he himself was dowered with the hate of hate, the scorn of scorn, the love of love.

Although the great friendship of Tennyson's life was early severed and remained a perpetual sorrow, and although he was sufficiently a recluse to draw upon himself the charge of personal pride, contemning his fellow-men, yet throughout his long life the poet was always surrounded by a circle of more than acquaintances and admirers. Friendships begun at College continued, friendships springing from like labours and enthusiasms strengthened, friendships slowly growing from exchange of thoughts, and interchange of sympathies ripened and matured. Tennyson's soul went forth unto all that was worthy, and he was willing to accept voluntarily as a friend the man whose work was his recommendation. Thus a visitor like Dr Oliver Wendell Holmes had no difficulty in penetrating the reserve in which the Laureate half-concealed himself; and equally he was in spiritual accord, if not in physical contact, with a score of others whose labours and learning had won his praise. At one time and another the circle of friends, broken only by departure or death, included Carlyle, Longfellow, Lord Houghton, Landor, Fitzgerald, Sir Henry Parkes, Whitman, Spedding, Lear, Woolner, Sir Henry Taylor, Palgrave, Rogers, Dickens, Thackeray, Sydney Dobell, Dean Alford, Brookfield, Browning, Garibaldi, Ruskin, Sir John Simeon, Bayard Taylor, Maurice, Lushington, and other leaders of thought in England and America; to say nothing of that inner circle of friends whose privacy we may respect. Innumerable anecdotes might be adduced for the purpose of showing how genial and happy was the poet's intercourse with these brother-workers and kindred spirits'; but surely enough is revealed in *In Memoriam*, in the lines to his brother Charles, in the sonnet upon Brookfield, in *A Dead Prophet*, in the words of sympathy to "J. S.," in the sonnet to "J. M. K.," in the stanzas to "E. L.," in the invitation to the Rev. F. D. Maurice, in the beautiful poem to Mary Boyle—surely, I say, enough is revealed in these poems, fresh from a heart warm with sympathy, to vindicate the poet from the charge of frigid exclusiveness and unamiability. Tennyson was no misanthrope. His greeting was always "men my brothers"; his aim was always to better the race; his ideal was universal federation, social purity, and complete happiness, wrongs redressed and right triumphant, the ushering-in of the Golden Year. How could such a man fail to be "one with his kind"? He, like Abou Ben Adhem, could be written down in the book of gold as

One that loved his fellow-men.

Longfellow left a record of his visit to Tennyson in a beautiful sonnet; Tennyson reminded us of the visit of Garibaldi in the lines *To Ulysses*, addressed to W. G. Palgrave, who died at Monte Video before he had read the poem of thanks for "tales of lands I know not." In this poem Tennyson contrasted his friend's experience "basking below the Line" with his own—"soaking here in winter wet," and thus described himself in his English home:

> I, tolerant of the colder time,
>   Who love the winter woods, to trace
>   On paler heavens the branching grace
> Of leafless elm, or naked lime,
>
> And see my cedar green, and there
>   My giant ilex keeping leaf
>   When frost is keen and days are brief—
> Or marvel how in English air
>
> My yucca which no winter quells,
>   Although the months have scarce begun,
>   Has push'd toward our faintest sun
> A spike of half-accomplish'd bells—
>
> Or watch the waving pine which here
>   The warrior of Caprera set
>   A name that earth will not forget
> Till earth has roll'd her latest year.

A footnote to these verses refers to the allusion to the warrior of Caprera thus :—"Garibaldi said to me, alluding to his barren island, 'I wish I had your trees.'" The pine which Garibaldi planted still flourishes amain, a conspicuous feature in one of the most delightful gardens that poet could have loved to call his own.

It was about the time that Tennyson was in his "grand,

but very gloomy" state that Edward Fitzgerald made an interesting record. "Alfred," he wrote, "seems to be independent of weather. In one of the great storms of this year, he walked all along the coast to the Needles, which is six miles off. With all his shattered nerves and weary gloom, he seems to have some sort of strength and hardihood. His tenderness is genuine as well as his simplicity; and he has *no hostilities*, and is never active, as against people. He only grumbles. He wants a story to treat, being full of poetry with nothing to put it in."

The story was found (I use the word "found" advisably, for Tennyson did not invent the plot), and in 1864 *Enoch Arden* appeared. In the nine years which had elapsed since the publication of *Maud*, he had written *Enid and Nimue, or, The True and the False* (1857), which was suppressed as soon as printed; the *Idylls of the King* (1859), to which I shall refer later; *The Grandmother's Apology* (now known as *The Grandmother*), to which Millais supplied an illustration (1859); *Sea Dreams* and *Tithonus* (1860); and an *Ode*, a *Welcome*, several small lyrics, an Epitaph, and the *Experiments* in classic metres.

Opinions of *Enoch Arden* differ widely. Bayard Taylor curtly dismissed it in his essay as Tennyson's "poorest narrative poem." Others have hailed it as his most masterly production, and there is no question that it is the most "popular" of all his sustained work—though Heaven forbid that this should be accounted conclusive testimony of its value. The Rev. George Dawson, whose knowledge and love of Tennyson was only exceeded by his knowledge and love of Shakespeare, unhesitatingly declared that *Enoch Arden* was "the noblest and best" of Tennyson's productions. "I find in it," he said, "almost every quality of the poet—true sympathy and all the rest. There is not a fine word in it. The conceits and affectations, and ringlet-within-ringlet of the earlier poems of Tennyson, are all gone. Some of his poems are too elaborate. Most people require to read them several times to understand what the poet means, and then they are not certain; but in *Enoch Arden* is brought to perfect clearness the last lesson of the true-hearted. It is the perfection of even narrative—neither break, nor flaw, nor pause—but calmly and quietly on goes the flow of verse— fit things in few words, and these words most apt. It is the last triumph of art to be perfectly simple and natural. In *Enoch Arden* we have an heroic soul in a simple dress, and a tale of love stronger than death, told in matchless language. It is an idyll of the noblest heroism, told by simplest people in simple circumstances, and in daily life. . . . I account it a far higher achievement to show this generation the deep things of the human soul in the dress of this generation, than to show the great things of humanity under the dress of knights, monks, and nuns. The one is an easy task; the other a very difficult one. Therefore I deliberately prefer those poems which treat of modern times, as Hood's *Song of the Shirt.* I account *Enoch Arden* a far greater poem than the *Idylls of the King.* These were grand beyond all description, but this is nobler because it finds the qualities of King Arthur in the rough and humble garb of the sailor, the miller, and the sailor's wife."

The story of *Enoch Arden* was familiar before Tennyson's time, and Enoch Ardens in real life have been abundant since. Adelaide Proctor had dealt with the same character and the same crisis in a man's life in one of her lyrics, *Homeward Bound;* but at the point when the hero sees his wife "seated by the fire, whispering baby-words and smiling on the father of the child," Tennyson departed from the main lines of the previous narrative. Miss Proctor made the three recognise each other, and the hero, after blessing her, departed again to roam "over the restless ocean." Tennyson's conception was still finer, for he made the broken-hearted man depart without a word. Said George Dawson in vindicating Enoch Arden for telling his story to the landlady just before his death,—"The conduct may be questionable, but the great beauty of the poem is this : here is a sailor, and a little dull town, and a miller, and a miller's wife ; and in that poor sailor's heart there beats the whole depth of passionate human love. Everything self-denial can do is done, the sorest stress ever laid on human heart is laid on his. The circumstances are almost too terrible to contemplate. God grant that you and I may never come anything near such a crisis of the soul."

Standing midway between the shorter and detached idylls and the massive work represented by the *Idylls of the King*, the idyll of *Enoch Arden*, purely English in tone and sentiment, and dealing with a humble drama of the day, specially appealed to a larger class of readers and students than those which had gone before or came after. The poem has its heights and its depths, yet it can always be understood of the people. Enoch Arden is himself a sublimely heroic and intensely pathetic figure — at once so masterful and so helpless, so strong and so weak, so resolute and so incapable. The whole poem is full of casuistry. The giant is defeated, the feeble man prevails, the victor is vanquished, the defeated is triumphant. There is no comparison between Enoch and his rival Philip. The one is headstong, impetuous, undaunted, unyielding ; the other is patient, submissive, gentle, and complaisant. The one can brook no delay, tolerate no doubt—he is full of manly passion and ardour, and until he has won his wife is unsatisfied. The other, though never reluctant or hesitating, can always wait, always subdue his feelings, always remain faithful and believe in the faith of others. Both men are heroes, both are men to admire, both are men of true heart and pure purpose, and yet they " stand off in difference so mighty." Both men had their victory and their defeat, and, knowing the spirit of each, who shall say which triumphed the more ? —Philip, with his wife won by years of waiting, or Enoch, knowing his power, and dying in secret to save the woman he loved from a moment's regret ?

As a poetical composition *Enoch Arden* is notable for its

compression, its concentrated force, its word-simplicity—all in keeping with the story told and the characters delineated. It opens with a description, clear and accurate as a photograph, of the little seaport Deal, where foam and yellow sands are seen in the chasm-broken cliffs, where red roofs cluster about a narrow wharf;—

> Then a moulder'd church; and higher
> A long street climbs to one tall-tower'd mill;
> And high in heaven behind it a gray down
> With Danish barrows; and a hazelwood
> By autumn nutters haunted, flourishes
> Green in a cuplike hollow of the down.

In this hazelwood, Philip Hay, the miller's son, Enoch Arden, "a rough sailor's lad Made orphan by a winter shipwreck," and Annie Lee, "the prettiest little damsel in the port," unconsciously worked out the drama of their later life. The boys quarrelled as to who should wed her, and Enoch "stronger made was master"; but Annie would bid them cease disputing, "and say she would be little wife to both." This was the faint adumbration of what was yet to pass. When the boys became men, Enoch won Annie for his wife, and Philip, too shy to speak and too late, "in their eyes and faces read his doom." But when Enoch was cast away on an island, and unheard of for many years, Philip, deeming him dead, asked for Annie's love. She, faithful to the man who had first won her, yet unable to speak harshly to the man who had been her best friend through years of sorrow and poverty, could only ask Philip to wait a little; and he, with the lifelong hunger in his heart, said—

> "Annie, as I have waited all my life
> I well may wait a little."

Convinced at last that Enoch was dead, and persuaded by Enoch's children to marry Philip, she became the miller's wife—and then Enoch, rescued after many years, returned from the island, "the loneliest in a lonely sea." His had been a hard fate: for years cut off from the world of life,

K

parted by the seas from home and wife, and waiting wearily
and vainly day by day, year by year, for the sight of a sail.
And when "his lonely doom Came suddenly to an end,"
when the

> Long-hair'd, long-bearded solitary,
> Brown, looking hardly human, strangely clad,
> Muttering and mumbling, idiotlike it seem'd,
> With inarticulate rage—

was taken aboard and brought to his home, what worse
doom awaited him?  He went home—home to the wife
and babes he had left years before.

> Then down the long street having slowly stolen,
> His heart foreshadowing all calamity,
> His eyes upon the stones, he reach'd the home
> Where Annie lived and loved him, and his babes
> In those far-off seven happy years were born ;
> But finding neither light nor murmur there
> (A bill of sale gleam'd thro' the drizzle) crept
> Still downward thinking "dead or dead to me" !

At last he found his way to Philip's dwelling, hearing first
from the good and garrulous hostess of the inn all the
changes which time had brought.  A thousand memories
"unspeakable for sadness" rolled upon him as he reached
the old loved haunts, and

> By and by
> The ruddy square of comfortable light,
> Far-blazing from the square of Philip's house,
> Allured him, as the beacon-blaze allures
> The bird of passage, till he madly strikes
> Against it, and beats out his weary life.

He had longed to see his wife again and know that she was
happy, and so he stole like a thief to the place where she
lived, and there he saw "that which he better might have
shunn'd."

> For cups and silver on the burnish'd board
> Sparkled and shone ; so genial was the hearth :
> And on the right hand of the hearth he saw
> Philip, the slighted suitor of old times,

> Stout, rosy, with his babe across his knees ;
> And o'er her second father stoopt a girl,
> A later but a loftier Annie Lee,
> Fair-hair'd and tall, and from her lifted hand
> Dangled a length of ribbon and a ring
> To tempt the babe, who rear'd his creasy arms,
> Çaught at and ever miss'd it, and they laugh'd :
> And on the left hand of the hearth he saw
> The mother glancing often toward her babe,
> But turning now and then to speak with him,
> Her son, who stood beside her tall and strong,
> And saying that which pleased him, for he smiled.

Enoch's sacrifice—his silent departure, and his holding of "his purpose" till he died—was the sacrifice of a strong heroic soul. The last two lines of the poem may jar upon sensitive minds, and seem to be in discord with the tone of the whole poem. The gewgaws of showy pageantry and a costly funeral are in such a case more of a hollow mockery than a sterling tribute to the inborn greatness of the humble sailor whose life was one long combat with hostile fortune.

The volume containing *Enoch Arden* and other poems was dedicated to the poet's wife.—

> Dear, near and true—no truer Time himself
> Can prove you, though he make you evermore
> Dearer and nearer, as the rapid of life
> Shoots to the fall—take this, and pray that he
> Who wrote it, honouring your sweet faith in him,
> May trust himself.

The more important of the poems included in the volume were *Aylmer's Field*, the stern, dark story of which had been related to Tennyson by his friend Woolner, the sculptor ; *Sea Dreams, Tithonus,* which Thackeray had previously published in *Cornhill Magazine ; The Grandmother,* one of Tennyson's favourite poems, and selected by him for recitation on several important occasions ; and the first of the semi-humorous dialect poems, the *Northern Farmer.* The last was a revelation to many of the poet's admirers. Except in the punning song of *The Owl,* he had not revealed a faculty for dry humour, but the *Northern*

*Farmer*, displayed capacity of an original kind. The prototype of the worldly-minded man who thought his son a fool to marry for "luvv" instead of for "munny" was John Baumber, a famous old character who dwelt in the Grange next to the Rectory at Somersby. But the "old style" Northern Farmer, whose boast was—

> I 've 'ed my point o' yaäle ivry noight sin' I beän 'ere,
> And I 've 'ed my quart ivry market-noight for foorty year—

is a general type, perhaps, rather than an individual study.

The volume contained a poem entitled *The Ringlet*, which was omitted afterwards—a vivacious set of verses, not of a very high order, but pleasant enough to read in spare moments. Among smaller pieces were *The Sailor Boy*, *The Islet*, and *The Flower*—the last a protest against the crowd of imitators of his style who had risen up and threatened to detract from the honours of the original poet. The flower he had sown had at first been called a weed, but when it grew and wore a crown of light, thieves took it from him and sowed it far and wide.

> Most can raise the flowers now,
> For all have got the seed.

Tennyson has seldom, however, had occasion for jealousy. Those who flattered him by their imitations were not able to reproduce the richness and luxury of *Tithonus*, the epic power of *Sea Dreams*, the passionate intensity of scorn and censure of *Aylmer's Field*. Nor had they the art to excel the master who gave the fanciful description of a wild, aimless voyage, full of unreality and designed exaggeration, crowded with charming pictures and flushed with the suggestive lights of a vivid but uncontrolled imagination. *The Voyage* is so entrancing that we could wish it were not a dream, and with the pursuers of the ideal we would sail evermore round the merry world. Such magic visions as came to the bewitched crew come but once, and are seen by enchanted eyes.

How oft we saw the Sun retire,
  And burn the threshold of the night,
Fall from his Ocean-lane of fire
  And sleep beneath his pillar'd light.
How oft the purple-skirted robe
  Of twilight slowly downward drawn,
As thro' the slumber of the globe
  Again we dash'd into the dawn.

New stars all night above the brim
  Of waters lighten'd into view;
They climbed as quickly, for the rim
  Changed every moment as we flew.

  .     .     .     .     .     .

And one fair Vision ever fled
  Down the waste waters day and night,
And still we followed where she led,
  In hope to gain upon her flight.
Her face was evermore unseen,
  And fixed upon the far sea-line;
But each man murmur'd, "O my Queen,
  I follow till I make thee mine!"

One of the chief effects of the 1864 volume was to demonstrate Tennyson's versatility and his deep human feeling. He had been charged in early life with a preference for unrealities and the toys of romance, and until the publication of *In Memoriam* he had done little to rebut the charge. But in that great poem his own grief had been the theme. In *Enoch Arden, Sea Dreams, Aylmer's Field*, and *The Grandmother* the griefs of others commanded his attention. He had forsaken dreams for the dramas of life; he had "felt with his kind," and expressed their sorrows, hopes, and emotions. No longer was he the cold and passive observer of men, but their active sympathiser, finding words for their passions, giving voice to their wrongs. No longer was he the philosopher standing apart and drawing morals from intellectual problems; the problems of humanity day by day engaged his attention. The poor sailor-hero, the humble city-clerk and his wife, the broken-hearted youth, Leolin, and his brother,—desolate homes of rich and poor, sundered lives of gentle and simple, sorrows and disasters of mankind all the world over : these supplied themes in the place of dreams and fancies and the simulated frenzies of youth.   Poet has given us no tenderer views of women than Annie Lee, Edith Aylmer, and the city-clerk's wife.   They stand out in their natural beauty and their true womanliness above all the Adelines and Margarets, and Lilians with their sudden pallors, their flushes, their curved frowns, and their faint smiles.   Taine had said what could now be said no longer—that Tennyson had supplied the world with "keepsake characters from the hand of a lover and an artist." Now he had given us quivering flesh and blood, and the very glory and utter pathos of life itself.

# CHAPTER IX.

## THE IDYLLS OF THE KING.

" With a melody
Stronger and statelier,
Led me at length
To the city and palace
Of Arthur the King ;
Touch'd at the golden
Cross of the churches,
Flash'd on the Tournament,
Flicker'd and bicker'd
From helmet to helmet,
And last on the forehead
Of Arthur the blameless
Rested the Gleam."

*—Merlin and the Gleam.*

THERE are great gaps in Tennyson's history. We travel along an ill-defined track, his works serving as guides and signs ; but the space between is oft-times dark and seemingly nothing but waste. Whether the blanks will ever be filled is now more than doubtful. The periods which apparently were uneventful were in reality times of great preparation. The results of strenuous toil, and of hard work performed in semi-seclusion, were to be seen later. Tennyson, it may safely be said, was never idle. He was always at a task, and however silent he may have been, he was eventually to be heard in strains as deep and sweet as ever. No year of his life was barren and unproductive. Though the world saw nothing of his work, he was ever sowing seed, tending, maturing, and perfecting flowers of poesy, though his patience, slowness, and persistency ill-suited the expectation and desire of his eager admirers. His industry was, indeed, marvellous. He was devoted to

his work, scheming new and improving old designs, studying deeply—for he was a wise man, always learning—and,
regardless of the world and indifferent to its counsel,
pursuing a course entirely his own as a poet and as
a man.

Tennyson had been attracted to the Arthurian legend
very early in life, as a boy having read Malory's romances.
In 1837 Landor recorded that "a Mr Moreton, a young
man of rare judgment, read to me a manuscript by Mr
Tennyson, very different in style from his printed poems.
The subject is the death of Arthur. It is more Homeric
than any poem of our time, and rivals some of the noblest
parts of the Odyssea." The poem, with its introduction
*The Epic*, appeared first in the 1842 volume, and in the prelude to it we gain, perhaps, a hint of the writer's opinions
and intentions.

> "You know," said Frank, "he burnt
> His epic of King Arthur, some twelve books "—
> And then to me demanding why? "O, sir,
> He thought that nothing new was said, or else
> Something so said was nothing—that a truth
> Looks freshest in the fashion of the day:
> God knows: he has a mint of reasons: ask.
> It pleased *me* well enough." "Nay, nay," said Hall,
> "Why take the style of those heroic times?
> For nature brings not back the Mastodon,
> Nor we those times: and why should any man
> Remodel models? these twelve books of mine
> Were faint Homeric echoes, nothing-worth,
> Mere chaff and draff, much better burnt."

There can be slight question that the publication of the
*Mort d'Arthur* was tentative. But Tennyson was brimful
of the romances of Malory. In the 1832 volume he had
printed *The Lady of Shalott*, a version of the Elaine
legend, and an allegory with meanings manifold, chief of
which is that as the facts of human life and history are
revealed idealism perishes, the mirror of poetry is shattered,
and the gleaming threads of which romance is woven are

tangled and snapped. Then, in the next edition, had been added the splendid ballad of the only perfect knight, Sir Galahad, who

> Kept fair through faith and prayer
> A virgin heart in work and will.

And in the same volume there was the magic fragment of enchanting verse describing the meeting of Sir Lancelot and Queen Guinevere, the suffused colour of the scene described being as rich, and pure, and vivid as in the pictures of Raphael. A stanza in the *Palace of Art* should also be noted. These were the preludes to the *Idylls of the King*, but seventeen years were to pass before the vibrations of the chords of that mighty symphony were first to be heard. In the interval had come *The Princess*, *In Memoriam*, and *Maud*, three masterpieces all different in style and tone; but the fourth, in some ways greater and better than all, was to be begun. Said George Dawson— "Almost all great writers may be divided into two great classes—those that leap into fame at once, whose first book is their best, whose first air is their only air, and all whose subsequent writings are variations more or less excellent upon the old and original theme ; others that climb slowly to fame, whose early work gives promise of after excellence. Tennyson's genius is slow to exhibit its fulness. Tennyson climbs slowly to fame, and it is easy to trace the progressive labour, the constantly accumulating success, and the constantly diminishing faults of all that he has written. Some of his earlier poems were feeble, the elaboration was overdone, and the meaning obscure. But he has since learned to clothe lofty thoughts in simple words. . . . Why did Tennyson choose the *Idylls of the King?* Probably from that deep-seated feeling which makes men take refuge in a far-off time, a far-off place, and far-off people from the vulgarity and meanness and commonplace of the hour in which they themselves live ; for there is no denying that every hour whilst present is a vulgar hour. . . . In thinking of old times, the meanness and vulgarity are all gone. Time and the grave take the coarse and the common sooner than the noble. . . . I would rather have a romance of King Arthur than the most precious book of antiquity. The same feeling probably led Tennyson to King Arthur. . . . He knew the vulgarity of wealth, the offensive obtrusiveness of the poor, the indifference of the well-born, the sneakishness of the low-born; and chilled, indignant, repelled, he fled from the vulgarity and impurity and corruption of modern times, to the nobler times of old."

Poets have in many ages hovered round the Arthurian legend, and some have alighted upon the subject, only perhaps to leave it again feeling that it was beyond their scope.

> The mightiest chiefs of British song
> Scorn'd not such legends to prolong;
> They gleam through Spenser's elfin dream,
> And mix in Milton's heavenly theme;
> And Dryden in immortal strain,
> Had raised the Table Round again.

Scott, Warton, Gray, the now forgotten or contemned Blackmore, Lytton, Arnold, Morris, and Swinburne felt the influence of the legend with "its dim enchantments, its fury of helpless battle, its almost feminine tenderness of friendship, its fainting passion, its religious ardours,— all at length vanishing in defeat, and being found no more." Tennyson lifted the romance into the highest and purest region of poetry, impregnated the stories with great meanings and suggestions, illuminated the history with rich interpretation. The *Idylls* are of lofty grandeur, of sweetest purity, of intensest and most radiant splendour. Malory wrote perfect prose; Tennyson transmuted that prose into perfect poetry.

Nearly forty years ago a stranger went to Caerleon, and without giving his name or stating his errand, took up his abode at the Hanbury Arms, one of the oldest hostelries in the kingdom. It faces the Usk, and originally stood at a point in the road commanding three approaches to the ancient city. Its low-browed windows with the stone mullions of unusual thickness, and the square hooded dripstones above, indicate that the house must date from the fourteenth or fifteenth century. Accommodation for travellers can only be obtained at this place, and the stranger was therefore compelled to take up his abode therein. I visited Caerleon in 1890, and in the Hanbury Arms read an account by a local chronicler of the visitor. "Quiet and unobtrusive to a degree," he said, "he soon attracted attention from his very reserved and seclusive habits. Day after day passed, and his figure was seldom seen. Frequently he would leave the house early in the morning, and go no one knew whither, and on his return partake of slight refreshment, and retire to his room until next morning. It was soon recognised that the stranger was fond of long walks, and there was not a hill in the neighbourhood up whose sides he did not climb. For a time no companion or friend seemed to notice him, but occasionally a letter arriving at the post-office was delivered to him. At first the name attracted no attention, but at length 'Alfred Tennyson' inscribed on successive missives seemed to have a special interest for the local post-master. He repeated the name until its familiarity led him to suspect that the stranger was no other than the Poet Laureate, and this ultimately proved correct. On the fact becoming generally known that Tennyson was staying at Caerleon visitors frequently called upon him, but he endeavoured to maintain his seclusion to the last." Tennyson afterwards became the guest of Mr John Edward Lee of the Priory. In 1859 the result of his sojourn at "the City of Legions" was seen when he produced the first of the *Idylls*. The room which the poet occupied remains in the same state as it was on Tennyson's visit. It was allotted to myself, and the landlord, with a touch of pride, pointed to the chair and table which Tennyson had used. Enterprising Americans had offered large sums for them, but the landlord, with a creditable sentiment of reverence for the old associations, had declined to sell.   Tennyson's favourite walks were shown to me, and I was able to obtain evidence of the fidelity and the scrupulous care with which he had described the scenery of the locality.   The Laureate can also be traced to Cornwall.   As early as 1848 he had been to Truro, where he was the guest of Mr Henry Sewell Stokes, himself a man of letters.   Tennyson was then preparing *In Memoriam* for publication, and it is stated that some portion of the elegy was written during this journey.   At Morwenstow, a primitive and picturesque sea-village between Clovelly and Kilkhampton, he was the guest of his friend the Rev. R. S. Hawker, one of the most remarkable of clergymen, best of men, and truest of poets; and he was frequently to be met about the rugged country between Bude and Tintagel.   The scenery could not fail to inspire him, and he must have felt that the real Arthur-land, in spite of the demonstrations of antiquaries to the contrary, is to be found in Cornwall and South Wales.   Tennyson accepted the current tradition, and he has described the wild and imposing scenery of the south-west country as he alone was capable of doing.

The story of Tennyson's visit to Cornwall has seldom been related, and the following extracts from an interview with the poet's host at Truro (Mr Stokes), may be read with interest, though I am bound to say that some parts of it strike me as apocryphal :—

"Once in Cornwall he lost his pipe, but the lady who found it so treasured her prize that she would not restore it.   His habits were of the simplest, though strange.   He would be down to dinner punctually at three o'clock of an afternoon, and he was visible from that time until he went to bed early or late the next morning.   Meanwhile he would be discussing all subjects that appealed to his active and imaginative brain.   When he bade farewell for the night he entered his room, and was not seen again until dinner next day.   So his stay in Cornwall was passed.   He drank sherry, and he smoked continuously.

He was never without the black dudeen, which his friends have come to recognise as part and parcel of the man. Whilst thus quietly, lazily lying on the stream of life, being gently carried forward, he was engaging in writing that grand eulogy to his dead friend, Arthur Hallam. Though engaged on this mastership, he was the best of company. He was always ready for discussion. Curiously enough, he was some time in doubt as to Robert Browning's claims as a great poet ; or if he had made up his mind, his opinion was not favourable. On one occasion he asked Mr Stokes, 'What do you think of Browning?' To which he got answer, 'I would rather suspend judgment. What do you think?' 'I would rather not say,' answered the future Laureate, and added, 'What's your opinion of my *Princess?*' His friend did not answer, and Tennyson remarked, 'I know ; you do not like it.' He was a great admirer of Burns and Gray. He once said the latter's *Elegy in a Churchyard*—that hackneyed task work of the elementary scholar —he would rather have written than any poem in the language. He had, indeed, a strong liking for Gray, and classed him and Burns as the two greatest lyric poets of any age or country. He much loved some of Burns's poetry. He would linger affectionately over the recital of *Ye Banks and Braes of Bonny Doon*, and was delighted with some of the Scotch poet's songs which the late Mrs Stokes used to sing. But before all Tennyson placed his Bible. He had also a great liking for Dante's *Inferno*, and knew it line for line. He would boast in his pleasant way that if anyone read one line he could give the next from memory. And he invariably did it. He had a marvellously retentive memory. He was a good German scholar, though apparently indifferent to French, and could recite whole passages from Goethe's *Faust*. His memory, he always said, was too strong to prove as useful as it might were it of a more ordinary character. He remembered so distinctly all that he read that he eschewed the perusal of new books, and browsed on the old pasturage of literature. He knew every stage play, it seemed, and could name every species of seaweed. What has perhaps been most widely noted relative to the Laureate's person is his beautifully-balanced head, the finest head in Europe, his enthusiastic admirers have often chimed. Once Mr Stokes said to him, 'You have the finest head I ever saw.' 'No,' answered the Laureate, 'it is defective behind. I shall never write a good drama. I have not enough passion.' What a strange commentary is this treasured remark of 1848 on events in later years, during which the Laureate has more than once proved the truth of his own words. He was of a somewhat (!) scientific leaning presumably, for he then carried with him Mary Somerville's book, in addition to the *Odyssey*."

For thirteen years, from 1859 to 1872, Tennyson was

engaged in producing his sequence of stories from the "noble hystorye" of King Arthur. The ten pieces were considered to form a perfect whole until, in 1885, in the *Tiresias* volume, the episode of *Balin and Balan* was added. This piece was intended to be read as an introduction to *Merlin and Vivien*, and only by so reading it can its use and purpose be recognised. The poem also served as a link between preceding lines where there was a faint whisper of Guinevere's imperfection, and those in which Vivien denounced the scandals of the Court

> Polluting, and imputing her whole self,
> Defaming and defacing, till she left
> Not even Lancelot brave, nor Galahad clean.

What is an Idyll? Many have doubted whether Tennyson was justified in using this term for his cycle of Arthur-poems. "Idyllic" is scarcely the name to apply to the guilty loves of Lancelot and Guinevere, or the scandal-mongering of Vivien and the doting frailty of Merlin. An idyll is a picture of rustic peace, of sylvan beauty, of primitive simplicity—"a picture-poem, Nature in the background, and in the foreground men and women of primitive manners and simple nobleness." Few of the Arthur-poems, as Tennyson wrote them, are therefore idylls at all in the strictest sense; but the poet no doubt felt himself fully justified in using the term because he presented to us in a series of scenes the leading incidents in what, after all, is a great drama. The meaning and object of the poems are on the surface apparent; but below the surface there are not unlikely mysteries of significance which few think of resolving or even of searching for. Thus a New York critic has contended that the *Idylls* are not to be taken literally or historically, but allegorically—that Arthur typifies the Soul; the Round Table, the Body; Merlin, Wisdom; the Lady of the Lake, Religion; and the three Queens, Faith, Hope, and Charity. What is more, this same critic received an autograph letter from Tennyson accepting his interpretation. On the other hand, Bayard Taylor, in a somewhat carping and querulous mood, declared that the *Idylls* were "an example of a lofty poetic theme weakened in exact proportion as it is carried beyond the limits of the first conception." He thought that all after the first four were an afterthought, and had lost freshness, resonance, and fluency. "There is more for us," we are surprised to hear him saying, "in the early ballad of *Sir Galahad* than in the later ballad (!) of *The Holy Grail*, for this, like a modern Madonna compared with those of Fra Angelico or Raphael, gives us technical imitation instead of unthinking faith." He found fault with the style :—"Tennyson's verse moves more cautiously in these added *Idylls*: the lines no longer beat, sharp-smitten with the dint of armed heels, as in the *Morte d'Arthur*; his Muse takes heed to her feet, picks her way, is conscious of her graceful steps and repeats them." And so forth. Edmund Clarence Stedman has called the *Idylls* unhesitatingly the Laureate's "master-work." "Nave and transept, aisle after aisle, the Gothic minster has extended until, with the addition of a cloister here and a chapel yonder, the structure stands complete. . . . It is the epic of chivalry—the Christian ideal of chivalry which we have deduced from a barbaric source—our conception of what knighthood should be, rather than what it really was; but so skilfully wrought of high imaginings, fairy spells, fantastic legends, and mediæval splendours, that the whole work, suffused with the Tennysonian glamour of golden mist, seems like a chronicle illuminated by saintly hands, and often blazes with light like that which flashed from the holy wizard's book when the covers were unclasped."

Henry Elsdale's *Studies in the Idylls* (1878) supplies us with the most exact and detailed account of the whole of the series, constituting in reality an epic. A rapid survey of each poem is taken in turn, and the complete set is then examined as "a single work of art." "This examination," it was claimed, "tended to bring fairly before us the lofty and noble purpose which underlies the whole work, and its essential unity, so that the various poems are but the different acts in one great drama. It showed us the artistic agreement and harmony between the action and progress of this drama, in the successive poems, and the attendant scenes and operations of outward nature. These again will be seen to be influenced by those changes of time, season, and weather, which the progressively unfolding cycle of a single complete year will bring before us, side by side with the progressively unfolded action of the general drama. We shall discern, as we proceed, more and more clearly, that these *Idylls* constitute essentially one long study of *failure*. They bring before us that sad doom of vanity, of disappointment, of blighted promises and withered prospects, which, here as elsewhere, is seen to await many bright hopes and noble enthusiasms. And they show us the secret of this failure, the dread working of that mystery of iniquity which mars and ruins the fairest of prospects. The Evil comes first ; but, following ever upon it, with slow and tardy, as it would appear, but certain and irresistible steps, we recognise the noiseless and stealthy tread of the avenging Nemesis of Retribution."

The flaw in the *Idylls* has been pointed out by Professor Ingram, among others. "The poet appears to have sacrificed Arthur to Launcelot. The warm and varied colour which plays about the latter is brought out more vividly by comparison with the white radiance in which the former is clothed. Perhaps a pure, cold exaltation seemed best to accord with the saintliness attributed to Arthur. But if such was the thought of the poet he was certainly in error. This kind of tenuity and colourless pallor is by no means essential to sanctity, which can quite well accord with hearty life and vigorous personality." Arthur's perfection, in short, supplies the excuse for Guinevere's frailty.

The Epic of King Arthur is divided into four portions, in each of which the characteristic of the four seasons of the year gives the clue to the tone of the poem. In the Spring comes the King and makes a realm and reigns. His Noble Order is founded; the Knights joust, champion the weak and suffering, and display their valour; Gareth wins the hand of Lynette. In the Summer King Arthur and his Knights are at the height of their power. Foes have found them irresistible. Their prowess and courtesy win for them the love of good and true women, though that love itself may be akin to pain for some. Geraint proves the constancy of Enid; Launcelot is loved with that love which was her doom by Elaine, the lily maid of Astolat. The quest for the Holy Grail begins. In the Autumn the first stage in decline is reached. Vivien is loud in her slanders; Ettarre is false to Pelleas; the Knights begin to return from a fruitless journey, hopeless, baffled, realising their imperfections and weakness. And in the Winter the King foresees his doom. The last tournament is fought; the bowers of Camelot are deserted; Mordred the usurper has arisen; the Queen is false; and the last battle is fought at night beside the winter sea. And thus could the last Knight, Sir Bedivere, lament—

> The true old times are dead,
> And now the whole Round Table is dissolved
> Which was an image of the mighty world,
> And I, the last, go forth companionless,
> And the days darken round me, and the years,
> Among new men, strange faces, other minds.

The stories as related are all to be found in Malory (the text of which is sometimes very closely followed), with the exception of *Geraint and Enid*, which is to be found in Lady Charlotte Guest's *Mabinogion*, from the Welsh of the *Llyfr Coch o Hergest* (The Red Book of Hergest). In the original the story is long and somewhat involved, and Tennyson has followed it very literally where it suited his purpose, but introduced new elements and suppressed some of the old episodes. It was at the private press of Sir Ivor Bertie Guest, the son of Lady Charlotte Guest, that in 1867 the cycle of songs written for Dr Arthur Sullivan, was printed under the title of *The Window ; or the Loves of the Wrens.* The poet said—" These little songs, whose almost sole merit—at least till they are wedded to music— is that they are so excellently printed, I dedicate to the printer." We thus have evidence of the personal as well as literary friendship existing between the poet and the translator of the *Mabinogion.*

The first four of the *Idylls* were—*Enid, Vivien, Elaine,* and *Guinevere,* and it is generally conceded by the critics that these have a truer Homeric ring than those which followed. The first of these pieces, *Enid and Nimue ; or the True and the False,* had been privately printed in 1857, and never permitted to get into the hands of other than a very few friends; while in 1858 Arthur Clough recorded that he had listened to Tennyson's reading of King Arthur's last interview with the faithless Queen. When Bayard Taylor visited Tennyson, " I spoke," he said, " of the Idyll of Guinevere as being perhaps his finest poem, and said that I could not read it aloud without my voice breaking down at certain passages. 'Why, I can read it and keep my voice!' he exclaimed, triumphantly. This I doubted, and he agreed to try, after we went down to our wives. But the first thing he did was to produce a magnum of wonderful sherry, thirty years old, which had been sent him by a poetic wine-dealer. Such wine I never tasted. 'It was meant to be drunk by Cleopatra or Catharine of Russia,' said Tennyson. We had two glasses apiece, when he said, 'To-night you shall help me drink one of the few bottles of my Waterloo —1815.' The bottle was brought, and after another glass all round, Tennyson took up the *Idylls of the King.* His reading is a strange, monotonous chant, with unexpected falling inflexions, which I cannot describe, but can imitate exactly. It is very impressive. In spite of myself I became very much excited as he went on. Finally, when Arthur forgives the Queen, Tennyson's voice fairly broke. I found tears on my cheeks, and Mr and Mrs Tennyson were crying, one on either side of me. He made an effort and went on to the end, closing grandly. 'How can you say,' I asked (referring to the previous conversation), 'that you have no surety of permanent fame? This poem will only die with the language in which it is written.' Mrs Tennyson started up from her couch. 'It is true!' she exclaimed; 'I have told Alfred the same thing.'"

In 1869 four new *Idylls* were published—*The Coming of Arthur, The Holy Grail, Pelleas and Ettarre,* and *The Passing of Arthur,* the original *Morte d'Arthur* fittingly being interwoven into the last of these, and forming the finale. Two years later the *Contemporary Review* printed *The Last Tournament,* and this with *Gareth and Lynette* was published in the volume of 1872. "It is probable," writes the author of *Tennysoniana,* "that these additional idylls were an afterthought, and that the first four were all that were originally contemplated." Carlyle found this fare unsatisfying, and complained that the poet was treating his readers "so very like infants, though the lollipops were superlative." Among the earliest and most discriminating of Tennyson's admirers was Prince Albert, and the *Idylls* heightened his opinion of the Laureate. He read the poems to the Queen, and to the Empress Frederick when she came to England in 1860, pointing out to his daughter at the same time what suitable subjects were suggested to her for pictures. Writing to the poet himself, he said—

"Will you forgive me if I intrude upon your leisure with a request which I have thought some little time of making—viz., that you would be good enough to write your name in the accompanying volume of your *Idylls of the King?* You would thus add a peculiar interest to the book containing those beautiful songs, from the perusal of which I derived the greatest enjoyment. They quite rekindle the feeling with which the legends of King Arthur must have inspired the chivalry of old, while the graceful form in which they are presented blends those feelings with the softer tone of our present age.—Believe me, always yours truly,                                   "ALBERT."

"BUCKINGHAM PALACE, *May* 17, 1860."

Soon afterwards it was fated that the "blameless Prince,"

Wearing the white flower of a blameless life,

should pass away ; and Tennyson wrote the touching Dedication which serves as elegy and monument to one who seemed "scarce other than his own ideal knight."  Twelve years later, when the series was closed, the concluding lines *To the Queen* were added, and her Majesty was asked, for the sake of the undying love borne to the dead Prince, to accept

This old imperfect tale
New-old, and shadowing Sense at war with Soul.

Perhaps the greatest compliment which Tennyson ever received was that conveyed to him by an old Breton woman, under the following circumstances :—

Renan (who, by the way, died but a few days before the poet) and Tennyson were friends, and the former a few years ago, on the visit of the Welsh archæologists to Brittany, related to them an anecdote which had much pleased him.  Tennyson had told him that he once stayed a night at Lannion, the birthplace of Renan's mother. Next morning he asked for his bill, but the landlady refused to accept anything.  "You are the man," she said, "who has sung our King Arthur, and I cannot charge you anything."

Nothing so tender, so powerful ; nothing so vigorous, so rich ; nothing so alluring, so stimulating, can be found in any literature as in the legendary history of Arthur—a history which trembles with human passions and glows with spiritual fires, which unites the real and the ideal by links so subtle and so strong—which, like a jewel of rarest workmanship, gathers and clusters the lights of day and emits them again in flashes of tripled splendour.  Every student finds new meanings in the theme : for those who seek there are ever bright truths lying beneath the vesture of romance.  Stage by stage these wonderful idylls rise to a climax of majestic height. Tennyson has made King Arthur of a greatness and nobility which causes him to stand forth as epochal—a pillar, a guide, a vision sublime, a reality intense, a faith and a religion for ever. From the shadows and the mists of the past he emerges, and before him spreads a track of light—a path towards that fair ideal we strive to attain.

# CHAPTER X.



> " The Voices of the day
> Are heard across the Voices of the dark."
> —*The Ring.*

IT has been the ambition of most of the successful lyrical poets to attempt dramatic work ; why, it would be difficult to explain. They have courted failure in this exacting department of literature with a persistency which, if otherwise directed, might have added greatly to their fame. Love of variety, anxiety to excel in new directions, the craving for public acclamation, the burning desire for life and reality to be given to their conceptions—these may be among the causes which induced poets like Byron, Shelley, Dryden, Coleridge, and Longfellow to leave for a while the Study for the Stage. As it happened, they only succeeded in producing poems cast in the dramatic form, though in justice to Byron it should be stated that he never desired his *Manfred* to obtain representation. Lord Tennyson's first dramas proved that he possessed the dramatic instinct but not the dramatic faculty. *Queen Mary* is incomparably ponderous and dull, Shakespearean in its antique garb, but lacking the Shakespearean vitality and spirit—a drama wholly classical in style, but cold, dry, and dead within as the Classics never were. Tennyson in drawing from the stores of the past neglected to give them an attraction for the present. There is no animation in *Queen Mary :* the men and women do not live and breathe again, but are phantoms of the dead long-ago. We gaze, not upon the mirroring of the past as it was, but upon the past revealed as it is. Instead of beholding the semblance of life we peer into a charnel-house. *Harold* and *Becket* possess the same faults, though happily not in the same degree. Becket and Rosamund are more human in guise, and there is something of the intensity of life in Harold and Edith. But even here we have studies and clever portrayals of character instead of men and women endued with warmth, invested with potentiality, vitalised and re-incarnated by the poet's art. As for *The Falcon*, its triviality of treatment and its staleness of subject would render it unmeet for serious criticism, even if it were redeemed by a single passage worthy of remembrance. These four dramas form a class by themselves, and the most devout Tennysonian would scarcely regret the disappearance of the greater portion of most of them. Yet, without being antilogous, I may add that the historical plays contain some of Tennyson's best thoughts, and they possess a high interest, for they reveal the progress, slow as it was, which the Laureate made in an important branch of literature; they mark the gradual development of his power in a given direction, and they prepare us for the reception and the understanding of those later dramas in which he came near achieving absolute success. *The Cup* is an exquisite poem; its characters are distinct, its arrangement effective, its climax powerful; and *The Promise of May* is a true drama shaped and contrived by a poet's hand. As for *The Foresters*, the last and the best of its class, though one of the least ambitious, it is almost a flawless piece of workmanship—an idyll glowing with colour, a poem sparkling and spontaneous, a drama skilful and impressive. An antique legend flowered out anew and put forth luxuriant blossoms; the unfolded leaves were odorous and bright with the sunlight and dew of morning upon them. In spite of a mournful undertone, in spite of hovering shadow, the play (or, more fittingly, the pastoral) ripples with gaiety and gleams with radiance. Prince John may scowl and conspire, but he cannot banish the merriment of the freedom-loving Foresters, or stifle the devoted affection of the outlaw Earl of Huntingdon and Marian, his " Maiden-wife."   It was gratifying to the poet's admirers that his labours to produce an English play were not all in vain.   Failure had followed many of his attempts, but success, long-awaited, came to cheer the last hours of his life.

Tennyson had only produced two dramas in 1877 when Bayard Taylor, in his enlightened critique, advanced the following judicious opinions :—

" Tennyson's two recent dramatic poems (*Queen Mary* and *Harold*) have been a surprise to all who have simply enjoyed his previous works without perceiving the nature of his dominant intellectual passion.   In the elaboration of poetic detail he had already reached the limit of his powers,—nay, whether conscious of the fact or not, he had passed the limit drawn by the higher law of proportion. He was compelled to turn to an untried form ; and, having made the selection, a true instinct next compelled him to acquire an untried manner.   He comes back to the simple language through which human character must express itself in the drama, resists (we cannot doubt) the continual temptations of metaphor and all other graces of his lyric genius, studies sharper contrasts and broader effects, and so narrowly misses a crowning success that his failure becomes a relative triumph.   The dramatic faults of *Queen Mary* have been generally recognised : they are partly inherent in the subject, into which no single, coherent tragic element can be forced, and partly in overweighting each one of the many characters with his or her own separate interest. *Harold* is constructed with more skill, and we do not readily see why it should not be regarded as a great dramatic poem.   It is full of strong and vivid passages ; the characters are carefully studied, the blank verse is admirable, and the gleams of pure poetry which brighten it are sobered to the true tone.   In execution it is almost wholly free from the faults which I have indicated.   The heroic pitch is maintained throughout, based upon that heroism in the author's nature which impels him to conquer the world's doubt. Its only defect is that of *composition*, in the sense used by painters—in the grouping of characters and the disposition of scenes, which should gain in action and intensity as they approach the overhanging doom. Thus, the closing description of the Battle of Hastings, a masterly piece of work, would quite destroy the effect of the tragedy if it were represented upon the stage. It is written for the brain and the ear, not for the eye."

However opinions may differ (and we must always expect controversy on this point) as to the value of Tennyson's plays and the place to be assigned them, we must not forget that George Eliot said they "run Shakespeare's close."[1] George Henry Lewes, who heard this, agreed with the remark, and after reading *Becket*, he prophesied that "the critics of to-morrow will unanimously declare Alfred Tennyson to be a great dramatic genius." Emphatic testimony to the value of the play was forthcoming also from another, and an unexpected, quarter, Mr J. R. Green the historian declaring that with all his researches into the annals of the twelfth century he had never arrived at so vivid a conception of the characters of Henry the Second and his Court as was embodied in Tennyson's *Becket*. These, however, are opinions, not judgments.

Tennyson wrote a drama when a boy. His friends relate that he had no mean knowledge of the histrionic art. "You are a good actor lost," one of Mr Irving's company said to him in 1879 when he went to the Lyceum Theatre to see *Hamlet* performed, and, at the conclusion of the play (as Mrs Ritchie records) "explained the art, going straight to the point in his own downright fashion, criticising with delicate appreciation, by the simple force of truth and conviction carrying all before him." His love for the stage,

[1] In Smalley's Letters (1891) we read : "I chanced to sit next to George Eliot on the first night of Tennyson's *Queen Mary* at the Lyceum. The acting of the piece did not please her, and she favoured me with a running commentary on the performance, which was more brilliant than either the play or the acting. Her criticisms disclosed a singular talent for sharp pleasantries."

and particularly his love for Shakespeare, may supply reasons for his own determined efforts to become an acknowledged playwright, though he had mournfully told a friend in Cornwall that he knew he would never write a great drama. "I have not passion enough," he said. At a time that the decline of the drama is so frequently discussed we could have wished that his had been the privilege, as it would have been the pride and glory, of restoring the best traditions of the stage, and elevating the public taste.

That Tennyson was very much in earnest we learn in many ways, and Mr T. H. S. Escott's interesting gossip on the Laureate's plans at this period is too good to be lost. He related that in 1883 the poet rented for six weeks a smart house in a fashionable quarter of London, where he entertained the Prime Minister, the Dean of St Paul's, and Mr Jowett, the Master of Baliol, together with divers luminaries of statesmanship, letters, and theology, at dinner. He went out and permitted himself to be entertained by others. "He was the central ornament of the garden parties at Clapham," continued Mr Escott, "and it was upon one of these occasions that he sat together with Mr Browning and Lord Houghton for an entire hour under a spreading mulberry tree, while the whole company, drawn around, gazed in mute admiration upon this trinity of veteran wielders of the plectrum, deeply occupied the while in their oral symposium. Lord Tennyson soon began to find the conventionalities of London society insufferably tedious and cramping. When he appeared in public it was still in the picturesque wide-awake of the Italian bandit, with which his portraits have familiarised the world. However warm the weather his shoulders were enveloped by the poetic cloak. Everyone noticed him as he drove by in a carriage of decidedly dowdy aspect, and obviously hired at so much per week. Many people recognised him and touched their hats respectfully. Had the Laureate not placed a curb upon his inclination he would most certainly have lit his pipe. It was even rumoured that he once did so.

"The explanation of the august apparition which, when the season of 1883 was at its zenith, flashed upon the London world, is that Lord Tennyson was seized with an ambition of adding new laurels to his wreath, and that he wished not only to write plays that will live for ever, but to see them acted. He had a notion that if he was to be successful in his rôle he ought to be *en évidence* in London himself. Tennyson also frequently received visitors beneath his roof from Saturday till Monday, and among this class of guests none was more frequent or welcome than Henry Irving. Some of the social usages of the Laureate's house are peculiar, and are never departed from. When dinner is over the company adjourn to another room for dessert—in the same way that at Oxford and Cambridge the 'dons' of the high table quit the dining hall when the meal is disposed of, to sip their wine in what is called on the Isis the Common Room, and on the Cam the Combination Room. Lord Tennyson is fond now of a glass of sound port. Upon one occasion he pressed Mr Irving to take a glass of the precious liquid. Mr Irving did as he was desired, but not being a port wine drinker, sipped it very slowly. Before he had finished it the decanter from which the bard had been automatically replenishing his goblet was empty. Lord Tennyson bade the butler bring a fresh supply, and, turning to his guest, said drily, 'Do you always drink a bottle of port, Mr Irving, after dinner?'"

*Queen Mary*, the first, and in some respects the most ambitious of the dramas, was published in 1875, and produced the following year at the Lyceum Theatre by Mr Irving, who had suggested that the piece, if condensed, would make a "magnificent play." In spite, however, of brilliant acting and splendid stage accessories the piece enjoyed but a short run. The story as told by Tennyson follows closely upon the *Tower of London* of Harrison Ainsworth in its purely historical portions, though, no doubt the poet went, as usual, to first sources for his facts. Queen Mary is a sombre figure throughout, disappointed and bitter, yet with a truly regal dignity ; Philip of Spain is a dark character continually meditating ill for the English race, while Simon Renard is a conspirator almost abandoned enough for transpontine melodrama. The play lacks relief. It is all gloom, and even the fine portrayals of gallant and patriotic noblemen of the age are not sufficient to bring distinguishable light into the dark and troubled scenes. We are continually reminded of the horrors of Mary's reign—

> A hundred here and hundreds hang'd in Kent.
> The tigress had unsheath'd her nails at last,
> And Renard and the Chancellor sharpen'd them.
> In every London street a gibbet stood.
> They are down to-day. Here by this house was one ;
> The traitor husband dangled at the door,
> And when the traitor wife came out for bread
> To still the petty treason therewithin,
> Her cap would brush his heels.

Yet there are passages of wondrous power and beauty to be found. Bagenhall's account of the death of Lady Jane Grey is full of tender pathos, and the diction is perfect.

> *Stafford.* Did you see her die?
> *Bagenhall.* No, no ; her innocent blood had blinded me.
> You call me too black-blooded—true enough
> Her dark dead blood is in my heart with mine.
>
> .    .    .    .    .    .    .
>
> Seventeen—and knew eight languages—in music
> Peerless—her needle perfect, and her learning
> Beyond the churchmen ; yet so meek, so modest,
> So wife-like humble to the trivial boy
> Mismatch'd with her for policy ! I have heard
> She would not take a last farewell of him,
> She fear'd it might unman him for his end.
> She could not be unmann'd—no, nor outwoman'd—
> Seventeen—a rose of grace !
> Girl never breathed to rival such a rose ;
> Rose never blew that equall'd such a bud.
> *Stafford.* Pray you go on.
> *Bagenhall.*                    She came upon the scaffold,
> And said she was condemn'd to die for treason ;

> She had but follow'd the device of those
> Her nearest kin : she thought they knew the laws.
> But for herself, she knew but little law,
> And nothing of the titles to the crown ;
> She had no desire for that, and wrung her hands,
> And trusted God would save her thro' the blood
> Of Jesus Christ alone.

*Stafford.*                    Pray you go on.
*Bagenhall.*    Then knelt and said the Miserere Mei—
> But all in English, mark you ; rose again,
> And when the headsman pray'd to be forgiven,
> Said, " You will give me my true crown at last,
> But do it quickly" ; then all wept but she,
> Who changed not colour when she saw the block,
> But ask'd him, childlike, " Will you take it off
> Before I lay me down ?"   " No, madam," he said,
> Gasping ; and when her innocent eyes were bound,
> She, with her poor blind hands feeling—" Where is it ?
> Where is it ?"—You must fancy that which follow'd,
> If you have heart to do it !

If there is a scene comparable with that between Griffith and Queen Katharine, surely it is this. The dialogue which follows almost immediately when the childless Queen, pathetically happy in her delusive hope of motherhood, endeavours to " thaw the bleak manners " of her husband, must also be regarded as evidence of true dramatic skill, and of a subtlety infrequently discovered in modern plays. On the other hand, the poet gives us no very pleasing or (to my thinking) careful delineation of the character of the Princess Elizabeth, who, from first to last, instead of being a foil to Mary, is herself either a suspicious intriguante or a frivolous dame. No doubt Philip was right when he declared—

> She troubles England ; that she breathes in England
> Is life and lungs to every rebel birth
> That passes out of embryo ;

but this scarcely justifies the poet in presenting her as a somewhat weak plotter and a vain coquette. His very last words are words of doubt as to Elizabeth's fitness for the crown and her reliability as a monarch—

> *Bagenhall.*   God save the Crown ! the Papacy is no more.
> *Paget (aside).* Are we so sure of that ?

In the light of history this is a needless question, and an unwarranted aspersion upon the great Protestant Queen.

There are choice thoughts in the drama, brightening out like gems, and illuminating many a dull discourse.  Renard reminds us that

> Whether
> A wind be warm or cold, it serves to fan
> A kindled fire ;

and that "The folly of all follies Is to be love-sick for a shadow."  Here is a lesson for statesmen :—

> Statesmen that are wise
> Shape a necessity, as a sculptor clay,
> To their own model ;

and, better still—

> Statesmen that are wise
> Take truth herself for model.

Bagenhall supplies a striking picture of the cravens of Mary's time :—

> These spaniel-Spanish English of the time,
> Who rub their fawning noses in the dust,
> For that is Philip's gold-dust, and adore
> This Vicar of their Vicar.  Would I had been
> Born Spaniard !  I had held my head up then.
> I am ashamed that I am Bagenhall,
> English.

A more scathing and scornful denunciation of the dastards would be hard to discover.  The long speech of Cranmer is finely conceived and worthy of the man ; while the utterances of Sir Thomas Wyatt are truly those of a soldier and poet.  When bidden to tear up "that woman's work," his verses, he replies—

> No ; not these,
> Dumb children of my father, that will speak
> When I and thou and all rebellions lie
> Dead bodies without voice.　Song flies you know
> For ages.

It is a fact of great interest that *Queen Mary*, though a failure on the English stage, achieved a great success in Australia, where it was produced by Miss Augusta Dargon, a talented Irish actress.　Not only did the piece have a long run in the Melbourne Theatre Royal, but when reproduced at the Bijou Theatre in the same city, it enjoyed a second lease of public favour.

After the experience with *Queen Mary*, a feeling of surprise and, perhaps, of dismay was created when it was known in the following year that the Laureate had completed and meditated publishing a second historical drama, *Harold*.　The work, however, duly saw the light in 1877, and was dedicated to Lord Lytton, Viceroy and Governor-General of India, in the following terms : " My dear Lord Lytton—After old-world records—such as the Bayeux tapestry and the Roman de Rose,—Edward Freeman's History of the Norman Conquest and your father's Historical Romance treating of the same times, have been mainly helpful to me in writing this Drama.　Your father dedicated his *Harold* to my father's brother ; allow me to dedicate my *Harold* to yourself."　The reference to Lord Lytton's father revived the history of the only literary squabble in which Lord Tennyson was provoked to take part.　In early years Tennyson's childish poem, *O Darling Room*, had given the envious and malicious an opportunity of decrying the young poet.　Lord Lytton was among those who resented the rapid popularity of the new-comer, and with all the venom of personal rivalry he recommended people to read *O Darling Room* in order to see "to what depth of silliness the human intellect could descend."　He was just publishing *The New Timon : a Romance of London*, and inserted the following malignant passage :—

> Not mine, not mine (O Muse forbid !) the boon
> Of borrowed notes, the mock-bird's modish tune,
> The jingling medley of purloin'd conceits,
> Outbabying Wordsworth, and outglittering Keats,
> Where all the airs of patchwork-pastoral chime
> To drowsy ears in Tennysonian rhyme !
> Am I enthralled but by the sterile rule,
> The formal pupil of a frigid school,
> If to old laws my Spartan tastes adhere,
> If the old vigorous music charms my ear,
> Where sense with sound, and ease with weight combine,
> In the pure silver of Pope's ringing line ;
> Or where the pulse of man beats loud and strong
> In the frank flow of Dryden's lusty song?
> Let School-Miss Alfred vent her chaste delight
> On "darling little rooms so warm and bright" !
> Chaunt "I 'm aweary," in infectious strain,
> And catch her "blue fly singing i' the pane."
> Tho' praised by Critics, tho' adored by Blues,
> Tho' Peel with pudding plump the puling Muse,
> Tho' Theban taste the Saxon's purse controuls,
> And pension Tennyson, while starves a Knowles,[1]
> Rather be thou, my poor Pierian Maid,
> Decent at least in Hayley's weeds array'd,
> Than patch with frippery every tinsel line,
> And flaunt, admired, the Rag Fair of the Nine !

There is no denying the severity of the attack, and the retort might be pardoned if it were equally personal and merciless. Tennyson had not hitherto been regarded as a "fighting" poet, but, choosing the suggestive name of Alcibiades he gave vent to his fury in the following lines which appeared in *Punch* :—

### THE NEW TIMON AND THE POETS.

> We know him, out of Shakespeare's art,
>   And those fine curses which he spoke ;
> The old Timon, with his noble heart,
>   That, strongly loathing, greatly broke.
>
> So died the Old ; here comes the New :
>   Regard him : a familiar face ;
> I thought we knew him ; what, it 's you,
>   The padded man—that wears the stays—

[1] These lines allude to the circumstances related on page 77.

Who killed the girls, and thrilled the boys
  With dandy pathos when you wrote.
O Lion, you, that made a noise,
  And shook a mane *en papillotes.*

And once you tried the Muses too ;
  You failed, Sir : therefore now you turn,
To fall on those who are to you
  As Captain is to Subaltern.

But men of long enduring hopes,
  And careless what this hour may bring,
Can pardon little would-be Popes
  And Brummels, when they try to sting.

An artist, Sir, should rest in Art,
  And waive a little of his claim ;
To have the deep poetic heart
  Is more than all poetic fame.

But you, Sir, you are hard to please ;
  You never look but half content ;
Nor like a gentleman at ease,
  With moral breadth of temperament.

And what with spites and what with fears,
  You cannot let a body be ;
It 's always ringing in your ears,
  " They call this man as good as *me !* "

What profits now to understand
  The merits of a spotless shirt—
A dapper boot—a little hand—
  If half the little soul is dirt ?

*You* talk of tinsel !—why, we see
  The old mark of rouge upon your cheeks.
*You* prate of Nature !—*you* are he
  That spilt his life about the cliques.

A Timon you ! nay, nay for shame ;
  It looks too arrogant a jest—
The fierce old man—to take his name,
  You bandbox.  Off, and let him rest.

We can scarcely pity the man who had invited this terrible onslaught and suffered by it so dreadfully.  But Tennyson himself was inclined to magnanimity ; he was the first to regret his own denunciation; and within a week of the infliction of the punishment he had written the poem which still appears among his works—

> Ah God! the petty fools of rhyme
> That shriek and sweat in pigmy wars
> Before the stony face of Time,
> And look'd at by the silent stars:
>
> Who hate each other for a song,
> And do their little best to bite
> And pinch their brethren in the throng,
> And scratch the very dead for spite:
>
> And strain to make an inch of room
> For their sweet selves, and cannot hear
> The sullen Lethe rolling doom
> On them and theirs and all things here:
>
> When one small touch of Charity
> Could lift them nearer God-like state
> Than if the crowded Orb should cry
> Like those who cried Diana great:
>
> And I too, talk, and lose the touch
> I talk of.   Surely, after all,
> The noblest answer unto such
> Is perfect stillness when they brawl.

The "Afterthought" was nobly conceived; and the dedication of *Harold* to Lytton's son gave practical effect in the most graceful manner to the old expression of regret and the wish for greater charity.

*Harold* was not written for the stage, though there are scenes capable of strong and effective representation. The character of the daring and not sinless Harold is full of power, while the rivals for his love, passionate Aldwyth and the gentle Edith, are admirably pourtrayed. There are fine passages, high thoughts, ringing lines, firm and clear delineations of famous personages. Count William, the fiery Tostig, and Edward the Confessor, are real enough; and the history they made is traced with precision.

> All things make for good

we read in the prefatory lines—an echo of the truth arrived at in *In Memoriam*—and though English sympathy will always be with the last great Saxon who fell at Hastings, his victory would not have been greatly the better for this land. Yet England might have had a milder fate than to be governed by the men whose dictum was—

> The voice of any people is the sword
> That guards them, or the sword that beats them down.

Tennyson has described with the utmost skill how the wily and ruthless Norman made Harold a victim, and few scenes are more impressive than those in which the Confessor's heir is tempted to lie, sell his honour, and take oaths of falseness to his beloved country, for the sake of reaching England again. Harold was tempted, and he fell; he vowed treason, never meaning to keep the vow. Terrible retribution followed. To his love, Edith, he said—

> Tho' somewhat less a King to my true self
> Than ere they crown'd me one, for I have lost
> Somewhat of upright stature thro' mine oath,
> Yet thee I would not lose, and sell not thou
> Our living passion. . . .
> Oh God ! I cannot help it, but at times
> They seem to me too narrow, all the faiths
> Of this grown world of ours, whose baby eye
> Saw them sufficient. Fool and wise, I fear
> This curse, and scorn it.

Edith's situation is equally distressful.

> The King hath cursed him, if he marry me ;
> The Pope hath cursed him, marry me or no !
> God help me ! I know nothing—can but pray
> For Harold—pray, pray, pray—no help but prayer,
> A breath that fleets beyond this iron world,
> And touches Him that made it.

The struggle with Tostig, the constant striving with Aldwyth and Edith, the weird prophecies of Hugh Margot the Monk, the imprecations of the Normans, all hurry on the fate of the unhappy King. Yet, with battle-axe in hand, he gave a good account of himself when enemies thronged round him.

> How their lances snap and shiver
> Against the shifting blaze of Harold's axe !
> War-woodman of old Woden, how he fells
> The mortal corpse of faces.   There ! and there !
> The horse and horseman cannot meet the shield,
> The blow that brains the horseman cleaves the horse,
> The horse and horseman roll along the hill,
> They fly once more, they fly, the Norman flies.

But this was not to be, and when the battle was over, two desolate heart-broken women were seeking the king they loved, who lay among the dead with an arrow in his heart.   The conclusion of Tennyson's drama is full of solemn grandeur.

Best in construction, most dramatic in tone, strongest in character, *Becket*, the third of Tennyson's historical dramas, will probably prove to be the piece upon which his fame as a playwright chiefly depends.   It is not so ambitious in some respects as either *Queen Mary* or *Harold*, but it has the compensating merit of being more skilfully designed.   The plot is one of intense interest, the situations are striking and well-conceived, the dialogue is crisp, the action fairly rapid, the climax powerful.   *Becket* was specially written for stage representation, with Mr Irving as the proud prelate ; though Tennyson himself informed Lord Selborne in a brief dedicatory epistle that in its present form it might not meet the exigencies of the modern theatre.   Curiously enough, where the poet this time hesitated the actors were more confident.   Lawrence Barrett, whose untimely death was mourned a short time ago, intended to produce *Becket* in America, and had written that he " foresaw a great success "; and Mr Irving always regarded the play as full of possibilities.   Tennyson found an agreeable subject in the "mitred Hercules" of Henry Plantagenet's time, just as in the gloomy character of Lucretius he found (as Mr Stedman puts it) a brooding character with which he was quite in sympathy. Thomas à Becket is, indeed, a fit hero for a great drama, a giant, a man of supreme intellectual force, an epoch-maker, whom Shakespeare himself might have portrayed as grandly as his Coriolanus. Tennyson was bold to undertake the task, but he was justified. He has helped us to realise the greatness of the prelate who ruled England and made a monarch tremble. Becket moves, a stately and imposing figure, fearless, daring, resolute, among friends, enemies, and rivals; he leads vast enterprises, forms high designs, and only falls at last when the King himself stoops to envy his power.

Interwoven with the main story are the threads of the romance associated with the name of Fair Rosamund. It was, indeed, the poet's original intention to make the fortunes of the King and Rosamund de Clifford of paramount interest; but he probably found that once Becket was introduced he was compelled, in order fitly to represent the character, to assign him a commanding position. Becket rules all; and just as easily as he could vanquish the King at chess, so could he defeat his plans of State. As Chancellor he was mighty; as Archbishop supreme. Said he—

> This Canterbury is only less than Rome,
> And all my doubts I fling from me like dust,
> Winnow and scatter all scruples to the wind,
> And all the puissance of the warrior,
> And all the wisdom of the Chancellor,
> And all the heap'd experiences of life,
> I cast upon the side of Canterbury—
> Our holy mother Canterbury, who sits
> With tatter'd robes.

The time soon came for the prelate to prove his independence, his courage, and his zeal. He braved the anger and the friendship of the King, defied the lords, subdued all men, and vauntingly exclaimed—

> If Rome be feeble, then should I be firm.

Had he been the Holy Father, he

> Would have made Rome know she still is Rome ;

but, as it was, he made Rome a power in England, and acted as Pope to people and the King.

Tennyson has idealised the loves of Henry and Rosamund, and sublimated the fate of the wife unwed. The scene between outraged Queen Eleanor and Fair Rosamund is of thrilling intensity, and the sudden intervention of Becket to prevent murder, if not warranted by history, is for dramatic purposes magnificent. Rosamund in return is sole mourner when her saviour is himself slain. The haughty prelate lies silent in death in the darkened cathedral. A terrific storm rages ; flashes of vivid lightning weirdly illuminate the scene ; and beside the dead man kneels Rosamund, bowed in sorrow and in prayer. Becket fell nobly. When the murderous horde surrounded him he cried—

> Ye think to scare me from my loyalty
> To God and to the Holy Father.  No !
> Tho' all the swords in England flash'd above me
> Ready to fall at Henry's word or yours—
> Tho' all the loud-lung'd trumpets upon earth
> Blared from the heights of all the thrones of her kings,
> Blowing the world against me, I would stand
> Clothed with the full authority of Rome,
> Mail'd in the perfect panoply of faith,
> First of the foremost of their files, who die
> For God, to people heaven in the great day
> When God makes up his jewels.

He was no craven. Knowing his fate—it had been foretold in a dream—he went forth with stateliness, unperturbed and unvexed, to meet it. "I am readier to be slain than thou to slay," he cried to one of the assassins, and, commending himself to his Creator, he knelt and received his death-stroke. Tennyson's Becket is worthy to rank with Shakespeare's Wolsey: what higher praise could be wished or awarded ?

Purely from the literary point of view the drama is one

of singular power. In the earlier scenes Becket is simply the keen adventurer struggling for political power ; but once he is made the Pope's ambassador and hierophant he changes, and his devotion to Church and Faith is devotion which the King himself cannot shake. The conflict between the monarch and the prelate is severe ; powers league themselves against the man who feeds beggars to show his humility and defies Henry Plantagenet to prove his fearlessness. Almost his last utterance is one of defiance to all who would make him swerve from loyalty to the Church ; and he exemplified, as he preached, that

> Valour and holy life should go together.

When in his hour of supreme danger, while he can hear the roar of the avenging Knights, and the battering of the great doors, his companions urge him to fly and hide in the darkened crypt, he calmly turns to them with the words—

> Oh, no, not either way, nor any way
> Save by that way which leads thro' night to light.
> Not twenty steps, but one.
> And fear not I should stumble in the darkness,
> Not tho' it be their hour, the power of darkness,
> But my hour too, the power of light in darkness !
> I am not in the darkness but the light,
> Seen by the Church in Heaven, the Church on earth—
> The power of life in death to make her free !

And when he falls prone and receives his death-stroke none are more appalled than the four Knights who hurriedly ride out into the storm and bear to their revengeful master the tidings which he had so bitterly to regret.

The drama was produced at the Lyceum Theatre by Mr Irving on February 6th, 1893, and at the close of the performance on the first night he said to an enthusiastic audience: " It has been to us a great privilege, a great honour, as we all feel, to produce this work, a work which we are assured will remain a lasting ornament to the stage and to English literature. For my comrades and myself I may say that we have laboured with all our hearts—it has been to us a labour of very great love—to endeavour to add one more laurel wreath to the brow of the master, who was so lately with us. I can only thank you all once more for the hearty, enthusiastic, ungrudging cordiality with which you have accepted our efforts to-night."

Mrs Kendal accepted a play from the Laureate's pen, and in 1879 produced *The Falcon* at the St James's Theatre, the talented actress herself appearing as the Lady Giovanna. Of this drama it is impossible to speak with any favour. The subject is unfortunate, and its treatment almost unavoidably unsatisfactory. The story of Ser Federigo and his falcon, as told by Boccaccio and Longfellow, is pre-eminently poetical, but does not easily lend itself to being dramatised. It is a story to tell or to read, not a story to resolve itself into form and connection by the words and actions of *dramatis personæ;* not one to see acted. As the drama stands, the Laureate seems to have done his best to impart and sustain interest in it by the introduction of a humorous foster-brother to the hero, and a loquacious nurse. The former is unnatural, the latter is not original. Furthermore, such characters lower the poetical tone of the piece, and when it is remembered that the chief scene represents Lady Giovanna dining on Count Federigo's favourite bird, it will be conceived that the piece appealed more to the mirth than to the sympathy of an audience. The Count converses, the lady eats, the foster-brother interposes his quips, and the nurse rambles. Amid all this the familiar story is slowly unravelled. There are few of those charming lines, those warm touches, or those suggestive phrases which contribute so much to make Longfellow's poem successful. Nor even is that sentiment expressed by Lord Tennyson which, it seemed to us, the story was intended to illustrate: "All things come round to him who will but wait."

*The Cup* and *The Falcon* are not dramas of such high aim as *Queen Mary*, *Harold*, and *Becket*, and cannot be compared with them. Of the two, the former is infinitely superior to the latter. *The Cup* is a short and somewhat impressive tragedy founded on a Roman story. Camma, a Galatian, the wife of Sinnatus, a Tetrarch, is beloved by Synorix, an ex-Tetrarch, who does not scruple to murder Sinnatus in order to gain his ends. Refusing to espouse her husband's murderer, Camma becomes a Priestess in the temple of Artemis ; but owing to the persistency with which Synorix urges his suit, allows the marriage ceremony to take place. It was the

> Ancient custom in Galatia
> That ere two souls be knit for life and death,
> They two should drink together from one cup,
> In symbol of their married unity,
> Making libation to the goddess.

Camma poisons the wine in the drinking cup, partakes of it herself, bids the newly-crowned Galatian king

> Drink, and drink deep—our marriage will be fruitful ;
> Drink, and drink deep, and thou wilt make me happy,

and by the success of her design saves herself from a union she loathes, and revenges the husband she loved. This little drama, which contains all the elements of pathos, lacks what is essential in all works designed for successful representation on the stage—warmth and incident. It is not until the final words are being spoken and the last deeds being enacted that one is really moved by what is occurring. The scenes of the first act are colourless and somewhat laboured, but happily relieved and redeemed by outbursts of genuine poesy. In one, and perhaps the finest, of these the nobility and patriotism of Camma are demonstrated, when, responding to the invidious suggestion of Synorix, that

> To submit at once
> Is better than a wholly hopeless war,

she says—

> Sir, if a state submit
> At once, she may be blotted out at once,
> And swallow'd in the conqueror's chronicle.

> Whereas in wars of freedom and defence
> The glory and grief of battle won or lost
> Solders a race together—yea—tho' they fail,
> The names of those who fought and fell are like
> A bank'd-up fire that flashes out again
> From century to century, and at last
> May lead them on to victory—I hope so—
> Like phantoms of the gods.

Camma is, in fact, a truly beautiful conception. In her purity, in her devotion, and in her beauty, she stands out in marked contrast to the sensual ex-Tetrarch who seeks her for his wife. Her life was good, her death is calm and hopeful ; she justifies her last act—tragic and pathetic—by her constancy to the dead Sinnatus. Rising with outspread arms, she exclaims—

> There—league on league of ever-shining shore,
> Beneath an ever-rising sun—I see him—
> "Camma, Camma !"  Sinnatus, Sinnatus !

and thus uttering his name expires in the arms of the Priestesses.

The drama was produced at the Lyceum Theatre by Mr Irving and Miss Terry, with magnificent scenery, in 1881, and was a legitimate success, running for over a hundred nights.

The task of criticising *The Promise of May*, produced by Mrs Bernard Beere at the Globe Theatre in 1882, is beset with difficulties. The piece revealed the Laureate's progress in stage-craft, and there are characters in the drama worthy of deep study. Tennyson was for almost the first time seen as a prose-writer, and it cannot be doubted that in *The Promise of May* his terseness and epigrammatic brightness show to considerable advantage. There are four or five distinct and subtle studies of character, and the management of dialect is as skilful as in the poems. The theme is painful, at times almost revolting, and it is not surprising to find that on the stage *The Promise of May* was no greater success than *Queen Mary* had been. Quite recently Mrs Beere in an interview declared that had she not been a novice in theatrical management at that time she would never have accepted the piece at all. She said that the production of *The Promise of May* was "an artistic success," but "an experience of two weeks was enough to convince me that I was on the wrong tack." One reminiscence of those days is worth preserving, "Lord Tennyson," Mrs Beere related, "was very amusing at rehearsals, and evinced the greatest interest in the way things were conducted on the stage. He came to most of the rehearsals, and, though against the rules, would sit in the pit smoking his pipe." The production of *The Promise of May* was fated to arouse curiosity and even excitement of not the most healthy or desirable character. Philip Edgar, the most important of the *dramatis personæ*, was the poet's conception of "a surface man of theories, true to none." He is an agnostic, cynical and heartless, and having seduced and basely deserted his pretty country sweetheart (whom he has bewildered with his high-sounding philosophy), he returns after a long interval, under another name, and woos her sister. On the night of November 14, 1882, a scene occurred in the Globe Theatre which has thus been described by the nobleman who caused it, the Marquess of Queensberry: "Towards the close of the first act when the gentleman representing the character of Edgar appeared on the stage, I instantly became deeply interested when I perceived the character he, Edgar, had come to represent, or rather, as I took it, most grossly to misrepresent. After listening a few minutes to the sentiments expressed by this gentleman freethinker and atheist of Mr Tennyson's imagination, I became so horrified and indignant that, rising in my stall, I simply, in a loud voice, made the following remarks apropos of Edgar's comments upon 'Marriage': 'These are the sentiments that a professing Christian (meaning Mr Tennyson) has put into the mouth of his imaginary freethinker, and it is not the truth.' My statement of the facts will, I presume, explain my motives. I am a secularist and a freethinker, and, though I repudiate it, a so-called atheist; and, as president of the British Secular Union, I protest against Mr Tennyson's abominable caricature of an individual who, I presume, he would have us believe represents some body of people, which, thanks to the good of humanity, most certainly does not exist among freethinkers."

The comments upon marriage in the mouth of Edgar, from which the Marquess of Queensberry so strongly dissented, are as follow :—

> The storm is hard at hand will sweep away
> Thrones, churches, ranks, traditions, customs, marriage,
> One of the feeblest ! Then the man, the woman,
> Following their best affinities, will each
> Bid their old bond farewell with smiles, not tears ;
> Good wishes, not reproaches ; with no fear
> Of the world's gossiping clamour, and no need
> Of veiling their desires.
>
>               Conventionalism,
> Who shrieks by day at what she does by night,
> Would call this vice ; but one time's vice may be
> The virtue of another ; and Vice and Virtue
> Are but two masks of self ; and what hereafter
> Shall mark out Vice from Virtue in the gulf
> Of never-dawning darkness?
>
>   .      .      .      .      .
>
>           And when the man,
> The child of evolution, flings aside
> His swaddling-bands, the morals of the tribe,
> He, following his own instincts as his God,
> Will enter on the larger golden age ;
> No pleasure then taboo'd : for when the tide
> Of full democracy has overwhelm'd
> This Old world from the flood will rise the New,
> Like the Love-goddess, with no bridal veil,
> Ring, trinket of the Church. but naked Nature
> In all her loveliness.

An American critic of considerable discernment has expressed the opinion that in the *The Promise of May* is to be found the supreme illustration of the influence of Theocritus upon Tennyson—an influence which he pronounces to be more or less visible in all the productions of the Laureate. He draws a comparison between *The Promise of May* and Renan's terrible story *L'Abbesse de Jouarre*, and declares that the conclusions of the English play are "miserable, hopeless, and immoral." This, and like criticisms, proceed from an imperfect understanding and appreciation of the character of Edgar, and from an absolute misconception of the Laureate's own intentions. What the poet thought, and what his Edgar is said to have thought are entirely different matters, and ought never to have been confused. The finest explanation of the poet's meaning appeared in the lucid article from the pen of a scholar now dead, published in the *St James's Gazette* in December 1886. He says :

"Edgar is not, as the critics will have it, a freethinker, drawn into crime by his Communistic theories. Edgar is not even an honest Radical, nor a sincere follower of Schopenhauer ; he is nothing thorough and nothing sincere. He has no conscience until he is brought face to face with the consequences of his crime ; and in the awakening of that conscience the poet has manifested his fullest and subtlest strength.

At our first introduction to Edgar, we see him perplexed with the haunting of a pleasure that has sated him. ' Let us eat and drink, for to-morrow we die ' has been his motto ; but we can detect that his appetite for all pleasure has begun to pall. He repeats wearily the formulæ of a philosophy which he has followed because it suits his mode of life. He plays with these formulæ ; but they do not satisfy him. So long as he had on him the zest of libertinism he did not, in all probability, trouble himself with philosophy. But now his selfishness compels him to take a step of which he feels the wickedness and repugnancy. He must endeavour to justify himself to himself. The companionship of the girl he has betrayed no longer gives him pleasure ; he hates her tears because they remind him of himself—his proper self. He abandons her with a pretence of satisfaction ; but the philosophical formulæ he repeats no more satisfiy him than they satisfy the poor girl whom he deserts. Her innocence has not, however, been wantonly sacrified by the dramatist. She has sown the seed of repentance in her seducer, though the fruit is slow in ripening. Years after he returns, like the ghost of a murderer, to the scene of his crime. He feels remorse. He is ashamed of it ; he battles against it ; he hurls the old formulæ at it ; he acts the cynic more thoroughly than ever. But he is changed. He feels a desire to 'make amends.' Yet that desire is still only a form of selfishness.

He has abandoned the 'Utopian Idiocy' of Communism. Perhaps, as he says with self-mockery that makes the character so individual and remarkable, 'because he has inherited estates.' His position of gentleman is forced on his notice : he would qualify himself for it— selfishly and without doing excessive penance. To marry the surviving sister and rescue the old father from ruin would be a meritorious act. He sets himself to perform it. At first everything goes well for him ; the old weapons of fascination that had worked the younger sister's ruin now conquer the heart of the elder. He is comfortable in his scheme of reparation, and lays 'that flattering unction to his soul.' Suddenly, however, the girl whom he had betrayed, and whom he thought dead, returns ; she hears him repeating to another the words of love she herself had heard from him and believed. 'Edgar !' she cries, and staggers forth from her concealment, as she forgives him with her last breath, and bids him make her sister happy.

Then, and not till then, the true soul of the man rushes to his lips ; he recognises his wickedness, he knows the blankness of his life that is his punishment. He feels then, and will always feel, aspirations after good which he can never, or only imperfectly fulfil. The position of independence on which he prided himself is wrested from him ; he is humiliated. The instrument of his selfish repentance turns on him with a forgiveness that annihilates him ; the bluff and honest farmer whom he despises triumphs over him, not with the brute force of an avenging hand, but with the pre-eminence of superior morality. Edgar quits the scene ; never again, we can believe, to renew his libertine existence, but to expiate with long life-contrition the monstrous wickedness of the past."

*The Promise of May* deserved a much better fate than to be misunderstood or regarded as a literary curiosity. Farmer Dobson and Farmer Steer, to say nothing of the labourers and servants who come upon the scene, are genuine specimens of the hearty, honest, plain-spoken, well-meaning men whom rural England still produces. Dora and Eva Steer are sweet and pathetic girls, and one cannot but feel a pang that a ravager like Edgar should take the happiness and sunshine from their lives. The villagers' views of the man who has "no respect for the Queen, or the parson, or the justice o' peace, or owt," are quaintly expressed with that touch of humour of which Tennyson was master. The air of Lincolnshire pervades the whole drama, and one cannot help thinking that the poet found his theme in a past experience or a tradition of his native place. The result of Communistic doctrines in a quiet Lincolnshire "-by" can easily be imagined. Beauty is betrayed, the wiseacres are bewildered, manly hearts are broken, and hopes are blasted. Edgar, a self-avowed "bundle of sensations," has no desire beyond self-gratification when first he is introduced, and like Faust, seeking a moment's delight, he ruthlessly spoils the fair and spotless flower which he finds. As time passes and he feels that the good he should have loved is irrevocably lost, he is filled with a morbid regret, and makes the horrible proposal to marry his victim's sister for a reason which we cannot believe to be genuine even if it is not deliberately fraudulent. Take Edgar's own argument, and see what it comes to in the end : a selfish apology for misdeeds.

> If man be only
> A willy-nilly current of sensations—
> Reaction needs must follow revel—yet—
> Why feel remorse, he, knowing that he *must* have
> Moved in the iron grooves of Destiny.
> Remorse then is a part of Destiny,
> Nature a liar, making us feel guilty
> Of her own faults.

That Edgar largely lacks the sense of personal responsibility is evident from the first. He believes himself the toy of fortune, the sport of chance, the victim of capricious fate, swayed hither and thither by the wind, carried neither willing nor unwilling by currents—a man without volition, whose " mortal house "

> Is haunted by
> The ghosts of the dead passions of dead men ;
> And these take flesh again with our own flesh
> And bring us to confusion.

When the man is freed from his Utopian dreams he is still despicable; his motives are doubtful, his desires base. Beside this dark character how splendidly shows Dobson, the sturdy, devoted, ignorant, but ever-noble lover of the two sisters! And how tender, the one in her trusting, the other in her love and honour, are Eva and Dora. Eva in her shame is not to be scorned, Dora in her crystalline purity of spirit is a type of the best of womankind.

In October 1891, Mr Theodore Watts announced that Lord Tennyson had written a new play which could be best described as "a woodland poem," and in a series of daintily-written though discursive articles prepared the public for *The Foresters*. We learnt that the comedy had been "written for some time," that "several titles were under discussion," and that the hero of the piece was Robin Hood. "As a Midlander," said Mr Watts (though Lincolnshire is not usually included in the Midland Counties), "Lord Tennyson could not fail to be in very especial sympathy with the spirit of those ballads which recount the doings and the glories of the Midland hero, Robin Hood, that prince of robbers, whose exploits under the greenwood tree have been impudently stolen by Northern ballad-mongers." Before the formal announcement had appeared, the fact was generally known that the Daly Company, with Miss Ada Rehan, intended to produce a new play by the Laureate. Mr and Mrs Daly and Miss Rehan had visited the poet and heard the play read, and it is said that Tennyson very minutely explained certain passages, and stated how the parts should be played. On one occasion Miss Rehan expressed the hope that the poet would be present when the play was first produced. "No, my dear," said Tennyson; "I am far too old to look into the future, and can promise nothing." And, to emphasise his meaning, he forthwith recited *Crossing the Bar*. The play was staged in America with complete success, and on the publication of the work early in 1892, the critics were almost unanimous that the Laureate had succeeded in producing a Pastoral full of freshness, vigour, and sweetness. The love of Robin Hood and Maid Marian is the love of two ardent and noble natures. What says the typical English girl when her lover, the Earl of Huntingdon, is banished and outlawed, and becomes plain Robin Hood ?—

> Forget him—never—by this Holy Cross
> Which good King Richard gave me when a child—
> Never !
> Not while the swallow skims along the ground,
> And while the lark flies up and touches heaven !
> Not while the smoke floats from the cottage roof,
> And the white cloud is rolled along the sky !
> Not while the rivulet babbles by the door,
> And the great breaker beats upon the beach !
> Never—
> Till Nature, high and low, and great and small,
> Forgets herself, and all her loves and hates
> Sink again into chaos.

Lord Tennyson has not departed to any extent from the main lines of the legend which lives in that fine English ballad, "A Lytell Geste of Robyn Hode"; but his slight deviations are thoroughly justified, for they lead to the disclosure of new beauties. The only regret can be that the lively, daring, reckless outlaw has an occasional tendency to moralise like a melancholy Jaques ; yet the following passage, whether it be in accord with the character of the speaker or not, is a fine piece of writing :—

> My lonely hour !
> The king of day hath stept from off his throne,
> Flung by the golden mantle of the cloud,
> And sets, a naked fire.   .   .   .
> .   .   .   .   It is my birthday.
> I have reign'd one year in the wild wood.  My mother,
> For whose sake, and the blessed Queen of Heaven,
> I reverence all women, bad me, dying,
> Whene'er this day should come about, to carve
> One lonely hour from it, so to meditate
> Upon my greater nearness to the birthday

> Of the after-life, when all the sheeted dead
> Are shaken from their stillness in the grave
> By the last trumpet.
>
>               Am I worse or better?
> I am outlaw'd.   I am none the worse for that.
> I held for Richard, and I hated John.
> I am a thief, ay, and a king of thieves.
> Ay! but we rob the robber, wrong the wronger,
> And what we wring from them we give the poor.
> I am none the worse for that, and all the better
> For this free forest-life, for while I sat
> Among my thralls in my baronial hall
> The groining hid the heavens; but since I breathed,
> A houseless head beneath the sun and stars,
> The soul of the woods hath stricken thro' my blood,
> The love of freedom, the desire of God,
> The hope of larger life hereafter, more
> Tenfold than under roof.

An excellent bit of philosophy follows—

>               I believe there lives
> No man who truly loves and truly rules
> His following, but can keep his followers true.
> I am one with mine.   Traitors are rarely bred
> Save under traitor kings.

In his loneliness Robin Hood passionately desires to see
Marian again—

> Gone, and it may be gone for evermore!
> O would that I could see her for a moment
> Glide like a light across these woodland ways!
> Tho' in one moment she should glance away,
> I should be happier for it all the year.
> O would she moved beside me like my shadow!
> O would she stood before me as my queen,
> To make this Sherwood Eden o'er again,
> And these rough oaks the palms of Paradise!

The wish is fulfilled, and Maid Marian reigns—but not be-
fore she has come disguised and tested her lover's fidelity.
But this sovereignty of the glades perturbs the Queen of
Fairyland, and a delightful fairy interlude follows like a

passing dream—the whole stage lights up, and fairies are
seen swinging on boughs and nestling in hollow trunks.
Titania and her elfs sing in the moonlight—

> We must fly from Robin Hood
> And this new queen of the wood.

The fairies have many plaints to make of the intruders.
The lusty bracken has been beaten flat, the "honest daisy
deadly bruised," the "modest maiden lily abused," and the
"beetle's jewel armour crack'd."   So the chorus swells—

> We be scared with song and shout.
> Arrows whistle all about.
> All our games be put to rout.
> All our rings be trampled out.
> Lead us thou to some deep glen,
> Far from solid foot of men,
> Never to return again,
>                         Queen.

And Titania acquiesces in tripping and melodious lines
with the refrain—

> Up with you, out of the forest and over the hills and away.

The Laureate has next depicted the forest life of Robin
Hood, his merry men, and his "maiden-wife."  The greedy
friars, the merchants, and the beggars pass by in procession,
and Friar Tuck, Little John, Much, and Scarlet live up to
their reputations and disport themselves jovially.  It is a
gay and gallant life, yet the Outlaw Chief often yearns for
King Richard to come and restore him to a better and
nobler career.  The valiant Crusader returns at last, and
good men get their own.  But, with remembrance of happy
days surging in their breasts, it is half with regret that the
merry men turn from the glades.  Then says Robin Hood,
Earl of Huntingdon once more,—

> Our forest games are ended, our free life,
> And we must hence to the King's Court.  I trust
> We shall return to the wood.  Meanwhile, farewell
> Old friends, old patriarch oaks.  A thousand winters

> Will strip you bare as death, a thousand summers
> Robe you life-green again.   *You* seem, as it were,
> Immortal, and we mortal.   How few Junes
> Will heat our pulses quicker !   How few frosts
> Will chill the hearts that beat for Robin Hood

And Marian takes up the theme—

> And yet I think these oaks at dawn and even,
> Or in the balmy breathings of the night,
> Will whisper evermore of Robin Hood.
> We leave but happy memories to the forest.
> We dealt in the wild justice of the woods.
> All those poor serfs whom we have served will bless us,
> All those pale mouths which we have fed will praise us,
> All widows we have holpen pray for us,
> Our Lady's blessed shrines throughout the land
> Be all the richer for us.   You, good friar,
> You Much, you Scarlet, you dear Little John,
> Your names will cling like ivy to the wood.
> And here perhaps, a hundred years away,
> Some hunter in day-dreams or half asleep
> Will hear our arrows whizzing overhead,
> And catch the winding of a phantom horn.

To which Robin Hood tenderly adds—

> And surely these old oaks will murmur thee
> Marian along with Robin.   I am most happy—
> Art thou not mine ?—and happy that our King
> Is here again, never I trust to roam
> So far again, but dwell among his own.

The curtain falls while harmonious voices are singing joyously, " Now the King is home again."

Lord Tennyson did nothing in its way better than this. He produced a Pastoral or Masque, for which, for a comparison, we must go back to Milton's *Comus*. He has done for Sherwood what Shakespeare did for Arden, and has written a pure idyllic English play where we seem to breathe the free gladsome air and smell the rich rare perfume of our matchless glades. And while the admired heroes and the winsome heroines of romance tread the sunlit stage, we listen to the quaint old-time speech and

hear the haunting measures of songs which almost set themselves to music.  Of these intercalary lyrics nothing but
the highest praise can be said.   The magic slumbrous
lines, *To sleep ! to sleep !* had seen the light before ; and
*There is no land like England* was one of the Laureate's
early pieces re-vestured and re-introduced.    But the
following stanzas were new :—

> Love flew in at the window
>     As Wealth walk'd in at the door.
> "You have come for you saw Wealth coming," said I.
> But he flutter'd his wings with a sweet little cry,
>     I 'll cleave to you rich or poor.
>
> Wealth dropt out of the window,
>     Poverty crept thro' the door.
> " Well now you would fain follow Wealth," said I.
> But he flutter'd his wings as he gave me the lie,
>     I cling to you all the more.

Considering Lord Tennyson's age, *The Foresters* was a
wonderful performance.   In the winter of his life the laurels
grew greener on his brow.

# CHAPTER XI.



> " I have climb'd to the snows of Age, and I gaze at a field in the Past."
>
> *—By an Evolutionist.*

> " Deed and song alike are swept
>   Away, and all in vain
> As far as man can see, except
>   The man himself remain.
>
> .     .     .     .     .
>
> The man remains, and whatsoe'er
>   He wrought of good or brave
> Will mould him thro' the cycle year
>   That dawns behind the grave."
>
> *—Epilogue to the Charge of the Heavy Brigade.*

TENNYSON'S literary activity continued to the end. His pen was never idle, and his voice rang out clearly and sweetly in song until the moment that death commanded silence. Sometimes, at the close of a long dull day, the sun as it is about to sink crimsons all the west and makes a glory in the sky : so the Poet Laureate, at the end of his long day, and after a sombre interval, flashed out thoughts of beauty and passed from among us while we were contemplating the radiant glory of his work. Some of his last lines will be the best remembered. The world will not willingly let die such poems as *Crossing the Bar* and *The Silent Voices*, or forget the assuring message of hope in *The Dawn, Faith,* and *God and the Universe.* After a life of doubt, of questioning, the poet heard the answer and received the promise—

Spirit, nearing yon dark portal at the limit of thy human state,
Fear not thou the hidden purpose of that Power which alone is great,
Nor the myriad world, His shadow, nor the silent Opener of the Gate.

Tennyson had already formally recanted of some of the

heresies of his youth. He had learnt that ideals could not be attained, that dreams must fade, that visions must die, and that a divine purpose was manifesting itself even through darkness and the ways of evil. In his youth he had despaired of many things, he had been rebellious, and he had turned pessimist. In his old age he saw that right slowly conquered wrong, that truth gradually overcame error, that the best of all things ultimately survived and grew in strength, and that the red of the dawn is ever turning " a fainter red," and may at last become the whiteness and purity of " a hundred thousand, a million summers away." He who had doubted, mourned, and despaired so much, cried with a last strong breath—

> Doubt no longer that the Highest is the wisest and the best,
> Let not all that saddens Nature blight thy hope or break thy rest,
>  Quail not at the fiery mountain, at the shipwreck, or the rolling
> Thunder, or the rending earthquake, or the famine, or the pest.

He who had revolted against destiny, who had questioned, protested, and even denied the wisdom of over-ruling Providence, could at the last pray to " My Father, and my Brother, and my God "—

> Steel me with patience ! soften me with grief !
> Let blow the trumpet strongly while I pray,
> Till this embattled wall of unbelief
> My prison, not my fortress, fall away !

The right note was struck in *Locksley Hall Sixty Years After*, a poem which drew from Walt Whitman one of the finest appreciations of the Tennyson both young and old whom he had known. Said the venerable author of *Leaves of Grass* :—

" Beautiful as the song was, the original *Locksley Hall* of half-a-century ago was essentially morbid, heart-broken, finding fault with everything, especially the fact of money's being made (as it ever must be, and, perhaps should be) the paramount matter in worldly affairs—

Every door is barr'd with gold, and opens but to golden keys.

First, a father having fallen in battle, his child (the singer)

Was left a trampled orphan and a selfish uncle's ward.

Of course, love ensues.   The woman in the chant or monologue proves a false one ; and, as far as appears, the ideal of woman, in the poet's reflections, is a false one—at any rate, for America.   Woman is *not* ' the lesser man.'   (The heart is not the brain.)   The best of the piece of fifty years since is its concluding line :—

For the mighty wind arises roaring seaward, and I go.

Then for this current 1886-7 a just-out sequel, which, as an apparently authentic summary says, ' reviews the life of mankind during the past sixty years, and comes to the conclusion that its boasted progress is of doubtful credit to the world in general, and to England in particular. A cynical vein of denunciation of democratic opinions and aspirations runs through the poem, in marked contrast with the spirit of the poet's youth.'   Among the most striking lines of this sequel, are the following :—

Envy wears the mask of Love, and, laughing sober fact to scorn,
Cries to Weakest as to Strongest : ' Ye are equals, equal-born.'

Equal-born ?   O yes, if yonder hill be level with the flat.
Charm us, Orator, till the Lion look no larger than the Cat,

Till the Cat, thro' that mirage of overheated language loom
Larger than the Lion,—Demos end in working its own doom.

.     .     .     .     .     .     .     .     .

Tumble Nature heel o'er head, and, yelling with the yelling street,
Set the feet above the brain and swear the brain is in the feet.

Bring the old dark ages back without the faith, without the hope,
Break the State, the Church, the Throne, and roll their ruins down the slope.

I should say that all this is a legitimate consequence of the tone and convictions of the earlier standards and points of view.   Then some reflections, down to the hard-pan of this sort of thing.

The course of progressive politics (democracy) is so certain and resistless, not only in America, but in Europe, that we can well afford the warning calls, threats, checks, neutralisings, in imaginative literature, or any department, of such deep-sounding and high-soaring voices as Carlyle's and Tennyson's.   Nay, the blindness, excesses of the prevalent tendency—the dangers of the urgent trend of our times—in my opinion, need such voices almost more than any.   I should, too, call it a signal instance of democratic humanity's luck that it has such enemies to contend with—so candid, so fervid, so heroic. But why do I say enemy? Upon the whole, is not Tennyson—and was not Carlyle (like an honest and stern physician)—the true friend of our age?

Let me assume to pass verdict, or perhaps momentary judgment, for the United States on this poet—a removed and distant position giving some advantages over a nigh one.

What is Tennyson's service to his race, times, and especially to America? First, I should say, his personal character. He is not to be mentioned as a rugged, evolutionary, aboriginal force—but (and a great lesson is in it) he has been consistent throughout with the native, personal, healthy, patriotic spinal element and promptings of himself. His moral line is local and conventional, but it is vital and genuine. He reflects the upper crust of his time, its pale cast of thought—even its *ennui*. Then the simile of my friend John Burroughs is entirely true, ' His glove is a glove of silk, but the hand is a hand of iron.' He shows how one can be a royal laureate, quite elegant, and 'aristo- cratic,' and a little queer and affected, and at the same time perfectly manly and natural. As to his non-democracy, it fits him well, and I like him the better for it. I guess all like to have (I am sure I do) some one who presents those sides of a thought, or possibility, differ- ent from our own—different, and yet with a sort of home-likeness—a tartness and contradiction offsetting the theory as we view it, and construed from tastes and proclivities not at all our own. To me, Tennyson shows more than any poet I know (perhaps has been a warning to me) how much there is in finest verbalism. There is such a latent charm in mere words, cunning collocutions, and in the voice ringing them, which he has caught and brought out beyond all others—as in the line "And hollow, hollow, hollow, all delight," in *The Passing of Arthur*, and evidenced in *The Lady of Shalott*, *The Deserted House*, and many other pieces. Among the best (I often linger over them again and again) are *Lucretius*, *The Lotos-Eaters*, and *The Northern Farmer*. His mannerism is great, but it is a noble and welcome mannerism. His very best work, to me, is con- tained in the books of *The Idylls of the King*, all of them, and all that has grown out of them, though, indeed, we could spare nothing of Tennyson, however small or however peculiar—not " Break, Break," not " Flower in the Crannied Wall," nor the old, eternally-told passion of Edward Gray—

> Love may come, and love may go,
>   And fly like a bird from tree to tree ;
> But I will love no more, no more
>   Till Ellen Adair come back to me.

Yes, Alfred Tennyson, is a superb character, and will help give illustriousness, through the long roll of time, to our nineteenth century. In its bunch of orbic names, shining like a constellation of stars, his will be one of the brightest.  His very faults, doubts, swervings, doublings upon himself, have been typical of our age.  We are like the voyagers of a ship, casting off for new seas, distant shores.  We would still dwell in the old suffocating and dead haunts, remembering and magnifying their pleasant experiences only, and more than once impelled to jump ashore before it is too late, and stay where our fathers stayed, and live as they lived.  Maybe I am non-literary and non-decorous (let me, at least, be human, and pay part of my debt) in this word about Tennyson.  I want him to realise that here is a great and ardent nation that absorbs his songs, and has a respect and affection for him personally, as almost for no other foreigner.  I want this word to go to the old man at Farringford as conveying no more than the simple truth ; and that truth (a little Christmas gift) no slight one either.  I have written impromptu, and shall let it all go at that. The readers of more than fifty millions of people in the New World not only owe to him some of their most agreeable and harmless and healthy hours ; but he has entered into the formative influences of character here, not only in the Atlantic cities, but inland and far West, out in Missouri, in Kansas, and away in Oregon, in farmer's house and miner's cabin.

Best thanks, anyhow, to Alfred Tennyson—thanks and appreciation in America's name."—

One of the most striking facts in Whitman's strange poetic career was his intense love for the songs of his contemporaries, who were in more than one sense his rivals. Though he himself disdained "dulcet rhymes" he admired the minstrelsy of others.  The friendship existing between him and Lord Tennyson was altogether remarkable. Their styles were so opposite that they seemed almost to be warring against each other.  Whitman hewed his rugged lines out of granite ; Tennyson fashioned his dainty verse from all things bright and fair.  Yet each found in the other's works great truths and manifold beauties.  Nor did they fear to express their feelings, and one of the rare instances on record of the Laureate's acknowledging a public criticism was occasioned by the "word sent to the old man at Farringford."  The cordial friendship existing between the two was the more noteworthy for the reason that in 1855 when *Leaves of Grass* was published Whitman compared his work with Tennyson's *Maud*, to the disadvantage of the Laureate. But the comparison was not intended to be offensive, nor was it ever resented. The message of 1887 was welcomed; though the "old man at Farringford" not only outlived its sender, but a day after the death of the "good, gray poet" issued his new work *The Foresters.* The Laureate's response has a deep pathetic interest. "Dear Walt Whitman," he wrote; "I thank you for your kind thoughts of me. I value the photograph much, and I wish that I could see not only this sun-picture, excellent as I am told it is, but also the living original. May he still live and flourish for many years to be. The coming year [1888] should give new life to every American who has breathed a breath of that soul which inspired the great founders of the American Constitution whose work you are to celebrate. Truly, the mother country, pondering on this, may feel that how much soever the daughter owes to her, she, the mother, has nevertheless something to learn from the daughter. Especially I would note the care taken to guard a noble Constitution from rash and unwise innovators." Lord Tennyson's kindly expressions went far to compensate Whitman for the unexpected attack which had just been made upon him by Mr Swinburne. But the Laureate gave a more practical token of his esteem for the poet in poverty by subscribing to the Christmas gift sent to him by English friends. In 1890, Whitman wrote again—"I have already put on record my notions of Tennyson and of his effusions; they are very attractive and flowery to me—but flowers, too, are at least as profound as anything; and by common consent Tennyson is settled as the poetic cream-skimmer of our age's melody, *ennui*, and polish—a verdict in which I agree, and should say that nobody (not even Shakespeare) goes deeper in those exquisitely touched and half-hidden hints and indirections left like faint perfumes in the crevices of his lines."

The most morbid, beclouded, and desponding of Tennyson's poems are *De Profundis* and *Vastness*, tinctured as they are with the melancholy of a life darkening at its close.  Happily, the poet recovered from his gloomy contemplation of the shadows of "the deep"; and "sunset and evening star" had no sadness for him.  *De Profundis*, perhaps, was the product only of a mood, not of confirmed convictions, for at the time it was written the old poet was giving the world those stirring ballads which kindled the enthusiasm of Carlyle.  Of this series it is difficult to say which is best, though the wonderful power of *Rizpah* has struck every reader, and excited the admiration of every critic.  Mr T. A. Trollope in his *What I Remember* (1887) relates that he was taken by the Leweses to see the Laureate just as he had finished this grand poem.  Tennyson read the lines to his visitors, but " laid strict injunctions on us to say no word to anyone of what we had heard, adding with a smile that was half *naif*, half funning, and wholly comic : 'The newspaper fellows, you know, would get hold of the story, and they would not do it as well.'"  Surely there was never woman's wail which sounded so fierce, so terrible, so pitiful, as the wail of the woman for the son " hang'd in chains for a show."

God 'ill pardon the hell-black raven and horrible fowls of the air,
But not the black heart of the lawyer who kill'd him and hang'd him
    there.

There is a wail also, more subdued, not defiant, but utterly sad, in the widow's account of *The First Quarrel*—the first quarrel that was the last, for

The boat went down that night—the boat went down that night.

But what is the sound we hear in *The Revenge*, a ballad of the fleet ?  A sound of triumph from brave lips and dauntless men who fought the Spaniard knowing that " to fight is but to die,"—who scorned to fly from the enemy though the little Revenge had but a " hundred fighters on deck and ninety sick below," and the whole Spanish fleet was massed against them.

Half of their fleet to the right and half to the left were seen,
And the little Revenge ran on thro' the long sea-lane between.

Thousands of their soldiers look'd down from their decks and laugh'd,
Thousands of their seamen made mock at the mad little craft
Running on and on,

but Sir Richard Grenville had never turned his back on Don or devil—

And the sun went down, and the stars came out far over the summer
    sea,
But never a moment ceased the fight of the one and the fifty-three.

Long as Britain's glory shall be remembered the story of the little Revenge will be recounted.

God of battles, was ever a battle like this in the world before ?

Sir Richard Grenville's name will live in the imperishable ballad of the Laureate. Macaulay sang the praise of the Roman who "kept the bridge," but Tennyson found an English Horatius crying "Fight on, fight on," when his vessel was a wreck, riddled with shot and shell, and when his own wounds were almost too great to be borne. But all round the little ship lay "the Spanish fleet with broken sides," and the little Revenge having done her best, yielded, though the Captain would have had her split in twain that he and his men might

Fall into the hands of God, not into the hands of Spain.

But "the lion there lay dying."

And the stately Spanish men to their flagship bore him then,
Where they laid by the mast, old Sir Richard caught at last,
And they praised him to his face with their courtly foreign grace ;
But he rose upon their decks, and he cried :
" I have fought for Queen and Faith like a valiant man and true
I have only done my duty as a man is bound to do ;
With a joyful spirit I, Sir Richard Grenville, die !"
And he fell upon their decks, and he died.

The Laureate might have sought in vain for a sublimer

hero ; the hero might have longed in vain for a better minstrel to sing his praise.   The ballad of *The Revenge* is one
that will live, one that will fire many an earnest spirit, and
one that will ever make a people proud of their valiant
sons in the brave days of old.   To the same category
belong the Laureate's *Defence of Lucknow*, and *The Charge
of the Heavy Brigade at Balaclava*, a noble tribute to
Scarlett's three hundred men who charged thousands of
Russians in the valley and on the heights.

> Scarlett was far on ahead, and he dashed up alone
> Thro' the great gray slope of men,
> And he wheel'd his sabre, he held his own
> Like an Englishman there and then ;
> And the three that were nearest him follow'd with force,
> Wedged themselves in between horse and horse,
> Fought for their lives in the narrow gap they had made,
> Four amid thousands ; and up the hill, up the hill,
> Galloped the gallant three hundred, the Heavy Brigade.

Lord Tennyson possessed the faculty in an eminent degree
of identifying himself with the heroes—seeming to feel the
thrill of martial ardour, to experience the exhilaration of
valiant deeds, and to understand the pain and the glory of
battle.   No one has sung of soldiers' deeds as he ; no one
has so filled his verses with trumpet tones ; the clash of
weapons, the clangour of arms, we hear them resound in his
ringing lines, in the breathless rush of his verse !  He should
be known as the soldiers' poet as well as the elogist of
heroes, for he was often at his best when making "a martial
song like a trumpet call" and

> Singing of men that in battle array,
> Ready in heart and ready in hand,
> March with banner and bugle and fife
> To the death, for their native land.

His lines to General Hamley attest his admiration of the
hero, and in the *Epilogue* to the *Charge of the Heavy
Brigade*, after telling of his hatred of war for war's own
sake, he exclaimed—

> But let the patriot-soldier take
>   His meed of fame in verse ;
> Nay—tho' that realm were in the wrong
>   For which her warriors bleed,
> It still were right to crown with song
>   The warrior's noble deed.

Contrasted with these passionate ballads, how stately seem pieces like *Sir John Oldcastle, Lord Cobham,* or even *Columbus;* while *The Sisters* is an exquisite sonata in words, and the lyrics commencing " O diviner air " and " O diviner light " can only be matched to the melodies of Mendelssohn. The whole poem is in Tennyson's finest strain, the diction superb, the current of thought rich, the story strange and moving. In the *Voyage of Maeldune* Tennyson found a weird Irish legend to his liking, and he has enriched it with many a bright and glowing detail. But the story of Emmie, told *In the Children's Hospital,* was provocative of controversy ; and though the poem has force and beauty, it is more than doubtful whether it does not cast un-warranted blame upon a body of men whose humanity, devotion, and tenderness are worthy of recognition. The rough doctor is an uncommon type ; the burly sceptic is still rarer ; while the "ghastly tools" of the surgeon are surely not to be regarded as useless horrors. On the publication of the poem a storm of disapprobation and protest arose, and however we may admire the poet's lines, we cannot but feel that their censure, direct or implied, is unjust.

When the *Tiresias* volume was published late in 1885, it was hailed as evidence of the sustained power and un-quenched fire of the poet's spirit. Full of melody and inspiration, the volume was a proof (as one critic said) that at seventy-seven Tennyson's muse still "mingled the fire of youth with the tenderness of age." " Never," wrote another, " did he touch the keys of passionate utterance with a firmer hand ; never did he clothe in more vividly poetic form the conceptions of a masculine intelligence. So splendid an old age is a welcome feature in the literary annals of our time." "Here, in *Tiresias* itself, and in many of the other poems," said a third, whom I take to be no other than Mr Lang, though I am quoting from an anonymous article, "are the same potent influences of style, and the music and charm of words, which have delighted fit ears ever since *Timbuctoo*, though a prize poem, gave the world assurance of a poet. Custom has not staled nor imitation debased the rich Tennysonian measure which haunts us as

> The rich Virgilian rustic measure
> Of *Lari maxime* all the way,

haunted the Laureate among the lakes of Italy. The new poems have, besides and above this, almost as personal a note as *In Memoriam*. The poet now and again speaks plainly of himself and for himself. Standing on the inner threshold of age, he looks back across more than seventy years, remembering friends, remembering griefs and sorrows, and still happy and fortunate in an old age, *nec cithara degentem*, and not uncheered by hope." There had been a fear that the sweet flow of verse had been embittered, and that in his declining years Tennyson would have been prone to dwell upon the tenebrous gathering of cloud and the threatenings of death. But a cheerful note was struck in the opening lines to "Old Fitz," the friend of former days, with whom he had once tarried and "tried the table of Pythagoras"; to whom he paid the hearty tribute of a true admirer of his literary gifts, and of whom he could say —thinking of "two voices heard on earth no more"—

> But we old friends are still alive,
> And I am nearing seventy-four,
>   While you have touch'd at seventy-five,
> And so I send a birthday line
>   Of greeting.

With that greeting was enclosed the poem of *Tiresias*, rescued from the "sallow scraps of manuscript" of a forgotten book. *Tiresias* is akin in style, in theme, and in treatment to *Tithonus* and *Ulysses*, those unapproachable English classics which best enable English readers to understand the luxury and splendour of Greek masterpieces. Tiresias was a blind Theban soothsayer, a prophet who with clear eye read the scroll of the future; and he foretold that if Menœceus would sacrifice himself Thebes would be victorious against Seven. The prophet's blindness is variously accounted for, but Tennyson accepted the legend that his sight was destroyed by Pallas Athene, at whom the presumptuous mortal had dared to gaze while she bathed. He has wandered in all lands; his wont, he says,

> Was more to scale the highest of the heights
> With some strange hope to see the nearer God.

Searching, craving for beauty, for a glimpse of the divine, he journeyed on, until the day came when his eyes rested upon a forbidden scene, and forthwith their light was extinguished. Here is the picture—as chastely sensuous, as vivid, yet as free from voluptuousness, as brilliant and beautiful, as the poet's art coud reveal it.

> One naked peak—the sister of the sun
> Would climb from out the dark, and linger there
> To silver all the valley with her shafts—
> There once, but long ago, five-fold thy term
> Of years, I lay; the winds were dead for heat;
> The noonday crag made the hand burn; and sick
> For shadow—not one bush was near—I rose
> Following a torrent till its myriad falls
> Found silence in the hollows underneath.
>
> There in a secret olive-glade I saw
> Pallas Athene climbing from the bath
> In anger; yet one glittering foot disturb'd
> The lucid well; one snowy knee was prest
> Against the margin flowers; a dreadful light
> Came from her golden hair, her golden helm
> And all her golden armour on the grass,
> And from her virgin breast, and virgin eyes
> Remaining fixt on mine, till mine grew dark
> For ever, and I heard a voice that said

> " Henceforth be blind, for thou hast seen too much,
> And speak the truth that no man may believe."

> Son, in the hidden world of sight, that lives
> Behind this darkness, I behold her still,
> Beyond all work of those who carve the stone,
> Beyond all dreams of Godlike womanhood,
> Ineffable beauty, out of whom, at a glance,
> As it were, perforce, upon me flash'd
> The power of prophesying. . . .

The old prophet, who has prophesied and been unheeded, is full of ripe wisdom ; and Menœceus, his companion, hears many a pregnant word fall from his lips. " To cast wise words among the multitude Was flinging fruit to lions," had been the seer's experience.

> Who ever turn'd upon his heel to hear
> My warning that the tyranny of one
> Was prelude to the tyranny of all ?
> My counsel that the tyranny of all
> Led backward to the tyranny of one ?

Here the Laureate found his opportunity of once more uttering a warning to democrats—a lesson from the past to the present.   And is not this applicable now, as then ?—

> Virtue must shape itself in deed, and those
> Whom weakness or necessity have cramp'd
> Within themselves, immerging, each, his urn
> In his own well, draw solace as he may.

The words impelling Menœceus to the sacrifice came from a noble mind—a mind that esteems no duty so high, no privilege so great, as serving the State by life or death.

> My son,
> No sound is breathed so potent to coerce,
> And to conciliate, as their names who dare
> For that sweet mother land which gave them birth
> Nobly to do, nobly to die.  Their names,
> Graven on memorial columns, are a song
> Heard in the future; few, but more than wall
> And rampart, their examples reach a hand
> Far thro' all years, and everywhere they meet

And kindle generous purpose, and the strength
To mould it into action pure as theirs.

Could heroes have greater, purer inspiration than this? Could their fate be more honourable, their victory more glorious, than for their names to be a song, and their deeds to be both example and monument? Tennyson's words are stimulating as a cordial; they impart strength to the faltering, and fire the ambition of the brave.

> The golden lyre
> Is ever sounding in heroic ears
> Heroic hymns.

The poem is followed by a reference to Fitzgerald's death, touching, sincere, kind, as all Tennyson's tributes to his friends were.

Three powerful narrative poems were included in the *Tiresias* volume—*The Wreck, Despair*, and *The Flight*. The first and last of these portrayed the effects of a marriage without sympathy and love. In the one case the husband was indifferent to his sensitive wife.

He would open the books that I prized, and toss them away with a
    yawn,
Repell'd by the magnet of art to the which my nature was drawn,
The word of the poet by whom the deeps of the world are stirr'd,
The music that robes it in language beneath and beyond the word!

My Shelley would fall from my hands when he cast a contemptuous
    glance
From where he was poring over his tables of trade and finance;
My hands when I heard him coming would drop from the chords or
    the keys,
But ever I fail'd to please him, however I strove to please.

The result of this misalliance is easily foreseen. The woman wanted warmth and sympathy, and when her husband denied it, she "threw herself all abroad," played her part "by the low footlights of the world," "caught the wreath that was flung"—and fell. *The Flight* is equally painful. It is the story of a woman who is to be purchased as a slave, under the name of wife and with the consent of holy church, by a man whom she loathes. The marriage morning has come, but unable to face her dreadful fate—a fate, it is to be feared, not so uncommon in society as to make the Laureate's stern denunciation unnecessary—she flies.

Shall I take *him?* I kneel with *him?* I swear, and swear forsworn
To love him most whom most I loathe, to honour whom I scorn?
The Fiend would yell, the grave would yawn, my mother's ghost would
    rise—
To lie, to lie—in God's own house—the blackest of all lies!

The curse of such unions, the horrors of such customs in the marriage-market of modern Babylon, called for the lash of the Laureate's scornful words. For these abuses *do* exist, and were there no Mammonite parents in these days of advance, the foul wrong would not be done. But fathers "pay their debts" with the honour and happiness of their daughters; and mothers obtain their recompense and reward by securing a buyer for their beloved children in the monster who seeks only the gratification of the basest passion.

    It is not Love but Hate that weds a bride against her will.

*Despair* tells the story of a man and his wife who, having lost all faith in God and a future, resolve to drown themselves. The woman dies; the man is rescued by a minister of the sect he had abandoned. In the poem the man relates to his preserver the history of his struggle against infidelity; and he is not grateful that his life was saved. Death to him was less terrible than the agony of living. "Why," he asks,

Should we bear with an hour of torture, a moment of pain,
If every man die for ever, if all his griefs are vain,
And the homeless planet at length will be wheel'd thro' the silence of
    space,
Motherless evermore of an ever-vanishing race,
When the worm shall have writhed its last, and its last brother-worm
    will have fled
From the dead fossil skull that is left in the rocks of an earth that is
   . dead?

Practically the questions are unanswered, and to men who will not "believe where they cannot prove," no answer is possible. This infidel had had a glimmer of "a God behind all," but the scanty, unsatisfying light, had only maddened him the more. Though the problem was unsolved in the poem, a possible solution might have been found in one that followed, a poem of wonderful beauty and bright with golden truths. *The Ancient Sage* is one of the best poems of its kind. The vexing doubts of youth are recalled only that the experience of life—a life of work and thought— may for ever lay these spectres of the mind. The perfection, the necessity of Faith, is the sermon preached and the lesson enforced. As if catching up the threads of the old argument in *In Memoriam* the poet says—

> Thou canst not prove the Nameless, O my son,
> Nor canst thou prove the world thou movest in,
> Thou canst not prove that thou art body alone,
> Nor canst thou prove that thou art spirit alone,
> Nor canst thou prove that thou art both in one :
> Thou canst not prove thou art immortal, no
> Nor yet that thou art mortal—nay, my son,
> Thou canst not prove that I, who speak with thee,
> Am not thyself in converse with thyself,
> For nothing worthy proving can be proven,
> Nor yet disproven : wherefore thou be wise,
> Cleave ever to the sunnier side of doubt,
> And cling to Faith beyond the forms of Faith.

In this poem we seem to get glimpses of the poet's own religion and its adaptation, and there is a hint of that form of "spiritualism" which has led more than one to believe that he was convinced of the invisible but tangible union between the material and immaterial worlds. Whether Tennyson was a "Spiritualist" or not in the ordinary or esoteric sense cannot be safely judged. His well-known letter of May 1874, referring to his "waking trance," and the fading away of his individuality into "boundless being," with the loss of personality ; his mysterious allusions in *In Memoriam ;* his sonnet on that condition of body or mind when

> We muse and brood,
> And ebb into a former life, or seem
> To lapse far back in some confused dream
> To states of mystical similitude ;

and the declaration in *The Ancient Sage*—

> More than once when I
> Sat all alone, revolving in myself
> The word that is the symbol of myself,
> The mortal limit of the Self was loosed,
> And past into the Nameless, as a cloud
> Melts into Heaven.　I touch'd my limbs, the limbs
> Were strange not mine—and yet no shade of doubt,
> But utter clearness, and thro' loss of Self
> The gain of such large life as match'd with ours
> Were Sun to spark—unshadowable in words,
> Themselves but shadows of a shadow-world :

—all these seem to favour the view that Tennyson believed the spirit could escape the fetters of the body for a while, and pass into higher stages, enjoy communion with higher beings, and hold converse, perhaps, with angels of song and light.

> Star to star vibrates light: may soul to soul
> Strike thro' a finer element of her own ?

"I believe," he told Miss Weld, "that beside our material body we possess an immaterial body. I do not care to make distinctions between the soul and the spirit, as men did in days of old, though perhaps the spirit is the best word to use of our higher nature, that nature which I believe in Christ to have been truly divine, the very presence of the Father, the one only God, dwelling in the perfect man. We shall have much to learn in a future world, and I think we shall all be children to begin with when we get to Heaven, whatever our age when we die, and shall grow on there from childhood to the prime of life, at which we shall remain for ever. My idea of Heaven is to be engaged in perpetual ministry to souls in this and other worlds." So we understand the meaning of those passionate lines of a grief-stricken man in *Maud*—

> Ah Christ, that it were possible
> For one short hour to see
> The souls we loved, that they might tell us
> What and where they be.

In *The Ancient Sage* the poet found the means of sending forth a message to the world to hope on and have Faith, to cleave to the belief in "the Nameless," to trust that despite our feeble wills, our veiled eyes, our stumbling steps, under guidance we were being led onward and upward for some grand and divine end. Darkness must not dismay: " the clouds themselves are children of the Sun." Life must be well used, all evil abstained from, the beast within curbed ; and thus men, laying their "uphill shoulder to the wheel," will "climb the Mount of Blessing." Men will inquire, but all mysteries will not be revealed—

> The key to that weird casket, which for thee
> But holds a skull, is neither thine nor mine,
> But in the hand of what is more than man,
> Or in man's hand when man is more than man.

Infinite trust, boundless confidence, are demanded by the Ruler of all from his subjects ; and in the giving of that trust, the submission to the Higher Will, lies all satisfaction. Faith

> Reels not in the storm of warring words,
> She brightens at the clash of "Yes" and "No,"
> She sees the Best that glimmers thro' the Worst,
> She feels the Sun is hid but for a night,
> She spies the summer thro' the winter bud,
> She tastes the fruit before the blossom falls,
> She hears the lark within the songless egg,[1]
> She finds the fountain where they wail'd " Mirage!"

One other poem in the volume calls for remark; a sad and moving story bearing the title of *To-morrow*. It is the only poem of the Laureate's in the Irish dialect, and, unlike his other dialect poems, it is tragic. The heroine is a Molly Magee whose "batchelor" was Danny O'Roon.

---

[1] *Cf.* "The music of the moon Sleeps in the pale eggs of the nightingale." —*Aylmer's Field.*

Her lover went away over the sea, telling her he would see her to-morrow ; but he never came back.   Others told her that she had been deserted, and that Danny had taken another wife; but Molly remained staunch, true, and trusting—

> I 'd his hand-promise, an' shure he 'll meet me again.

Her mind gave way at last, and then "To-morra, to-morra, machree," became her incessant, dolorous cry. Danny was found at last—forty years after the parting. He had fallen into a bog after drinking, and had died there.   The body was laid by the chapel-door.   None of the new generation could recognise it.

> But Molly kem limpin' up wid her stick, she was lamed iv a knee,
> Thin a slip of a gossoon call'd " Div ye know him, Molly Magee ?"
> An' she stood up strait as the Queen o' the world—she lifted her
>     head—
> " He said he would meet me to-morra !" an' dhropt down dead an
>     the dead.

The poet's aftermath had all the richness and luxury of the harvest.   No one contributed so long and so well to the " Renascence of Wonder " or to the philosophy of the times ; no one so pitilessly indicted the evils of the age, or so sublimely sang its hopes.   He was one of the great buttresses of religion despite the doubts which ever intruded, and will ever intrude.   Like Clough he could have said—" Let us ascend the clouded hill and expect the voice of him who entered into the cloud.   Perhaps he will descend the mount with sacred light shining from his countenance, bearing the tables of the new law ; meanwhile, let us not turn back to Egypt, not dance at the bidding of the first priest around a Golden Calf."   This seems to have been Tennyson's attitude, and tempted as he was to forsake the stronghold of religion from time to time, he remained steadfast, faintly trustful of the "larger hope." " Poetry will die with Tennyson," said Mr Augustine Birrell; while Mr Froude has delivered the opinion that of all great men of the past century Tennyson and Carlyle are alone likely to live. If this be true, it must be for a better reason than that supplied by a critic who, while admitting that Tennyson was great as a singer, denied that he was a teacher. " It would have been better for him and for all of us," wrote Mr Salt, "if he had thought it well to follow the wise example of Gray, and Collins, and Keats, and restrict himself to that art of poetry in which he has so few rivals. For if ever a poet has come near to perfection in his work, Lord Tennyson has done so in those poems where a great but simple thought had to be expressed, and where there was no room for the introduction of any controversial matter. For example, in *Ulysses* we have a splendid representation of the indomitable energy of the will; in the *Lotos-Eaters*, of rest; in *St Agnes' Eve*, of purity and resignation; in *Rizpah*, of horror, and pity, and love. But, unfortunately, the Poet Laureate was not content with this simplicity of subject; he has deliberately descended into the arena of strife, and must be judged accordingly. Indeed, it was so obviously useless to attempt to exonerate him from this criticism, that his earlier and more enthusiastic admirers boldly took the bull by the horns, and claimed for him the position of a great teacher and thinker. It will be found, I fear, that his thoughts, when sifted, are light as chaff; and that his philosophical system is a mixture of opportunism and shallow optimist theories."

Mr Arthur Galton, too, believes that "Tennysonian lasciviousness of style is to disguise poverty of thought and to conceal the absence of virility and vigour"; but while it is admitted that Tennyson said little absolutely new, it is false to state that his poetry was not weighted with thought and illuminated with the most radiant of truths. His were no "barren commonplaces," but fruitful lessons, no matter how or whence derived. Novelty is not necessarily a charm or a virtue, and the fact remains that but for Tennyson many a pearl of wisdom would have been lost, or, untouched by his consummate art, would have been esteemed of little worth. "Tennyson is the one supreme poet of the day," said Mr Swinburne, and the tribute came not only from a fellow-poet and an acute critic, but from one who might have been his rival. The judgment of the age was certainly in concurrence with this verdict: the "one supreme poet" without a successor, the peerless craftsman whose "jacinth work of subtlest jewelry" will fascinate the eyes of wondering witnesses to be.

It was thought that a period was put to Tennyson's work with the issue of the *Tiresias* volume, but he had other poems in reserve, and his productiveness had not ceased. *Locksley Hall Sixty Years After*, which drew forth the tribute from Whitman, followed in a twelvemonth, and perhaps on account of its association in name and character with an old favourite, no less than on account of its merits, achieved a remarkable and immediate popularity. Whatever apprehension had existed as to the Laureate's powers, or as to the nature of his experiment, with its obvious risks, was dispelled the moment the new *Locksley Hall* was read. Like Anacreon of old, the Laureate was able to prove that though winter was on his brow spring was in his heart. Ancient founts of inspiration still welled through his fancy, and he could fittingly conclude at seventy-seven what he began at seventeen. *Locksley Hall* was the adumbration of a drama full of the passion, the bluster, and the frenzy of hot youth; the *Sixty Years After* was an epilogue in which the events of intervening years were recalled in the serenity and wisdom of age. Said one discerning critic:—

Taken together, the two pieces will remain a marvellous picture of the chastening power of time on the impulses and hopes of an ardent soul. There is not the smallest incongruity between the two portraits. Life has not quelled the spirit or quenched the hope; but it has taught the madness alike of wild hope and sheer despair. The same problems press upon the mind of the veteran which fired the spirit of the young man ; but the superstitious confidence in this or that solution has been dissipated, and all the rancour bred of purblind enthusiasm has passed away.  If there ever was any excuse for the notion, religiously held by many a votary of Tennyson, that the hero of *Locksley Hall* was none other than the poet himself, there is surely the fullest warrant for the belief that in this pendant to the masterpiece we have on record the ripe life-thoughts of the Laureate. If he was not the disappointed lover and the wild dreamer, he at any rate entered with dramatic intensity into all the emotions and aspirations of his hero ; and now, 'sixty years after,' when experience and disillusionment, it may be, have done their work, when it is possible to contemplate with clear eyes the condition of the world after it has spun for half-a-century ' down the ringing grooves of change,' we are invited to hear what false hopes have vanished, and, in their stead, what true and firm grounds of assurance, undiscerned, or, at least undescribed, in the hot, fanciful days, remain to us."

The experience which brought the lover of Amy so much sorrow is now an old man's dim memory; the persons who played their part in a life-drama are phantoms; only one man lives to close the story and tell of those who are dead.  If there are no retractions there are repentances, and *Sixty Years After* is less a palinode than a development.  What was Amy's fate ?  What her husband's ?

Dead—and sixty years ago, and dead her aged husband now,
I this old white-headed dreamer stoopt and kissed her marble brow.
Gone the fires of youth, the follies, furies, curses, passionate tears,
Gone like fires and floods and earthquakes of the planet's dawning
 years.
Gone the tyrant of my youth, and mute below the chancel stones,
All his virtues—I forgive them—black in white above his bones.

In *Locksley Hall* a young disappointed lover, frantic, jealous, despairing, spoke in sorrow and hate.  His is a thoroughly human outburst, which commands, in spite of its fury and false reasoning, in spite of its dogmatism and bias, the genuine sympathy and compassion of his hearers. The interest is human.  The poet sways the reader at will; his irony is appreciated, his foolish braggartism applauded.  All this is changed sixty years after.  The old man has disowned the young, remodelled his philosophy, and reconciled himself to his destiny. The memory of Amy shines star-like through the mist of time and sorrow; but the broken chain that bound the mourner to his kind has been linked again by an Edith—

She with all the charm of woman, she with all the breadth of man.

He possesses a heart of charity. No longer are his feelings stirred by the tumult of passion; no longer is he an impossible idealist. *Sixty Years After* is full of wholesome sentiment and honest feeling, and the thoughts are enshrined in word-caskets such as only could be wrought by the Laureate. "The writer of the second *Locksley Hall*," said Professor Dowden, "has again given back as a river that which he received from men about him as a vapour—the fears of faith in presence of a revolution inspired by selfish greeds, the fears of art in presence of a base naturalism which only recognises the heart in man."

The sequel to *Locksley Hall* had been prophesied more than twenty years before by Professor Japp, and the vaticination is worth recalling, for it proves that the afterthought was a natural and logical process. "Upon his scathed heart dawns the glory of a great moral truth, that, though the individual withers under limitation and wrong, the world still progresses. The poet has here carried the poem to the strict limit of his experience at the time it was written. It closes but it does not cease. It abounds with suggestions as to a higher result in prospect. It points to a region of lofty possibility. If the poet ever again wrote on a kindred theme it would test at once his insight and fuller experience whether he would conduct his hero to a more worthy goal."[1] Mr Gladstone's learned review of the two *Locksley Halls* is a separate study, and it forms a most interesting and valuable footnote to the poems.

"No greater calamity could happen to a people than to

---

[1] "Three Great Teachers of Our Age," by A. H. Japp (1865).

break utterly with its past," wrote the veteran statesman. " Our judgment on the age that preceded us should, however, be strictly just; but it should be masculine, not timorous. This rule particularly applies to the period which precedes our own." Again, he declared that "each generation or age of men is under a two-fold mistake—the one to overrate its own performances and prospects, the other to undervalue the times preceding or following its own." Mr Gladstone asked whether it was just on the part of the poet, or even needful, to "open so dark a prospect for the future," or to pronounce so "decided a censure on the past"? While reserving his judgment on the changes in the world of thought and of inward conviction, the statesman declared that in the main the business of the half-century had been "a process of setting free the individual man that he might work out his vocation without wanton hindrance, as his Maker would have him do." After all, Mr Gladstone's conclusions are not unlike the conclusion at which Tennyson ultimately arrived—

All things make for good.

Three years of almost complete silence followed the publication of *Locksley Hall Sixty Years After*, though there were rumours from time to time that the poet was preparing another volume. It was again in the month of December that the new work saw the light, the December of 1889. The slim volume with the familiar green covers bore the title of *Demeter*, and contained twenty-eight poems, of which number four had previously been published—*On the Jubilee of Queen Victoria, Vastness, The Throstle*, and the lines on W. G. Ward. None of these chips from the poet's workshop had excited enthusiasm, but the volume contained superior material. "Illustrious and consummate " had been the words applied to the Laureate by the greatest of his brother-poets, Browning, and these words seemed most befitting at this period with the new evidence of the poet's capacity presented. The opening lyric to the Marquess of Dufferin and Ava possessed a pathetic interest from the fact that it was an expression of thanks from a bereaved father to the friend of his dead son, Lionel. Lady Dufferin had written on March 30, 1886—"We left Calcutta very early this morning. Poor Mr Tennyson's bed was pulled to the window that he might see us off. He is still very ill, but as the hot weather is coming on he must go home, and he is to start on Sunday. He has had a long, sad illness, borne most patiently." He died on the homeward journey, and was buried at sea.

It was not only to the statesman that the poet did honour, but that

> You and yours may know
> From me and mine, how dear a debt
> We owed you, and are owing yet
> To you and yours, and still would owe.

Then comes the sad but proud reference to the beloved son whose sudden death occasioned such deep regret—

> A soul that, watch'd from earliest youth,
> And on thro' many a brightening year,
> Had never swerved for craft or fear,
> By one side-path, from simple truth :
>
> Who might have chased and claspt Renown
> And caught her chaplet here—and there
> In haunts of jungle-poison'd air
> The flame of life went wavering down.

Dying, Lionel Tennyson spoke of the kindness of Lord Dufferin ; and the father delivered thanks for the son. It is a poem written in all tenderness of feeling, and the closing lines—

> To question, why
> The sons before the fathers die,
> Not mine ! and I may meet him soon—

were an outburst such as had seldom come in late years from the most reserved and restrained of men.

The story of *The Ring* served to remind us that Lord Tennyson's love-stories have mostly the same plot. If

*Locksley Hall* be analysed, it will be found to contain the germ of the story told in *Lady Clara Vere de Vere, Maud, Aylmer's Field, The Sisters*, and several others, the main idea existing in each case, and the theme varying but slightly.

*The Ring* bears more than a casual resemblance to the story of *The Sisters* (Edith and Evelyn), which was published ten years or more before. In that poem a father tells to his prospective son-in-law the story of his own wooing—of how he was betrothed to Edith, and afterwards, seeing her twin-sister, fell more violently in love with her and married her. The young wife died within two years, and the deserted sister had in the meantime pined away. In *The Ring* a father and his daughter (Muriel) converse on the eve of the latter's wedding, and the father is induced in this case also to tell the story of his own marriage. There is a legend connected with the ring which he is about to present to his daughter.

> Long ago
> Two lovers parted by a scurrilous tale
> Had quarrell'd, till the man repenting sent
> This ring " Io t'amo " to his best beloved,
> And sent it on her birthday.  She in wrath
> Return'd it on her birthday, and that day
> His death-day, when, half frenzied by the ring
> He wildly fought a rival suitor, him
> The causer of that scandal, fought and fell ;
> And she that came to part them all too late,
> And found a corpse and silence, drew the ring
> From his dead finger, wore it till her death,
> Shrined him within the temple of her heart,
> Made every moment of her after life
> A virgin victim to his memory,
> And dying rose, and rear'd her arms, and cried
> " I see him, Io t'amo, Io t'amo."

Muriel's father, becoming possessed of the ring, intended to present it to Miriam, but by mistake her sister Muriel received it,

> And flaunted it
> Before that other whom I loved and love.

The man was obliged to undo the error, and Muriel fled, after giving up the ring to the sister for whom it was intended. The end of the episode seems almost to be in the identical language of Lord Tennyson's previous poem, with which I have already instituted the comparison.

<blockquote>
Miriam loved me from the first,<br>
Not thro' the ring; but on her marriage-morn<br>
This birthday, death-day, the betrothal ring,<br>
Laid on her table overnight, was gone ;<br>
And after hours of search and doubt and threats,<br>
And hubbub, Muriel enter'd with it.   "See ?—<br>
Found in a chink of that old moulder'd floor !"<br>
My Miriam nodded with a pitying smile,<br>
As who should say "that those who lose can find."<br>
   Then I and she were married for a year,<br>
One year without a storm, or even a cloud ;<br>
And you, my Miriam, dead within the year.<br>
   I sat beside her dying, and she gaspt :<br>
"The books, the miniature, the lace are hers ;<br>
My ring, too, when she comes of age, or when<br>
She marries ; you—you loved me, kept your word.<br>
You love me still ' Io t'amo.'—Muriel—no—<br>
She cannot love ; she loves her own hard self,<br>
Her firm will, her fix'd purpose.   Promise me<br>
Miriam not Muriel—she shall have the ring."<br>
And there the light of other life, which lives<br>
Beyond our burial and our buried eyes,<br>
Gleam'd for a moment in her own on earth.<br>
I swore the vow, then with my latest kiss<br>
Upon them, closed her eyes, which would not close,<br>
But kept their watch upon the ring and you.<br>
Your birthday was her death-day.
</blockquote>

The sequel, too, is not unfamiliar to students of the poet's works, but the interwoven incident of the ring allows of pleasing variations and developments, and the close of the poem has a weird intensity. The daughter herself expresses this in describing a half-fantastic fear that a ghost

<blockquote>
Had floated in with sad reproachful eyes,<br>
Till from her own hand she had torn the ring<br>
In fright, and fallen dead.   And I myself<br>
Am half afraid to wear it.
</blockquote>

The story was a fit companion to those that the Laureate had previously written, and it was one more significant instance of the continuous dwelling of his thought upon a series of melancholy incidents that almost suggested a personal acquaintance or experience.

The poems *Happy* and *Forlorn* must be classed with the previous narrative pieces of which *The Wreck* and *The Flight* are types. The former poem consists of the monologue of a leper's bride, eager to rejoin her afflicted husband, and not unwilling to share his irremediable fate.

> I shall hardly be content,

exclaims the impassioned and devoted wife—

> Till I be leper like yourself, my love, from head to heel.
>
> O foolish dreams, that you, that I, should slight our marriage oath :
>   I held you at that moment even dearer than before ;
> Now God has made you leper in His loving care for both,
>   That we might cling together, never doubt each other more.
>
> The Priest who joined you to the dead, has joined our hands of old ;
>   If man and wife be but one flesh, let mine be leprous too,
> As dead from all the human race as if beneath the mould ;
>   If you be dead, then I am dead, who only live for you.

This is the woman's "happiness,"—a terrible but beautiful idea of devotion. In *Forlorn* a very sad note is also touched, and the speaker, half-delirious with pain and shame, tells of the nameless wrong done to a trusting woman. The awful thoughts that pass through the mind of an injured and distracted mother, not wife, in her hour of agony, are expressed with tragic power. Tennyson had treated a like subject in his early volume in the grim poem on *The Sisters*, with its weird refrain "O the Earl was fair to see." But *Forlorn* is not a story of revenge; it is of the dark fears which haunt a guilty mind, and the dread of a helpless woman in the most pitiable state.

Of *Demeter and Persephone*, which gives the title to the volume, it need only be said that it is a poem of that

luxurious nature which makes everyone revel in *Œnone.*
What could be better than

> The sun
> Burst from a swimming fleece of winter gray?

or such " cunning collocutions " as " A league of labyrinthine
darkness "? or such happiness of imagery as is contained in
this delightful passage ?—

> A sudden nightingale
> Saw thee, and flash'd into a frolic of song
> And welcome ; and a gleam as of the moon,
> When first she peers along the tremulous deep,
> Fled wavering o'er thy face, and chased away
> That shadow of a likeness to the King
> Of shadows, thy dark mate.

The legend is a familiar one, but as treated by the Laureate
it has a freshness and beauty—ay, and a splendour also—
which makes it doubly dear.   Could lines like these fail to
impart life and charm to the ancient myth ?—

> So in this pleasant vale we stand again,
> The field of Enna, now once more ablaze
> With flowers that brighten as thy footstep falls,
> All flowers,—but for one black blur of earth
> Left by that closing chasm, through which the car
> Of dark Aïdoneus rising rapt thee hence.
> And here, my child, tho' folded in thine arms,
> I feel the deathless heart of motherhood
> Within me shudder, lest the naked glebe
> Should  yawn once more into the gulf, and thence
> The shrilly whinnyings of the team of Hell,
> Ascending, pierce the glad and songful air ;
> And all at once their arch'd necks, midnight-maned,
> Jet upward thro' the midday blossom.   No !
> For, see, thy foot has touched it ; all the space
> Of blank earth-baldness clothes itself afresh,
> And breaks into the crocus-purple hour
> That saw thee vanish.

Beautiful indeed were the lines on *The Progress of
Spring* which the poet had rescued from his half-forgotten
manuscripts—

Found yesterday—forgotten mine own rhyme
    By mine own self,
As I shall be forgotten by old Time,
    Laid on the shelf—

A rhyme that flower'd betwixt the whitening sloe
    And kingcup blaze,
And more than half-a-hundred years ago.

The poem was written at the time when the war between capital and labour was at its fiercest, and the burning of the farmers' ricks was the easiest way for the labourers to manifest their hostility. All this time of riot and trouble came back to the poet's recollection, and he remembered

      That red night
  When thirty ricks,

All flaming, made an English homestead Hell—
    These hands of mine
Have helpt to pass a bucket from the well
    Along the line,

When this bare dome had not begun to gleam
    Thro' youthful curls.

In these lines *To Mary Boyle* the poet dedicated "this song of Spring." It is almost a pity to make extracts from the exquisite lyric, and one fears to hear a cry of pain as when Dante broke a branch from the living trees. Let this one stanza suffice:

She floats across the hamlet. Heaven lours,
  But in the tearful splendour of her smiles
I see the slowly-thickening chestnut towers
  Fill out the spaces by the barren tiles.
Now past her feet the swallow circling flies,
  A clamorous cuckoo stoops to meet her hand;
Her light makes rainbows in my closing eyes,
  I hear a charm of song thro' all the land.
Come, Spring! She comes, and Earth is glad
  To roll her North below thy deepening dome;
But ere thy maiden birk be wholly clad,
  And these low bushes dip their twigs in foam,
  Make all true hearths thy home.

Miss Boyle, a life-companion of the poet's, died very shortly after these verses to her had been published. She could claim among her close and honoured friends, Landor, Browning, and Dickens, and was both a novelist and poetess herself, some verses of hers in the *Tribute*, entitled *Our Father's at the Helm*, having exceeded in popularity the contribution of Tennyson himself to that miscellany. The poem, which was of the didactic order, with a very obvious "moral," is not one which would be likely to suit the taste of readers now. Mary Boyle will owe her fame to the monument fashioned for her in exquisite verse by the Laureate, who remembered her when she was

> A lover's fairy dream,
> His girl of girls,

and to whom he could then say—

> Close are we, dear Mary, you and I
> To that dim gate,

though *how* close the one was he knew not.

# CHAPTER XII.

THE SWAN-SONGS.

"Sunset and evening star,
    And one clear call for me !
And may there be no moaning of the bar,
    When I put out to sea.

.      .      .      .      .

Twilight and evening bell
    And after that the dark !
And may there be no sadness of farewell,
    When I embark."

*—Crossing the Bar.*

IT is recorded that when Tennyson heard Byron was dead he "thought the whole world was at an end." "I thought," he said, "everything was over and finished for everyone— that nothing else mattered. I remember I walked out alone and carved 'Byron is dead' into the sandstone." In October 1892 came the news that Tennyson was dead, and we too felt that there was a void, a gap, a "something lost" so great, so commanding, that for the moment everything seemed over and finished, nothing mattered, the impenetrable darkness of night enveloped us. "Tennyson is dead" were words that carved themselves upon many a heart. The sweetest singer, the purest poet, had passed into the silent land, and left us longing in vain for the touch of a vanished hand, craving in despair for a sound of the voice that is still. The "spectre fear'd of man" came in no dread guise to the aged poet, whose greatest work was to prove the glory and the excellence of death. Fitting indeed was it for him who had sung the psalm of triumph *In Memoriam* that the grave should have no terrors. The silvery light of the moon fell upon the dying poet's face; now and then a smile flitted across his tranquil features; an open volume of Shakespeare lay in his hand; and as the gray October morning broke "God's finger touched him, and he slept." The flood had borne him onward, and, crossing the bar, he saw his Pilot face to face. For forty-two years he had worn the laurel crown, receiving it "greener from the brows Of him who uttered nothing base." Scholar, philosopher, idealist as he was, he had still been the poet of the people, voicing their hopes and fears, espousing their cause, expressing their sorrows, proclaiming their joys, finding fitting words for all emotions. The foremost fact in Tennyson's long life was his consistency. He pursued one ideal, and he might have said with the voyagers of whom he sang—

> One fair Vision ever fled
>   Down the waste waters day and night,
> And still we follow'd where she led,
>   In hope to gain upon her flight.
> Her face was evermore unseen,
>   And fixt upon the far sea-line;
> But each man murmur'd, " O my Queen,
>   I follow till I make thee mine."

The poet never doubted his mission and never swerved from his purpose. Known or unknown, rich or poor, courted or neglected, he was a poet always, feeling within himself something of a sacred designation and distinction. Carlyle discovered that he was "a true human soul to whom your soul can say Brother." When his triumph came—the triumph over prejudice, indifference, and all those other obstacles which the world loves to place in the path of genius—it was unequivocal. His songs, with their delicious cadences, their dreamy sensuousness, and their suffusion of exquisite colour, were at once a revelation and an enchantment. The stanzas had a haunting melody; the very words seemed to sparkle to the eye; a sense of luxury and rest was borne on the languorous lines. There had been nothing like it since the music-laden verses of

*The Faery Queen* gushed from the soul of Edmund Spenser, and the consummate art of the poet could not fail to obtain acknowledgment. Yet the lyrics were no more than the promise of spring: the glory of summer, the abundant autumn harvest, and even the splendour of a long and genial winter, were to follow. Upon which of Tennyson's works will his fame last? Perhaps on all, for he wrote little that was unworthy, though *In Memoriam, Maud*, and the Arthurian series will stand out as the most conspicuous pillars. These poems are as much for the future as the present, and the pinnacle of the poet's fame will gleam, high and shining, through the ages. The great magician is dead, and the temple of his body deserted.

> Life and Thought have gone away
>     Side by side.
>     Leaving door and windows wide—
> Careless tenants they !

and we can only cry out with the poet—

>     Life and Thought
>     Here no longer dwell ;
>     But in a city glorious—
> A great and distant city—have bought
>     A mansion incorruptible.
> Would they could have stayed with us !

Three weeks after Tennyson's death his last collection of poems was published—*The Death of Œnone, Akbar's Dream, and other Poems*. This posthumous volume excited the highest interest, and no doubt the pieces included in it will always claim a special attention. They were full of reminiscences, and awakened old memories ; they touched anew the sweet familiar chords and gave out the gathered harmony of the minstrel's life. The delight felt when the music of the early lyrics, sixty years before, cast a spell upon the soul stole to us again, and we were amazed and charmed to find that the skill of the minstrel and the freshness of the voice of the singer remained unimpaired. We do not pretend that those hundred odd pages, containing but twenty-three poems, would have made any poet's fame, or that they can add to the Laureate's. The writer of them, whoever he might have been, would not have escaped recognition; but as the last gift of the octogenarian poet who had given us so much, the volume has a value, a pleasure, and a pathos all its own. And if this can be said for the world in general, how much more must these words apply to that lone companion of his life to whom the poems are dedicated! In 1864 Tennyson dedicated *Enoch Arden* to one who was "near, dear, and true," and could be made no truer "by Time itself"; and with Romney he might have said, "The world would lose, if such a wife as you Should vanish unrecorded." Eight-and-twenty years later we find him saying that as he looked at the high blue of a June sky and the bright bracken and brown heather at his feet—

> I thought to myself I would offer this book to you,
> This, and my love together,
> To you that are seventy-seven,
> With a faith as clear as the heights of the June-blue heaven,
> And a fancy as summer-new
> As the green of the bracken amid the gloom of the heather.

Could anything be more tender, more delicate, and more beautiful?

When Tennyson was a young man, only recognised as a genius among a small circle, Carlyle introduced Sir John Simeon to him at Bath House with the uncouth observation—"There he sits upon a dung heap, surrounded by innumerable dead dogs." The "dead dogs" were the translations and adaptations from the classics, chief among which was *Œnone*, a long blank-verse poem published in the volume of 1832. The *Quarterly Review*, in its famous onslaught on Tennyson, specially attacked this poem, and with shafts of stinging ridicule assailed the form in which the subject was treated, the long descriptions of inanimate beauties, and the refrain, "sixteen times repeated"—

Dear Mother Ida, hearken ere I die.

Tennyson ten years later republished the piece with many amendments and some remarkable elaborations, and *Œnone* took its place as an English classic. It is, in fact, an incomparably beautiful composition, as purely Greek in its grace and chasteness as the Greek-fashioned masterpieces of Keats. Œnone, the rarely beautiful goddess, addresses a soliloquy to Mount Ida, in which she relates how she has been deserted by Paris for the rival whom he judged to exceed all others in beauty. Edgar Allen Poe, most exacting of critics, declared that "by the enjoyment or non-enjoyment of *Œnone* he would test anyone's ideal sense." Just sixty years after the first lines on Œnone saw the light, we had given to us a volume treating of Œnone's death. "Oh, Mother Ida, hearken ere I die" was the haunting refrain of the first piece, and in the last we find the goddess sinking into the arms of death. She is alone in a cave, and the vines "which on the touch of heavenly feet had risen" had long ago withered. And while she gazed at the desolate scene and the changed landscape

> Her Past became her Present, and she saw
> Him, climbing toward her with the golden fruit,
> Him, happy to be chosen Judge of Gods,
> Her husband in the flush of youth and dawn,
> Paris, himself as beauteous as a God.

Then, from out the long ravine below a wailing cry reaches her, a cry that

> Seem'd at first
> Thin as the batlike shrillings of the Dead
> When driven to Hades, but, in coming near,
> Across the downward thunder of the brook
> Sounded "Œnone";

and then Paris, the deceiver, once the pride of men, but now "no longer beauteous as a God," appeared before his deserted wife "like the wraith of his dead self." He had been struck by a poison'd arrow, and now, not in repentance but in deadly fear, the wanton had come to beseech the woman he had wronged to save his life.   He had no allegiance to his first love, but he was dying, and she had learnt the secret—

> Taught by some God, whatever herb or balm
> May clear the blood from poison, and thy fame
> Is blown thro' all the Troad.

His life is in her hand, and he appeals to her, nay, he demands her assistance.

> The Gods
> Avenge on stony hearts a fruitless prayer
> For pity.   Let me owe my life to thee.

But Œnone is unrelenting, unforgiving, obdurate.

> I am poison'd to the heart,

wailed Paris.

> "And I to mine," she said.   "Adulterer,
> Go back to thine adulteress and die !"

Paris could bear no more.   He knew his fate.

> He groan'd, he turn'd, and in the mist at once
> Became a shadow, sank and disappear'd,
> But, ere the mountain rolls into the plain,
> Fell headlong dead.

Shepherds on Ida raised him, and "forgetful of the man whose crime had half unpeopled Ilion," built him a funeral pile, kindled it, and called upon his name.   But Œnone sat within the cave "like a creature frozen to the heart Beyond all hope of warmth"; then, sleeping, she heard a ghostly murmur, "Come to me!"

> She rose and slowly down
> By the long torrent's ever-deepen'd roar,
> Paced, following, as in trance, the silent cry.
> She waked a bird of prey that scream'd and past;

> She roused a snake that hissing writhed away ;
> A panther sprang across her path, she heard
> The shriek of some lost life among the pines,
> But when she gain'd the broader vale, and saw
> The ring of faces redden'd by the flames
> Enfolding that dark body which had lain
> Of old in her embrace, paused—and then asked
> Falteringly, " Who lies on yonder pyre ? "
> But every man was mute for reverence.

At last she was told that the corpse was of him whom she would not heal, and even as the words were uttered

> *The morning light of happy marriage broke*
> *Thro' all the clouded years of widowhood,*

and with an exulting cry of " Husband " she leapt into the flames

> And mixt herself with him and past in fire.

The poem has not the jewelled splendour of the first which Tennyson wrote on Œnone, for it is less ambitious, more subdued in colour, less ornate and more chaste in design. It contains ringing lines and lofty images, and the same limpidity yet strenuousness of speech which is so characteristic of all his " faint Homeric echoes." The *Death of Œnone* was dedicated in a poem cast in classic mould to the Master of Balliol, who was bidden—

> To-day, before you turn again
> To thoughts that lift the soul of men,
>     Hear my cataract's
> Downward thunder in hollow and glen,
>
> Till, led by dream and vague desire,
> The woman, gliding toward the pyre,
>     Find her warrior
> Stark and dark in his funeral fire.

Among Tennyson's ethico-theological poems I am inclined to rank *Akbar's Dream* very high. The poet's hatred of dogmas, bigotry, sectarianism, and religious forms which take the place of religion itself and all true worship, is well known to every student of his life and works.  He had toleration for all, and it was he who sang the praise of honest doubt. Righteousness is to be found more in works than in faith, and those who live well can scarcely hold a false creed.  So thought Akbar, the great Mogul Emperor of the sixteenth century, whose " abhorrence of religious persecution put our Tudors to shame."  He invented " a new eclectic religion by which he hoped to unite all creeds, castes, and peoples : and his legislation was remarkable for vigour, justice, and humanity."  In this person Tennyson found a man well-suited for his purpose of teaching the people of to-day to display a truer spirit of love and charity, and to trust more to the results of a man's life than to external forms and empty professions.  Lip-worship and genuflections may be no worship at all—may be mere heathenism, hypocrisy, and irreverence.  Let us listen to Akbar as he speaks of the beginning of all mysteries and the cause of all dissensions—" The Alif of thine alphabet of Love," which we " scarce can spell "

> He knows Himself, men nor themselves nor Him,
> For every splinter'd fraction of a sect
> Will clamour " *I* am on the Perfect Way,
> All else is to perdition."
>                        Shall the rose
> Cry to the lotus " No flower thou "? the palm
> Call to the cypress " I alone am fair "?
>
> .        .        .        .        .
>
> Look how the living pulse of Alla beats
> Thro' all His world.   If ever single star
> Should shriek its claim " I only am in heaven,"
> Why that were such sphere-music as the Greek
> Had hardly dream'd of.   There is light in all,
> And light, with more or less of shade, in all
> Man-modes of worship.

Akbar, who permitted freedom and decreed that each philosophy and mood of faith might hold its own, listened apart to the contentions of men blurting " their furious formalisms," but that rage of words was simply to his cars

> The clash of tides that meet in narrow seas,—
> Not the Great Voice, not the true Deep.

Therefore he hated the "rancour of their castes and creeds," and prayed for a time when "the mortal morning mists of earth" shall "fade in the noon of heaven,"

> When creed and race
> Shall bear false witness, each of each, no more,
> But find their limits by that larger light,
> And overstep them, moving easily
> Thro' after-ages in the love of Truth,
> The truth of Love.     .     .     .     .
>
> .     .     .     .     .     .     .     .     .
>
> .     .     .     I can but lift the torch
> Of Reason in the dusky cave of Life
> And gaze on this great miracle, the World,
> Adoring That who made, and makes, and is,
> And is not, what I gaze on—all else Form,
> Ritual, varying with the tribes of men.
>
> Ay but, my friend, thou knowest I hold that forms
> Are needful : only let the hand that rules,
> With politic care, with utter gentleness,
> Mould them for all his people.
>
> And what are forms ?
> Fair garments, plain or rich, and fitting close
> Or flying looselier, warm'd but by the heart
> Within them, moved but by the living limb,
> And cast aside, when old, for newer,—Forms !

There are many fine passages in lines which follow, but I must forbear to quote them. A more powerful plea for indulgence and patience among professing religious nations cannot be read. It is a rebuke to all bigots, and a glorious example to all liberal-minded men who fear not to believe that men of all race and creed

> In *some* way live the life
> Beyond the bridge, and serve that Infinite,
> Within us, as without, that All-in-all,
> And over all, the never-changing One

> And ever-changing Many, in praise of Whom
> The Christian bell, the cry from off the mosque,
> And vaguer voices of Polytheism
> Make but one music, harmonising " Pray."

Akbar's " dream " is a vision of things to come, when the good he has established shall be overthrown and the rules he has ordained be violated. He saw with prophetic eye his son and those who followed " loosen, stone from stone, all my fair work," and he heard from the ruin that arose the " shriek and curse of trampled millions." This was to be; yet, the Monarch saw the dawn of another era, when an alien race in the west should fit stone to stone again and make a Temple wherein Truth, Peace, Love, and Justice might reside. But how far has this prophecy of things to come been fulfilled ? *Akbar's Dream* is a poem to be treasured because it undoubtedly gives us Tennyson's own cherished faith—his abundant reverence without orthodoxy, and his firmness of belief without dogmatism. He was the better Christian for being no bigot, and his fervour was not to be questioned because he refused to be fanatical.

*St Telemachus* would serve as a companion picture to *St Simeon Stylites.* Again the poet tells of a saint who served God with fasting, prayer, and mortification of flesh. He did not chain himself to a pillar, but he was a haggard anchorite who " never changed a word with men," and haunted a desolate fane. At length he heard a call to Rome, and turning to the west he followed

> A hundred sunsets, and the sphere
> Of westward-wheeling stars ; and every dawn
> Struck from him his own shadow on to Rome.

Only Tennyson could have described the westward journey thus. Telemachus reached the Christian city, and saw men fight with lions and gladiators in the arena—

> And eighty thousand Christian faces watch
> Man murder man.

Is not this phrase as good as Byron's " butchered to make

a Roman holiday"? Telemachus called upon them to forbear in the name of Christ Jesus.

> For one moment afterward
> A silence follow'd as of death, and then
> *A hiss as from a wilderness of snakes,*
> Then one deep roar as of a breaking sea,
> And then a shower of stones that stoned him dead,
> And then once more a silence as of death.

But his death was not in vain: "His dream became a deed that woke the world," and Honorius the Emperor decreed

> That Rome no more should wallow in this old lust
> Of Paganism, and make her festal hour
> Dark with the blood of man who murder'd man.

*The Bandit's Death* is dedicated to Sir Walter Scott in four commonplace lines only removed from triviality by their heartiness. The poem is adapted from a story narrated in Scott's last Journal, and is gruesome in the extreme. There is power in the poem, but it is only the power which we expect from fifth-rate singers who provide amateur reciters with verses for undiscriminating audiences. The average man who believes in Mr Sims will think Tennyson has done well, and *The Bandit's Death* would be highly popular at a Penny Reading. One can imagine the sensation that would be caused when, with proper dramatic action, an ambitious amateur rendered the final verse, supposed to be spoken by the bandit's wife—

And the band will be scatter'd now their gallant captain is dead,
 For I with this dagger of his—do you doubt me? Here is his head!

It is a relief and a delight to turn to the next poem, *Charity*, which is a woman's wail at man's baseness; but the widow of the man who had wronged her—" The tenderest Christ-like creature that ever stept on the ground "—was her salvation. *Kapiolani*, a short ode on a great chieftainess, is another proof of what Tennyson might have done, had he cared, as a writer of classical verse—Greek, Latin, and Anglo-Saxon. *The Dawn* is something of a diatribe and a lament. Its tone reminds us of the opening lines of *Maud* and the furious outbursts in *Locksley Hall* against the iniquities of the day.

Dawn not Day,

While scandal is mouthing a bloodless name at *her* cannibal feast,
And rake-ruin'd bodies and souls go down in a common wreck,
And the press of a thousand cities is prized for it smells of the beast,
Or easily violates virgin Truth for a coin or a cheque.

There are other doubtful or wholly pessimistic poems, like some with which we are already familiar— *Vastness, Despair,* and *De Profundis.* But in the end Tennyson has presented us with a sublime incitement to have faith, and these strong words, uttered almost from the grave, will fortify and stimulate many a faltering pilgrim and many a trembling heart.

Doubt no longer that the Highest is the wisest and the best,
Let not all that saddens Nature blight thy hope or break thy rest,
  Quail not at the fiery mountain, at the shipwreck, or the rolling
Thunder, or the rending earthquake, or the famine, or the pest !

Neither mourn if human creeds be lower than the heart's desire !
Thro' the gates that bar the distance comes a gleam of what is higher.
  Wait till death has flung them open, when the man will make the
    Maker
Dark no more with human hatreds in the glare of deathless fire.

One or two of the final poems in the volume formed the poet's own dirge, and undoubtedly *The Silent Voices* has taken its place with *Crossing the Bar* as one of the purest of hymn-like poems. It was fittingly chanted when the poet was laid to rest in Westminster Abbey, and it would not be surprising to find that it is in future used on similar occasions, for it has beauty of diction, consolation, and sweetness of sentiment.

When the dumb Hour, clothed in black,
Brings the Dreams about my bed,

> Call me not so often back,
> Silent Voices of the dead,
> Toward the lowland ways behind me,
> And the sunlight that is gone !
> Call me rather, silent voices,
> Forward to the starry track
> Glimmering up the heights beyond me,
> On, and always on !

The poem entitled *God and the Universe* is a questioning and an answering. "Will my tiny spark of being wholly vanish in your deeps and heights?" is the characteristic query of the poet. Once he might have confessed a mystery, but the "sunset of life gave him mystical lore," and he could say triumphantly to his spirit "nearing yon dark portal,"

Fear not thou the hidden purpose of that Power which alone is great.

Tennyson sang in many keys and many moods, but an undercurrent of melancholy was always audible, and served as accompaniment to his lays. If ever his joyousness seemed unrestrained, it was in some of those brief mellow preludes in which he first made his charm and power known. But even his earliest work gave forth sad and weary sounds which prepared the listener for the great threnodies to come. A poet who in his youth could compose *Mariana* and *Œnone* was already master of the art of transmuting the heart's deepest sorrow into language which itself glistened like tears. But his faith in the future of man and the divine righteousness grew firmer, and his last words are an assurance that life is not vain, and that after death all is not dark.

"He has worthily fulfilled his mission," said a critic. "He has devoted himself to his art, and striven with honest effort to give us the best he could. He has ever sought, by presenting high ideals, and inspiring pure sentiments, to do the noblest work—to raise us above ourselves, above vulgar aims, and selfish narrowness, and low-thoughted cares." Tennyson took his farewell of us with a cry of joy and triumph, and now that he has passed from among us " to where beyond these voices there is peace," those last jubilant words will ring in our ears and echo down the ages. We hear the poet and we see the hero, and we rejoice that his last words were as good and true, and his teaching as plain and pure, as ever they were.   He fitly finished his work: revealing to us his surpassing strength and grandeur to the close, and departing with a cherished message of hope and trust.

# CHAPTER XIII.

## TENNYSON AS A STUDENT.

" I hear a charm of song thro' all the land,

. . . . . .

Across my garden ! and the thicket stirs,
The fountain pulses high in summer jets,
The blackcap warbles, and the turtle purrs,
The starling claps his tiny castanets."
*—The Progress of Spring.*

" A full-cell'd honeycomb of eloquence."
*—Edwin Morris.*

THACKERAY once said to Bayard Taylor, " Tennyson is the wisest man I know." His wisdom was of no common order. It manifested itself in surprising ways, lurking in unexpected expressions, and taking a sudden turn in unlooked for directions. Tennyson was a linguist, naturalist, geologist, astronomer, theologian, and skilled in the sciences. Nor did he neglect the lighter forms of literary study, for he was an assiduous novel-reader, like Macaulay, and could delight in the masterpieces of fiction whether English or French. But, like his great predecessor Wordsworth, he was above and beyond all the lover of nature, knowing by instinct the wonder and beauty of tree and star, and realising the miracle alike of the "flower in the crannied wall," which could be plucked and held " root and all " in the hand, and of the vast evolutionary changes in the world's history. I believe it is a fact that nowhere among his multitude of allusions to nature in all her varying forms and emanations is there a single false statement. His word can always be accepted whether he simply name the colour of a leaf, the plumage of a bird, or the characteristic of a mountain. Apparently he delighted in minutiæ, but this was because his knowledge was deep and founded on personal investigation. " The meanest flower that blows" had for him a charm, a significance, a wonder all its own.  Scores of poems contain lines which in a perfectly casual manner convey striking scientific facts.  Tennyson was so full of information that he was quite unpretentious in his use of it ; and he has cast into the most attractive poetic shape many a hard dry truth.  Nothing, perhaps, could be more wonderfully expressed than that somewhat curious discovery that water, when exposed to cold more than enough to freeze it, may still retain liquidity if kept still, while the slightest motion will set the particles in motion, and, by helping their molecular change of position, instantly cause the water to solidify.  What I have tried to explain in this involved sentence Tennyson has condensed into the magic lines—

> Break, thou deep vase of chilling tears
> That grief hath shaken into frost.

"Shaken into frost" is worthy to be accepted as a chemical formula.

"Yes, Tennyson is a great student of Nature," wrote William Cullen Bryant.  But Charles Kingsley had discovered the fact before, and in his now famous essay had written—

"This deep simple faith in divineness of Nature as she appears, which, in our eyes, is Mr Tennyson's *differentia*, is really the natural accompaniment of a quality at first sight its very opposite, and for which he is often blamed by a prosaic world ; namely, his subjective and transcendental mysticism.  It is the mystic, after all, who will describe Nature most simply, because he sees most in her ; because he is most ready to believe that she will reveal to others the same message which she has revealed to him.  Men like Behmen, Novalis, and Fourier, who can soar into the inner cloud-world of man's spirit, even though they lose their way there, dazzled by excess of wonder— men who, like Wordsworth, can give utterance to each subtle anthropologic wisdom as the *Ode on the Intimations of Immortality*, will for that very reason most humbly and patiently 'consider the lilies of the field, how they grow.'  And even so it is just because Mr Tennyson is, far more than Wordsworth, mystical, and what our ignorant and money-getting generation, idolatrous of mere sensuous activity, calls 'dreamy,' that he has become the greatest naturalistic poet which England has seen for several centuries. The same faculty which enabled him to draw such subtle subjective pictures of womanhood as Adeline, Isabel, and Eleanor, enabled him to see, and therefore simply to describe, in one of the most distinctive and successful of his earlier poems, how

> The creeping mosses and clambering weeds,
> And the willow-branches hoar and dank,
> And the wavy swell of the soughing reeds,
> And the wave-worn horns of the echoing bank,
> And the silvery marish-flowers that throng
> The desolate creeks and pools among,
> Were flooded over with eddying song.

The same faith in Nature, the same instinctive correctness in melody, springing from that correct insight into Nature, ran through the poems inspired by mediæval legends. The very spirit of the old ballad writers, with their combinations of mysticism and objectivity, their freedom from any self-conscious attempt at reflective epithets or figures, runs through them all."

Hain Friswell, on the other hand, in his captious criticism, affected to scorn this fidelity to Nature, just as in the days gone by the *Quarterly* reviewer had ridiculed the "gummy" chestnut-trees and the "four-handed" mole. "It is enough for Mr Tennyson's truly English spirit," said the cynic, "to see how

> On either side the river lie
> Long fields of barley and of rye,
> That clothe the wold and meet the sky ;
> And through the field the road runs by
>     To many-tower'd Camelot ;

or how

> In the stormy east wind straining,
> The pale yellow woods were waning,
> The broad stream in his banks complaining,
> Heavily the low sky raining
>     Over tower'd Camelot.

Give him but such scenery as that which he can see in

every parish in England, and he will find it a fit scene for an ideal myth, subtler than a casuist's questionings, deep as the deepest heart of woman." But it may fairly be asked whether the very capacity complained of was not a merit, and in itself demonstrated the highest quality which goes to the making of a true poet. Had not Tennyson been a keen observer and deeply versed in nature-lore, he could never have written *Amphion* and talked with such ease of the "gouty oak," the "pirouetting ashes," the "stiff-set sprigs," and the "scirrhous roots and tendons." Never could he have related the grotesque effect of Amphion's fiddling, when

> The birch-tree swang her fragrant hair,
>   The bramble cast her berry,
> The gin within the juniper
>   Began to make him merry,
> The poplars in long order due,
>   With cypress promenaded,
> The shock-head willows two and two
>   By rivers gallopaded.
>
> Came wet-shot alder from the wave,
>   Came yews, a dismal coterie ;
> Each pluck'd his one foot from the grave,
>   Poussetting with a sloe-tree :
> Old elms came breaking from the vine,
>   The vine stream'd out to follow,
> And, sweating rosin, plump'd the pine
>   From many a cloudy hollow.

Take every adjective in turn, and you find the distinctive characteristic of the tree ; take every verb, and you find the only possible act of the timber fiddled into motion ! No dull reader of

> Botanic Treatises,
> And Works on Gardening through there,
> And Methods of transplanting trees,
> To look as if they grew there,

was giving us his facts and fancies in this poem. No lover

of "arbours clipt and cut," faded alleys, and the "garden-squirt" was he:

> Better to me the meanest weed
>   That blows upon its mountain,
> The vilest herb that runs to seed
>   Beside its native fountain.

When Oliver Wendell Holmes visited the poet at Farringford, he gained evidence of the Laureate's love of trees—a love so great that he refused to allow them to be cut, but liked to see them in all their luxuriance of growth. "He took delight," wrote Dr Holmes, "in pointing out to me the finest and rarest of his trees, and there were many beauties among them. In this garden of England, where everything grows with such a lavish extravagance of green, I felt as if weary eyes and over-taxed brains might reach their happiest haven of rest." In the "careless-order'd garden" could be seen the "dry-tongued laurel" and "the waving pine which here The warrior of Caprera set," while around the lawn blossomed crocus, anemone, and violet. Tennyson's early love for trees was displayed in *A Dream of Fair Women*, when he spoke with such joy of the enchanted forest of his dream:

> Enormous elm-tree boles did stoop and lean
>   Upon the dusky brushwood underneath
> Their broad carved branches, fledged with clearest green,
>   New from its silken sheath;

and again in *Sir Launcelot and Queen Guinevere*, when he spoke of the May morning when

> Drooping chestnut-buds began
> To spread into the perfect fan
>   Above the teeming ground,
>
> .    .    .    .    .
>
> And, far in forest-deeps unseen
> The topmost elm-tree gathered green
>   From draughts of balmy air.

Of how many trees has Tennyson sung? We might

take them in alphabetical order, and thus find almost every tree in turn from ash to yew.  At night he saw the trees "lay their dark arms about the field"; and at dawn he first perceived that the breeze trembled o'er "the large leaves of the sycamore,"

> And gathering freshlier overhead,
>   Rock'd the full-foliaged elms, and swung
>   The heavy-folded rose, and flung
> The lilies to and fro.

The "hoary knolls of ash and haw" helped to make up the Somersby scene which breathed "some gracious memory of my friend"; and when the old home was left, his fear was that

> Unloved, the beech will gather brown,
>   The maple burn itself away.

The beech is a favourite tree.  "The winds were in the beech," sweeping the winter land that sad Christmas when "one mute Shadow" watched over all.  We read of "the leavy beech" and the "serpent-rooted beech," each description being true to nature.  The statement of an acute observer is found in *The Princess*, when Ida is asked why she lingers "to clothe her heart with love"—

> Delaying as the tender ash delays
> To clothe herself, when all the woods are green.

The "witch-elm" of the Lincolnshire flats—the "windy tall elm-tree" where rooks build—and the larch with its "rosy plumelets"—the "perky larch" also of "formal cut"—are often referred to; but the lime, "a summer home of murmurous wings" is more tenderly loved.  The "large lime feathers low";[1] "a million emeralds break from the ruby-budded lime";—how exquisite is the description!  Then we learn of the "towering sycamore," and, better still, of

---

[1] No one has made a choicer use of the verb "feathers" than Tennyson. See the repeated line in *Enoch Arden*:

> "The prone edge of the wood began
> To *feather* toward the hollow."

> The pillar'd dusk of sounding sycamores,

forming a fit avenue to Audley Court. The oak, "stubborn-shafted," the giant of the woods, has been invested by Tennyson almost with animate charms. It is the garrulous talker—"a babbler in the land"—who told Walter of his Olivia, and swore

> By leaf, and wind, and rain,
> That, tho' I circle in the grain
> Five hundred rings of years—
>
> Yet, since I first could cast a shade,
> Did never creature pass
> So slightly, musically made,
> So light upon the grass.

The descriptions of this veteran of the Chace are most happy. His "knotted knees" are half hidden in fern; he is "so broad of girth" that he "could not be embraced"; but, when Olivia strove to span his waist—

> I wish'd myself the fair young beech
> That here beside me stands,
> That round me, clasping each in each,
> She might have lock'd her hands.

The poem abounds with delicate humour, and yet it is mingled with the wisdom of the scholar. What subtle touches are here!—

> Her kisses were so close and kind,
> That, trust me on my word,
> Hard wood I am, and wrinkled rind,
> But yet my sap was stirr'd :
>
> And even into my inmost ring
> A pleasure I discern'd,
> Like those blind motions of the Spring,
> That show the year is turn'd.
>
> I, rooted here among the groves,
> But languidly adjust
> My vapid vegetable loves
> With anthers and with dust :

> But could I, as in times foregone,
>   From spray, and branch, and stem,
> Have suck'd and gather'd into one
>   The life that spreads in them,
>
> She had not found me so remiss ;
>   But lightly issuing thro',
> I would have paid her kiss for kiss
>   With usury thereto.

The hollow oak in which Merlin, by the wicked arts of Vivien, found his living tomb, and the giant oak furrowed by a bolt from heaven, the forecast of his doom, need only this scant reference.   But how prominent is the part which the poet has assigned to that most solemn of trees, the "world-old yew," reputed to last for thousands of years and to be the emblem of sorrow.   It was in a "yew-wood black as night," the warrior-hero of Oriana met his death ; it was a "black yew" which "gloom'd the stagnant air" when the desponding lover in *The Letters* looked forth for an omen ; and in *In Memoriam* the solemn tree stands forth in a weird picture, the central and most impressive feature.

> Old Yew, which graspest at the stones
>   That name the under-lying dead,
>   Thy fibres net the dreamless head,
> Thy roots are wrapt about the bones.
>
> O not for thee the glow, the bloom,
>   Who changest not in any gale,
>   Nor branding summer suns avail
> To touch thy thousand years of gloom.

The poet was the communicant with Nature, not the book-scholar.   His sense was keen enough to know where hidden violets lay; he detected the odour and recognised the hue of all that bloomed ; he even perceived, as it were, the spirit of the flowers, and could give to rose and lily, acacia and jessamine, a sensibility and a voice.   The exquisite stanzas *Come into the garden, Maud*, are almost wholly a flower-song.   The waiting lover alone at the gate feels the influence of the woodbine spices wafted abroad and the musk of the roses blown. It is the roses which heard through the night the harmony of flute, violin, bassoon; and it is the casement jessamine which has "stirr'd to the dancers dancing in tune." It is to the lily that the lover confesses his hopes, to the rose that he reveals his faith. His tender thoughts fly to the meadow where he and Maud have walked, and where the March-wind has

> Set the jewel-print of your feet
> In violets blue as your eyes;

and it is Maud herself who is "Queen rose of the rosebud garden of girls"—"Queen lily and rose in one."

> There has fallen a splendid tear
> From the passion-flower at the gate,
> She is coming, my dove, my dear;
> She is coming, my life, my fate;
> The red rose cries "She is near, she is near";
> And the white rose weeps, "She is late";
> The larkspur listens, "I hear, I hear";
> And the lily whispers, "I wait."

The beautiful imagery is continued to the end, for, like a flower crushed to earth, the lover's heart would, at Maud's coming,

> Start and tremble under her feet,
> And blossom in purple and red.

Who but the naturalist could have written such a song of flowers?

Often, however, Tennyson is more subtle, or, at all events, his design is not so easily perceived. He could tell of the "lines of green that streak the white Of the first snowdrop's inner leaves"; of the

> Foxglove spire,
> The little speedwell's darling blue,
> Deep tulips dash'd with fiery dew,
> Laburnums, dropping-wells of fire.

He knew "the smell of violets, hidden in the green," he knew the red anemone as it burned "at the root thro' bush green grasses," and he knew

> The tearful glimmer of the languid dawn
> On those long, rank, dark wood-walks drench'd in dew
> Leading from lawn to lawn.

A Tennyson Flora could easily be compiled,[1] and the excellence and exactness of the descriptions would be serviceable to the enthusiasts in botany. Bayard Taylor was surprised that all forms of knowledge should have been pursued by Tennyson for the sake of poetry, but surely no higher purpose could be wished. If the Muse was not worthy, where shall worth be found? Yet Taylor himself did not weary of pointing out how elegantly the knowledge had been applied, how profusely its riches were lavished, how aptly its suggestions had been employed. "All objects," he wrote, "present themselves to Tennyson with such distinctness of illustration that he forgets the unfamiliarity of the reader with their qualities. When he writes of 'a clear germander eye,' how many are there who know or remember that a germander is a wild plant with a blue flower? He speaks of hair 'more black than ash-buds in the front of March,' and we are obliged to pause and consider whether ash-buds are black." A newspaper correspondent recently gave an instance of the poet's acuteness of observation. Tennyson and the Rev. Stenton Eardley spent a month together in Switzerland, and once, when rambling over the mountains, the poet was seen by his companion on his hands and knees intently looking at something in the grass. "Look here," he exclaimed, "I can see the colour of the flower through the creature's wings." The creature was a dragon-fly, and the flower an Alpine rose. The dragon-fly, I may here incidentally mention, was a favourite with the poet, who beheld this insect as he flew—

---

[1] See Leo H. Grindon's Essay.

> With his clear plates of sapphire mail,
> A living flash of light.

What a study the fly must have been before such a description could be given !

There is a veritable anthology in *The Gardener's Daughter*, and on the May morning of the lover's journey he traversed a fairy-land of flowers.

> A well-worn pathway courted us
> To one green wicket in a privet hedge ;
> This, yielding, gave into a grassy walk
> Thro' crowded lilac-ambush trimly pruned ;
> And one warm gust, full-fed with perfume, blew
> Beyond us, as we enter'd in the cool.
> The garden stretches southward.   In the midst
> A cedar spread his dark green layers of shade.
> The garden grasses shone, and momently
> The twinkling laurel scatter'd silver lights.

*The May Queen, The Miller's Daughter, The Talking Oak,* and others of a like character would each supply a dainty bouquet ; while we may pick up the withered leaves and drooping flowers of autumn in the *Song* of the Spirit who haunts the yellowing bowers—

> Heavily hangs the broad sunflower
>   Over its grave i' the earth so chilly;
> Heavily hangs the hollyhock,
>   Heavily hangs the tiger-lily.

But the poet is happier still in his allusions to the coming of Spring, when first

> The tented winter-field is broken up
> Into that phalanx of the summer spears
> That soon should wear the garland.

In 1885 the *Youth's Companion*, an American magazine for young people, published a delightful poem called *The Progress of Spring*, for which it declared it had paid Tennyson £2 a line.  The poem is one of great natural beauty, and showed that the poet's eye was keen to behold the marvels of the season, and his voice sweet and clear to sing its praise.   It is indeed a glorious burst of melody, telling how

> Once more the Heavenly Power
>   Makes all things new,
> And domes the red-plow'd hills
>   With loving blue ;
> And blackbirds have their wills,
>   The throstles too.
>
> Opens a door in Heaven ;
>   From skies of glass
> A Jacob's ladder falls
>   On greening grass,
> And o'er the mountain walls
>   Young angels pass.
>
> Before them fleets the snow
>   And burst the buds,
> And shine the level lands,
>   And flash the floods ;
> The stars are from their hands
>   Flung thro' the woods.

All the eight verses seem almost to be a musical prelude to that poem, with its magic cadence and gleaming lines, called also *The Progress of Spring*, and telling how

> She comes ! The loosen'd rivulets run ;
>   The frost-bead melts upon her golden hair ;
> Her mantle, slowly greening in the Sun,
> Now wraps her close, now arching leaves her bare
> To breaths of balmier air.
>
> Up leaps the lark, gone wild to welcome her,
>   About her glance the tits, and shriek the jays,
> Before her skims the jubilant woodpecker,
>   The linnet's bosom blushes at her gaze,
> While round her brows a woodland culver flits,
>   Watching her large light eyes and gracious looks,
> And in her open palm a halcyon sits,
>   Patient—the secret splendour of the brooks.

The poet's birds would be subject for a chapter themselves.   His ears had been early familiarised with the incessant cawing in the "wrangling rookery," for the copses

round about the Somersby home are the domain of the
"black Republic."     I need scarcely tell again Mrs
Ritchie's story of the half-amused scorn of the poet when
a lady ventured to suggest that it was nightingales who
called "Maud, Maud, Maud."     "What a Cockney you
are," he exclaimed.  He had been thinking of the rooks
with their incessant "Caw, Caw, Caw."  Let us contrast
their harsh notes with

> The moan of doves in immemorial elms,

the onomatopœous line which haunts the ear with its low-
toned music; or even with the "Tuwhoo, tuwhit" of the
white owl.     There is the wild carol of the dying swan—
the "death-hymn," the coronach, "with a music strange
and manifold"; and there is a nest of birds piping their
sweetest and loudest in the lyrics gathered under the
name of *The Window*.  Tennyson knew something of the
mysteries of bird-life also.   We read in *In Memoriam*,

> When rosy plumelets tuft the larch,
>   And rarely pipes the mounted thrush;
>   Or underneath the barren bush
> Flits by the sea-blue bird of March.

What is "the sea-blue bird of March"?   The kingfisher,
whose blue in spring is more vivid than at other periods,
Spring being the pairing season.  So in *Locksley Hall—*

> In the Spring a fuller crimson comes upon the robin's breast;
> In the Spring the wanton lapwing gets himself another crest;
>
> In the Spring a livelier iris glows upon the burnish'd dove.

Mrs  Ritchie  tells  this  story:  "Once  when  Alfred
Tennyson was in Yorkshire—so he told me—as he was
walking at night in a friend's garden he heard a nightingale singing with such a frenzy of passion that it was
unconscious of everything else, and not frightened though
he came and stood quite close beside it; he could see its
eye flashing, and feel the air bubble in his ear through the
vibration.  Our poet, with his short-sighted eyes, can see
further than most people.  Almost the first time I ever

walked out with him he told me to look and tell him if the field-lark did not come down sideways upon its wing." Yet he has told us that the poet's song exceeds the nightingale's.   It is a song which

> Made the wild swan pause in her cloud,
>     And the lark drop down at his feet ;
> The swallow stopt as he hunted the bee,
>     The snake slipped under a spray ;
> The wild hawk stood with the down on his beak,
>     And stared, with his foot on the prey ;
> And the nightingale thought, " I have sung many songs,
>     But never a one so gay ! "

And was it not the sweet voice of Enid which made Geraint feel like a man abroad at morn ?—

> When first the liquid note beloved of men
> Comes flying over many a windy wave
> To Britain, and in April suddenly
> Breaks from a coppice gemm'd with green and red,
> And he suspends his converse with a friend,
> Or it may be the labour of his hands,
> To think or say, " There is the nightingale."

None but a poet country-bred could have written these lines—lines full of beauty and conveying a familar truth to the mind.   The voice of the sweet singer flying over the wave to Britain, and suddenly, in April, breaking upon the ear from a coppice bright in its hues of Spring ; the man ceasing his work, looking up in pleasure as the rapturous melody reaches him, and exclaiming, " There is the nightingale " :—these are small and precise details which, to my mind, are more convincing of the poet's knowledge than any formal display of learned information.

Tennyson has told of the clear-voiced mavis, of the lark that becomes a " sightless song," of the pealing and chirruping of the nightingale, of the blackbird and thrush, of the trilling linnet, of the tender moan of the dove, of the swallow winging south, of the calling curlew and the clamouring daw, and of all birds that slide o'er lustrous woodland, and that warble "liquid sweet." Nor did he love small animals less, but watched the field-mouse and the hedgehog, the mole, the rabbit, and the weasel, the mouse, the lizard, and the grasshopper. Few lines are more impressive in their pathos than those which describe the final ruin in *Aylmer's Field:*

> The great Hall was wholly broken down,
> And the broad woodland parcell'd into farms ;
> And where the two contrived their daughter's good,
> Lies the hawk's cast, the mole has made his run,
> The hedgehog underneath the plantain bores,
> The rabbit fondles his own harmless face,
> The slow-worm creeps, and the thin weasel there
> Follows the mouse, and all is open field.

An animate picture of desolation complete! The mouse, again, in *Mariana* was the symbol of ruin and regret—

> The mouse
> Behind the mouldering wainscot shriek'd,
> Or from the crevice peer'd about ;

while in *Maud* we find the disconsolate lover listening to "The shrieking rush of the wainscot mouse." When sorrowing Œnone grew weary of life and lay down as it were to die upon Mount Ida in the silence of noon, how silent we realise that noon to have been, when even—

> The grasshopper is silent in the grass,
> The lizard with his shadow on the stone
> Rests like a shadow, and the cicala sleeps.

But when the scene was to be one of destruction or of remorseless rapacity, the smallest creatures could be made to suggest a truth.

> Nature is one with rapine.
> The Mayfly is torn by the swallow, the sparrow spear'd by the shrike,
> And the whole little wood where I sit is a world of plunder and prey.

The miracle of minute life is also to be revealed. The expatriated lover of Maud on the Breton strand is not moved by the roll of the breakers so much as by the

> Lovely shell,
> Small and pure as a pearl,
> Lying close to my foot,
> Frail but a work divine,
> Made so fairily well
> With delicate spire and whorl,
> How exquisitely minute,
> A miracle of design !

"What is it ?" he asks, and we have the researches of science explained to us, its speculations expressed, in the dainty stanzas which follow.

> The tiny cell is forlorn,
> Void of the little living will
> That made it stir on the shore.
> Did he stand at the diamond door
> Of his house in a rainbow frill ?
> Did he push, when he was uncurl'd,
> A golden foot or a fairy horn
> Thro' his dim water-world ?
>
> Slight, to be crush'd with a tap
> Of my finger-nail on the sand,
> Small, but a work divine,
> Frail, but of force to withstand,
> Year upon year, the shock
> Of cataract seas that snap
> The three-decker's oaken spine
> Athwart the ledges of rock,
> Here on the Breton strand !

The ability to turn science to such poetical account has been possessed by few, and the additional gift of transmuting hard scientific facts into gleaming lines of verse is rare indeed. Tennyson never seems constrained or pretentious in this use of learning ; the burden of knowledge to him was "light as a flower," and his happiest illustrations were those derived from the lore of nature's own book. He drew on the resources of geology in writing of

> Dragons of the prime
> That tare each other in their slime,

and again when he asked, beholding the seeming waste of nature,—

So careful of the type ?   But no !
  From scarpèd cliff and quarried stone
  She cries, " A thousand types are gone !
I care for nothing—let them go."

He has condensed in a few lines the nebular theory of the origin of the solar system, and the Darwinian theory of human evolution.   In *Maud* we read—

A monstrous eft was of old the Lord and Master of Earth,
For him did the high sun flame, and his river billowing ran,
And he felt himself in his force to be Nature's crowning race.
As nine months go to the shaping an infant ripe for his birth,
So many a million ages have gone to the making of man :
He now is first, but is he the last ? is he not too base ?

In *In Memoriam* the summing-up is this :

                  They say,
The solid earth whereon we tread,

In tracts of fluent heat began,
  And grew to seeming-random forms,
  The seeming prey of cyclic storms,
Till at the last arose the man ;

Who throve and branch'd from clime to clime
  The herald of a mightier race,
  And of himself in higher place,
If so he type this work of time

Within himself, from more to more :
  Or, crown'd with attributes of woe,
  Like glories, move his course, and show
That life is not as idle ore,

But iron dug from central gloom,
  And heated hot with burning fears,
  And dipt in baths of hissing tears,
And batter'd with the shocks of doom

To shape and use.

And he has summed up the world's changes in the course of geological periods in those fine and impressive lines on mutability—

There rolls the deep where grew the tree.
  O earth, what changes hast thou seen !

> There where the long street roars, hath been
> The stillness of the central sea.
>
> The hills are shadows, and they flow
> From form to form, and nothing stands ;
> They melt like mist, the solid lands,
> Like clouds they shape themselves and go.

Among Lord Tennyson's acquirements was a knowledge of astronomy. None but a " silent watcher of the skies " could have so beautifully turned to account the phenomena represented by the ever-varying constellations, and the appearance and disappearance of the planets.

> Many a night from yonder ivied casement, ere I went to rest,
> Did I look on great Orion sloping slowly to the West.
>
> Many a night I saw the Pleiads, rising thro' the mellow shade,
> Glitter like a swarm of fire-flies tangled in a silver braid.

The beautiful picture presented by the autumn sky could not be more poetically described. The grand constellation of Orion was a favourite one with the poet. The lover in *Maud*, wandering all the night in his frenzy and doubt,

> Walk'd in a wintry wind by a ghastly glimmer, and found
> The shining daffodil dead, and Orion low in his grave,

—a fact which at once informs us of the season and of the hour of the journey. In one of the early poems we find the following verse, which almost reaches sublimity :—

> Each sun which from the centre flings
> Grand music and redundant fire,
> The burning belts, the mighty rings,
> The murmurous planets' rolling choir,
> The globe-filled arch that, cleaving air,
> Lost in its own effulgence sleeps,
> The lawless comets as they glare,
> And thunder through the sapphire deeps
> In wayward strength, are full of strange
> Astonishment and boundless change.

In *The Hesperides* we find the reference to Hesper and Phosphor—

Hesper hateth Phosphor, evening hateth morn

—which afterwards was turned into so beautiful a simile in *In Memoriam.*

> Sad Hesper o'er the buried sun
> And ready, thou, to die with him,
> Thou watchest all things ever dim
> And dimmer, and a glory done :
>
> The team is loosen'd from the Wain,
> The boat is drawn upon the shore ;
> Thou listenest to the closing door,
> And life is darken'd in the brain.
>
> Bright Phosphor, fresher for the night,
> By thee the world's great work is heard
> Beginning, and the wakeful bird ;
> Behind thee comes the greater light :
>
> .    .    .    .    .    .
>
> Sweet Hesper-Phosphor, double name
> For what is one, the first, the last,
> Thou, like my present and my past,
> Thy place is changed ; thou art the same.

The allusion is to the evening and the morning star, Venus. The first of the *Poems by Two Brothers* opens with a reference to the evening star which " beams mildly from the realms of rest," and in the same volume references to the stars are numerous, the most striking and important being the following—

> The stars of yon blue placid sky
> In vivid thousands burn,
> And beaming from their orbs on high,
> On radiant axes turn :
> The eye with wonder gazes there,
> And could but gaze on sight so fair.
>
> But should a comet brighter still,
> His blazing train unfold,
> Among the many lights that fill
> The sapphirine with gold ;
> More wonder then would one bestow
> Than millions of a meaner glow.

Take again these lines from the ode on *Sublimity*—

> I love the starry spangled heav'n, resembling
> A canopy with fiery gems o'erspread,
> When the wide loch with silvery sheen is trembling,
> Far stretch'd beneath the mountain's hoary head.

The rapture of the boy remained the rapture of the man. How often the planets and the stars are mentioned in the *Idylls* ("the seven clear stars of Arthur's Table Round"); how fine a part they play in *The Voyage*, and what a pleasant reference to Charles's Wain may be found in *The May Queen!*[1] The poet's ideas are not commonplace. It would have been easy enough for him to speak of stars in the casual and indefinite manner adopted by most men, but his references gleam with intelligence and abound in information. "I well remember," says a friend, "one particular night on which there was a total eclipse of the moon, when he was so much struck by the number of constellations rendered visible to the naked eye through the veiling of the moon's light that he insisted on his youngest son being got out of bed to look at the sight." It is also recorded that when the Laureate paid his last visit to London he sent for Mr Norman Lockyer in order to discuss with that famous astronomer the temperature of the sun. Mr Lockyer left the poet's presence with the impression that he knew as much about astronomy as he did himself. Tennyson's poem to the Princess Beatrice on the occasion of her wedding is altogether in the astronomical vein, and though involved and somewhat obscure, contains the superb image of a

> Conjectured planet in mid-heaven
> Between two Suns,

which,

> Sway'd by each Love, and swaying to each Love

draws from both

> The light and genial warmth of summer day.

[1] See also *The Two Voices*, *The Princess*, and other poems for many striking allusions and illustrations.

The somewhat curious attempt, however, to expound how "two Suns of Love make day of human life" called forth the criticism that "the poet assumed a truly thaumaturgical rôle by presenting awe-struck humanity with a boon to which we must go back even into the era of creation to find a parallel. . . . *Two* suns, according to this sublime poetical postulate of his, make up the *day* of which he sings. Poetry, however closely allied it may be to the faculty of fancy, must not violate any condition which it may have voluntarily prescribed for itself." In his daily conversation Tennyson loved to have science, philosophy, and metaphysics for his theme; his mind ever seemed to dwell upon the wonders of the universe, the teachings of Nature, and the baffling questions of the hereafter. He speculated much, and in the end was forced to confess that "all was mystery." Geology and astronomy were in particular delightful to him; their wondrous secrets, as disclosed, filled him with awe, and he declared that the "freedom of the human will and the starry heavens were the two greatest marvels which come under human observation." "When I think," he said (according to Miss Weld, his kinswoman), "of all the mighty worlds around us, to which ours is but a speck, I feel what poor little worms we are, and ask myself, What is greatness?" Of his wondering, faltering faith in religion I have already spoken, but though he doubted much, he never lost anchorage in the belief of a Creator and His goodness. "I do not like," he said, "such a word as *design* to be applied to the Creator of all these worlds, it makes Him seem a mere artificer. A certain amount of anthropomorphism must, however, necessarily enter into our conception of God, because, though there may be infinitely higher beings than ourselves in the worlds beyond ours, yet to our conception man is the highest form of being. Matter, time, and space are all illusions, but above and beyond them all is God, who is no illusion. We can readily understand the existence of spirit much better than that of matter, which is to me far more incomprehensible than spirit.  We see nothing as it really is, not even our fellow-creatures."  "My love for Nature is as old as I," said the man who was

> A full-cell'd honeycomb of eloquence
> Stored from all flowers ;

and we are tempted to think that the poet was giving an unconscious portrayal of himself, or of his *alter ego*, when he wrote the lines.  The acquisition of knowledge was with him a life-craving.  He might have said—

> I knew the flowers, I knew the leaves, I knew
> The tearful glimmer of the languid dawn,

and have felt the thrill of joy when a voice whispered

> The wood is all thine own,
> Until the end of time.

Yet, early he had recognised that "knowledge comes but wisdom lingers," and in his great life-sorrow he had felt how unsatisfying was learning and how vain was intellectual power.

> Who loves not Knowledge?  Who shall rail
> Against her beauty?  May she mix
> With men and prosper !  Who shall fix
> Her pillars ?  Let her work prevail.
>
> But on her forehead sits a fire ;
> She sets her forward countenance
> And leaps into the future chance,
> Submitting all things to desire.
>
> Half-grown as yet, a child, and vain,
> She cannot fight the fear of death.
> What is she, cut from love and faith,
> But some wild Pallas from the brain
>
> Of Demons? fiery-hot to burst
> All barriers in her onward race
> For power.  Let her know her place ;
> She is the second, not the first.
>
> A higher hand must make her mild,
> If all be not in vain.

Again—

> Let Knowledge grow from more to more,
> But more of reverence in us dwell ;
> That mind and soul according well,
> May make one music as before,
>
> But vaster.

"The poet's sympathy with science," said Professor Dowden, "is ardent in an age when science reaches forth her arms to feel from world to world ; and yet once or twice his spirit is vexed by doubts as to the possibility of reconciling scientific observations with his spiritual faiths and hopes.  Happily as yet science has not grown the remorseless antagonist of faith, undermining by her reasonings the very conscience and the religious sentiment, therefore it suffices the heart, in Tennyson's poems, should stand up as the champion of the soul :—

> A warmth within the breast would melt
> The freezing reason's colder part,
> And like a man in wrath the heart
> Stood up and answered, " I have felt ! "

Largely viewed, science cannot but minister to human welfare if only its freedom be in harmony with spiritual order. The 'crowning race,' as conceived by Tennyson, is one that shall look, eye to eye, on knowledge ; holding the earth under command, reading nature like an open book ; possessing majestic order in a system of vast federations which shall bind nation to nation in peace, and having a reverent faith in

> One God, one law, one element,
> And one far-off divine event,
> To which the whole creation moves."

It has been said that to Shelley Nature was Love ; to Wordsworth she was Thought ; but to Tennyson she was neither : yet it seems to me that Tennyson was almost as much a Nature-worshipper as both.  He knew all the beauty, all the miracle, and as much as any of the meaning of " all things great and small," and if he restrained himself it was because of his firm faith in " Nature's God," who demanded his highest reverence.  He was more artist than interpreter, but what a faithful, inspiring, enlightening artist he was !  He was veritably the Meissonier of poets, giving us in microscopic detail and with marvellous fidelity the photograph, rather than the picture, of things as they are.  He was not the first to observe them, but he was the first to present many perfect scenes in words and reproduce impressions which we deemed to be beyond adequate explanation in language.  Thus we get—

> A fiery dawning, wild with wind,

the

> Little clouds, sun-fringed,

a

> Death-dumb, autumn-dripping gloom,

and like gleams which in a single flash reveal wonders of views.  Splendid revelations come in longer passages.

> A moon, just
> In crescent, dimly rained about the leaf
> Twilights of airy silver ;

the morning drives

> Her plough of pearl
> Far-furrowing into light the mounded rack,
> Beyond the fair green field and eastern sea.

King Arthur, gazing

> O'er the illimitable reed,
> And many a glancing plash and sallowy isle,

saw the glare of

> The wide-wing'd sunset of the misty marsh

upon a huge machicolated tower ; and an intent watcher of the sea observes

> The crest of some slow-arching wave
> Heard in dead night along the table-shore,
> Drop flat, and after the great waters break
> Whitening for half a league, and thin themselves,

> Far over sands marbled with moon and cloud,
> From less and less to nothing.

The thunder-clouds

> Floating thro' an evening atmosphere,
> Grow golden all about the sky ;

or, at night, a rising cloud may

> Topple round the dreary west,
> A looming bastion fringed with fire.

The succession of pictures in *St Agnes, Sir Galahad, Sir Launcelot and Queen Guinevere, The Two Voices, The Daisy,* and all such pieces, are too familiar to need disclosing anew.

" At the root of most of his excellence," said Professor Ingram, " lies his keen sense and exquisite enjoyment of every species of beauty—of all that is lovely in form, or graceful in movement, or rich in colour, or harmonious in sound. His finely-tuned organisation seemed tremblingly alive to those more delicate shades and tones of external nature which are scarcely distinguished by obtuser sensibilities. Connected with this gift is his power of painting the appearances of the outer world, not merely with general truthfulness, but with an almost magic reality of detail. Yet he does not fall—at least in his mature works—into pre-Raphaelite excess. He is saved from this by his practice of presenting every aspect of nature, not simply as it is in itself, but in relation to human feeling. He shows us the landscape as it is seen by the actors in his poems, and the features he exhibits are selected with relation to their dominant emotions. His moral sensibilities are not less fine than his physical— he notes with accuracy the subtle play of feeling, and those minor involuntary indications which are its natural language. And often he brings out most effectively the character—or, might I say? the soul—of a situation by some slight fugitive trait—some evanescent touch of attitude, or gesture, or expression. He is a master of orderly and lucid narrative; nothing is left hazy or indistinct in the stories he tells—everything is adequately prepared by previous explanations, everything is maturely worked out to its natural close."

Tennyson's poems open unto our eyes a matchless gallery where we are fascinated, tranced, dazzled, and ever delighted as in brightest dreams. His art is high and noble, his skill superb, his touch true. If he transports us into fairyland and brings visions before us, if, like the necro-mancer of old, he bids us gaze upon what never was and never will be, it is only because his scenery is too rich, his subjects too ideal, his colours too pure. He is never grotesque, never wholly artificial; luxurious fancy casts a glamour over realities, and like Will Waterproof we

> Look at all things as they are,
> But thro' a kind of glory.

The charm is complete. All grossness disappears, and under the poet's spell the scales fall from our eyes and we catch a glimpse of heaven.

# CHAPTER XIV.



"Something so mock-solemn."
—*The Princess.*

"The Muse, the jolly Muse it is !
She answer'd to my call,
She changes with that mood or this,
Is all-in-all to all."
—*Will Waterproof's Lyrical Monologue*

THE attempts at humour in the dramas I consider to be, without exception, failures. The by-play of words is trivial, the situations are unprovoking, and the jests mirthless. Some of the Shakespearean clowning is unintelligible, but it is possible to believe that we are at fault, not the dramatist, and that what a former age could understand and enjoy we in later times fail to appreciate. But it is not so with Tennyson. He mistook uncouthness for humour, and bad burlesque for wit. The lighter passages in his dramas are intolerable, and nothing is more depressing than the fooling in *The Falcon*. All this is the more remarkable because Tennyson was at heart a genuine humourist, or rather, he had a vein of genuine humour by no means easily exhausted. He was dry, grim, and subtle ; and if his wit did not bubble over it was at least spontaneous in its flow and sparkling. Its unexpectedness was not the least of its good qualities, for, like a sudden light, it surprised, amazed, and seemed doubly brilliant. Tennyson never lost dignity, never indulged in persiflage, never wrote a nonsense rhyme. His was an amusing cleverness, and, after all, taking the humourous pieces by turn, we can only conclude that they were studies or experiments in a style, just like the experiments in metre. We can imagine that Tennyson was quite serious when he sat down and began the task of writing his dialect poems. He chose his motif, he selected his type of character, he prepared his points. He did not, like the genial Dr Holmes, begin a poem in a light-hearted and haphazard way; he accomplished a set task. And when *The Northern Farmer, Will Waterproof's Lyrical Monologue, Owd Roä*, and *The Churchwarden and the Curate* were duly finished, they would need revising, polishing, amending, their effects heightening, and all the rest of it, before they would be ready for the public. What I wish to make clear is that Tennyson was always the man with a purpose, whether grave or gay, and that even in his humourous moments he did not forget his office. And it is for this very reason that his failure in writing light dramatic scenes can be understood. Whether he was in the mood or not he knew that the "relief" must be given—and his resources were not equal to the demand.

Strictly speaking, Tennyson's humourous poems are very few in number. Passing by the *Second Song* on *The Owl*, with its word-play on "tuwhoo" and "tuwhit," the list begins with *The Talking Oak*, which is written in a gleesome, light-spirited manner, and contains some cleverly-amusing lines. The poem as a whole, however, scarcely comes under the heading, and in the volume of another poet might have been classed as altogether serious. *Amphion*, too, with all its frolicsome fancies, is far too ingenious to be called amusing, but in *Will Waterproof's Lyrical Monologue* we get such delightful confessions and quaint conceits that it is only human to smile at them. The legend of the Cock and the Head Waiter is a happy conception, and when the fanciful Will, drinking his pint of port, exclaims—

> I ranged too high : what draws me down
>   Into the common day ?
> Is it the weight of that half-crown,
>   Which I shall have to pay?

the change is too ludicrous to be other than irresistible.

The first of the dialect poems was published in 1864, and the poet's old neighbour, John Baumber, of Somersby Grange, served as the prototype of the *Northern Farmer.*

> Git ma my aäle, fur I beänt a-gooin' to breäk my rule,

was the cry of Tennyson's rare old character; but it is not unlikely that the poet (as was usual with him) obtained the suggestion for his story from a once popular book in which the following passages occur: "One of the strongest instances I have seen of such a deliberate practice of the *Dum vivimus, vivamus,* was mentioned by the clever and humourous surgeon, Mr Wadd. He was called to a respectable lusty farmer who had indulged in his strong home-brewed ale till a serious illness came upon him. After some attendance his medical friend told him that it was clear that unless he gave up his favourite beverage he would not live six months. 'Is that your serious professional opinion?' 'I am certain of it.' The farmer thought a few minutes, tears came into his eyes; he sighed heavily, and at last said, 'I am sorry for it—very sorry; it's very sad, but I cannot give up my ale." So with the old Lincolnshire farmer.

> I 've 'ed my point o' aäle ivry noight sin' I beän 'ere,
> An' I 've 'ed my quart ivry market-noight for foorty year,

and he "weänt breäk rules fur Doctor." *The Northern Farmer*, new style, is the selfish, grasping man of a later period, obstinate and worldly-minded, greedy for gain and a despiser of sentiment. To his lovesick son, who has committed the heinous offence of becoming "sweet on Parson's lass," when she "'ant nowt, an' she weänt 'a nowt when 'e 's deäd," the old man explains his "noätions." His morality is summed up in

> Proputty, proputty sticks, an' proputty, proputty graws,

and he reminds his offspring that he can

> Luvv thy lass an' 'er munny too,
> Maakin' 'em goä togither as they've good right to do.
> Could'n I luvv thy muther by cause o' 'er munny laaïd by?
> Naäy—fur I luvv'd 'er a vast sight moor fur it : reäson why.

Taking the humourous poems in turn, for convenience, we come next to *The Northern Cobbler*, the plot of which was undoubtedly plagiarised. But the inimitable Tennysonian style, the language, and the quaint observations, make the piece the poet's own. Only Tennyson could have put into the mouth of the reformed drunkard the lines—

> An' then I minded our Sally sa pratty an' neät an' sweeät,
> Straät as a pole an' cleän as a flower fro' 'eäd to feeät :
> An' then I minded the fust kiss I gied 'er by Thursby thurn ;
> Theer wur a lark a-singin' 'is best of a Sunday at murn,
> Couldn't see 'im, we 'eärd 'im a-mountin' oop 'igher an' 'igher,
> An' then 'e turn'd to the sun, an' 'e shined like a sparkle o' fire.
> "Doesn't tha see 'im," she axes, "fur I can see 'im," an' I
> Seeäd nobbut the smile o' the sun as danced in 'er pratty blue eye ;
> An' I says, "I mun gie tha a kiss," an' Sally says "Noä, thou moänt,"
> But I gied 'er a kiss, an' then anoother, an' Sally says "doänt !"

Even more felicitous in its phrasing and curious ideas is *The Village Wife ; or, The Entail*, in which an inquisitive and talkative dame tells the story of the " owd Squire's " ruin. The matter-of-fact woman chatters on and on, vain of her knowledge of the affairs of other folks, vain of her " butter an' heggs," and vain of her dealings " wi' the Hall." It is needless to say that the busybody and gossip considers herself a highly superior person, and that she is the self-constituted critic of the misguided man who lived in his books and antiquities, and to the horror of all good Christians " bowt owd money, es wouldn't goä, wi' good gowd o' the Queen."

I have before expressed the opinion, and time and further investigation have done much to confirm me in it, that there was something more than a reminiscence of Tennyson's own father, " the owd Doctor," in the portrait of the " owd Squire " who

Niver looökt ower a bill, nor 'e niver not seed to owt,
An 'e niver knawd nowt but booöks, an' booöks, as thou knaws, beänt
    nowt.

Occasional lines in the poem are slyly humorous. Says
the gossip—

Hoffens we talkt o' my darter es died o' the fever at fall :
An' I thowt 'twur the will o' the Lord, but Miss Annie she said it wur
    draäins.

The old dame was decidedly muddled as to what an "entail"
meant, and her opinion was divided as to whether it was
some dread legal formality or an appendage which could be
" cut off "—

    Squire were at Charlie ageän to git 'im to cut off 'is taäil ;

and when Charlie broke his neck—

    Theer wur a hend o' the taäil, fur 'e lost 'is taäil i' the beck.

The superior wisdom of the village wife is manifested in
her cool criticism of all the Squire's "gells," especially of
the one who was "stuck oop." And

Molly the youngest she walkt awaäy wi' a hofficer lad,
An' nawbody 'eärd on 'er sin', sa o' coorse she be gone to the bad !
An' Lucy wur laäme o' one leg, sweet-'arts she niver 'ed none—
Straänge an' unheppen Miss Lucy ! we naämed 'er " Dot an' gaw
    one ! "
An' es fur Miss Annie es call'd me afoor my awn foälks to my faäce
" A hignorant village wife as 'ud hev to be larn'd 'er awn plaäce,"
Hes fur Miss Hannie the heldest hes now be a-grawing sa howd,
I knaws that mooch o' sheä, es it beänt not fit to be towd !

What revenge is crowded into the two last lines, and made
emphatic with repeated aspirates. One can imagine the
spiteful woman worked up into frenzy at the thought of
Miss Annie's unjust aspersion, and retaliating with all the
force in her nature—" I knaws that mooch o' sheä, es it
beänt not fit to be towd ! "

    The pleasantry in *The Spinster's Sweet-arts* is altogether
of another kind, and when published in the *Tiresias* volume

S

of 1885 revealed new capacity on the part of the poet.
The spinster's "Sweet-arts" are a number of cats named
"arter the fellers es once was sweet upo' me"—

Tommy the fust, an' Tommy the second, an' Steevie an' Rob.

They remind the dame of the characteristics of her old
lovers, and in her prattling to them we discover the humour
and the pathos of her past history.   The Spinster had
had "two 'oonderd a-year," and Rob was the first to angle
for the prize—

Niver wur pretty, not I, but ye knaw'd it wur pleasant to 'ear,
Thaw it warn't not me es wur pretty, but my two 'oonderd a-year.

The dame espied the man's flattery, and though once she
was "nigh saäyin' Yis," the clumsy man spoilt her carpet,
and she gave him "a raätin" that "sattled his coortin'."
Then came Steevie, but he was a widower, and the particular maid could not have taken to the "bouncin' boy
an' a gell."  "I hevn't naw likin' fur brats," she says—
"A haxin' me hawkard questions, and saäyin' ondecent
things."   Then her thoughts revert to the two quarrelsome,
fighting Tommies, and she has no regret that she declined
to become their slave—"Horder'd about, an waäked, when
Molly 'd put out the light" by a man "coomin' in wi' a
hiccup"—

An' the taäble stäin'd wi' 'is aäle, an' the mud o' 'is boots o' the stairs,
An' the stink o' 'is pipe i' the 'ouse, an' the mark o' 'is 'eäd o' the chairs.

So she remained a spinster, sitting in her "oän little
parlour," doing her little charities, and being held in more
esteem than a "graäter Laädy" who would have "allus to
hax of a man how much to spare or to spend."

The dialect poem of *Owd Roä* can only be included in
the category of humorous poems on account of incidental
passages.   The sleepy farmer thinking of Free Trade, and
wondering

> Howiver was British farmers to stan' ageän o' their feeät,

is a capital study.

> An' I slep' i' my chair ageän wi' my hairm hingin down to the floor,
> An' I thowt it was Roäver a-tuggin' an' tearin' me wuss nor afoor,

> An' I thowt 'at I kick'd 'im ageän, but I kick'd thy Moother istead.
> "What arta snorin' theere fur? the house is afire," she said.

> Thy Moother 'ed beän a-naggin' about the gell o' the farm,
> She offens 'ud spy summut wrong when there warn't not a mossel o'
>    harm;

> But Moother was free of 'er tongue, as I offens 'ev tell'd 'er mysen,
> So I kep i' my chair, fur I thowt she was nobbut a-rilin' ma then.

But the house was on fire—"An' I wasn't afeärd, or I thinks leästwaäys as I wasn't afeärd"; but the general panic was intense, and "Moother was naggin' an' groänin' an' moänin' an' naggin' ageän." Old Rover the dog was the hero of that night, and saved the life of a child to whom the story is told; but "Moother" "cotch'd 'er death o' cowd that night, poor soul, i' the straw."

The last of this delightful series of poems appeared in the volume of Swan-songs, *The Death of Œnone and other Poems.* In *The Churchwarden and the Curate* we are presented exactly with the same type of character as the Northern Farmer, and the dialect is confessedly "that which was current at Spilsby and in the country about it" in the poet's youth. Spilsby is a small market town about seven miles across the wolds from Somersby, Tennyson's birthplace; and it was here that Sir John Franklin was born, the uncle of Tennyson's wife. The poet has written few stories which are more delightful than this of the old churchwarden turned from being a Baptist—

> I can't abeär 'em, I can't, fur a lot on 'em coom'd ta-year—
> I wur down wi' the rheumatis then—to *my* pond to wesh thessens
>    theere—
> Sa I sticks like the ivin as long as I lives to the owd church now,
> Fur they wesh'd their sins i' *my* pond, an' I doubts they poison'd the
>    cow.

The joke is not original—it is told by Julian Young in his Memoirs, of a farmer's wife who laboured under the same delusion. But the churchwarden is an excellent type. He recognises in the new curate an audacious lad who was wont to steal his apples and take fish surreptitiously out of Howlaby beck—but he was not going to be severe on the " Parson's lad." He can now give him some good worldly advice, and we detect in it the satire against certain of the clergy which is thoroughly characteristic of Tennyson :—

An' I reckons tha 'll light of a livin' somewheers i' the Wowd or the
    Fen,
If tha cottons down to thy betters, an' keeäps thysen to thysen.
But niver not speäk plaain out, if tha wants to git forrards a bit,
But creeäp along the hedge-bottoms, an' thou 'll be a Bishop yit.

Naäy, but tha *mun* speäk hout to the Baptises here i' the town,
Fur moäst on 'em talks ageän tithe, an' I 'd like tha to preäch 'em
    down,
For *they*'ve been a-preächin' *mea* down, they heve, an' I haätes 'em
    now,
Fur they leäved their nasty sins i' *my* pond, an' it poison'd the cow.

The old man's advice to the curate is exquisite in its way, and his explanation as to how he himself " coom'd to the top o' the tree " is too good to be quoted in fragments. It is incomparable in its quaintness and its worldly wisdom, and is in Tennyson's best style.

Saw by the graäce o' the Lord, Mr Harry, I ham wot I ham

is the boast of the sly old fellow, and there is a sting of satire in the poet's explanation of how the words came to be uttered.

Within limits, and in his special domain, we must regard Tennyson as a humourist of a genuine and uncommon order. As in other things, he was punctilious even in his merry-making, and in consequence it was only when really inspired that he was seen to advantage. The triviality or dullness which passes for humour in the dramas is the obvious result of a set task being formally carried out. The contrast is great indeed when the grim and subtle humour of the poems is turned to; and *The Northern Farmer* series alone would support Tennyson's reputation for keen wit and the masterly delineation of quaint characters.

# CHAPTER XV.

## SOME CHARACTERISTICS OF TENNYSON.



"TENNYSON has re-made the English language," wrote Mr Galton. Although there are undoubtedly mannerisms and conceits in Tennyson's verse—taking "conceits" in Kingsley's sense to mean an image not true and abiding but for a mood and occasion only—yet, even in these details, he was consistent and correct. What at first seemed to be purely affectation, proved to be part of a deep-laid plan, and we have to thank the poet who was originally described as artificial for bringing back into use simple, strong Saxon words which had fallen into desuetude or been held up to contempt. No finnicking poet, after all, was the writer of album verses, the minstrel of fair women, and the rhymer of the boudoir. *Enoch Arden* is a vigorous Saxon poem ; so are the *Idylls* one and all. For the sake of compactness all words with Tennyson are contracted as much as possible. He was no lover of polysyllables and sesquipedalian adjectives. In his earlier volumes he wrote each word fully, but when he commenced revising, every "though" was shortened to "tho'," every past participle ending in "ed" was written "'d" or "t"; the word "toward" became in every place a monosyllable, and wherever an abbreviation could be allowed it was made. Consequently there is no waste in the lines ; there is no sense of profusion, but every passage seems exact, concentrated, crisp, compressed. False display was abhorrent to the poet; his pruning-knife was always in use, cutting away every needless part, clipping and trimming in every possible place. How pregnant short passages became in consequence of this! Take the description of Enoch Arden's life on the desert island—

> No want was there of human sustenance,
> Soft fruitage, mighty nuts, and nourishing roots ;
> Nor save for pity was it hard to take
> The helpless life so wild that it was tame.
> There in a seaward-gazing mountain-gorge
> They built, and thatch'd with leaves of palm, a hut,
> Half-hut, half native cavern. So the three,
> Set in this Eden of all plenteousness,
> Dwelt with eternal summer, ill-content.

How many pictures are crowded upon this morsel of canvas, and each picture is complete, precise, worthy of microscopic examination. Here, again, is a scene displayed in a flash of light—

> I saw the spiritual city and all her spires
> And gateways in a glory like one pearl

—a scene which no elaboration could make more resplendent and no further vision render more entrancing. Who could explain all the suggestiveness, all the beauty and fullness, of the revelation conveyed in this short passage?—

> I found a mighty hill,
> And on the top, a city wall'd : the spires
> Prick'd with incredible pinnacles into heav'n,
> And by the gateway stirr'd a crowd.

To depict this the artist would need abundant scope for the vast scene of the wall'd city, the "incredible pinnacles," and the swarming crowd. Yet these twenty odd words disclose everything. Tennyson had the art of revealing scenes rather than describing them. There is no laborious delineation or colouring in any of his scenes, yet those scenes are wonderfully vivid, beautiful, and finished. In *Mariana* he suggests the desolation instead of depicting it, and we understand how lonely and ruinous was the moated grange when we read that

> The broken sheds look'd sad and strange;
> Unlifted was the clinking latch;
> Weeded and worn the ancient thatch.

No picture could more perfectly realise than these words a louring Autumn noon—

> In the stormy east-wind straining,
> The pale yellow woods were waning,
> The broad stream in his banks complaining,
> Heavily the low sky raining
> Over tower'd Camelot;

or than these words realise the tropical splendour of evening—

> There all in spaces rosy-bright
> Large Hesper glitter'd on her tears,
> And deepening thro' the silent spheres
> Heaven over Heaven rose the night.

But a whole volume would be needed to treat the subject properly. Tennyson was always an artist—an artist by nature and by training—and though his hand was not unfamiliar with the brush, it is his pen-pictures, glowing and beautiful, which will always fascinate the eye.

Tennyson's scenery is mostly typical English; his characters are typical English; his names are typical English. In his Lincolnshire dialect poems it is worthy of noting that the names of places always end in "by," this termination being most common in the county. Thus we have "Thurnaby," "Wrigglesby," "Thursby," "Harmsby," "Hutterby," "Gigglesby," and "Howlaby," the last-named occurring in two of the poems. So far as the names of people go, Tennyson was careful to select favourite and not uncommon ones. We get no more Chloes and Dorindas, Strephons and Florizels, but charming and simple names with a homely English music of their own, such as Ellen Adair, Emma Moreland, Laurence Aylmer, Edward Morris, and Enoch Arden. Tennyson was seemingly fond of the names of Edith and Alice for girls, Edward and Lionel for men, as he uses these several times. Then, without counting the Claribel, Adeline, and Rosalind of early days, we have Letty, Clara, Evelyn, Ida, Dora, Amy, Olivia, Annie, and Maud—all with a pleasant ring and a familiar sound. It is this which adds to the human interest we feel in Tennyson's characters. Amaryllis and Damon and Celia are not akin; but one recognises Tennyson's men and women as real flesh and blood, from the wealthy miller, with his double chin and portly size, to Edith Aylmer, whose

> fresh and innocent eyes
> Had such a star of morning in their blue ;

or Lilia, "a rosebud set with little wilful thorns, And sweet as English air could make her."

In Tennyson's first volume his bias was detected, and his characteristics noticed by his friend Spedding, who found, however, that the bias was likely to prove profitable, and that the characteristics were uncommon and decidedly worthy.

"The human soul, in its infinite variety of moods and trials, is his favourite haunt," wrote Spedding ; "nor can he dwell long upon any subject, however remote apparently from the scenes and objects of modern sympathy, without touching some string which brings it within the range of our common life. His moral views, whether directly or indirectly conveyed, are healthy, manly, and simple ; and the truth and delicacy of his sentiments is attested by the depth of the pathos which he can evoke from the commonest incidents, told in the simplest manner, yet deriving all their interest from the manner of telling. See, for instance, the story of *Dora*, and *The Lord of Burleigh*. What is there in these that should so move us ? Quarrels and reconciliations among kindred happen daily. Hopeless affection, secretly, without complaint, cherished to the end, is a grief commoner than we know of. Many a woman marries above her natural rank, and afterwards dies of a decline. How is it that we do not pass these stories by as *commonplace*—so like what we see every day that we want no more of them?  It is because they are disclosed to us, not as *we* are in the habit of seeing such things, through the face they present to the outward world—but as they stand recorded in the silent heart, to whose tragic theatre none but itself (and the poet) may be admitted as a spectator. . . . But there are four poems in which Mr Tennyson has expressly treated of certain morbid states of the mind; and from these we gather, not indeed his creed, but some hints concerning his moral theory of life and its issues, and of that which constitutes a sound condition of the soul. These are the *Palace of Art*, the *St Simeon Stylites*, the *Two Voices*, and the *Vision of Sin*. . . . As the *Palace of Art* represents the pride of voluptuous enjoyment in its noblest form, the *St Simeon Stylites* represents the pride of asceticism in its basest. . . . In the *Two Voices* we have a history of the agitations, the suggestions and counter-suggestions of a mind sunk in hopeless despondency, and meditating self-destruction; together with the manner of its recovery to a more healthy condition. . . . The *Vision of Sin* touches upon a more awful subject than any of these;—the end, here and hereafter, of the merely sensual man.  The picture is of the youth, the winged steed, and the palace—the warm blood, the mounting spirit, and the lustful body— now chilled, jaded, and ruined: the cup of pleasure drained to the dregs; the senses exhausted of their power to enjoy, the spirit of its wish to aspire: nothing left but 'loathing, craving, and rottenness.' His mental and moral state is developed in a song, or rather a lyric speech, too long to quote; and of which, without quoting, we cannot attempt to convey an idea;—a ghastly picture (lightened only by a seasoning of wild inhuman humour) of misery and mockery, impotent malice and impenitent regret; 'languid enjoyment of evil with utter incapacity to good.'"

It was only to be expected that Tennyson's verse, having undergone so much revision, should be free from verbal flaws and in technique well-nigh perfect.  His rhyming is excellent, and he speedily overcame that want of exactness in rhythm for which Coleridge rebuked him. It is therefore rather surprising to find so obvious a defect as has been permitted to remain in *The Palace of Art*, where a clumsy device is adopted in order to complete the scansion of a line.  The poet speaks of a traveller in a strange land who hears the " moan of an unknown sea,"

> And *knows* not if it be thunder, or a sound
> Of rocks thrown down, or one deep cry

> Of great wild beasts ; then *thinketh*, " I have found
>     A new land, but I die."

At the risk of being considered hypercritical I must also point out one small irregularity in *Come into the garden, Maud.* Maud is addressed in the second person plural, " you," throughout the poem, except in one line when, it would seem, the task of finding a rhyme to " me " caused the poet to resort to an expedient scarcely allowable.   We therefore get this medley :

> But the rose was awake all night for *your* sake,
>     Knowing *your* promise to me ;
> The roses and lilies were all awake,
>     They sigh'd for the dawn and *thee.*

A trifle, truly ; but a false note is struck.

Sir Edward Hamley in an article on *False Coin in Poetry* declares that a favourite passage in *The Princess* is " remarkable for confusion."   We are told of

> jewels five words long
> That on the stretched forefinger of all Time
> Sparkle for ever.

" No doubt," says Sir Edward, " Time, who has always possessed a forelock, may also possess a forefinger ; but *all* time—that is, time not figurative but abstract—cannot ; the word ' all ' annihilates the personification, and with it all claim to the digit.   But, granting the forefinger, why are the jewels to be placed on it ?   True, the forefinger is used for pointing—but it cannot point at the rings upon itself.   Moreover, the forefinger can hold but a very limited number of jewels ; yet the novel office assigned to Time is that of perpetually holding out the member, to the neglect of his established duties with his scythe, hour-glass, &c., in order to exhibit these favoured vocables.   Lastly, to fill up the tale of slips in the passage, ' sparkle for ever ' is wrong in referring to a circumstance of time, and unnecessary as an indication of duration, after the phrase ' all Time.' " The criticism seems to me to be arbitrary, but the favourite passage certainly has its defects as a metaphor.

Tennyson had one or two favourite ideas, and he repeated them several times. One was the idea of a coming time when

> The war-drum throbb'd no longer, and the battle-flags were furl'd,
> In the Parliament of man, the federation of the world.
>
> There the common-sense of most shall hold a fretful realm in awe,
> And the kindly earth shall slumber, lapt in universal law.

Thus in *Locksley Hall*; and we get a repetition in *The Golden Year*:

> Ah ! when shall all men's good
> Be each man's rule, and universal peace
> Lie like a shaft of light across the land,
> And like a lane of beams athwart the sea,
> Thro' all the circle of the Golden Year?

The thought again occurs in the *Ode* sung at the opening of the International Exhibition:

> O ye, the wise who think, the wise who reign,
> From growing commerce loose her latest chain,
> And let her fair white-wing'd peacemaker fly
> To happy havens under all the sky,
> And mix the seasons and the golden hours ;
> Till each man find his own in all men's good,
> And all men work in noble brotherhood,
> Breaking their mailed fleet and armed towers,
> And ruling by obeying Nature's powers,
> And gathering all the fruits of earth and crown'd
>     with all her flowers.

And the echo is repeated once more in *Locksley Hall Sixty Years After*, when the poet dreams of

> Earth at last a warless world, a single race, a silent tongue,
> I have seen her far away—for is not Earth as yet so young?—
>
> Robed in universal harvest up to either pole she smiles,
> Universal ocean softly washing all her warless Isles.

"Is not earth as yet so young?" That, also, is an echo from the past. In the concluding portion of *The Day Dream* we learn that

> We are Ancients of the earth,
> And in the morning of the times.

In *The Princess* we are told,

> This fine old world of ours is but a child
> Yet in the go-cart,

and in the last volume of all, " Dawn not Day " is a theme in itself—

> Is it shame, so few should have climb'd from the dens in the level
>     below,
>   Men, with a heart and a soul, no slaves of a four-footed will?
>   But if twenty million of summers are stored in the sunlight still,
> We are far from the noon of man, there is time for the race to grow.

The doctrine of evolution is taught throughout Tennyson's works, and the old question is often discussed of man's rising from the beast and reeling back into the beast again. Another idea which recurs is that most succinctly expressed in *The Coming of Arthur*—" Man's word is God in man " ; a condensation of the thought in *Enoch Arden*, " Where God in man is one with man in God."

Next to his hatred of Napoleon, Tennyson hated all "tonguesters," and girded at them with might and main. Wild talk, specious phrases, deceptive watchwords, irresponsible chatter, and mob-oratory he regarded as positive diseases. " Through the tonguesters we may fail." A dozen similar expressions will occur to the mind of every student. Peace, Brotherhood, Purity, Honesty in thought and deed, Truth, and Sincerity—these are the leading points in Tennyson's doctrines, and form the most frequent of his allusions. Hatred of Despotism, Deception, and Unmanliness in all its insidious phases, flashes out in many a burning line and scornful word. " Every sophister can lime " the " wild hearts and feeble wings " of the herd ; the "dogs of Faction " can always bay ; but the wise man will always strive for peace, settled government, freedom, and the extension of knowledge—loving

> The gleams of good that broke
> From either side, nor veil his eyes.

Profusion of rhyme is the prevailing characteristic of some of the poems, especially the earlier ones. *The Lady of Shalott* consists of nine-lined verses ; the first four rhyme successively ; the fifth and last lines end in Camelot (once only in Lancelot) and Shalott respectively ; and the remaining three rhyme with each other. The length of the poem makes this feat more remarkable. It is repeated in *Fatima* and *Sir Launcelot and Guinevere.* Triple rhymes are the characteristic of *The Two Voices ;* rhymes clever and uncommon, yet used with elegance, surprise and delight in *Amphion* and *The Brook.* There are some ingenious alternations in *Maud,* a sort of regular-irregularity indicative of the poet's skill. The fourth section of Part I. consists of ten six-line stanzas, the first line rhyming with the fourth, the second with the fifth, and the third with the sixth, throughout the poem. There are minor variations of this style in succeeding sections, but in the second section of Part II. the placing of the rhymes is a refinement of art. The ear, too, can detect the sweetest of ripples and tender repetitions in the flow of such lines as—

'Tis a morning pure and sweet,
And a dewy splendour falls
On the little flower that clings
To the turrets and the walls ;
'Tis a morning pure and sweet,
And the light and shadow fleet ;
She is walking in the meadow,
And the woodland echo rings ;
In a moment we shall meet ;
She is singing in the meadow
And the rivulet at her feet
Ripples on in light and shadow
To the ballad that she sings.

Dr Mann has shown in his *Maud Vindicated* how the poet has made rhythm expressive of passing moods : how it becomes abrupt when the lover refers to Maud's brother, and how, " when the song passes on from this rough and disagreeable topic to the more pleasing theme, the verse at once softens into a sweetly flowing stream that makes one or two little contracted leaps, and then glides on with the most absolute smoothness." Doubtless this was all designed, though I think the poet's emotion rather than his art was responsible for it. Dr Mann also has pointed out that in the opening stanzas word-painting and word-music are combined to produce a most notable effect, and he quotes—

I remember the time, for the roots of my hair were stirr'd
By a shuffled step, by a dead weight trail'd, by a whisper'd fright,
And my pulses closed their gates with a shock on my heart as I
    heard
The shrill-edged shriek of a mother divide the shuddering night.

" Here the steps that bear the stiff burthen are shuffled " (we read), " the dead weight is trailed, and the fright is whispered to the scared boy's soul, in the very sounds that are embodied in the words. Any one who has ever seen some massive flood-gate flung back by the regurgitant stream with a shock, will at once recognise the symbolising power of this language. Every one who catches the complete rhythm of the tones in the concluding line of the stanza will be helped to the conception of what the shrill-edged shriek is which can divide the shuddering night." The two *Locksley Halls* supply similar examples of the Laureate's masterly use of rhythm to aid his effects and emphasise or symbolise his sentiment. Such poems are to be entirely dissociated from pure experiments in quantity, such as the " barbarous hexameters " which were "the strong-wing'd music of Homer," the Miltonic alcaics, the fantastical and dainty " metrification of Catullus," and the lines of the poems *Boädicea*, *Battle of Brunaburh*, *Merlin and the Gleam*, and *Kapiolani*.

Tennyson's metres are worthy of some consideration, though they do not afford much scope for special study. In the early poems his stanzas were noted for their daintiness of construction, but, without supplying anything actually original, he newly adapted olden forms and improved upon them. Occasionally he was able to surprise the ear with a delightful turn, either by transposition of rhymes, or by the unexpected suppression or addition of a syllable.  Mr Venables, in his Memoir of Henry Lushington, records that one day when he had read aloud *The Daisy* and the lines *To the Rev. F. D. Maurice*, Lushington said—" How the simple change in the last line from a dactyl to an amphibrachys changes a mere experiment into a discovery in metre." Tennyson was very happy in this discovery, and used it with excellent effect.   There is something almost enchanting in the three rhymed lines and the one, ending in a double syllable, unrhymed :

> How faintly-flush'd, how phantom-fair,
> Was Monte Rosa, hanging there
>     A thousand shadowy-pencill'd valleys
> And snowy dells in a golden air.

A modification of this form of verse is found in the dedicatory Lines *To the Master of Balliol*—

> Dear Master in our classic town,
> You, loved by all the younger gown
>     There at Balliol,
> Lay your Plato for one minute down,
>
> And read a Grecian tale re-told,
> Which, cast in later Grecian mould,
>     Quintus Calaber,
> Somewhat lazily handled of old.

The metre of *In Memoriam*, simple as it is, has at all times excited much attention.  The wonder is, not that Tennyson made it his own, but that it was not in common use before.  That Tennyson deliberately chose it as best suited for his purpose cannot be questioned.  *In Memoriam* was the work of seventeen years, written at divers times and in sundry places, some of it at Somersby, some at Barmouth, some in Cornwall, some in London, some at Clevedon, some at Cheltenham.[1]   The metre was not

<hr>

[1] A small volume has been published bearing the title *The Golden Decade of a Favoured Town*.  The town is Cheltenham, and the golden decade was 1843 to 1853, during which time Tennyson, his mother, and several brothers

actually new, for Ben Jonson had written an *Elegy* in the same form, the first verse running thus:

> Though beauty be the mark of praise,
> And yours, of whom I sing, be such
> As not the world can praise too much,
> Yet is 't your virtue now I raise.

In Smollett's translation of *Don Quixote* there are two stanzas formed similarly, and it is even said that Prior originally wrote a portion of a poem in like manner. These, however, constitute the only instances known of the use of the metre which will evermore be associated with Tennyson's *In Memoriam*. That this choice was both wise and happy all are agreed. Charles Kingsley said:—"The poems seem often merely to be united by the identity of their metre, so exquisitely chosen, that while the major rhyme in the second and third lines of each stanza gives the solidity and self-restraint required by such deep themes, the mournful minor rhyme of each first and fourth line always leads the ear to expect something beyond, and enables the poet's thoughts to wander sadly on, from stanza to stanza and poem to poem, in an endless chain of

> Linked sweetness long drawn out."

Mr Stedman added his tribute. "The author's choice of the transposed-quatrain verse was a piece of good fortune," he said. "Its hymnal quality, finely exemplified in the opening prayer, is always impressive, and, although a monotone, no more monotonous than the sounds of nature —the murmur of ocean, the soughing of the mountain pines. Were *In Memoriam* written in direct quatrains, I think the effect would grow to be unendurable." In spite

and sisters, lived there. "He was often in the habit of walking in Jessop's gardens, and no doubt many of the stanzas of *In Memoriam* were either born there or frequently subjected to that *labor limæ* which brought it into a state of almost absolute perfection. . . . What is still more interesting is that the local scenery helped to suggest and furnish some of the thoughts and images of the poems themselves." See *ante*, page 58.

of its length *In Memoriam* is never tedious.  If the poet, to avoid monotony, had changed the metre from time to time the whole sombre, quiet, calm, and even effect of the poem would have been irreparably ruined.  As it is, we pass on from hymn to hymn, and follow without weariness the

> Short swallow-flights of song that dip
> Their wings in tears, and skim away.

In regard to Tennyson's blank verse, I am disposed to accept the statement of Mr Stedman, that it "surpasses other blank verse in strength and condensation," and that it was "the poet's own invention, derived from the study of Homer and his natural mastery of the Saxon element in our own language."  The Homeric echoes are audible enough in the Arthurian idylls, from first to last, and in eclogues like *Edwin Morris* and *Ulysses* they are only fainter because of their sweetness.  Of the latter poem Mr Stedman said it had no equal for "virile grandeur and astonishingly compact expression; conception, imagery, and thought are royally imaginative, and the assured hand is Tennyson's throughout."  Equally beautiful and equally perfect, each in its way, is *Tithonus, St Simeon Stylites*, and *The Gardener's Daughter.  Love and Duty, Audley Court*, and *Dora* do not reach so high a level, and *Walking to the Mail* does not pass the average.  The blank verse of the dramas is much looser, is less polished, and lacks that strenuousness and concentration with which the earlier poems were replete.  In *The Princess* Tennyson seems, at times, almost too economical of his words.  He disdained to make plain that "he *said*" or "she *replied*," and omitted the verb, with the result that the abrupt "Then he:" and "And she:" at first grate upon the ear.  The imitation of Tennyson in mannerisms of this sort has been far from successful, and has exposed both the poet and his flatterers to ridicule.  Much as I object to parody, I cannot refrain from quoting a few inoffensive pages from Dr Oliver

Wendell Holmes's novel, *The Guardian Angel,* in which the Tennysonian school is ironically dealt with. Gifted Hopkins, the village poet, may be taken as a rude disciple of the Laureate's, reproducing all his mannerisms without making them the vehicle for wisdom. Thus, in Vol. ii. p. 21, we get—

"'Perhaps you will like these lines,' he said, 'the style is more modern :—

> Oh daughter of the spiced South
>     Her bubbly grapes have spill'd the wine
>     That staineth with its hue divine
> The red flower of thy perfect mouth.'

And so on, through a series of stanzas like these, *with the pulp of two rhymes between the upper and lower crust of two others.*"

So much for the *In Memoriam* style of the Laureate. But *The Princess* is travestied more openly in Gifted Hopkins's *Triumph of Song.*

> I met that gold-haired maiden, all too-dear ;
> And I to her : Lo ! thou art very fair,
> Fairer than all the ladies in the world
> That fan the sweetened air with scented fans,
> And I am scorched with exceeding love,
> Yea, crisped till my bones are dry as straw.
> Look not away with that high-arched brow,
> But turn its whiteness that I may behold,
> And lift thy great eyes till they blaze on mine,
> And lay thy finger on thy perfect mouth,
> And let thy lucent ears of carven pearl
> Drink in the murmured music of my soul,
> As the lush grass drinks in the globed dew ;
> For I have many scrolls of sweetest rhyme
> I will unroll and make thee glad to hear.
> Then she : Oh shaper of the marvellous phrase
> That openeth woman's heart as doth a key,
> I dare not hear thee—lest the bolt should slide
> That locks another's heart within my own.
> Go, leave me—and she let her eyelids fall,
> And the great tears roll'd from her large blue eyes.
> Then I : If thou not hear me, I shall die,
> Yea, in my desperate mood may lift my hand
> And do myself a hurt no leech can mend ;

> For poets ever were of dark resolve,
> And swift stern deed—
>           That maiden heard no more,
> But spake : Alas ! my heart is very weak,
> And but for—Stay !  And if some dreadful morn,
> After great search and shouting through the wold,
> We found thee missing—strangled—drowned i' the mere—
> Then should I go distraught and be clean mad !
> O poet, read ! read all thy wondrous scroll !
> Yea, read the verse that maketh glad to hear !
> Then I began and read two sweet, brief hours,
> And she forgot all love save only mine !

For the elegant trifles of verse Tennyson had never much affection.  In later life he almost entirely neglected the sonnet; while he was guiltless of the composition of ballade, kyrielle, pantoum, rondeau, sestina, triolet, villanelle, and all the artificial forms of verse adopted more for fantasy and pastime than for serious purpose.  On the other hand, he displayed a capacity for reproducing the "riddling triplets of old time," and he could imitate to a marvel the Mantuan poet, "lord of language," and "wielder of the stateliest measure ever moulded by the lips of man." His love of alliteration never became a craze.  It was effective because it was not strained and laboured, and it was used just often enough to display the poet's power, just seldom enough to please the reader's taste.  Tennyson, on the other hand, made a speciality of double-words, and excelled even his master, Spenser, in the number and richness and power of his combinations.  Freely admitting the mannerisms and peculiarities of the poet, I still find it extremely difficult to understand the criticism of Hain Friswell who in his *Men of Letters honestly criticised* confined himself to sweeping denunciation of the poet's work.

"An age," he said, "that calls Dickens *deep* reading, and picks up the sixpences, will appreciate Alfred Tennyson.  Look at his photograph.  Deep-browed, but not deep-lined ; bald, but not grey ; with a dark disappointment and little hopeful feeling on his face ; with hair unkempt, heaped up in the carriage of his shoulders, and with his figure covered with a tragic cloak, the Laureate is pourtrayed, gloomily peering from two ineffective and not very lustrous eyes, a man of sixty, looking more like a worn and a more feeling man of fifty. His skin is sallow, his whole physique not jovial nor red like Shakespeare and Dickens, but lachrymose and saturnine ; lachrymose ! and yet as regards fame and reward, what a successful man he has been ! At an age at which Shakespeare was holding horses, he was a pensionary of the Court. When he was very young the critics killed a far greater poet, John Keats, so that they might shower down repentant and self-recalcitrant praise on the successor. When he was but young, an old worn-out poet—a true prose man, but a poet still—contended for the Laureateship after years of toil and pen labour, but the young singer was crowned, and received the Laureate's wreath, the Laureate's fame and pension—the glory of which wreath was made purer and higher from that of his predecessor, Wordsworth. Tennyson's access to fame was sudden. 'Lorsque Tennyson publia ses premiers poèmes,' says M. Taine, 'the critics spoke mockingly of them,' and let us say the critics were right. 'He was silent,' continues the French author, 'and for ten years no one saw his name in a review, nor even in a catalogue, his books had burrowed their way alone ('avaient fait leur chemin tout seuls et sous terre '), and on the first blow Tennyson passed for the greatest poet of his country and his age.' It was because the age had been sinking in verve and true poetic feeling that Tennyson, great as he is in some points, at once rose to the level of its highest appreciation. It has cost long years for Tennyson to free himself from the drawing-room style of poetry. Indeed the ' Keepsake' and 'Book of Beauty' haunt him for ever, and have effectually forbidden him to be a *great* poet. And yet he had something of a chance that way once. There is the divine *afflatus* perceptible, but he has been educated too much, and is too careful and too timid. They write of him as of one who lies on the sofa all day, and smokes cigars. Tennyson's popularity, as a poet, grew down from the higher classes. A few young people of high life began to admire him, and Moxon sold his books slowly ; then the next stratum of society under these took [the fever, and found in the Laureate's poems easy things to understand ; and then again, and again, a wider but a commoner circle took up his songs. By his books he made at last much money. His brothers, Charles and Septimus,[1] both singers, were at one time rivals, but he soon distanced them and others. It was whispered that the Queen admired and that Prince Albert read his poems, and then with the loyal English-speaking people his fame was made. Moxon died, and the house paid Tennyson all that his books brought, save a percentage of fifteen per cent. ; so that for some years the poet found his lines golden. When *Macmillan* and the *Cornhill* magazines were

---

[1] An error—Frederick is no doubt meant.

started, their proprietors wanted names to attract, and they paid the Laureate a guinea a line for some weak kickshaws :

> I stood on a tower, in the wet,
> When the old year and the new year met,

and a weak story about a City clerk, which were hardly worth printing. The magazines did themselves good as regards advertising, but much harm to the Laureate. In 1830 the Laureate published poems, chiefly lyrical, with prose notes full of egotism, which were properly laughed at, and since then, it is said, Tennyson has abandoned prose for ever. Yes, Tennyson is a greatly successful, but he is not a great poet. The next age will surely reverse the verdict of this. He is sugar-sweet, pretty-pretty, full of womanly talk and feminine stuff. Lilian, Dora, Clara, Emmeline [1]—you can count up thirty such pretty names, but you cannot count any great poem of the Laureate's. No, he is no great poet. Mr Tennyson has been very discreet, and a very good Court poet,—for a manufactured article really none better ; but he is like the lady who did not want to 'look frightful when dead,' and so put on the paint and the fucus, and he will take no deep hold of the world. What did sweet Will Shakespeare do? Did he not say that he had

> gored mine own thoughts ;
> Sold cheap what is most dear,
> And made myself a motley to the view.

Did he not give us blood and passion with his poetry? But says Tennyson : 'Nor can it suit me to forget' that I am admired by all young ladies, and am a Laureate. Further he adds,

> I count it crime
> To mourn for any overmuch.

And posterity will count it folly to place a half-hearted and polished rhymster amongst her shining great ones, who were fellows with poverty and disrespect in this life, and who learnt in suffering that they might teach in song."

Tennyson could afford to disregard "criticism" of this character. His best answer to such censors was "silence when they rave"; yet such outbursts taught him that

> Sing thou low or loud or sweet,
> All at all points thou canst not meet,
> Some will pass and some will pause.

---

[1] Adeline is no doubt intended.

> What is true at last will tell :
> Few at first will place thee well ;
> Some too low would have thee shine,
> Some too high—no fault of thine—
> Hold thine own and work thy will !

These lines from the last volume might almost be the poet's answer to the critics, who could not "place him well" at the beginning, who misunderstood him at many stages of his life, but who found in the end that the man who "held his own and worked his will" was the victor over all.

# CHAPTER XVI.

## LABOR LIMÆ: SUPPRESSED AND REVISED POEMS.

" And here the Singer for his art
Not all in vain may plead,
' The Song that nerves a nation's heart,
Is in itself a deed.'"
—*Epilogue.*

TENNYSON'S suppressed poems, and his constant revision, curtailment, and extension of those retained and published, are a study in themselves. He composed slowly and laboriously, and as a rule had a verse completely shaped in his mind before he committed it to paper. Once it was written out he set about polishing it, finding new places for words, new words for places, and making change upon change until not infrequently the original disappeared entirely, and the whole verse was recast. His favourite mode of composition was to walk about in his garden, smoking vigorously, and revolving his ideas until they took shape. At such times he was unapproachable. When engaged on a sustained work he would lock himself in his study, and neither be heard nor seen for days at a time. His love of revision was almost a mania, and it was one of the tasks of his life to

> Add and alter, many times,
> Till all be ripe and rotten.

His caligraphy was quaint and neat, the letters being distinct, small, and Greek-like, and to the expert revealing the love of exactness, minuteness, and care of the writer. No hurried, passionate, excitable man could have written every word with such evident control and restraint. Byron, who always composed in a fever, sent illegible scrawls to the printer, but Tennyson's manuscripts were models of pictur-esque neatness and legibility. The interpolations and cor-rections were not very numerous; alterations were usually made at a much later period. Yet even at this stage the *labor limæ* was sometimes evident, as, for example, in the manuscript of the cycle of songs *The Window*. In the "copy" there is a verse of eight lines scored through which has never appeared in any published edition, and there are also autograph corrections of seventeen lines, while six, left untouched, now differ from the printed form. Whether this is true art or not need not now be discussed. Tenny-son, at all events, could claim as an example Virgil, who

> Would write ten lines, they say,
> At dawn, and lavish all the golden day
> To make them wealthier in his readers' eyes.

It is known that the *Æneid* was once twenty times longer than Virgil left it, and it was by years of paring, erasure, and condensation that it was brought to perfection ; and Virgil spent three whole years, not in composing, but in revising the five or six hundred verses of his *Pastorals*. After this we need not blame Tennyson for spending more years in improving his poems than in writing them.

But the deviations in text are full of suggestion and interest, and give us an insight into the poet's methods, his self-criticism, and his development. No one profited more by criticism than Tennyson, and if the harsh strictures of the *Quarterly* reviewer and Christopher North need any justification, that justification will best be found in Tenny-son's own amendments. The poet wrote at one time and another positive absurdities. I doubt whether more ridiculous lines could be found than *The Skipping Rope*, or more childish lines than *O Darling Room*. Not only were there incongruities of thought in these early compositions, but in not a few the rhymes were bad and the metre imper-fect. Remembering how careful Tennyson was in after years, and that not a defective rhyme or a false quantity exists in his poems as we now know them, we can simply view with amazement the stupidities and blunders of which he was once guilty.

"Regarded as a crop of wild oats," said Spedding, " Mr Tennyson's first collection of poems, as originally published, cannot but be accounted a production of unusual promise. The natural faults of youth—exuberance, prodigality, lightness of heart and head, ingenuity wasted upon nothing, the want of sustained effort and a determined course, together with some vanities and fopperies—it may well afford to be charged with. The untried genius needed to be assured of its powers by putting them forth—to feel itself alive through all its capacities by living acts of creation. Hence his early efforts are, many of them, rather exercises than works—gymnastic exercises for the fancy, the intellect, the imagination, the power of language, and even for the feelings—valuable, as the games and tasks of schoolboys are valuable, not for the thing done, but for the practice, strength, and dexterity acquired in doing it. Here we have a succession of vague melodies, in which the power of musical expression tries how far it can go ; there a group of abstract ideas, turned, for the satisfaction of the creative genius, into shape ready for the sculptor—here a conceit, in which the fancy admires its own ingenuity ; there a thought, of no great worth or novelty perhaps, but expressed with curious felicity :—presently we find ourselves surrounded by a bevy of first loves—Adelines, Madelines, and Lilians, more than we can remember—phantoms of female grace in every style, but all belonging to the land of shadows ; then again come delineations of every state of mind, from that of the mystic who has nearly reached the highest circle, to the 'second-rate sensitive mind not in unity with itself' ; and of every variety of untried being, on earth or in water, or on the earth under the water, from the grasshopper with his 'short youth, sunny and free,' to the Kraken sleeping for ages in the central depths, among millennial sponges and giant-finned polypi : whilst at intervals we recognise a genuine touch of common humanity—a *Character*, a *Circumstance*, or a sketch truly drawn from homeliest nature, which needs, however, no fancy dress to make it beautiful, but will remain for ever fresh when all that 'airy stream of lively portraiture' has faded before the increasing daylight.

The superiority of his second collection of poems lay not so much in the superior workmanship (it contained perhaps fewer that were equally perfect in their kind), as in the general aim and character. If some of the blossom was gone, it was amply repaid by the more certain promise of fruit. Not only was the aim generally larger, the subjects and interest more substantial, and the endeavour more sustained, but the original and distinctive character of the man appeared more plainly. His genius was manifestly shaping a peculiar course for itself, and finding out its proper business ; the moral soul was beginning more and more to assume its due predominance—not in the way of formal preaching (the proper vehicle of which is prose)—but in the shape and colour which his creations unconsciously took, and the feelings which they were made insensibly to suggest.  Considerable faults, however, still remained ; a tendency, for example, arising from the fullness of a mind which had not yet learned to master its resources freely, to overcrowd his composition with imagery ; a habit also (caused by that dissatisfaction with himself, which, so long as it does not depress the spirits too much, a poet ought to cultivate rather than to repress) of adding, altering, and retouching, till in trying to improve the form he lost the spirit and freshness of his work, and blurred the impression ;—to which may be added an over-indulgence in the luxuries of the senses—a profusion of splendours, harmonies, perfumes, gorgeous apparel, luscious meats and drinks, and such 'creature comforts,' which rather pall upon the sense, and make the glories of the outward world a little too obscure and overshadow the world within.  The poems originally published in 1832, are many of them largely altered, generally with great judgment, and always with a view to strip off redundances—to make the expression simpler and clearer, to substitute thought for imagery, and substance for shadow. *The Lady of Shalott*, for instance, is stripped of all her finery ; her pearl garland, her velvet bed, her royal apparel, and her 'blinding diamond bright,' are all gone ; and certainly, in the simple white robe which she now wears, her native beauty shows to much greater advantage.  The *Miller's Daughter*, again, is greatly enriched by the introduction of the mother of the lover ; and the following beautiful stanzas (which many people, however, will be ill satisfied to miss) are displaced, to make room for beauty of a much higher order :—

> Remember you the clear moonlight
>   That whiten'd all the eastern ridge,
> When o'er the water, dancing white,
>   I stepp'd upon the old mill-bridge ?
> I heard you whisper from above,
>   A lute-toned whisper, 'I am here !'
> I murmur'd 'Speak again, my love,
>   The stream is loud ; I cannot hear !'
>
> I heard, as I have seem'd to hear
>   When all the under-air was still,
> The low voice of the glad new year
>   Call to the freshly-flowered hill.

> I heard, as I have often heard
> The nightingale in leafy woods
> Call to its mate, when nothing stirr'd
> To left or right but falling floods."

The *Poems by Two Brothers* contained nothing so foolish and, seemingly, so hopeless as some of the now-excluded verses which were given a place in the *Poems chiefly Lyrical.* If such verses were included in any volume again the composer would justly expose himself to the sternest censure or to killing ridicule ; and because Tennyson afterwards scaled so great a height there is no need to protest, as has been often done, against the crushing comments of Lockhart and Wilson. Tennyson practically admitted the justice of their criticisms when he amended all the faults he could of which they had spoken, and rigidly suppressed those pieces which he found irremediable.

The discarded poems number no fewer than sixty, without including Tennyson's share in the *Poems by Two Brothers.* In some half-dozen instances pieces, suppressed for many years, have been permitted to reappear. The *Supposed Confessions of a Second-rate sensitive mind* (1830), *Nothing will Die* (1830), *All Things will Die* (1830), *The Kraken* (1830), *We are Free* (1830), *Mine be the strength of Spirit* (1833), *Buonaparte* (1833), *The Third of February* (1852), *Literary Squabbles*, *The Bridesmaid*, and other occasional pieces, belong to this category. They may all be found now in the authorised editions ; yet at one time or another they had been excluded. Tennyson appeared to have a particular aversion to republishing, or even acknowledging, his patriotic poems, probably because they were written rather in his official capacity as Laureate than from personal choice. Yet in the last of his volumes *The Death of Œnone* he rescued *Riflemen, Form,* from the neglect in which it had long lain, and thus set at rest for ever the doubt as to whether he or Trench was the writer of the stirring lines. It would have been still more gratifying had a place been found for *Hands all Round,* which

Lady Tennyson had set to music, and for *Britons, guard your own.* We would also have willingly substituted either of these for the *Jubilee Ode*, but Tennyson could be capricious in his own choice as well as discriminating.

There was good reason for the omission of *The "How" and the "Why,"* for the final verse is not good poetry even if it is good sense.

> Why the life goes when the blood is spilt?
>     What the life is? where the soul may lie?
> Why a church is with a steeple built?
> And a house with a chimney-pot?
> Who will riddle me the how and the what?
>     Who will riddle me the what and the why?

If the poet had wished to burlesque his own poem he could not have done better than this. But we must regret the loss of *The Burial of Love*, which, if not uniformly excellent, is a poem of great tenderness and rare diction.

> His eyes in eclipse,
> Pale cold his lips,
> The light of his hopes unfed,
>     Mute his tongue,
>     His bow unstrung
> With the tears he hath shed,
> Backward drooping his graceful head,
>                     Love is dead :
>     His last arrow is sped ;
>     He hath not another dart ;
> Go—carry him to his dark deathbed ;
>     Bury him in the cold, cold heart—
>                     Love is dead.
>
> Oh, truest love ! art thou forlorn,
>     And unrevenged? thy pleasant wiles
>         Forgotten, and thine innocent joy?
>         Shall hollowhearted apathy,
> The cruellest form of perfect scorn,
> With languor of most hateful smile,
>                 For ever write,
>                 In the withered light
>                 Of the tearless eye,

> An epitaph that all may spy?
> No! sooner she herself shall die.
>
> For her the showers shall not fall,
> Nor the round sun shine that shineth to all;
> Her light shall into darkness change;
> For her the green grass shall not spring,
> Nor the rivers flow, nor the sweet birds sing,
> Till Love have his full revenge.

The stanzas "*To*———," commencing "Sainted Juliet!" contain the pretty image, or conceit,—

> Love unreturned is like the fragrant flame
> Folding the slaughter of the sacrifice
> Offered to gods upon an altar-throne.

A song, beginning—

> I' the glooming light
> Of middle night
> So cold and white,
> Worn Sorrow sits by the moaning wave,

is in that vein of melancholy which we find in *A Spirit haunts the year's last hours* and similar dirge-like pieces. The whole poem is powerful, and the deathlessness of despair is cunningly explained.

> Death standeth by;
> She will not die;
> With glazed eye
> She looks at her grave: she cannot sleep
> Ever alone
> She maketh her moan:
> She cannot speak: she can only weep,
> For she will not hope.
> The thick snow falls on her flake by flake,
> The dull wave mourns down the slope,
> The world will not change and her heart will not leap.

Another song, *The Lintwhite and the Throstlecock*, has less claim to attention. It is archaic and affected in style, and unless it is a deliberate imitation of the old-fashioned ballad it has little merit of its own. The third verse is best.

> Fair years, with brows of royal love,
>   Thou comest, as a king,
>     All in the bloomèd May.
>   Thy golden largess fling,
>   And longer hear us sing ;
>   Though thou art fleet of wing,
>     Yet stay.
>   Alas ! that eyes so full of light
>   Should be so wandering !

This is followed by a third song—

> Every day hath its night :
>   Every night its morn ;

with a refrain—"Ah ! welaway !" The piece is scarcely beyond the level of a drawing-room ballad.

Very different is the workmanship in *Hero and Leander*, a poem with many bright lines and truly poetic in its conception.

> Oh go not yet, my love,
>   The night is dark and vast ;
> The white moon is hid in her heaven above,
>   And the waves climb high and fast.
> Oh ! kiss me, kiss me once again,
>   Lest thy kiss should be the last.
> Oh kiss me ere we part ;
> Grow closer to my heart.
> My heart is warmer surely than the bosom of the main.
>   O joy ! O bliss of blisses !
>   My heart of hearts art thou.
> Come bathe me with thy kisses,
>   My eyelids and my brow.
> Hark how the wild rain hisses,
>   And the loud sea rolls below.
>
> Thy heart beats through thy rosy limbs,
>   So gladly doth it stir ;
> Thine eye in drops of gladness swims.
>   I have bathed thee with the pleasant myrrh.
> Thy locks are dripping balm ;
> Thou shalt not wander hence to-night,
>   I 'll stay thee with my kisses.
> To-night the roaring brine
>   Will rend thy golden tresses ;

> The ocean with the morrow light
>   Will be both blue and calm ;
> And the billow will embrace thee with a kiss as soft as mine.
>
>     No Western odours wander
>       On the black and moaning sea,
>     And when thou art dead, Leander,
>       My soul must follow thee !
>     Oh go not yet, my love,
>       Thy voice is sweet and low ;
>     The deep salt wave breaks in above
>       Those marble steps below.
>     The turret-stairs are wet
>       That lead into the sea.
>     Leander ! go not yet.
>     The pleasant stars have set :
>     Oh ! go not, go not yet,
>       Or I will follow thee.

A slight piece, *The Grasshopper*—described as " The Bayard of the meadow " for no very obvious reason—and two verses on *Love, Pride, and Forgetfulness*, call for no particular notice.  Following these is a *Chorus*, to which is prefixed a note that it formed part of an unpublished drama " written very early," a statement which is worth bearing in mind, as it casts a light upon the poet's later, and almost hopeless, infatuation for writing dramatic pieces. Perhaps the predilection was a much earlier one than has been supposed.  The *Chorus* itself has a fine ring.  Take the second verse—

>     The day, the diamonded night,
>       The echo, feeble child of sound,
>     The heavy thunder's griding might,
>       The herald lightning's starry bound,
>     The vocal spring of bursting bloom,
>       The naked summer's glowing birth,
>     The troublous autumn's sallow gloom,
>       The hoarhead winter paving earth
>             With sheeny white, are full of strange
>             Astonishment and boundless change.

There are several small poems, some only consisting of

eight lines, which have no particular value and can easily be spared. Such are *Lost Hope, The Tears of Heaven, To a Lady Sleeping,* and *Love and Sorrow*—the last-named yielding the single thought that " They never learned to love who never knew to weep." But this was scarcely an original discovery. Tennyson has preserved so few sonnets that it might be considered he had seldom attempted that form of composition, in this way presenting a contrast to his brother Charles, who preferred the " poet's humble plot of ground."[1] Yet at one time Alfred Tennyson was a sonneteer, but his productions are very uneven. Four sonnets appeared in the 1830 volume which were afterwards excluded. The second of these, descriptive of night, is the best. What could be better than these two lines?

> All night through archways of the bridgèd pearl,
> And portals of pure silver, walks the moon.

The poet bade his soul so to " walk on,"—

> Turn cloud to light, and bitterness to joy,
> And dross to gold with glorious alchemy,
> Baring thy throne above the world's annoy.

In another sonnet we find a flow of words which afterwards turned into more familiar music.

> The wise, could he behold
> Cathedralled caverns of thick-ribbed gold
> And branching silvers of the central globe,
> Would marvel from so beautiful a sight
> How scorn and ruin, pain and hate, could flow.

The fault of these sonnets is that the constant straining after effect is visible. Strange and uncouth words and combinations are introduced. We read of " The wan dark coil of faded suffering," of " sheeny snakes,"

---

[1] Archbishop Trench said in one of his Lectures on Literature and Art, delivered in 1867, that " Tennyson never seems to have cared much for the Sonnet ; at least, he has very rarely clothed his own thoughts in this verse." The Archbishop knew only two of the poet's sonnets, but there were then fully a dozen in existence.

of "woven glooms," of "an honourable eld," of "salient blood," of "blastborne hail," of "heated eyne," and of "pallid thunderstricken sighs."   Words like "pleached," "yronne," "blosmy," "evanisheth," "bloomèd," "empery," "pleasaunce," show the influence of Shelley upon the poet, but they are not employed with the ease and spontaneity necessary to make them acceptable.

A long poem on *Love*, in spite of many mannerisms, is so far removed from the commonplaces written on the subject by a young man that it scarcely deserved its fate.

> Thou foldest, like a golden atmosphere,
> The very throne of the eternal God,

wrote the poet, and in a still finer strain he continued—

> Passing through thee the edicts of his fear
> Are mellowed into music, borne abroad
> By the loud winds.

One wonders how a youth of twenty, or perhaps younger, could have written—

> To know thee is all wisdom, and old age
> Is but to know thee.          .          .          .          .
>
> .          .          .          .          .          .          .          .          .
>
> As dwellers in lone planets look upon
> The mighty disk of their majestic sun
> Hollowed in awful chasms of wheeling gloom,
> Making their day dim, so we gaze on thee.

The first volume contained two patriotic songs—the *English War-Song*, exuberant and vaunting in tone, and the *National Song*, which, after sixty years of neglect, suddenly reappeared in the pastoral drama of *The Forresters*.   Both pieces manifest the poet's pride in his country, and his unshaken belief that "there is no land like England."

> Come along ! we alone of the earth are free,

he exclaimed exultingly, and picked out the French as the most enslaved and contemptible of men.   The poems will be read with more amusement than admiration.

The poem entitled *Dualisms* appears to have been after-wards condensed into the nine fine lines entitled *Circum-stance*—the history in brief of two lives, beginning and ending undivided : " So runs the round of life from hour to hour."   Here is the original thought in its original garb :

Two bees within a crystal flowerbell rocked,
　Hum a lovelay to the westwind at noontide.
　　Both alike, they buzz together,
　　Both alike, they hum together,
　Through and through the flowered heather.
Where in a creeping cove the wave unshocked,
　Lays itself calm and wide.
　Over a stream two birds of glancing feather
　Do woo each other, carolling together,
　Both alike they glide together,
　　　Side by side :
Both alike, they sing together,
Arching blue-glossed necks beneath the purple weather.

Two children lovelier than Love adown the lea are singing,
　As they gambol, lily garlands ever stringing :
　　Both in blossomwhite silk are frockèd :
　Like, unlike, they roam together
　Under a summer vault of golden weather ;
　Like, unlike, they sing together
　　　Side by side,
Mid May's darling golden lockèd,
Summer's tanling (*sic*) diamond eyed.

The poems omitted from the edition of 1833 were numerically smaller, but the list contains at least one poem of greater importance than any others.   We could willingly forego the pleasure, if such it be, of reading the diatribe on Buonaparte, but the long lyrical poem on *The Hesperides*, with its ringing musical lines, ought not to have been consigned to oblivion.   A few of its passages are en-shrined in other poems of a later date, and there are references which will easily be recognised.   The allusion to Hesper and Phosphor, to the dragon older than the world, and to the full-faced sunset, are repeated elsewhere.   The conclusion of the song sung by the three daughters of Hesperus is instinct with music.

> Every flower and every fruit the redolent breath
> Of this warm sea-wind ripeneth,
> Arching the billow in his sleep ;
> But the land wind wandereth,
> Broken by the highland-steep,
> Two streams upon the violet deep :
> For the western sun and the western star,
> And the low west wind, breathing afar,
> The end of day and beginning of night
> Make the apple holy and bright ;
> Holy and bright, round and full, bright and blest,
> Mellowed in a land of rest ;
> Watch it warily day and night ;
> All good things are in the west.
> Till mid noon the cool east light
> Is shut out by the tall hillbrow ;
> But when the full-faced sunset yellowly
> Stays on the flowering arch of the bough,
> The luscious fruitage clustereth mellowly,
> Golden-kernelled, golden-cored,
> Sunset-ripened above- on the tree
> The world is wasted with fire and sword,
> But the apple of gold hangs over the sea.

The poem serves as a preparation for *The Lotos-Eaters*. The writer of the one could only have been the writer of the other. There are weaknesses in *The Hesperides*, but only the hypercritical would have deemed them fatal. Tennyson was too severe upon himself when he rejected lines in which others could scarcely fail to find genuine delight.

Two portraits, *Rosalind* and *Kate*, were suppressed, because they obviously fell short of the standard set in the series to which *Lilian*, *Margaret*, and *Eleänore* belong. Yet both are graceful and pretty poems despite their imperfections. "My falcon Rosalind," however, with "wild eyes" and "bitter words" is not a very attractive lady. Angry Kate is preferable.

> I know her by her angry air,
> Her bright black eyes, her bright black hair,
>     Her rapid laughters wild and shrill,
> As laughters of the woodpecker

From the bosom of a hill.
  'Tis Kate—she sayeth what she will :
For Kate hath an unbridled tongue,
  Clear as the twanging of a harp,
  Her heart is like a throbbing star.
Kate hath a spirit ever strung
  Like a new bow, and bright and sharp
  As edges of the scymetar.
Whence shall she take a fitting mate ?
  For Kate no common love will feel ;
My woman-soldier, gallant Kate,
  As pure and true as blades of steel.

Kate saith " the world is void of might."
  Kate saith " the men are gilded flies."
    Kate snaps her fingers at my vows ;
  Kate will not hear of lovers' sighs.
I would I were an armed knight,
  Far famed for well-won enterprise
And wearing on my swarthy brows
The garland of new-wreathed emprise ;
  For in a moment I would pierce
The blackest files of clanging fight,
And strongly strike to left and right,
  In dreaming of my lady's eyes.
  Oh ! Kate loves well the bold and fierce ;
But none are bold enough for Kate,
She cannot find a fitting mate.

Of the two sonnets on the Polish Insurrection, with
which Tennyson had the warmest sympathy, it is difficult
to understand why the one should be taken and the other
left ; but there was good reason for not reproducing the
lines on Christopher North, and the " Darling Room "
might most fitly remain unhonoured and unsung. *No
More,* an echo from Shelley, and the *Anacreontics* (both
originally published in the *Gem* of 1831) are merely trifles ;
but the *Fragment* which appeared in the same annual
might have been redeemed from obscurity.

Where is the Giant of the Sun, which stood
In the midnoon the glory of old Rhodes,
A perfect Idol with profulgent brows
Farsheening down the purple seas to those

> Who sailed from Mizraim underneath the star
> Named of the Dragon—and between whose limbs
> Of brassy vastness broadblown Argosies
> Drave into haven?  Yet endure unscathed
> Of changeful cycles the great Pyramids
> Broadbased amid the fleeting sands, and sloped
> Into the slumbrous summer noon : but where,
> Mysterious Egypt, are thine obelisks
> Graven with gorgeous emblems undiscerned?
> Thy placid Sphinxes brooding o'er the Nile?
> Thy shadowing Idols in the solitudes,
> Awful Memnonian countenances calm
> Looking athwart the burning flats, far off
> Seen by the high-necked camel on the verge
> Journeying southward?  Where are thy monuments
> Piled by the strong and sunborn Anakim
> Over their crowned brethren On and Oph?
> Thy Memnon when his peaceful lips are kist
> With earliest rays, that from his mother's eyes
> Flow over the Arabian bay, no more
> Breathes low into the charmed ears of morn
> Clear melody flattering the crisped Nile
> By columned Thebes.  Old Memphis hath gone down :
> The Pharaohs are no more : somewhere in death
> They sleep with staring eyes and gilded lips,
> Wrapped round with spiced cerements in old grots
> Rock-hewn and sealed for ever.

The mystical sonnet, " Me my own fate to lasting sorrow doometh," was a contribution to *Friendship's Offering* in 1833, in the pages of which also appeared that sonnet which seems like a page from the poet's history—

> Check every outflash, every ruder sally
>   Of thought and speech ; speak low and give up wholly
> Thy spirit to mild-minded melancholy ;
> This is the place.  Through yonder poplar valley
>   Below the blue-green river windeth slowly :
> But in the middle of the sombre valley
> The crisped waters whisper musically,
>   And all the haunted place is dark and holy.
> The nightingale, with long and low preamble,
>   Warbled from yonder knoll of solemn larches,
>   And in and out the woodbine's flowery arches
> The summer midges wove their wanton gambol

> And all the white-stemmed pinewood slept above—
> When in this valley first I told my love.

I have too much reverence for Tennyson to quote a single line of the poem entitled *The Skipping Rope*. The marvel is that he could have written it; the greater marvel that he could have ever permitted it to be published. It is not even clever nonsense; it is ridiculous without gaiety— vapid, foolish, dull. The verses were omitted from the edition of 1842, and should never see the light again. The Farewell to Macready, a sonnet read by John Foster at a dinner given to the actor on his retirement, the stanzas contributed to the *Keepsake* so late as 1851, "What time I wasted youthful hours," and the two additional verses to *God Save the Queen*, written for the marriage of the Princess Royal of England with the Crown Prince of Prussia (the Emperor Frederick) in 1858, call for no attention. Tennyson appears to have sent his inferior wares to the periodicals, and the fact that he deemed them unfit for preservation and acknowledgment goes far to show that he had scant respect for such means of publication. Even late in his life he often acted on a plan which can only be open to this explanation.

At one time it seemed likely that all the patriotic poems would be lost—even the best of them, *Britons, guard your Own* and *Hands all Round*. They were worth saving if only to give posterity the opportunity of understanding how vigorous the Laureate could be in dealing with the events of the day; and many would have been well pleased had the appeals to Englishmen to save their land and unite their forces not have been allowed to die away in silence.

Another poem dating from early days the world should not " willingly let die "—the poem on *The Mystic*, in a strain with which we afterwards became familiar, but which seems remarkable in one so young.

> Angels have talked with him, and showed him thrones :
> Ye knew him not, he was not one of ye,
> Ye scorned him with an undiscerning scorn :
> Ye could not read the marvel in his eye,
> The still serene abstraction : he hath felt

The vanities of after and before ;
Albeit, his spirit and his secret heart
The stern experiences of converse lives,
The linked woes of many a fiery change
Had purified, and chastened, and made free.
Always there stood before him, night and day,
Of wayward vary-coloured circumstance
The imperishable presences serene,
Colossal, without form, or sense, or sound,
Dim shadows, but unwaning presences
Fourfaced to four corners of the sky : [1]
And yet again, three shadows, fronting one,
One forward, one respectant, three but one ;
And yet again, again and evermore,
For the two first were not, but only seemed,
One shadow in the midst of a great light,
One reflex from eternity on time,
One mighty countenance of perfect calm,
Awful with most invariable eyes.
For him the silent congregated hours,
Daughters of time, divinely tall, beneath
Severe and youthful brows, with shining eyes
Smiling a godlike smile (the innocent light
Of earliest youth pierced through and through with all
Keen knowledges of low-embowèd eld)
Upheld, and ever hold aloft the cloud
Which droops lowhung on either gate of life,
Both birth and death : he in the centre fixt,
Saw far on each side through the grated gates
Most pale and clear and lovely distances.
He often lying broad awake, and yet
Remaining from the body, and apart
In intellect and power and will,[2] hath heard
Time flowing in the middle of the night,
And all things creeping to a day of doom.
How could ye know him ?  Ye were yet within
The narrower circle : he had wellnigh reached
The last, which with a region of white flame,
Pure without heat, into a larger air
Upburning, and an ether of black blue,
Investeth and ingirds all other lives.

[1] Compare with the *Ode* on Wellington.
[2] These three lines favour the poet's idea of spiritualism.

Tennyson's process of refining his poems, of incessantly polishing and improving lines, is one to which we scarcely like to accord praise ; and yet its effects were so wonderfully good that we cannot regret the labour which produced them. Whether a poet writes in a frenzy, or whether he toils tediously and mechanically to produce something worthy, it is the actual result which must be ultimately regarded, and upon that, and that alone, judgment will be passed. The end always justifies the means. A pleasant fancy may be destroyed when we see the poet or the artist or the inventor in his workshop, and watch his many devices to bring to perfection a poem with ringing lines, a picture of glowing colour, a novelty to make time or distance of no account. But, after all, the composer and the inventor are but workmen, and we must permit them to labour at their schemes like others who are busy with hand and brain. Shakespeare was a great refiner, and had he not engaged in alteration and revision the world would have lost the richness and beauty of much that he wrote. There is a common but entirely erroneous idea that poets, in a fit of inspiration, " dash off " sublime compositions in a complete condition needing no further amendment or elaboration. Yet Wordsworth was not ashamed to tell a young friend that he often spent three weeks over a few lines, and Mr Russell Lowell declared that the poet revised his early work so frequently that he destroyed all its interest as a juvenile production.[1] If Gray was seven years writing his *Elegy*, has not the world the advantage ? Genius is "an infinite capacity for taking pains," and we need not be surprised when we learn that Tennyson re-wrote *Come into the Garden, Maud*, over fifty times, or that *Locksley Hall* cost him six weeks' continuous labour. Tennyson was a hard and a slow worker—almost a drudge. He devoted hours

---

[1] When Emerson first visited Wordsworth he told the poet '' how much the few printed extracts had quickened the desire to possess his unpublished poems. He replied he never was in haste to publish ; partly, because he corrected a good deal, and every alteration is ungraciously received after printing.— *English Traits.*

and hours to the smallest details.   A good example is supplied by the short dedicatory poem *To the Queen*, every verse of which has been altered—almost every line—and one verse, originally published, suppressed.   Colonel John Hay, who possesses the original manuscript, says—"The first verse is completely transformed by subsequent interlineations and erasures, being erected by magic touches from a quatrain of commonplace prose, such as you or I or anybody might write, into the radiant jewel of poetry that it is. The first two words in the original version are ' Revered Victoria,' a weak salutation indeed.   In another verse we have a touch of sycophancy as well as of commonplace, both of which disappear under revision, the first reading—

> And if your greatness and the care
>   That yokes with splendour yield you time
>   To seek in this, your Laureate's rhyme,
> For aught of good that can be there,

and the amended copy reading, very much improved,

> And should your greatness and the care
>   That yokes with empire yield you time
>   To make demand of modern rhyme,
> If aught of ancient worth be there."

When the original manuscript of this poem was sold in June 1889 two verses were found not published in the revised edition.   The first of these (No. 3 in the MS.) ran thus—

> Nor should I dare to flatter state,
>   Nor such a lay would you receive
>   Were I to shape it, who believe
> Your nature true as you are great.

The second verse refers to the Crystal Palace, and has lost much of its significance.   The last line, also, is weak.

> She brought a vast design to pass
>   When Europe and the scatter'd ends
>   Of our fierce world were mixt as friends
> And brethren in her halls of glass.

In the first edition, "were mixt as friends" appeared as "did meet as friends."   It was this manuscript which contained a concluding note to the publisher asking if the "yous and yours and hers" ought not to be in capitals.[1]

The manuscript of *The Daisy* contained very few alterations, but the stanzas to the Rev. F. D. Maurice had been much improved, while several verses had been obliterated from *Maud.* One of those deleted verses ran—

> What use for a single mouth to rage
> At the rotten creak of the State machine,
> Though it makes friends weep and enemies smile
> That here in the face of a watchful age
> The sons of a gray-beard-ridden isle,
> Should dance in a round of old routine,
> While a few great families lead the reels,
> And pauper manhood lies in the dirt,
> And Fawn and Wealth with gilded heels
> Trample service and tried desert.

The verse might not have strengthened the poem, but it would have been thoroughly in keeping with the tone of despair and vexation in the opening portions.

How, by re-casting a poem, Tennyson could make it more animated and beautiful, can be seen in the two following examples. The lyric in *The Princess* commencing

> Thy voice is heard through rolling drums
> That beat to battle where he stands,

originally was in this form—

> When all among the thundering drums
> The soldier in the battle stands,
> Thy face across his fancy comes,
> And gives the battle to his hands.

Yet another version was—

> Lady, let the rolling drums
> Beat to battle where thy warrior stands ;
> Now thy face across his fancy comes,
> And gives the battle to his hands.
>
> Lady, let the trumpets blow,
> Clasp thy little babes about thy knee :
> Now their warrior father meets the foe,
> And strikes him dead for thine and thee.

[1] See page 347.

Neither of these versions is worthy to rank beside that which now appears. Take again the famous song, also from *The Princess*, " Home they brought her warrior dead." The original poem stood thus—

> Home they brought him slain with spears,
>   They brought him home at even-fall.
> All alone she sits and hears
>   Echoes in his empty hall,
>     Sounding on the morrow.
>
> The sun peep'd in from open field,
>   The boy began to leap and prance,
>   Rode upon his father's lance,
> Beat upon his father's shield—
>   " O hush, my joy, my sorrow."

How infinitely superior was the afterthought. Both the poet and his readers were gainers by such excisions and emendations as were made time after time.

> Poets lose half the praise they should have got,
> Could it be known what they discreetly blot,

said Waller, and Tennyson deserves thanks for ever striving to give the world his best, even at the risk of drawing too much attention to his process of workmanship. The first drafts of a poem may be rough and crude, and it is decidedly interesting to observe how a mere hint may be caught up and used with powerful effect, how a colourless detail assumes shape and hue under the master's hand, how the nugget of thought is made to gleam as the refiner fits it into place and prepares it for use. A year or two ago Mr Aubrey de Vere sent to the State Library of Iowa a Tennysonian manuscript containing sixteen stanzas of the *Two Voices*. The chirography was described as " very clear, correct, and beautiful," and the number of corrections was small. But " distant " in the line, " The distant battle flasht and rung," was originally " swaying," and the words " a merely selfish " in the line " Nor in a merely selfish cause," were " an honourable." A more important alteration had

been made midway between these two lines, for the
stanza—

> To search thro' all I felt and saw
> The springs of life, the depths of awe,
> And reach the law within the law,

was a substitution for, and transformation of,

> To search the law within the law,
> The soul of what I felt and saw,
> The springs of life, the depths of awe.

There had also been a change in the order of the verses,
for the stanza had originally preceded the one it now
follows. Only Tennyson himself could have realised the
necessity of this.

In regard to minor changes, the alteration of single words
and single lines, the excellent work done by the author
of *Tennysoniana* can scarcely be bettered. It is almost
a tedious task to trace the multitudinous revisions, yet to
the student such labour has its compensations and advantages. Whoso cares to read the original *Lady of Shalott*
side by side with the present version will have some conception of the extraordinary pains Tennyson must have
taken in choosing and rejecting mere words, in pruning
lines, and in introducing new stanzas. No fewer than
seventy lines are new or changed. The last verse is an
addition, and takes the place of one much inferior.—

> They crossed themselves, their stars they blest,
> Knight, minstrel, abbot, squire, and guest ;
> There lay a parchment on her breast,
> That puzzled more than all the rest—
> The well-fed wits at Camelot.
> " The web was woven curiously,
> The charm is broken utterly ;
> Draw near and fear not, this is I,
> The Lady of Shalott."

On several occasions the poet changed his mind again and
again, and re-inserted poems which he had previously rejected, or re-admitted lines in their original form and

abandoned a later revision.   He excluded, for instance, the second verse of the lyric, "As thro' the land at eve we went,"—

> And blessings on the falling out,
>   That all the more endears,
> When we fall out with those we love,
>   And kiss again with tears !

and after some years suddenly and unexpectedly included it again.   The re-admission secured popular approval.   On the other hand, we should be sorry to find the introduction to *A Dream of Fair Women* or *The Miller's Daughter* inserted afresh, and we can dispense with those portions of the *Palace of Art* which only served to enrage the *Quarterly* reviewer.

Although *In Memoriam* was the work of so many years it was only long after its publication that it was brought to its present condition of verbal excellence.   There are something like forty minor corrections and improvements, some of them only consisting of a change of tense, or an altered preposition or conjunction, but nevertheless deemed essential by the nice sense of the poet.   There were also additions to be made, sections xxxix. and lix. (as now numbered) not appearing in the original edition.   No poem was too small for the poet's attention, and no poem was too great to escape his further consideration.   He inserted new lines, erased old ones, chose better words, amended phrases, and thus did all that skill and art could accomplish to make the work of his life flawless and enduring.   How marvellous was the change wrought may be best understood by comparing the opening lines of *Œnone*, published in the 1833 volume, with those which appeared in the volume of 1842.   Originally the first passage was—

> There is a dale in Ida, lovelier
> Than any in Ionia, beautiful
> With emerald slopes of sunny sward, that lean
> Above the loud glen river, which hath worn
> A path thro' steep-down granite walls below,
> Mantled with flowering tendril twine.

And this has since been expanded into—

> There lies a vale in Ida, lovelier
> Than all the valleys of Ionian hills.
> The swimming vapour slopes athwart the glen,
> Puts forth an arm, and creeps from pine to pine,
> And loiters, slowly drawn.   On either hand
> The lawns and meadow ledges midway down
> Hang rich in flowers, and far below them roars
> The long brook fall'n thro' the cloven ravine
> In cataract after cataract to the sea.

Take another instance of scrupulous care in polishing what was written.  In the *Morte d'Arthur*, 1842, appeared the two lines—

> Then went Sir Bedivere the second time,
> Counting the dewy pebbles, fix'd in thought.

In the eighth edition, 1853, the line had been added, and placed between—

> Across the ridge and paced beside the mere,

simply a luxury supplied out of the poet's affluence.  But Tennyson could be no less painstaking in his excisions.  It may have been something of a sacrifice to him to withdraw those five powerful lines from the *Ode* on Wellington which run—

> Perchance our greatness will increase ;
> Perchance a darkening future yields
> Some reverse from worse to worse,
> The blood of men in quiet fields,
> And sprinkled on the sheaves of peace.

Boswell, quoting Johnson, said that "amendments are seldom made without some token of a rent," but so skilful and judicious a workman as Tennyson was not likely thus to impair the fabric which he wrought.  His revisions may best be likened to the addition of ornaments or to the placing of original beauties in a clearer light.  He had a keen eye for the radiance, and a sensitive ear for the melody, of words.  This is why the poems are magically bright and mystically musical.  Well might Emerson declare that no one had a finer ear, nor more command of "the keys of language" than Alfred Tennyson.

# CHAPTER XVII.

## WAS TENNYSON AN ORIGINAL POET?

> " He thought that nothing new was said, or else
> Something so said 'twas nothing—that a truth
> Looks freshest in the fashion of the day."
>
> —*The Epic.*

READERS of the *Poems by Two Brothers*, published by
Alfred and Charles Tennyson in 1827, cannot have failed
to observe that the youthful poets were particularly susceptible to the influences of those ancient and modern
writers whom they admired. They had brooded over the
works of Horace, of Virgil, of Lucretius, of Cicero, and of
Juvenal; of Byron, of Cowper, of Beattie, of Milton, and
of Gray. Out of the hundred and three poems, no fewer
than sixteen are prefaced with mottoes from Homer,
while scholiast-wise, the two brothers had supplied in an
abundance of footnotes the classical authority for their
statements, and explanations of their allusions. Thus the
faculty of imitation was speedily developed, and the boy-
poets who had admitted in their preface that "it were no
easy task to light upon any novel combination of images,
or to open any vein of sparkling thought untouched
before," were content to adopt styles and methods from
which they had derived pleasure, and which they deemed
worthy of perpetuation. They plucked a few pinions from
the wings of others wherewith they themselves might soar,
and they succeeded in making a very respectable though
in nowise a noteworthy first flight. By examining the
*Poems by Two Brothers*, we learn with some exactness the
course of reading the writers had pursued, and we discover
under whose spell they had fallen. And this little volume

supplies a clue to the whole of the Laureate's literary work. Like Montaigne he could say, "I number not my borrowings, but I weigh them." It is evidence of his disposition to trust to others, to seek suggestion, to gather the threads of olden thought and weave them into new and brighter patterns of truth. Lord Tennyson worked from well-recognised models. He invented but little ; his was not the gift of creating but of reproducing. No one can surpass him in literary workmanship, and the stamp of his individuality is impressed upon all that he did. He uttered old thoughts, but the utterance is new. It rings out clearly, and surprises the ear with its delightful cadence. Often when he re-introduced an ancient truth he adorned it with the jewellery of magic words, and vestured it in sumptuous apparel. But the fact remains that he never told a new story or constructed an original plot ; his wisdom was centuries old, and his imagery would be deemed trite but for its splendour and its charm.

> Shadows haunting fairily
> The brain, new stuffed in youth, with triumphs gay
> Of old romance,

as Keats sang, have always been the Laureate's stock-in-trade.

"I assume," wrote Bayard Taylor, "that Tennyson's studies in literature have been very thorough and general, for I have been surprised by suggestions of his lines in the most unexpected places. Every author is familiar with the insidious way in which old phrases or images, which have preserved themselves in the mind, but forgotten their origin, will quietly slip into places where the like of them is needed." I do not think Tennyson ever wished to be considered an original thinker. May he not have been expressing a secret conviction when he wrote *The Epic ?*

> He thought that nothing new was said, or else
> Something so said 'twas nothing—that a truth
> Looks freshest in the fashion of the day.

X

The most casual reader will speedily recognise that Tennyson, as Socrates said of himself, was " but the mid-wife of men's thoughts."   The longest prose letter he is ever known to have written was penned to defend himself from a charge of plagiarism.[1]   But Tennyson is not a plagiarist, and those who understand him best will be the last to consider him such.   From first to last he confined himself to the task of casting truth into new moulds, of enduing it with new significance, of bringing it into a purer light.   He coins delicious phrases, which pass into current speech ; he vivifies ancient wisdom, rescues thoughts in danger of perishing in a dead tongue, and restores in richer beauty the crumbling fabrics of past philosophy. This is no unworthy mission.   The truth which in its primitive state existed in a rough but serviceable shell he presented in a golden casket, and the whole world, attracted, hastened to accept it.   We welcome the gift that Tennyson offered, not because it was new, but because it enchanted the sense either with delicate gleams of light or the ripple of delicious melody.   The novelty in literature is, as Pope defined it, " what oft was thought but ne'er so well expressed."   Judged by this standard we might even rank Tennyson, had he desired it, among the archetypal chiefs.

But whoso has the advantage of a complete set of the Laureate's works will be able, picking up each volume in turn, to say—" This shows the influence of Spenser, this of Keats, this of Shelley, this of Byron, this of the classical Greek and Roman writers."   It will be remembered that Lytton in his furious and afterward-regretted onslaught on his young rival for the laurel crown, caustically wrote—

> Not mine, not mine (O Muse forbid ! ) the boon
> Of *borrowed notes*, the mock-bird's modish tune,
> *The jingling medley of purloined conceits,*
> Out-babying Wordsworth, and out-glittering Keats,
> Where all the airs of patchwork-pastoral chime
> To drowsy ears in Tennysonian rhyme.

[1] See Appendix B.

The "purloin'd conceits" were not an imagined fault upon which to indict the poet.   At that time Tennyson had published two volumes.   One of the best-known and most admired of the poems was *Mariana* with its mournful refrain.   The motif of that poem (putting aside the single line in *Measure for Measure*) may surely be found in Robert Henryson's *From the Testament of Cresseid*, be-ginning—

> Thus chiding with her dreary destiny,
> Weeping, she woke the night from end to end,
> But all in vain : her dole, her careful cry,
> Might not remëid, nor yet her mourning mend.

Tennyson was fond of the lyrics of old English writers in those days.   In Skelton's *Isabell* and *To Mistress Margaret Hussey* he appears to have found at least a hint for his poem-pictures of female beauty.   "His early poems showed a considerable amount of intellectual struggle," wrote Bayard Taylor.   "We find in them traces of the influence of Milton, Shelley, and Barry Cornwall, but very rarely of Keats, of whom Tennyson has been called singularly enough, the lineal poetical child.[1]   Indeed he and Keats have little in common except the sense of luxury in words, which was born with both, and could not be outgrown.   But the echoes of Shelley, in the poems afterwards omitted from the volume which Tennyson published in 1830, are not to be mistaken.   Take this stanza as an example :—

> The varied earth, the moving heaven,
>   The rapid waste of roving sea,
> The fountain-pregnant mountains riven
>   To shapes of wildest anarchy,
> By secret fire and midnight storms
>   That wander round their windy cones,
> The subtle life, the countless forms
>   Of living things, the wondrous tones

---

[1] In 1889 a correspondent, in reply to an inquiry, received an autograph note from Tennyson—"Keats and Horace were great masters, but not my masters."

> Of man and beast, are full of strange
> Astonishment and boundless change.

The sign-manual of Barry Cornwall is even more distinctly set in the following :—

> When will the stream be aweary of flowing
> Under my eye?
> When will the wind be aweary of blowing
> Over the sky?
> When will the clouds be aweary of fleeting?
> When will the heart be aweary of beating,
> And nature die?
>
> Never, oh ! never, nothing will die :
> The stream flows,
> The wind blows,
> The cloud fleets,
> The heart beats :
> Nothing will die.

The poems from which these stanzas are taken, as well as *The Burial of Love, Hero and Leander,* and *Elegiacs* are written from the inspiration which dwells in melody and rhythm : the latter is not a wholly unsuccessful attempt to add rhyme to the classic elegiac metre :—

Creeping through blossomy rushes and bowers of rose-blowing
> bushes,
> Down by the poplar tall, rivulets babble and fall.
Barketh the shepherd-dog cheerly ; the grasshopper carolleth clearly ;
> Deeply the turtle coos ; shrilly the owlet halloos ;
Winds creep : dews fall chilly : in her first sleep earth breathes stilly :
> Over the pools in the burn water-gnats murmur and mourn.
Sadly the far kine loweth : the glimmering water outfloweth :
> Twin peaks shadowed with pine slope to the dark hyaline.
Low-throned Hesper is stayed between the two peaks : but the Naiad
> Throbbing in wild unrest holds him beneath in her breast.

Here the conception, as a picture, is so obscure that two different landscapes are suggested. Yet in the fragment we seem to discover the seed out of which Swinburne's poetry might have germinated. Where, then, shall we look for the seed of Tennyson's? I do not refer to imitation or even to unconscious influence; but there is usually something in each generation of poets—

often some slight, seemingly accidental form of utterance
—which, in the following generation expands into a characteristic quality. Examples of poetry written for pure
delight in sound and movement are rare before Shelley's
day ; and his influence upon Tennyson was very transient.
Before him no poet dared to use sound and metre in the
same manner as the architect and sculptor use form, and
the painter form and colour."

Mr Churton Collins in his *Illustrations of Tennyson*, a
work of the most scholarly character, finds traces of Shelley
in the Laureate's *Isabel*, but they are very slight. Thorough
as Mr Collins's work is, and valuable as every student will
find it, there are—as was inevitable—omissions which
another traversing the same path will be sure to remark.
Mr Collins had set himself a great task, and he fulfilled it
with infinite credit to himself. Every page bears evidence
of his rare scholarship and his indefatigable zeal. He has
left but little for others to do, especially in tracking
Tennyson along devious ways to the classical source of
his inspiration. But, if anything, Mr Collins has overlooked the importance of the Laureate's English reading,
and this portion of Mr Collins's works can be supplemented.
I can but hope, however, to assist in completing what
perhaps can never be complete.

Starting with the assumption that Tennyson's mastery
is in assimilative skill, Mr Collins has devoted many pages
to proving that the poet chose Virgil for a guide. But his
English model was Edmund Spenser, and, through him,
his two best disciples, Shelley and Keats. Recent com-
mentators have shown to what an extent the Laureate has
been indebted to Shakespeare for words, allusions, and
thoughts ; and the Rev. George Lester in his volume[1] has
given no fewer than four hundred and fifty Biblical parallels.
Mr Collins, it will be found, entirely ignores this part of
his subject, and he deals inadequately with Spenser and
Shelley.

<hr>

[1] *Tennyson and the Bible.* By the Rev. George Lester.

In that section of the Laureate's works known as *Juvenilia*, there are several pieces of which Mr Collins has failed to detect the prototypes, and he has not allowed for the all-pervading influence of the author of *Prometheus Unbound*. That Tennyson had absorbed the beauties, and some of the mannerisms, of this matchless poem, a hundred instances, seeming trifles in themselves, could be made to prove. Here and there only a word or a line, a hint subtly conveyed in passing, or a casual allusion, has sufficed for the poet in search of a theme. These minutiæ cannot be considered now, and they only serve, when accumulated, to signalise a discovery which can be made by a more direct process.

Tennyson conceived the Kraken "battening upon huge sea-worms in his sleep," but Shelley had spoken of "the dull weed some huge sea-worm battens on." The sea-fairies with their "Sweet faces, rounded arms, and bosoms prest To little harps of gold," were surely kin to

> The Nereids under the green sea
> Their white arms lifted o'er their streaming hair,
> With garlands pied and starry sea-flower crowns.

The now-suppressed poem, "Oh sad No More! Oh sweet No More," seems to have had its central idea drawn from Shelley's *Lament;* while the leaping fountain, in the Poet's mind,

> Like sheet lightning
> Ever brightening,

might have been the fountain of Shelley's which

> Leaps . . . with an awakening sound,
> And there is heard the ever-morning air
> Whispering without from tree to tree, and birds
> And bees.

Again, "bright as light and clear as wind" is reminiscent of Shelley's "light and wind within some delicate cloud"; while the Laureate's *Eleänore* is but a beautiful elaboration of Shelley's stanzas *To Constantia*.

On the other hand, it is worthy of note that a poet and
a poetess of the first rank are indebted to Tennyson for
themes and thoughts from this early volume of his lyrics,
Mr Russell Lowell having closely followed him in *The
Sirens*, and Mrs Browning having crystallised the ideas of
*The Ode to Memory* in her sonnet on *The Poet*.  And, in
regard to Mrs Browning, it is fair to ask whether she has
not annexed the idea of Tennyson's *Palace of Art* in her
*House of Clouds*.

> I would build a cloudy House
> For my thoughts to live in,
> When for earth too fancy loose
> And too low for heaven,

is but a slight variation in thought and treatment of the
Laureate's " sort of allegory."   But Tennyson cannot complain, for Mr Collins finds "the framework" of the poem
was fashioned in the *Book of Ecclesiastes*, while his pictures
are copies, not inferior to the originals, but copies notwithstanding.

One of the most hackneyed of Tennysonian lines is

> 'Tis only noble to be good,

which of course is old as virtue itself, and has found expression a thousand times.   Mr Collins traces it to
Menander, but surely it is more likely that the poet was
only repeating a line in the *Percy Reliques*—

> And to be noble we 'll be good.

As for the " claims of long descent," has not the dramatist
Rowe made one of his characters scorn them in the
words ?—

> Were honour to be scann'd by long descent
> From ancestors illustrious, I could claim
> A lineage of the greatest.

It will always be more or less a matter of speculation to

whom Tennyson is most indebted for the ideas and the style of *The Lotos-Eaters*. Mr Collins finds four operative influences, the most potent being those of Spenser and Thomson. To these may be added Shelley; while Dr Bayne believes that the poet derived his suggestion from *The Songs of the Fates*, repeated by Iphigenie at the end of the fourth act of Goethe's drama. "The gods," he says, "are therein described as sitting at golden tables, in everlasting feast, or striding along from peak to peak of the mountains, while up through gorge and chasm streams to them, like clouds of altar-smoke, the breath of strangled Titans." This is going too far afield, as well as overstraining the facts. Reference to Thomson and Spenser is perfectly conclusive; and as Mr Collins has quoted from *The Castle of Indolence*, I will confine my illustration to a single verse from the *Faëry Queen*—a verse which is itself a key to Tennyson's lyrical style:

> And, more to lull him in his slumber soft,
> A trickling stream from high rock tumbling down
> And ever drizzling rain upon the loft,
> Mixt with the murmuring wind much like the soun [sound]
> Of swarming bees did cast him in a swoon,
> No other noise, nor people's troublous cries,
> As still are wont to annoy the wallèd town,
> Might there be heard : but careless quiet lies
> Wrapt in eternal silence far from enemies.

Spenser has been constituted "the poet's poet." Milton did not disdain to learn from him, and Jonson wrote in his praise. His influence extends over a wide range of literature, and his lyrical effluence percolates through the poetry of the centuries that followed him. He gave words, dignity, sentiment, and form to the many who were not ashamed to be called his disciples. To read the poetry of the seventeenth, eighteenth, and nineteenth centuries, is to read in varied style what Spenser inspired and what Spenser exemplified. It is an old saying that all began in Homer, and certainly we can trace back point by point the succession of thought, as the traveller can trace back peak by peak the extent of a mountain-chain. We need not take into account the smaller pinnacles; the towering heights mark with unbroken regularity the wonder we would know. Giant intellects uplifted above the level of everything that lacks genius rise in stately progression, and we trace with ease the connection of Chaucer and Spenser, Milton and Shakespeare, Dryden and Wordsworth, Keats and Shelley, and the heir of all those ages—Tennyson. Spenser himself was a great borrower. In his methods as well as in his life the poet of our time who has just passed away resembled him. The poet-life lived apart, the poet-necromancy, with "heavenly alchemy" transmuting the real into the ideal, the poet-mystery clothing life with the strange and beauteous robes of wonder and fancy, the poet-wealth glorifying every theme, illuminating every text, and stringing pearls of truth and jewels of wit on old tradition :—are not these the character and attributes alike of the singer who won the praise of Elizabeth, and of the singer who won the laurel from Victoria? Each is a consummate artist ; each has given us truths in allegory ; each has enriched the language with majestic words, each has taught that beauty is holiness and that purity is joy. Yet neither possesses fundamental ideas, and they devoted themselves to brightening truths that had grown dull or had never shone with sufficient lustre. The object of the *Faëry Queen* was "to fashion a gentleman of noble person in virtuous and gentle discipline."

> Abroad in arms, at home in studious kind,
> Who seeks with painful toil shall Honour soonest find.

The object of the *Idylls of the King* was to restore the old chivalry, to make men faithful and pure-hearted, haters of wrong—

> To break the heathen and uphold the Christ.

Tennyson never invented a plot. The stories he tells are all old—*Dora, Godiva, Lady Clare, Enoch Arden, The*

*Lover's Tale, Voyage of Maeldune,* and the dramas, with perhaps the exception of the *Promise of May.* Then there are familiar love-pieces requiring no definite plot. Such are the *Miller's Daughter, Edwin Morris, Locksley Hall,* and *Edward Gray.* Even in a simple song the poet still preferred a theme chosen by another. "Home they brought her warrior dead" is merely a paraphrase of Scott's lines, but Scott had taken the idea from an Anglo-Saxon fragment.[1] Mr Collins has found a trace of Homer in *Love thou thy Land,* but he does not appear to know that this poem, along with *You ask me why tho' ill at ease* is merely a speech of James Spedding's cast into rhyme! In like manner Tennyson laid the speeches of Arthur Hallam under contribution, and thus Sir Henry Taylor was led to remark that he doubted Tennyson's competency to form opinions on political questions.

The *English Idylls* are admittedly "faint Homeric echoes." But this is not all. The echoes come from all sides. Mr Collins traces them back to a score or more of the world's great singers, but he does not exhaust the list. In *Ulysses* we read—

> How dull it is to pause, to make an end,
> To rust unburnish'd, not to shine in use !
> As tho' to breathe were life.

The idea is old enough. Massinger wrote in *The Maid of Honour*—

> Virtue, if not in action, is a vice.
> And, when we move not forward, we go backward ;
> Nor is this peace, the nurse of drones and cowards,
> Our health, but a disease.

In the same poem Tennyson writes—"I am a part of all that I have met," which is identical with an expression of Byron's ; and to this poet he is also indebted for the thought —"Strange good that must arise from out Its deadly opposite." Certain lines in *Locksley Hall* have been the subject of much contention, and with all diffidence I must confess

---

[1] See *The Lay of the Last Minstrel,* canto i. part ix.

that I cannot agree with some of the conclusions arrived at. The germ of the slight story may, perhaps, be found in Shelley's *Stanzas, April* 1814—a wild, passionate outburst with a dark suggestion of hopeless love and bitter estrangement. But it is to individual lines that I wish more particularly to direct attention.

Gold . . . gilds the straitened forehead of the fool,

though common as a thought, is evidently refined by Tennyson from the observation of Feltham—"Gold is the fool's curtain, which hides all his defects from the world." The pretty conceit, " Whom to look at was to love," may have been abstracted from Burns's lines *To Nancy*, but it must not be forgotten that Rogers and Scott also used the phrase. Mr Collins has found a parallel to

Our spirits rush'd together at the touching of the lips

in Guarini's *Pastor Fido*, which I should not be surprised to hear was unknown to Tennyson. Is it not more likely that the poet once more had recourse to Shelley, or was unconsciously reproducing the thought in that charming line—

When soul meets soul on lovers' lips?

There is another line in *Locksley Hall* which merits attention on account of its suggestiveness. Mr Collins is probably justified in attributing

I will take some savage woman, she shall rear my dusky race,

to Beaumont's *Philaster*, although this is not a new and independent discovery. The line in question, however, seems to have formed a text for Thackeray's *Esmond*. In one of the last chapters the hero says—" I am thinking of retiring into the plantations, and building myself a wigwam in the woods, and perhaps, if I want company, suiting myself with a squaw. . . . I may find a place for myself in the New [World] and found a family there. When you are a mother yourself, and a great lady, perhaps I shall send you over from the plantation some day a little barbarian that is half Esmond half Mohock, and you will be kind to him for his father's sake, who was, after all, your kinsman, and whom you loved a little." Is not Esmond's hopeless pursuit of his kinswoman Beatrix like the *Locksley Hall* lover's hopeless pursuit of Cousin Amy? Does not failure arouse in each the same spirit of despair?—are not their circumstances of hope and disappointment the same? The story of *Locksley Hall* is surely the story of *Esmond* without its details. That fine expression,

> A sorrow's crown of sorrow is remembering happier things,

is only Tennyson's own by reason of its excellence, for the idea has filtered through Chaucer, Dante, Boethius, and half-a-dozen others. Mr Collins can generally be depended upon to find what is both recondite and remote ; but while directing his telescope to far-off objects, he not infrequently forgets that there are objects close at hand worthy of his attention. Tennyson tells us that he was indebted to a poet for the truth he sang again. To Dante, therefore, must be ascribed the honour of supplying the thought which he re-fashioned and beautified. But Tennyson was not the first Englishman who had clothed the idea in English speech, for Henry Brooke in his *History of the Man of Letters* had anticipated him with the following rendering—" I imagine that the recollection of past happiness rather heightens than alleviates the sense of present distress." There is one other passage which has also become Tennyson's by merit, but which has experienced endless permutation—

> I held it truth, with him who sings
> To one clear harp in divers tones,
> That men may rise on stepping-stones
> Of their dead selves to higher things.

The poet alluded to is Goethe," says Mr Collins, "though there is no reference to any particular passage, but to his general teaching." For this curious declaration Mr Collins has the authority of Lord Tennyson himself, who wrote to a correspondent—"As far as I can recollect, I referred to Goethe." But let us look at the history of the thought. It seems to have originated, or at all events to have taken concrete form, in one of the sermons of St Augustine— "De vitiis nostris scalam nobis facimus si vitia ipsa calcamus." In the Sanskrit, line 1085 of the Hit'opadésa, the same idea occurs—

By their own deeds men ascend, and by their own deeds men do fall,
Like the diggers of a well, and like the builders of a wall.

Longfellow acknowledges St Augustine as his authority for writing—

> Of our vices we can frame
> A ladder, if we will but tread
> Beneath our feet each deed of shame.

Coventry Patmore, in the *Angel in the House*, has slightly varied the thought in the words—

> One dead joy appears
> The platform of some better hope.

Mr Russell Lowell, following the original more closely, has written—

> 'Tis sorrow builds the ladder up,
> Whose golden rounds are our calamities.

Instances might be multiplied, and we have therefore to decide whether we can trust to Tennyson's vague "recollection," or whether we should not decide for ourselves that the poet, as others have done, was recalling the passage which can be identified and with which he must have been familiar.

Lord Beaconsfield wisely said in *Lothair*, that the "originality of a subject is in its treatment." Consequently no apology is needed for showing how the Laureate, like the Stephen of one of his later poems, "coined into English gold some treasures of classical song." It is commonly supposed that the idea of *The Princess* was suggested in the concluding portion of *Rasselas*, but if so (as Mr Collins thinks) Tennyson constructed his masterpiece upon a very poor and frail basis. It is said that in 1662 the Duchess of Newcastle aired the idea of a university with "prudes for proctors, dowagers for dons." But putting this aside as being probably unknown to the poet, I venture to think that in *The Princess* he was catching up some of the wild, plausible doctrines expounded in the *Revolt of Islam*, and that his object was to enforce their impracticability.[1]

> Woman ! she is a slave, she has become
>   A thing I weep to speak—the child of scorn,
> The outcast of a desolated home      .      .
>
>   .      .      .      .  .  .      .      .
> This need not be.

Princess Ida is engaged in a struggle against convention. "You men have done it: how I hate you all!" is the cry of Lilia.   And the poet's aim is to teach that

> In the long years liker must they grow ;
> The man be more of woman, she of man.

Ida was but the Cythna of a later day.   And whereas the Princess asked—

> If she be small, slight-natured, miserable,
> How shall men grow ?—

Cythna had put the question in another form—

> Can men be free if woman be a slave ?

This, indeed, was a text from which both Tennyson and Shelley preached, and I cannot resist the conclusion that one poem resolves itself into a sequel of the other.   Mr Collins points out, and my own notes, if reproduced, would supply confirmation, that throughout *The Princess* there are reminiscences of Shelley.   The same images are employed, the same thoughts are introduced and re-discussed; only, while Shelley always soars away into idealism, Tennyson, in his materialistic way, strives after sober sense.

[1] See *ante*, pages 65, 66.

One of the most noteworthy of Tennyson's borrowings
—and in this case I had almost ventured to use the
obnoxious word plagiarism—is to be found in connection
with the curious little story related in *The Northern Cobbler.*
Five years before this poem appeared, Mr Robert Crompton published some verses in the Irish dialect entitled
"Facing the Inimy." The story was of a cobbler, and
of how he

> Hammered and stitched and hammered away,
>> Whilst, labelled "Potheen,"
>> A bottle was seen
> On his small window-shelf, that was
>> Painted green.
>
> "That's the Inimy!" Micky Muldoon would say :
>> "May its shadow be never
>> A jot less, for ever !"
> And I noticed the spirit from day to day—
>> It never grew less, no, never !

The explanatory story which follows is exactly, to a
detail, the story that Tennyson has re-told in Lincolnshire
dialect. The Rev. F. Langbridge has pointed this out
in his *Ballads of the Brave,* in which volume Crompton's
verses can be read. Tennyson was charged with plagiarism
when he published *Columbus.* A very strong *prima facie*
case was made out, but I can fortunately give a simple
explanation. The fact is, Lord Tennyson and Mr Ellis
(the poet from whom the Laureate is assumed to have
stolen his ideas) both went to a common source for
inspiration—the diary of Columbus !

*The Charge of the Light Brigade* was modelled upon
Drayton's *Agincourt;* the chess-playing scene[1] in *Becket*
is apparently a close imitation of the chess-playing scene
in Lessing's *Nathan the Wise,* the same trickery with
moves and in the use of names being employed. Tennyson
wrote of "the herd"—

> Wild hearts and feeble wings
> That every sophister can lime ;

---

[1] Tennyson himself was an accomplished chess-player.

and Milton had proclaimed the people—

> But a herd confused,
> A miscellaneous rabble, who extol
> Things vulgar    .    .    .    .
> They praise and they admire they know not what,
> And know not whom, but as one leads the other.

"The little rift within the lute," is obviously Cowper's

> Breach, though small at first, soon opening wide
> In rushes folly with a full-moon tide,

and the same poet seems to have supplied more than the theme of *St Simeon Stylites* in the lines beginning—

> What is all righteousness that men devise ?
> What but a sordid bargain for the skies ?

and followed by that picture of the anchorite—

> His dwelling a recess in some rude rock,
> Book, beads, and maple dish his meagre stock ;
> In shirt of hair and weeds of canvas dress'd,
> Girt with a bell-rope that the Pope has bless'd ;
> Adust with stripes told out for every crime ;
> And sore tormented, long before his time.
>
> .    .    .    .    .    .
>
> See the sage hermit, by mankind admir'd,
> With all that bigotry adopts inspir'd.
> Wearing out life in his religious whim,
> Till his religious whimsy wears out him.

Mr Collins allows very little for Wordsworth's influence in the lyrical portion of *The Brook*. The key-note seems to have been struck in the quatrain—

> Down to the vale this water steers,
>   How merrily it goes ;
> 'Twill murmur on a thousand years,
>   And flow as now it flows.

Tennyson's lines have a more perceptible ripple, but both the poets have tried to "match the water's pleasant tune." Burns did the same, but Wordsworth in one of his sonnets had given Tennyson another idea when he tracked the streamlet "dancing down its *waterbreaks*." In the *Ode* on the death of the Duke of Wellington we find the man praised who

> Gain'd a hundred fights,
> Nor ever lost an English gun,

forcibly reminding us of Massinger's hero, whose "fights and conquests hold one number."

> Not once or twice in our rough island-story
> The path of duty was the way to glory,

was a crystallising of the Iron Duke's own remark on being told that the word "glory" never occurred in his despatches. "If glory had been my object," he said, "the doing my duty must have been the means." Again, in the same poem, the Laureate puts words into the lips of the dead Nelson—

> Who is he that cometh, like an honour'd guest,
> With banner and with music, with soldier and with priest,
> With a nation weeping, and breaking on my rest?

Tickell, writing of Addison's interment in Westminster Abbey, had written—

> Ne'er to these chambers, where the mighty rest,
> Since the foundation came a nobler guest.

Coming to *In Memoriam*, I again find that all the coincidences have not been noted.

> Tears of the widower when he sees
>     A late-lost form which sleep reveals,
>     And moves his doubtful arms and feels
> His place is empty     .     .     .     .

irresistibly reminds one of Milton's pathetic lines—

> Methought I saw my late espoused wife
>
> .     .     .     .     .     .     .     .
>
> But oh! as to embrace me she inclined,
> I waked, she fled, and day brought back my night.

Campbell, in a well-worn phrase, has told us that distance

lends enchantment to the view; Tennyson informs us that
"the past will always win A glory from its being far."
Thackeray twice over wrote that 'twas better to have loved
and lost than never to have loved at all; the second of the
references is usually overlooked—"To love and win is
the best thing, to love and lose is the next best" (*Pendennis*, vol. ii. cap. ii.).  The beautiful stanzas commencing
"Calm is the morn without a sound" is Wordsworth's
sonnet with exquisite variation—

> Calm is all nature as a resting wheel.
>
> .   .   .   .   .   .   .   .
> .   .   .   .   .   .   .   .
>
> Now, in this blank of things, a harmony,
> Home-felt, and home-created, comes to heal
> That grief for which the senses still supply
> Fresh food ; for only then, when memory
> Is hush'd, am I at rest.

Next come the well-known lines—

> There lives more truth in honest doubt,
> Believe me, than in half the creeds.

The most likely parallel is from Bailey's *Festus*—

> Who never doubted, never half believed,
> Where doubt, there truth is—'tis her shadow.[1]

Lastly, there is the section dealing with the mutability of
the things of earth :

> There rolls the deep where grew the tree.
>   O earth, what changes hast thou seen !
>   There where the long street roars, hath been
> The stillness of the central sea.

Tennyson might have come fresh from the reading of
Beattie's lines—

> Art, empire, earth itself to change are doomed ;
> Earthquakes have raised to heaven the humble vale,
> And gulfs the mountain's mighty mass entombed,
> And where the Atlantic rolls wide continents have bloomed.

---

[1] Tennyson was a great admirer of *Festus*.  He said he dare not trust himself to express all that he thought of it.

Two parallels with Emerson's writings are rather striking. Thirty years before Tennyson had stored a mighty truth in those compact lines—

> Little flower . . . if I could understand
> What you are, root and all, and all in all,
> I should know what God and man is,—

the transcendental philosopher had written—

> Through a thousand voices
> Spoke the universal dame :
> Who telleth one of my meanings,
> Is master of all I am.

The Laureate has told us

> We are ancients of the earth,
> And in the morning of the times.

Emerson in his essay on *Politics* had quite as strikingly expressed a like opinion—"We think our civilisation near its meridian, but we are yet only at the cock-crowing and the morning star."

There is danger in pushing these conclusions too far, and were it not that Tennyson's method of working was well understood, there would doubtless be more hesitation in proclaiming the discovery of a "parallel" when probably there is only a mere coincidence. "Are not human eyes all over the world looking at the same objects, and must there not consequently be coincidences of thought and impressions and expressions?" The shells upon the shore of the ocean, Knowledge, are free to all who will gather them ; it is only the pearls of the great deep which the mighty can find, and which to them must belong when found. Tennyson's mission has been to seize upon good ideas conceived in other times, and impart to them a modern aspect. He recommends to our understanding what otherwise we might ignore, and presents in favourable form what in its original state we might have been loth to receive. In his hands ancient dogmas appear as shining truths, he gives splendour to uncouthness, and makes melodious the harsh

utterance of bygone ages.   His spell is irresistible.   Passed
through the Tennysonian sieve the coarse ore of literature is
refined, the dull hue disappears, and touched by his fingers
sparkles with animating fire.   Surely that service is not
small or to be contemned which rescues treasures from the
dust in which they are buried, and skilfully fashions them
into images of rarest beauty.[1]

[1] While this work was passing through the press Mr Harold Littledale's
*Essays on Lord Tennyson's Idylls of the King* was published.   I am disposed
to think that the chief value of the essays will be found in the numerous
parallelisms which Mr Littledale has discovered in the *Idylls*.   He shows
that the poet was specially indebted to Spenser, Milton, Wordsworth, and
Shelley.   (*Vide* pp. 184-191, 235, 297, &c.)   See also *Literary Coincidences*,
by W. A. Clouston (p. 93); *Alfred Tennyson*, by Walter E. Wace (cap. xiv.);
and *Tennysoniana*, by R. H. Shepherd (cap. xi.).   I ought to add that my
own chapter does not traverse the ground already covered in these volumes.

# CHAPTER XVIII.



> " Sallow scraps of manuscript,
> Dating many a year ago."
>
> —*To E. Fitzgerald.*

ALTHOUGH Lord Tennyson spoke slightingly of the "love of letters, overdone," and seemed to regard bibliography as an abused art, he had no reason to regret the interest displayed in the various editions of his works. Enthusiastic collectors have had to pay very dearly for their hobby. The value of the first editions of Tennyson's poems has been constantly rising, and what would seem to the man of the world an extravagant price has been willingly paid to procure those rare slim green volumes which were issued before "popular" editions were contemplated. Possessors of *Poems by Two Brothers*, *Poems chiefly Lyrical*, in two volumes, *In Memoriam* (noted for its dark binding), and of copies of those earliest productions, *Timbuctoo* and *The Lover's Tale*, must deem themselves extremely fortunate. These are the prizes. Not long ago a collection of Tennysoniana was offered for 12 guineas, this being almost at the rate of a guinea a page. There were the original proof-sheets of *The Window; or, the Loves of the Wrens*, with numerous corrections and addenda in the Laureate's own writing. It was doubtless the latter circumstance that made the 13 pages so precious, for the poet's autograph was seldom seen, and even the contents of his waste-paper basket were not permitted to pass into vulgar hands. An edition of Tennyson's poems for 1833 once fetched £26, 10s. ; the *Poems chiefly Lyrical*, in two volumes, 1842,

£64 ;[1] and the *Poems by Two Brothers*, £21, 10s. Some years ago Charles Tennyson's own copy of the last-named, with pencilled notes as to the authorship of each poem, was offered to a gentleman in Birmingham for £7. It would be interesting to know into whose hands this valuable copy has fallen. In 1887, when the library of the late Master of Trinity (Dr Thompson) was sold, some editions of Tennyson found their way into new quarters, among those dispersed being a copy of *The Lover's Tale*, purchased for £64 by Mr Quaritch for a well-known poet ; and there were copies of the volumes for 1827, 1830, 1833, 1842, all of which obtained high prices. Curious to relate, the copy of *The Lover's Tale* (a booklet of 60 pages) was bound at the end of another Tennysonian volume, and had escaped the notice of the cataloguer. Who among Tennyson collectors, however, possesses a copy of the privately-printed edition of *In Memoriam* (1849) ? This is probably the rarest of all editions of the Laureate's works, except *Enid and Nimue; or, The True and the False*, which was printed in 1857, but never actually published.

Now that "complete" editions of Tennyson's works may be expected—that is, as complete as the poet would allow them to be—it may be interesting to place on record a few facts relating to previous issues. The *Poems by Two Brothers*, containing 228 pages, saw the light in 1827, and the volume was never republished, nor was the authorship formally admitted. It was my privilege in 1890 to be the first to describe the original manuscript of these poems, consisting of about 90 pages covered closely with the "screwy" Greek-like caligraphy characteristic of the Tennysons. Jackson of Louth paid £20 for the manuscript : after the poet's death it was sold for £480. A full account of this manuscript is supplied in *In Tennyson Land*, and need not be repeated here. *Timbuctoo*, the Cambridge prize poem, was published in 1829, and was declared to be

---

[1] These prices are altogether exceptional, and must not be taken as the market value. See page 346.

" By A. Tennyson, of Trinity College," while two lines from Chapman prefaced it—

> " Deep in that lion-haunted inland lies
> A mystic city, goal of high emprise."

*Poems chiefly Lyrical,* a thin volume of 154 pages, in a buff cover, was issued from the press by Effingham Wilson, in 1830. It was almost unheeded, save by the poet's friends, but three years later the re-issue of the poems gave the *Quarterly* reviewer his chance. In after years the poems were rigidly revised ; others were suppressed, and of these a few were not permitted to be re-inserted until Messrs Macmillan published an eight-volume edition of the poet's works in 1887. The "afterthought" so often exercised by the Laureate in regard to the publication of doubtful pieces was represented by the inclusion of the *Leonine Elegiacs, The Confessions of a second-rate sensitive mind, Rosalind,* and a few others which have only intermittently appeared. The series of "portraits" in the first volume is still incomplete by reason of the omission of *Kate—* Kate who is known by her "angry air," who "sayeth what she will "—the "woman-soldier, gallant Kate, As pure and true as blades of steel." The "note" originally affixed to *Rosalind* has disappeared too—thirty-three lines that are decidedly worth reading, though " manifestly improper" as part of the text.

Anyone who has examined the several editions of Tennyson cannot but have been struck with the extremely modest way in which they made their appearance. The set of these green-covered volumes looks so unobtrusive that it stands revealed that no art of the printer or binder was employed to make its poetic merit known. "Poems, by Alfred Tennyson, in two volumes," runs the title of the famous edition issued by Edward Moxon in 1842. Turning another leaf we simply find the announcement, " Poems (published 1830)." It was this edition of 1842 which secured Tennyson's recognition as a poet. Nevertheless it contained some weak verses, notably *The Skipping Rope,* happily now suppressed.   At the end of Volume I. is the following note :—" The second division of this volume was published in the winter of 1832.  Some of the poems have been considerably altered, others have been added, which, with one exception, were written in 1833."  In 1848 the first one-volume edition of the poems was published, and in the same year *The Princess*, published in 1847, passed through a second edition.  This gave the Laureate an opportunity of dedicating that noble work to Mr Henry Lushington, and of making a few emendations in the text.

The style in which Moxon published the successive works of Tennyson was followed by the firms to whom the poet afterwards transferred his publications.  Mr Moxon, we have it on the authority of Miss Mitford, thought Tennyson " a great torment, keeping proofs a fortnight to alter, and then sending for revises."  Nevertheless, he declared that Tennyson was the only poet by whom he had never lost money.  It was he who printed *The Lover's Tale* in 1833 ; he saw the *Poems*, published in 1842, pass through eight editions ; and he published in turn *The Princess, in Memoriam, Maud*, and *The Idylls of the King.*  Then, after Sir Ivor Bertie Guest (now Lord Wimborne) had printed *The Window* at his private press, Strahan and Co. became Tennyson's publishers, and his connection with them is chiefly notable on account of their assistance in bringing to justice the American " pirates."  In 1872 Messrs Strahan published a handsome library edition of the poet's works, bound in green, and printed on superb paper in large type.  In the first of the volumes it is stated that the edition would be complete " in five volumes," but on the title page of the fifth is the correction, " in six volumes."  Six volumes there are, accordingly, although no doubt only five were originally in contemplation.  Such instances of printers' miscalculations are exceedingly rare, although it is probable that in this case the poet's " afterthought " may have been responsible for the error.  Tennyson's connection with this firm lasted until 1875. He had published very little in the meantime, being occupied with his first drama, *Queen Mary*. This was published by Henry S. King & Co., whose business was afterwards taken over by Kegan Paul & Co. To the last-named firm is due the praise of bringing the Laureate's works within reach of the people. They published an " Author's Edition," in six volumes ; an " Imperial Library Edition," in seven volumes ; a " Cabinet Edition," in twelve volumes ; and a " Miniature Edition," pocket size, in thirteen volumes. In 1878, when the shilling volumes made their appearance, the issue of cheap books had not begun, and the fact that Messrs Paul felt justified in venturing to lead the way with the works of Tennyson, is a significant commentary on the growing demand at that time for his poems. It is reported that at this time he was receiving £4500 a year from the sale of his books. Later on Lord Tennyson again changed his publishing house, and Messrs Macmillan acquired the privilege of taking charge of the Laureate's business arrangements. As we have seen, Jackson of Louth published the *Poems by Two Brothers; Timbuctoo* was printed in the *Cambridge Chronicle*, and thereafter never saw the light in any authorised form ; Effingham Wilson published the first edition of the *Poems, chiefly Lyrical,* and various magazines, periodicals, and newspapers have had the advantage of first printing some of the shorter pieces, half of which, however, have never been acknowledged.

Undoubtedly the most interesting, and at the same time the most audacious, edition of Tennyson is that which was published by Messrs Harper of New York, in 1878. It is actually, as opposed to nominally, " complete." The various English editions are complete only in a Tennysonian sense —perfect as a garden may be when the weeds have been extirpated and the trees pruned. Messrs Harper have left the flowers and the weeds, and have introduced some worthless additions in the way of illustrations. It is an unfair book, although it indirectly testifies to the interest that is taken in the whole of the Laureate's *disjecta membra*. It contains several portraits of the poet, who, in the frontispiece, is represented surrounded by the characters in the *Idylls*. All his known productions, up to the date of the publication of the book, are given, the number (including the *Poems by Two Brothers*) being 315. Deducting the latter, we have 203 pieces, as compared with about 150 poems printed in the authorised editions of that date. Among the more notable pieces printed in the American edition are the following, only with the titles of which English readers are, at the most, familiar :—*The Ringlet* ; two versions of songs now published in *The Princess* —" Lady, let the rolling drums " "and Home they brought him slain with spears "—*Timbuctoo* complete, and sixty-two other pieces, to which is prefixed the note that they are printed exclusively in this work. The poems are not all revised, and in the song, *We are free*, occurs the line, " Leaning upon the wingèd sea." The adjective now reads "ridgèd." The sour verdict of Hain Friswell, " It was because the age had been sinking in verve and true poetic feeling that Tennyson rose to the level of its highest appreciation," has never been regarded as a just one. The admirers of the Laureate have increased steadily year by year, and few of them escape the infection for obtaining rare editions.

For the convenience of collectors I may briefly summarise the rare volumes of Tennyson's with the highest prices they have fetched :—*Poems by Two Brothers*, 1827, £28-£32 , *Timbuctoo*, 1829, £6, 10s.; *Poems, chiefly Lyrical*, £5 ; *The Lover's Tale*, 1833, £41 ; *Poems*, 1833, £16 ; *Poems*, 1842, £9, 10s.; *Poems*, 1843 (2nd edition), £4, 12s. 6d.; and so on down to £1, 10s. or a little less ; *The Princess*, £6, 10s.; *In Memoriam* (anonymous), £5 ; *Poems*, 1857, illustrated by Mulready and others, £5 ; *Ode* on the Death of the Duke of Wellington (1d. leaflet), £2, 5s.; *Poems*, 1862, £4, 4s.; *The Window*, £36 ; *The Victim*, £32 ; the two latter having been privately printed.

Tennysonian manuscripts, as might be expected, have fetched very high prices. His autograph alone has been valued at £2, though Sir Henry Taylor records[1] in his autobiography that the Laureate was "very violent with the girls on the subject of the rage for autographs. He said he believed every crime and every vice in the world were connected with the passion for autographs and anecdotes and records." Late in his life, to his intense disgust, the manuscript of a number of his poems was thrown upon the market, and there was very keen competition to obtain possession of it. In June 1889 half-a-dozen of these manuscripts were offered for sale. The first was that of the *Dedication to the Queen*, and it was found that the MS. varied in many lines and words from the published version. One entire verse had not been printed, and a second had ceased to appear in later editions. To add to the interest of the MS. there was a footnote at the end of the page addressed to Mr Moxon the publisher—"I send you the three last stanzas of the *Dedication*. Ought not all the yous and the yours and the hers to be in capitals?—A. TENNYSON. Send the revises." This MS. was purchased for £30. The MS. of that favourite poem, *The Daisy*, occupying four and a half pages octavo, and containing several lines which were omitted in the published version, fetched £24, 10s.; while the copy of *The Letters* was valued at £18, 10s. The *Lines to the Rev. F. D. Maurice*, covering two pages, and differing from the published poem in several small details, went for £23. The MS. of *The Brook*, as might be expected, was deemed worthy of a higher price, and it was eventually secured for £51. Lastly came *Maud*. The MS. was incomplete, but by way of some compensation it contained a few unpublished verses. The price paid for this literary treasure was no less than £111. The autograph MSS. had previously been valued at £200; they actually realised £248. If these veritable scraps are so precious, what would be the value of the autograph copy,

---

[1] See page 4.

say, of *In Memoriam* or *The Idylls of the King ?*  In regard
to the sale just mentioned, it is worthy of note that the
Hon. Hallam Tennyson wrote to the *Times* as follows :—
" Sir,—With reference to the recent sale of my father's
manuscripts, he desires me to express his surprise and
indignation that unpublished verses of his have been made
public, and the manuscripts sold without his leave.  Some
of the corrections, moreover, appear not to be his."  This
protest did not, however, prevent a further sale taking
place in the following year, when most of the songs of *The
Princess* were purchased for 20 guineas.  Soon afterwards
a brief letter written by Tennyson was sold for £7, 7s.
Tennyson wrote very little prose which has been made
public, and his communications on plagiarism and suggestion alone can be deemed important.  In regard to his
poems, however, there seems no likelihood at present of his
fears being realised that the printed leaves

> May bind a book, may line a box,
> May serve to curl a maiden's locks.

# APPENDIX A.

## LOCALISING THE LAUREATE'S POEMS.

IT is far from my wish to raise controversy in this volume, but inasmuch as the Laureate's letter, as well as my own motives, have been greatly misunderstood, and as whatever Tennyson wrote must be regarded as having some historical value, I venture to reproduce his communication to me on the question of "localising." Lord Tennyson (through the medium of his son) informed me that "however pleasant my volume ["In Tennyson Land"] might be, he thought I had ridden my hobby to death. The *Ode to Memory* and *In Memoriam* alone of his poems contain any reference to Somersby. All the poems quoted . . . have nothing of Lincolnshire about them and are purely imaginative inventions." To which I venture to reply : No poet can be accepted as a judge of his own characteristics. The cumulative evidence against the Laureate's assertion is convincing, and it is remarkable that if the Lincolnshire element in the poems is an "imaginative invention," the poet waited until he was eighty years old before declaring it. Forty years previously Charles Kingsley had stated that the poems showed the colour and tone of Lincolnshire, and Tennyson did not correct him. The Rev. Drummond Rawnsley, Tennyson's particular friend, and himself a native of the same county, wrote seventeen years before—"As a Lincolnshire man, and long familiar with the district in which Mr Tennyson was born, I have often been struck with the many illustrations of our county's scenery and character to be found in his poems. What Wordsworth has done for the English Lakes and Scott for the Highlands, our poet has done for the homelier scenes of his boyhood and early manhood in Mid-Lincolnshire. They live for us in his pages, depicted with all the truth and accuracy of a photograph." Dr Peter Bayne, in *Lessons from the Masters* says—"The poems of the *first* volume bear curiously vivid marks of the Lincolnshire birth-land of the poet. . . . We seem as we read these early verses of Tennyson's to be actually transported to the scenes. . . . He trusts nothing to random strokes. . . . He sees the landscape, and details its features. He localises the moated grange for us by minute specific touches." The Rev. J. W. Dawson asserts that "Wordsworth never drew a picture of mountain solitude or lake scenery more simply true than the Lincolnshire poet gives of the great open spaces of the Fen country. His scenery is specially characteristic of Lincolnshire." So said Edmund Clarence Stedman, and many others : in short, there seems to have been a conspiracy upon the part of those who knew Lincolnshire to "localise" the Laureate's poems. I fail to see that the practice is pernicious. Tennyson's letter was honest : he was unconscious to what a great extent Lincolnshire entered into his poetry. But what can be said of the few so-called students of his works who accepted his denial and also declared that they could *find* no such evidence in support of my contention ? Happily their number was extremely small ; and I have to thank the many who readily and spontaneously came to my aid and justified me in my work. We must have heroes and be allowed to worship them, and there are few modes more disinterested and less obnoxious than that of making their homes classic shrines. If authors and poets consciously or unconsciously describe the scenery of a locality, or if the spirit of a place is infused into their work and recognisable, what harm can come of identification ? Scenes are the more inspiring for their associations, and there can be no more elevating pursuit than tracing their influence upon gifted minds. Nor can it be urged that we detract from a poet's merits by believing in his fidelity to nature and his ability to pourtray its beauty. We do not ask or expect the poet to be hard and restrained, and we do not deny him imagination ; we only search for truth in fairest and purest guise, and discovery wrongs no one. Great artists in words and colours have bequeathed to us real pictures of visible things—Shakespeare, Milton, Scott, Thomson, Keats, Shelley, Byron, Wordsworth, and Tennyson, and the legacy to be treasured must be fully understood.

## APPENDIX B.

### TENNYSON'S LETTER ON PLAGIARISM AND SUGGESTION.

THE following important letter on Plagiarism is referred to in the chapter on Tennyson's originality. It was addressed to Mr S. E. Dawson, author of *A Study of "The Princess,"* published at Montreal.

ALDWORTH, HASLEMERE, SURREY, *Nov.* 21, 1882.

DEAR SIR,—I thank you for your able and thoughtful essay on *The Princess.* You have seen, among other things, that if women ever were to play such freaks the tragic and the burlesque might go hand in hand. I may tell you that the songs were not an afterthought.

Before the first edition came out, I deliberated with myself whether I should put songs in between the separate divisions of the poem ; again, I thought, the poem will explain itself ; but the public did not see that the child, as you say, was the heroine of the piece, and at last I conquered my laziness and inserted them.  You would be still more certain that the child was the true heroine, if, instead of the first song as it now stands,

As thro' the land at eve we went,

I had printed the first song which I wrote, *The Losing of the Child.* The child is sitting on the bank of the river and playing with flowers —a flood comes down—a dam has been broken through—the child is borne down by the flood—the whole village distracted—after a time the flood has subsided—the child is thrown safe and sound again upon the bank, and all the women are in raptures.  I quite forget the words of the ballad, but I think I may have it somewhere.

Your explanatory notes are very much to the purpose, and I do not object to your finding parallelisms.  They must always recur.  A man (a Chinese scholar) some time ago wrote to me saying that in an unknown, untranslated Chinese poem there were two whole lines of mine almost word for word.  Why not ?  Are not human eyes all over the world looking at the same objects, and must there not consequently be coincidences of thought and impressions and expressions ?  It is scarcely possible for anyone to say or write anything in this late time of the world to which in the rest of the literature of the world a parallel could not somewhere be found.  But when you say that this passage or that was suggested by Wordsworth or Shelley or another, I demur, and, more, I wholly disagree.  There was a period in my life when, as an artist—Turner, for instance—takes rough sketches of language, &c., in order to work them eventually into some great picture, so I was in the habit of chronicling, in four or five words or more, whatever might strike me as picturesque in nature.  I never put these down, and many and many a line has gone away on the north wind, but some remain, *e.g.*:—

A full sea glazed with muffled moonlight.

Suggestion : The sea one night at Torquay, when Torquay was the most lovely sea village in England, though now a smoky town ; the sky was covered with thin vapour, and the moon was behind it.

A great black cloud
Drags inward from the deep.

Suggestion : A coming storm seen from the top of Snowdon.

In the *Idylls of the King* :—

> With all
> Its stormy crests that smoke against the skies.

Suggestion : A storm which came upon us in the middle of the North Sea.

> As the water-lily starts and slides.

Suggestion : Water-lilies in my own pond, seen in a gusty day with my own eyes. They did start and slide in the sudden puffs of wind till caught and staved by the tether of their own stalks—quite as true as Wordsworth's simile, and more in detail.

> A wild wind shook—
> Follow, follow, thou shalt win.

Suggestion : I was walking in the New Forest. A wind did arise and—

> Shake the songs, the whispers, and the shrieks
> Of the wild wood together.

The wind, I believe, was a west wind, but because I wished the Prince to go south, I turned the wind to the south, and naturally the wind said "Follow." I believe the resemblance which you note is just a chance one. Shelley's lines are not familiar to me, though, of course, if they occur in the *Prometheus* I must have read them.

I could multiply instances, but I will not bore you ; and far indeed am I from asserting that books, as well as nature, are not, and ought not to be, suggestive to the poet. I am sure that I myself and many others find a peculiar charm in those passages of such great masters as Virgil or Milton where they adopt the creation of a bygone poet, and reclothe it, more or less, according to their own fancy.

But there is, I fear, a prosaic set growing up among us, editors of booklets, bookworms, index hunters, or men of great memories and no imagination—who impute themselves to the poet, and so believe that he, too, has no imagination, but is for ever poking his nose between the pages of some old volume in order to see what he can appropriate.

They will not allow one to say "Ring the bells," without finding that we have taken it from Sir P. Sydney, or even to use such a simple expression as the ocean "roars " without finding out the precise verse in Homer or Horace from which we have plagiarised it. (Fact !)

I have known an old fishwife who had lost two sons at sea clench her fist at the advancing tide on a stormy day and cry out, "Ay, roar ; do ! How I hates to see thee show thy white teeth !" Now, if I had adopted her exclamation, and put it into the mouth of some old woman in one of my poems, I daresay the critic would have thought it original enough, but would most likely have advised me to go to nature for my old woman, and not to my imagination ; and, indeed, it is a strong figure. Here is another little anecdote about suggestion. When I was about twenty or twenty-one I went on a tour to the Pyrenees. Lying among these mountains before a waterfall that comes down 1000 feet or 1200 feet, I sketched it (according to my custom then) in these words :—

Slow-dropping veils of thinnest lawn.

When I printed this a critic informed me that "lawn" was the material used in theatres to imitate a waterfall, and graciously added, " Mr T. should not go to the boards of a theatre, but to nature herself, for his suggestions."

And I had gone to nature herself. I think it is a moot point whether, if I had known how that effect was produced on the stage, I should have ventured to publish the line.—I beg you to believe me, &c.,

A. Tennyson.

*P.S.*—By the by, you are wrong about "the tremulous isles of light" ; they are isles of light, spots of sunshine coming through the eaves, and seeming to slide from one to the other, as the procession of girls " move under the shade." And surely the " beard-blown goat " involves a sense of the wind blowing the beard on the height of the ruined pillar

# A TENNYSONIAN CHRONOLOGY.

PRINCIPAL FACTS IN, AND CONNECTED WITH, THE LIFE
OF THE POET LAUREATE.

1778.  George Clayton Tennyson born at Market Rasen (December 10).

1781.  Elizabeth Fytche born.

1805.  Rev. G. C. Tennyson married at Louth to Elizabeth Fytche (August 6).

1806.  George Tennyson born (died in infancy).

1807.  Frederick Tennyson born.

1808.  Charles Tennyson (afterwards known as Rev. Charles Tennyson-Turner) born (July 4).

1809.  ALFRED TENNYSON BORN (August 6).

1810.  Mary Tennyson born (died 1884).

1811.  Arthur Hallam born (February 1).
       Emily (or Emilia) Tennyson born (died 1887).

1813.  Edward Tennyson born (died 1890).

1814.  Arthur Tennyson born.

1815.  Alfred Tennyson goes to Clark's School.
       Septimus Tennyson born (died 1866).

1816.  Alfred Tennyson enters Louth Grammar School.
       Matilda Tennyson born.

1817.  Cecilia Tennyson born.

1819.  Horatio Tennyson born.

1820.  Alfred Tennyson leaves Louth Grammar School.

1826–7.  *Poems by Two Brothers* published at Louth.

1827–8.  Frederick Tennyson gained the Bronze Medal for a Greek Ode on the Pyramids.

1828.  Alfred Tennyson enters Trinity College, Cambridge (October 28).
       Meets Arthur Hallam.
       Writes *The Lover's Tale*.

1829.  Wins Chancellor's Gold Medal for poem on *Timbuctoo*.
       Poem is criticised in *Athenæum* (July 22).

1830.  *Poems chiefly Lyrical* published (London : Wilson).
       Tennyson and Hallam visit Pyrenees.
       *Sonnets* published by Charles Tennyson (Cambridge).

1831. Poems criticised in *Westminster Review* (January), in
    *Englishman's Magazine* (August) by Hallam, in *Tatler*
    by Leigh Hunt.
    Tennyson leaves Cambridge University.
    Rev. G. C. Tennyson died (March 16), aged 52.
    Miscellaneous poems published in magazines :—*Check every*
    *Outflash, No More, Anacreontic,* and *Fragment.*
1832. Poems criticised in *Blackwood's Magazine* by Wilson (May).
    Hallam leaves Cambridge, and proceeds to London.
    Tennyson publishes several sonnets.
    Edward Tennyson contributes a sonnet to the *Yorkshire*
    *Literary Annual.*
1832-3. *Poems* published (Moxon).
1833. *Quarterly Review* critique appears (April).
    Hallam proceeds to the Continent with his father.
    Hallam dies at Vienna (September 15).
    *The Lover's Tale* printed and suppressed.
1834. Hallam buried at Clevedon (January 3).
1835. Charles Tennyson-Turner becomes Vicar of Grasby.
    Tennyson's poems criticised in *London Review* (July).
    Tennyson goes to Cumberland.
1836. The Rev. Charles Tennyson-Turner marries Louisa Sellwood
    of Horncastle.
1837. *St Agnes* published in *The Keepsake.*
    The Tennyson family depart from Somersby, and reside at
    Beech Hill House, High Beech, Essex.
1838. Tennyson joins the " Anonymous " Club, and resides part of
    his time in London.
1840. Mrs Tennyson leaves High Beech, and resides at Tunbridge
    Wells.
1841. Mrs Tennyson removes to Boxley, near Maidstone, and
    meets the Lushingtons.
1842. *POEMS* PUBLISHED IN TWO VOLUMES (Moxon).
    Criticised by James Spedding in the *Edinburgh Review,* by
    John Sterling in the *Quarterly Review,* and by R. Monck-
    ton Milnes in the *Westminster Review.*
    Cecilia Tennyson married to E. L. Lushington (October 10).
    Tennyson introduced to Carlyle.
1843. Tennyson meets Wordsworth.
    Second edition of *Poems* (revised).
1844. Mrs Tennyson (mother) removes to 10 St James's Square,
    Cheltenham ; stays until 1850.
    Edgar Allan Poe criticises Tennyson in " Marginalia " of
    New York *Dramatic Review.*

1845.   Third edition of *Poems* published.

Pension of £200 granted.

Lytton attacks Tennyson in *The New Timon*.

*Bon Gaultier Ballads* published, containing parodies of, and references to, Tennyson.

The poet is a guest at Holland House.

1846.   Fourth edition of *Poems* (*The Golden Year* first included).

Tennyson replies to Lytton in *Punch:—The New Timon and The Poets* (February 28), and *Afterthought* (March 7).

James Russell Lowell criticises Tennyson in *Conversations on the Poets*.

1847.   *THE PRINCESS* PUBLISHED (September 23).

1848.   *Poems* issued in one volume, fifth edition.

Second edition of *The Princess*, dedicated to Henry Lushington.

Review of *The Princess* in *Quarterly Review*, by Sara Coleridge.

Tennyson goes to Cornwall; stays at Truro, Tintagel, and Morwenstow.

1849.   Lines in *Examiner* (March 24), "You might have won the poet's name."

1850.   (*Annus Mirabilis*).

TENNYSON PUBLISHES *IN MEMORIAM* (June 1).   Three editions called for.

MARRIES Miss EMILY SELLWOOD of Horncastle at Shiplake Church (June 13).

Appointed POET LAUREATE (November 19).

Sixth edition of *Poems*, and third edition of *The Princess*—songs added, and the poem entirely re-written.

Kingsley criticises Tennyson in *Fraser's Magazine* (September).

Lines contributed to *Manchester Athenæum Album*—"Here often, when a child."

Tennyson takes up his residence at Chapel House, Twickenham.

1851.   Tennyson presented to the Queen (March 6).

Seventh edition of *Poems*, containing dedicatory lines *To the Queen*.

Lines to Macready in *The Keepsake*, and "What time I wasted youthful hours."

Tennyson and his wife live abroad, chiefly in Italy.   Death of their first child.

Fourth edition of *The Princess* (altered), and fourth edition of *In Memoriam*, with the section now numbered LIX. added.

1851. Gerald Massey criticises *The Princess* in the *Christian Socialist.*

1852. *Britons, guard your own,* by "Merlin," in *Examiner* (January 31); *The Third of February* and *Hands all Round* in *Examiner* (February 7).

Tennyson returns to England; stays at Malvern with Carlyle and others.

Hallam Tennyson born at Twickenham (August 11).

*Ode on the Death of the Duke of Wellington* published in the *Times.*

Tennyson meets Bell Scott and other Pre-Raphaelites at Coventry Patmore's.

1853. Tennyson removes to Freshwater.

Eighth edition of the *Poems;* fifth edition of *The Princess.*

Tennyson visits the Highlands.

1854. *The Charge of the Light Brigade* published, and copies sent to the soldiers before Sebastopol.

Rev. F. D. Maurice dedicates his volume of Sermons to Tennyson.

Lionel Tennyson born at Freshwater (March 16).

Frederick Tennyson publishes *Days and Hours* (Parker and Sons).

Dr Kane names an Arctic landmark after Tennyson.

1855. University of Oxford confers on Tennyson the D.C.L. degree.

*MAUD* PUBLISHED (July 25), and severely criticised for its "war passages."

1856. *Maud* re-published with additions.

Dr Mann's *Maud Vindicated* issued. Tennyson writes letter of thanks.

1857. Bayard Taylor visits Tennyson at Freshwater.

Tennyson goes to Manchester, and encounters Nathaniel Hawthorne.

*Enid and Nimue; or, the True and the False* printed privately and withdrawn.

1858. Two verses added to the National Anthem on the occasion of the Princess Royal's marriage.

Tennyson visits the Duke of Argyll at Inverary.

1859. *IDYLLS OF THE KING* PUBLISHED (July 11)—four in number (Moxon).

*The War* printed in the *Times,* signed " T " (for some time attributed to Trench).

Tennyson goes to Portugal with F. T. Palgrave (August).

*The Grandmother* published in *Once a Week* (July 16).

1859. Frederick Tennyson settles in Jersey.

1860. *Sea Dreams* printed in *Macmillan's Magazine* (January).

*Tithonus* printed in *Cornhill Magazine* (February).

Tennyson goes to Cornwall.

1861. Tennyson revisits the Pyrenees ; also stays at Mont-les-Bains Cauteretz, &c., with his wife and children.

*The Sailor Boy* printed in *Victoria Regia* (Christmas).

1862. *Idylls of the King* dedicated to the late Prince Consort.

The *Exhibition Ode* published.

Analysis of *In Memoriam* by Robertson published.

Tennyson travels in Yorkshire and Derbyshire.

1863. *A Welcome* published (March 7), on the arrival of Princess Alexandra.

"Attempts at Classic Metres in Quantity," printed in *Cornhill Magazine* (December).

1864. Garibaldi visits Tennyson.

ENOCH ARDEN PUBLISHED (August 1).

Epitaph on the late Duchess of Kent published in the *Court Journal* (March 19).

Taine's *Histoire de la Litterature Anglaise* published, containing criticisms of Tennyson.

The Rev. Charles Tennyson-Turner publishes a volume of sonnets dedicated to Alfred Tennyson.

1865. Mrs Tennyson (mother) died, aged 84, at Hampstead ; buried at Highgate.

Baronetcy offered to Tennyson and declined.

*Selections from Works* published, containing several new poems (January 24).

Tennyson visits Weimar and Dresden.

1866. Tennyson subscribes to Governor Edward John Eyre's testimonial.

1867. Tennyson purchases Sussex estate.

*The Window; or, the Loves of the Wrens* privately printed by Sir Ivor Bertie Guest ; set to music by Sullivan, and published in 1871.

Tennyson visits Dartmoor.

1868. Longfellow visits Tennyson at Farringford.

Tennyson contributes a number of short pieces to magazines : —*The Victim* to *Good Words* (January) ; *On a Spiteful Letter* to *Once a Week* (January); *Wages* to *Macmillan's Magazine* (February) ; "1865-6" to *Good Words* (March); and *Lucretius* to *Macmillan's Magazine* (May).

1869. Tennyson elected Honorary Fellow of Trinity College, Cambridge ; and his bust by Woolner placed in the Library.

*Concordance* to Works issued by Brightwell.

1869.  Tennyson sojourns in North Wales.
       Frederick Tennyson contributes a poem to a magazine,
           *Grave and Gay*.
1870.  Tennyson takes legal proceedings against American "pirates."
       *The Holy Grail* published ; 40,000 copies ordered before
           publication.
1871.  *The Last Tournament* printed in the *Contemporary Review*.
1872.  *Gareth and Lynette* published.
       " Library edition " of Tennyson's works issued in six volumes
           (Strahan & Co.).
1873.  Charles Tennyson-Turner publishes his last volume of
           sonnets.
1874.  *A Welcome* to the Duchess of Edinburgh published.
       " Cabinet Edition " of works issued (H. S. King & Co.).
1875.  *QUEEN MARY* PUBLISHED (H. S. King & Co.).
       " Author's Edition " of works issued.
1876.  *Queen Mary* produced at the Lyceum Theatre (April).
       Tennyson again visits the Pyrenees.
1877.  *Harold* published.
       Bayard Taylor's critique of Tennyson published in the *Inter-
           national Review*.
       Lines on Sir John Franklin, and sonnet on the death of the
           Rev. W. H. Brookfield published.
       *Victor Hugo, Introductory Sonnet, Montenegro,* and *Achilles
           over the Trench* appear in *Nineteenth Century*.
1878.  *Becket* published.
       *The Revenge* printed in *Nineteenth Century* (March).
       Mr Lionel Tennyson marries Miss Eleanor M. B. Locker.
       *Studies in the Idylls* by Elsdale published (H. S. King & Co.).
       Tennyson spends some time in Ireland.
1879.  Charles Tennyson-Turner died at Cheltenham (April 25).
       Tennyson writes elegy, *Midnight* (June 30).
       *The Lover's Tale* re-published.
       *The Falcon* produced at St James's Theatre (December).
       Tennyson proceeds against the *Christian Signal* for publish-
           ing some of his suppressed poems.
1880.  *Ballads and Poems* published (Kegan Paul & Co.).
       Tennyson declines to be nominated for the Lord Rectorship
           of Glasgow.
       Charles Tennyson-Turner's Poems collected in one volume,
           with memoir.
1881.  *The Cup* produced at the Lyceum Theatre.
       Tennyson becomes Vice-President of the Welsh National
           Eisteddfod.

1881.   *Despair* published in the *Nineteenth Century.*
1882.   *The Charge of the Heavy Brigade* published in *Macmillan's Magazine* (March).
Tennyson goes to Lombardy.
Tennyson meets Sir Henry Parkes.
Writes letter to Teetotalers.
Santley sings *Hands all Round*, music by Mrs Tennyson.
*The Promise of May* produced at the Globe Theatre (November).   The Marquess of Queensberry protests.
Tennyson writes letter on Plagiarism and Suggestion to Mr S. E. Dawson (November 21).
1883.   Tennyson takes sea trip with Mr Gladstone, and meets the King of Denmark, the Czar and Czarina, the King and Queen of Greece, and the Princess of Wales at Copenhagen.   By request recites several poems, including *The Grandmother.*
Tennyson rents a house in Lower Belgrave Street, London, and entertains distinguished company.
1884.   TENNYSON IS RAISED TO THE PEERAGE AS BARON TENNYSON OF ALDWORTH (January 18).
Takes seat in the House of Lords, March 11.
*The Cup* and *The Falcon* published.
*Complete Works*, revised, issued.
The Hon. Hallam Tennyson marries Miss Audrey G. F. Boyle, granddaughter of Admiral Hon. Sir Courtney Boyle.
1885.   *Tiresias* published.
*Vastness* published in *Macmillan's Magazine* (November).
Tennyson writes to Mr Bosworth Smith on Disestablishment, which he believes would " prelude the downfall of much that is greatest and best in England."
The Hon. Lionel Tennyson writes a poem, *Sympathy;* the Hon. Hallam Tennyson contributes anonymously to *Macmillan's Magazine* a sonnet, *Orange-blossom.*
1886.   *Locksley Hall Sixty Years After* published (December 14).
Lionel Tennyson died at sea (April 20).
Tennyson writes *Ode* on Princess Beatrice's marriage (June).
1887.   Mr Gladstone writes on Tennyson's Retrospect in the *Nineteenth Century* (January).
Tennyson publishes a *Jubilee Ode* in *Macmillan's Magazine* (April) under the title of *Carmen Seculare*—universally condemned.
Tennyson visits the Channel Islands.
1888.   New edition of Poems, containing several at one time suppressed, issued in eight volumes (Macmillan).

1889.  *Demeter* published (December 12); 20,000 copies sold in a week.

Tennyson writes to the *Times* on railways (April).

His eightieth birthday commemorated (August 6).

Early MSS. sold for £250—invokes protest from the Laureate (June).

A "Tennyson Colony" founded in South Africa by Mr Arnold White.

Tennyson sends greetings to Russell Lowell on his seventieth birthday.

*The Throstle* published in the *New Review* (October).

1890.  More MSS. sold (May).

Tennyson's friend, Miss Mary Boyle died.

Frederick Tennyson publishes *The Isles of Greece.*

1891.  Tennyson is elected an honorary member of the Spalding Gentlemen's Society.

MSS. and rare volumes sold (March).

Lines *To Sleep* published in the *New Review* (March).

Swinburne writes a Birthday Ode on Tennyson (August).

Tennyson condemns the Russian persecution of the Jews (October 1).

Mr Daly and Miss Rehan visit the Laureate (October).

Frederick Tennyson publishes *Daphne and other Poems.*

Tennyson revisits Devonshire.

1892.  *The Foresters* published.  Produced in New York by the Daly Company in March.

*Lines on the Death of the Duke of Clarence* published in the *Nineteenth Century.*

TENNYSON DIED, October 6 ; buried in Westminster Abbey, October 12.

*The Death of Œnone, Akbar's Dream, and other Poems,* published October 28.

The manuscript of *Poems by Two Brothers* sold for £480.

# INDEX.

[Reference is not made in this index to individual poems, except where they give their title to a volume. Nearly all the Laureate's poems are mentioned, and will be found in the chapters chiefly in chronological order.]

          *INDEX.*

www.ingramcontent.com/pod-product-compliance
Lightning Source LLC
Chambersburg PA
CBHW051222120726
47905CB00004B/1228